HE LAZILY BRACED HIS HANDS
ON THE SHELF BEHIND HER HEAD

"You're telling me that you're willfully going to ignore my request?"

"Yup."

"I am so glad you said that."

She glanced up sharply. "Why?"

"Because it's settled. And now we can go with your idea." In one swift move, Jordan leaned down and brushed his lips over hers.

Kat stood frozen in the moment, aware of nothing but the warm, soft caress of his mouth. The rasp of his flannel shirt against her bare arms. The crisp scent of pine soap and warm, male skin. His kiss was subtle, yet insistent. Coaxing. Intoxicating. Heat bloomed inside her, spiraling out in every direction like a sensual drug too powerful to resist. She slid her hands around his neck and pressed closer.

This was madness; she knew it. But she just couldn't bring herself to care. All rational thoughts seemed to slip away like wispy clouds on a stiff breeze, until the only things left were the hot, bright taste of him and the feel of his powerful arms around her and the thudding beat of her heart. In that moment, only one thing was achingly clear.

Jordan Prescott knew how to kiss.

Don't Give Me Butterflies

The Holloway Girls

TARA SHEETS

ZEBRA BOOKS
KENSINGTON PUBLISHING CORP.
www.kensingtonbooks.com

ZEBRA BOOKS are published by

Kensington Publishing Corp.
119 West 40th Street
New York, NY 10018

All Kensington titles, imprints, and distributed lines are available at special quantity discounts for bulk purchases for sales promotion, premiums, fund-raising, educational, or institutional use.

Special book excerpts or customized printings can also be created to fit specific needs. For details, write or phone the office of the Kensington Sales Manager: Attn.: Sales Department. Kensington Publishing Corp., 119 West 40th Street, New York, NY 10018. Phone: 1-800-221-2647.

Zebra and the Z logo Reg. U.S. Pat. & TM Off.

First Printing: August 2019
ISBN-13: 978-1-4201-4630-1
ISBN-10: 1-4201-4630-0

ISBN-13: 978-1-4201-4631-8 (eBook)
ISBN-10: 1-4201-4631-9 (eBook)

10 9 8 7 6 5 4 3 2 1

Printed in the United States of America

To Brandon:
On this wild, beautiful roller coaster called life,
I'm glad I chose to sit next to you.

Chapter One

Kat Davenport was many things, but wealthy wasn't one of them. After plunking down her last twenty bucks at the store that morning for dog food, Cheetos, and shampoo, she vowed to take whatever job came her way, no matter what it was.

"Beggars can't be choosers," she told her dog, Hank, as they left their motel room that afternoon. "And anything's better than being hungry and homeless."

But now, as she yanked on the ridiculous yellow chicken costume and prepared to stand in the sweltering August heat at the Pine Cove Island farmer's market, the life of a hobo wasn't looking all that bad.

"Your beak's broken," her supervisor said in a voice like fine grit sandpaper.

Kat glanced at the woman lounging on the single fold-out chair inside their booth. Smitty Bankston was on the hard side of sixty, with a sour expression that said she knew it. Deep lines etched her face, and her hair was teased and sprayed into a frothy style that had seen better days and wanted to go back.

"Your chicken beak," Smitty said. "It's all crunched up." She took a long drag on her cigarette and flicked the ashes into the grass.

Kat blinked through the fumes. "I'll figure something out." If she'd learned one thing in her twenty-six years, it was how to improvise. She zipped the feathered costume up to her neck. The chicken head was a stuffed hood that snapped under her chin, but the plastic beak was crushed beyond repair.

"Just wear it without the beak, so your face shows," Smitty said, exhaling another plume of smoke. "That way people can hear you better when you ask for donations."

"Great." Kat tucked her frizzing red hair into the chicken hood, wondering how it had all come to this. When she saw the ad for a one-day job working with the Daisy Meadows Pet Rescue, she'd jumped at the chance. Animals were her specialty. She was born with the magical ability to communicate with them, and she'd always taken jobs involving animals. But this wasn't the cakewalk she'd expected. It was more like a pie in the face.

"Here's your basket," Smitty said, handing her a pink basket with the words PLEASE PAWS FOR DONATIONS on one side, and THANK YOU FURRY MUCH on the other. "Now get out there and work the crowd."

Thirty-seven minutes later—because she was counting—Kat had exactly zero dollars in donations. The afternoon sun was brutal, and the costume chafed in all the worst places. She wandered past vegetable stands, candlemakers, and flower booths, trying not to make eye contact with people.

"Big Bird!" a small child said, pointing at her.

"No, honey." His mother gave Kat a tight smile, then pulled him away. "That's something else."

A baby in a stroller stared at Kat with wide eyes, then started to howl.

Kat hurried past as fast as her chicken feet would allow. This gig was going on her Worst Jobs Ever list, no question. She felt like one of those costumed scam artists wandering

Times Square in New York City. Only a crazy person would "paws" and donate.

An old man with a cane hobbled over and tossed a quarter in her basket. "Shake those tail feathers, Bessie!" He wiggled his bushy eyebrows and grinned.

Kat glanced at the single coin. How had she fallen this low? Oh, yeah. Because she was the Queen of Impulsive Decisions. Three weeks ago, she was working as a pet sitter on *Hollywood Houseboat*, a reality show from Southern California. Then on a crazy whim, she'd decided to stay in the Pacific Northwest for good. Pine Cove Island was far away from the drama of L.A., and therefore, blissful, but now her bank account was empty again. And there was nothing blissful about that.

She shoved a sweaty lock of hair from her face and pushed on through the crowd.

On her second lap around the market, Kat had no further donations to show for her efforts. Fed up and needing a break from the sun, she made a beeline toward a shady spot underneath a large tree. A white farmer's tent filled with bundles of lavender stood beside it, but no one was there.

She plopped down on a bale of hay underneath the tree, then yanked off her chicken hood and shook out her hair.

A sudden gust of wind kicked up, and the fresh scent of lavender soothed her heated emotions.

She closed her eyes and breathed deeply, trying to embrace the moment. She needed to find her zen, or whatever it was called. But she also needed to find a permanent job, and a place that actually felt like home. A hollow ache settled in her chest. If a place like that even existed.

Leaning forward, Kat dropped her face into her hands. *Zen.* She massaged her temples with her fingers, trying to quiet her mind, but it didn't work. It was like asking a tornado to stop spinning. *Zen harder.* She tried for several more seconds, then let out a heavy sigh. It was no use. Maybe she could just hang out here in the shade for an hour or five.

"Excuse me," a deep voice said behind her. "I believe you're sitting on my lunch."

Kat spun around, or at least she tried. The costume's bulk made it difficult to maneuver. Her spiky tail feathers swished in an arc, sending her donation basket, a paper plate, and a sandwich flying into the grass.

"Oh!" She scrambled for the crushed sandwich and plate, setting them back on the bale of hay. Then she glanced up to apologize, but the words died in her throat.

The man loomed over her like a thundercloud, with broad shoulders, deeply tanned skin, and dark hair. He wore black jeans and a charcoal gray T-shirt, and he was so tall, Kat took an involuntary step back.

"I'm sorry," she managed. "I didn't notice your sandwich. It's this stupid costume. I can't even see my feet."

His gaze swept slowly over her.

She tried to appear calm and unfazed, but it wasn't easy. He was one of those gorgeous-by-accident types of people. The kind who didn't even have to try. Not like the carefully groomed pretty boys she'd worked with in L.A. Certainly not like her ex-boyfriend who had more clothes and hair products than she did. Nothing about this man was soft or pretty. He had sharp, masculine features, unusual amber eyes, and a thin scar across his left cheekbone. He was in need of a haircut and his face was unshaven, which— paired with the scar—made him look like some wicked character from a fairy tale.

The Beast, Kat decided. He reminded her of the dark prince who got turned into a beast because of his wicked ways.

His mouth curved into an almost-smile, and a fluttering sensation began in the pit of Kat's stomach.

Uh-oh. Butterflies. This was not a good sign. In fact, getting butterflies in her stomach was the exact opposite of a good sign. The Queen of Impulsive Decisions started to smile back, but Kat shut her down fast. She was here to start fresh. That was the plan. She was not going to get all fluttery over a hot guy. Been there, done that, bought the T-shirt too many times to count.

"Why are you dressed like a turkey?" he asked.

Heat scorched up the back of her neck. Here she was, fantasizing about him as a dark prince being all edgy and epic, and all he saw was a stuffed turkey. So much for fairy tales.

"I'm not—" She broke off with a sigh. Really, what did it matter? She grabbed her toppled basket off the ground and set it on the bale of hay. Unfortunately, her only donation of twenty-five cents was now lost somewhere in the grass. She searched the grass, aware that he was still watching her.

"Did you lose something?" he asked.

Just my dignity. She abandoned her search for the quarter. "It's not a big deal." With quick, frustrated movements, she began twisting her hair into a bun. If she didn't get back out there soon, Smitty was going to smoke her on a spit.

"You look pretty hot in that," he said.

She glanced sharply at him.

His face was all polite concern, but there was a glint of mischief in his eyes. "The costume." He gestured to the pear-shaped mess of feathers. "It's really hot."

Was he teasing her? She ignored him and shook out the chicken hood, preparing to put it on. The sooner she escaped into the boiling sea of humanity, the better. It was one thing to feel ridiculous, but another thing entirely to have a man like him witness it.

"But why a turkey?" he asked conversationally, leaning one shoulder against the tree trunk. "I don't get it."

"It's for a rescue shelter," she said, securing her hair with an elastic band from her wrist. "They thought it would draw attention to help get donations."

"For turkeys." He did not seem impressed.

"No." She threw him a look like *he* was the ridiculous one, then jammed on the feathered hood. "It's a rescue facility for animals. Mostly cats and dogs. And I'm a chicken, if you must know."

"Ah." He nodded solemnly, but she had the distinct feeling he was laughing at her. "I see that now."

She took a deep breath and let it out fast. "I know it's dumb, all right? Just give me five seconds and I'll be off to terrorize small children and leave you in peace."

He shrugged. "Take your time. I like chickens." He looped his thumbs into the pockets of his jeans and glanced at the crumpled plate. "My sandwich was chicken."

She tried to snap the hood under her chin. The clasp wouldn't catch. She tried again, muttering under her breath.

He pushed off the tree and stepped closer. "Do you need some help?"

"No," she said quickly. If he had to help, her humiliation would be complete. Why couldn't he just go away?

He kept watching as she fumbled with the clasp under her chin. Spiky feathers poked her neck. Brushed against her nose. Scraped along her collarbone. She bit the insides of her cheeks, frustration mounting with every second.

"Maybe you should consider an easier costume next time," he said.

She almost laughed. There wasn't going to be a "next time." Even if that meant she had to pack up a bindle stick and go moseying down the train tracks with her dog, Hank.

A prickly feather jabbed her ear. She plucked the offending feather out, tossed it to the ground, and continued trying to snap the hood.

"You could try a flamingo costume," he said amiably.

Another feather dug into her temple. She shoved it back. Sweat trickled between her shoulder blades. Her arms itched. Everything itched.

"Or an albatross," he suggested. "You know, something that really says 'cat and dog shelter.'"

Kat slapped feathers away from her face. It was too much. She was fed up. With the job. The day. Her life.

"Look." She pierced him with a glare, fighting to steady her voice. "I get that this might be entertaining to you, but it's no picnic for me. I took this gig because I needed the money. I'm supposed to be collecting donations and so far, all I've gathered is twenty-five cents from an old man who told me to shake my tail feathers. So just give me a break, okay? This is not my idea of a fun afternoon."

She turned her back on him, still grappling with the hood clasp. After several moments in which she considered ripping the hood off, dousing it with gasoline, and lighting it on fire with one of Smitty's cigarettes, it finally snapped closed. Hallelujah! Now she could get on with her glorious day.

"What is?" he asked.

She spun to face him, plucking a downy feather from her mouth. "What is what?"

He was studying her with those whiskey-colored eyes, his head cocked to one side like he was trying to figure out a puzzle. A dark lock of hair fell over his brow, and Kat was struck again by how attractive he was. Or, would be. If she were into those wild, wicked beast types. Which, she wasn't.

The butterflies in her stomach started to say otherwise, but she drew out a mental flyswatter and shut them up, fast.

"What is your idea of a fun afternoon?" he asked.

Kat blinked. It had been a long time since anyone asked her opinion on something like that. There were so many ways to answer it. She'd rather be almost anywhere right now. Like the beach, or an outdoor music concert, or a sidewalk café. She'd rather be curled up with her dog watching old black-and-white movies, or browsing thrift stores for treasures nobody wanted. But none of these things would seem particularly interesting to someone who looked like he roamed the halls of enchanted castles and slayed dragons in his spare time.

Instead she just shrugged. "I don't know. Watching movies. Shopping."

His expression faded to a look of mild boredom. "Of course."

Kat bristled. His dismissive tone bothered her. *He* bothered her. She lifted her chin. "Oh, is that not exciting enough for you?"

He lifted his hands. "Hey, whatever floats your boat. Not everyone has the same idea of fun, that's all. You are who you are."

She pressed her lips together. He had no idea who she was. "Well, what's your idea of a fun afternoon? Swimming with sharks? Jumping off cliffs in a wingsuit?"

His lips twitched. He ran a hand through his hair and looked away.

Kat couldn't help noticing his muscular arms, and how broad his shoulders were in comparison to his lean hips. He was built like a professional athlete. Maybe he really did do extreme sports.

"Nothing that complicated," he said, turning back to her. A soft smile played at the corners of his mouth. "Sometimes I just like to hang out and enjoy lunch with friends, or . . ." His gaze flicked to her costume, then back up to her face. "A hot chick."

Kat rolled her eyes. She grabbed her basket and marched away, tail feathers bouncing with each step.

A deep, masculine chuckle followed her until she lost herself in the crowd.

She was on the other side of the farmer's market before she looked in her basket. On the bottom was a folded twenty-dollar bill.

By six o'clock that evening, the farmer's market vendors were packing up for the day. Kat stood in the Daisy Meadows Pet Rescue booth and unzipped her chicken costume with a tortured sigh. The cool air felt like heaven on her sweaty skin. It was good to finally be free.

Smitty sucked on a cigarette and dug through the donation basket with her free hand. She held up the twenty-dollar bill. "Who's the big tipper?"

"I didn't catch his name," Kat said. In fact, she didn't see Mr. Tall, Dark, and Bothersome again after their first encounter.

Smitty shoved the donations into a glass jar and screwed the lid shut. "Well, old man Winthrop didn't donate twenty bucks, that's for sure. Bessie never got more than a quarter out of him."

Kat glanced up from tying her shoes. "Bessie?"

Smitty's expression curdled. "The gal who normally works the fair. She up and quit yesterday, which is why we needed a stand-in. And good riddance to her, if you ask me." She opened a metal box on the table and pulled out several bills. "Here's your pay. You did all right today."

"Thanks." Kat took the money and stuffed it in her pocket. Not a bad haul for an under-the-table gig.

Hank crawled out from his sleeping spot behind the tablecloth, tail spinning in joy to see her.

She scooped him up and kissed him on the head.

Smitty eyed her closely. "You good with animals?"

"I'm excellent with animals," Kat said. "It's kind of my

thing." And by "thing," she meant superpower. At least, that's what she liked to call it. By some freak of nature, she just always knew what animals were feeling, and she could communicate with them. Usually just by touching them, she received visual images of memories or things they were experiencing. But that's not something she could come right out and say. That was the kind of thing that got you beat up on the playground, or kicked out of a house.

"I need to hire another receptionist," Smitty said. "You good with paperwork and office stuff?"

"Sure." Kat pasted an extra-big smile on her face, hoping it would make up for the lie. Organization was not a close friend of hers, but work was money. And money was security. And security was everything. "I'm good with animals, and office stuff."

Smitty reached into her bedazzled denim purse, pulled out a business card, and handed it to her. "Come by Monday morning. Eight o'clock sharp. It's a full-time position, if you want it."

Kat glanced at the card with the words DAISY MEADOWS PET RESCUE across the top. This time, her smile was genuine. "Sounds perfect."

Chapter Two

"Room for Rent," Kat read aloud from her laptop screen later that evening. She was leaning against the headboard of her motel room, scrolling through the Pine Cove Island classified ads. "Looking for someone to share light chores."

She glanced down at her dog, Hank, on the coverlet beside her. "That sounds promising, right? I'm fine with light chores."

Hank thumped his tail in agreement.

She grabbed a chip from a bag on the nightstand and continued reading aloud. "Cooking a plus. Daily massage a must. Big tool provided . . ." Kat began to frown and continued reading under her breath. "For more details call X. L. Dickerson." She made a face and set the laptop aside.

Hank whined and shook his head.

"Yeah, that one's a definite no." Kat scrubbed her hands over her face. She'd been searching for a cheap room to rent for the past hour. Most of the rooms available were either too expensive or too far away from her new job. She'd purchased an ancient Ford sedan with the last of her savings, but it wasn't the most reliable commuter vehicle.

Hank crawled into her lap, and she scratched him under the chin.

An ad suddenly popped up at the top of the rental list. Kat glanced over at her laptop, reading aloud with hesitation. "Room for Rent. Willowbrook Lavender Farm, 37 Griffin Road. Discount on rent in exchange for light help with barn animals. Prior knowledge a must. All utilities included."

Kat sat up straighter. The animal shelter was on Griffin Road. She leaned sideways and typed in the farm's address on her laptop. It was less than a quarter of a mile away from the shelter. Quickly, she fired off an e-mail asking if the room was still available. Almost immediately, she got a response from an O. Prescott, and within minutes she had a plan to meet the following day to see the room.

"Hank, this might just work." Kat shut her laptop. She snuggled under the covers with her dog and whispered, "We live another day."

On Saturday around noon, Kat parked her car in front of Willowbrook Lavender Farm with mixed feelings.

The fresh, herbal scent of lavender permeated the air, and the field beyond the house was beautiful. Rows of lavender in varying shades of purple and blue stretched for an acre along the west side of the property. A red barn with white trim stood near the south field, its doors chained shut with a padlock. Outside there was a trailer and a bright green wheelbarrow.

But the farmhouse had seen better days. It was a dingy white structure with a wraparound porch. The flower boxes on the railing were cracked and empty. The three shallow steps leading to the porch were sagging with age, and the turquoise front door was faded and peeling.

Next to the house was a detached garage with an apartment above it. Her future living space, if things worked out. She eyed the single window above the garage, hoping the room was decent. For the rental price, she wasn't expecting much.

Kat crossed the lawn, trying to shove off the mantle of disappointment settling over her. She had hoped Willowbrook Lavender Farm would be a little more cheerful. Maybe a purple farmhouse with fluffy chickens pecking around in the yard. Come to think of it, there were no barn animals anywhere. Strange, considering that was part of the rental arrangement. Even the fenced paddock beside the house was empty and overgrown with weeds. The place looked abandoned.

She approached the front door where a silver dragonfly knocker hung at eye level. A mermaid wind chime beside the door danced in the breeze, its cheerful, tinkling sound eerily out of place in the somber atmosphere.

Kat paused to gather her thoughts, tried to smooth her frizzing curls, then knocked three times.

A few moments later, the door swung open and a man appeared.

Her mouth fell open in surprise.

Mr. Tall, Dark, and Bothersome stood on the threshold. He was younger than she'd first assumed—maybe in his late twenties or early thirties. His hair was damp and smoothed back, and he was clean shaven, so the angles of his face were more clearly defined. He wore jeans and an unbuttoned flannel shirt, revealing a glimpse of muscled torso and tanned skin. Kat thought he'd been attractive before, but now he looked downright sinful.

His gaze traveled over her hair, her clothes, her shoes.

She shifted self-consciously on her feet. She was wearing an old tank top, shorts, and chunky boots. All her clothes were black, which was a requirement for her last job as part of the working crew on the houseboat. She hadn't had the time or money to buy new clothes yet. Now, under his scrutiny, she felt inappropriately dressed, which was absurd, considering he barely had a shirt on.

"I didn't expect to see *you* here," she blurted.

He lifted a dark brow. "Sorry to disappoint you."

"I'm not," she said quickly. But it wasn't entirely true. She'd expected a wizened old farmer in overalls with a grandpa smile. Or maybe a little old lady in an apron with lots of cats. Someone sweet and comforting. This man was the exact opposite. He gave her that unsettling, butterflies-in-her-stomach feeling.

Kat cleared her throat and tried to sound calm, even though she wasn't. "I just didn't expect . . . I mean, you don't seem like a lavender farm type of person."

His expression flickered with bitter amusement. "I won't argue with that." He began buttoning his shirt. "You're early."

Kat glanced away. Watching him dress felt almost as intimate as if she were watching him undress. "I was supposed to come at noon, right?" She pulled her phone from her pocket and checked the time. Eleven forty. She must have rushed through the morning in her eagerness to see the room. "I didn't realize how early it was. Do you want me to come back in twenty minutes?"

"No need." He finished buttoning his shirt and held out a hand. "I'm Jordan Prescott."

"Kat Davenport." She reached out to shake his hand. It was a simple, everyday gesture, but the sudden skin-on-skin contact made her hyperaware of how big and warm he was, and how close they were standing. She quickly let go. "I thought I was meeting with an O. Prescott."

"My grandmother, Opal," Jordan said. "I posted the ad for her."

"You live here with your grandmother?" Another oddity.

He looked away. "Not for long."

Kat suddenly wondered what his story was. Everybody had a story. Some people got the happy Hallmark Channel ones with the parents and the family traditions and the fresh-baked cookies after school. Other people got *Les Misérables*. But that's what made them resourceful and self-sufficient and strong. That's what made them capable of handling whatever life threw their way.

She squared her shoulders and lifted her chin. "Is your grandmother here?"

"No. She's at the community center playing bingo. Or knitting." He shook his head in dismissal. "Whatever it is, she'll be back by twelve."

Kat nodded in relief. A little old lady who knitted and played bingo made sense. That was the kind of landlord she'd expected. A sinfully attractive, slightly annoying grandson wasn't part of the plan, but Kat wasn't going to let that stop her. She needed the room. It was cheap, which was her favorite price, and she had no problem taking care of animals. She had to make this work. Besides, he said he wasn't going to be there for long.

"I'm heading out, Jordan," a sultry female voice said from down the hall.

A pretty woman in a red dress suit and mile-high stilettos sauntered up beside him. She had sleek, dark hair and lips painted the exact shade of her dress. "Who's this?"

"Kat Davenport. She's here about the room for rent," Jordan said. "Ms. Davenport, this is Layla Gentry."

"Oh, that's right," Layla mused. "The room above the garage. I forgot about that." She swept Kat from head to toe in an appraisal so thorough, Kat felt like she was on an auction block. Apparently, Layla decided she wasn't worth the investment, because she tipped her head in a brief acknowledgment, then promptly dismissed her.

Layla placed a hand on Jordan's upper arm and squeezed.

"I have to run. Come by my office later." She brushed past Kat and sailed away on a river of Chanel No. 5.

"Does she live here, too?" Kat asked.

"No. She was just doing some work for me."

Kat wasn't going to ask what kind of work. It wasn't any of her business. He could do whatever he wanted with as many friends as he wanted. All she cared about was having a convenient place to live.

"Come in." Jordan stood back and waved her into the house. "I'll show you around."

Kat paused in the doorway. It was dark in the hall, except for a splash of sunlight from a window on the upstairs landing. She stole a glance at Jordan Prescott. Her potential new roommate.

He was standing half in shadow. An errant sunbeam slanted across his face, which made his eyes appear even brighter and more golden than usual.

"Are you coming in, or . . . ?"

She hesitated for a few heartbeats.

His expression lit with amusement, and his mouth curved into a smile. It wasn't the sweet, comforting kind of smile one would expect from grandpa farmers and little old cat ladies. It was an enchanted, wicked-prince smile. The kind that could lure a woman into all sorts of delicious trouble, if she were willing.

"Chickening out?" he asked softly.

Kat narrowed her eyes. She could think of several good reasons why she might be better off with a different living arrangement. But the Queen of Impulsive Decisions just tossed her hair, stepped over the threshold, and followed the beast into his lair.

Jordan watched Kat Davenport breeze past him, head high, fiery curls tumbling around her shoulders.

He almost smiled again, which would be more than twice in one day. A miracle. The last thing he'd wanted to do was come back to this godforsaken place. There hadn't been much to feel good about since his return, but meeting her was proving to be entertaining, if nothing else.

She was all bravado, and he knew it. Yesterday at the farmer's market, she'd been hot and bothered, and angry at the world.

When he first saw her sitting on the hay bale covered in those yellow feathers, he'd wanted to laugh. But the moment she spun around and locked her emerald green eyes on his, he'd felt an instant jolt of . . . something. He'd never seen her before. She wasn't someone he could easily forget. She had a beautiful, fallen-angel face. The kind that made a man's good sense go flying out the window just so he could get closer, even though he knew it might be his undoing. But that's not what caught him by surprise. Something about the way she stood felt familiar—the tilt of her chin, balled fists, eyes wide and assessing. There was a fierce determination in her that he'd recognized. It had been a long time since he'd seen that kind of grit in someone else. He was so caught by surprise that his knee-jerk reaction had been to tease her. He'd wanted to make her smile, but all he could do was stand there, asking her dumb questions. And then when he'd tried to charm her, that was even worse. No wonder she'd stomped away. He was an idiot.

Jordan shut the door and followed Kat into the foyer of his family's farmhouse. She was like a bright flame in the hallway, her beautiful heart-shaped face glowing with curiosity as she took in her surroundings. Jordan got the feeling she charged through life like this—full speed ahead, treating every challenge like a new adventure, even in the face of uncertainty.

"Whoa," Kat said, stopping in the foyer in front of the hall table. "This is stunning. What is this?"

The huge canvas painting was at least five feet by five feet. Brilliant strokes of color were splashed across the center of the canvas in golds and reds and varying shades of brown. Beyond it, stretching from end to end, were rows and rows of compact brushstrokes in every shade of blue and violet and other colors with names he couldn't remember if he tried.

Jordan watched her scrutinize the painting up close—the uneven, layered pigments and textured brushstrokes. When a person stood directly in front of it, the painting was a bright jumble of abstract shapes and color. But Jordan knew the intent was to surprise the viewer. It was a secret in plain sight. If she stood back several feet, she might see the truth emerge.

It was an impression of the farm. The red barn. The fields of lavender stretching beyond the horizon. A bright sunny day. A wheelbarrow. It was a cumulation of warm summer days, where all one could do was sip lavender lemonade and joke about watching the paint dry.

A familiar ache unfurled inside his chest, grabbing hold of any momentary lightness. It was a reminder of what life on the farm could have been, but never was. A reminder of wishes he'd long since outgrown.

"It's a painting," he managed.

Kat cocked a hip and threw him a sassy grin. "Thanks for the clarification." She went back to studying the image, then took a couple of steps back. "I love it. It's so bright and cheerful. I especially like the detail of the white chickens near the wheelbarrow."

"The chickens?"

"Right here," Kat said, pointing to blobs of creamy paint beside a slash of geometric earth tones.

Jordan frowned. He'd never noticed before.

"It's amazing how abstract it seems at first," she continued. "But really it's the farm and the lavender fields. Who did this? I think I love it." She flashed him a brilliant smile that did something to the ache in his chest. Whatever it was, he shut it down fast.

He pointed down the hall. "The kitchen is this way. The room above the garage has a full working bathroom, but no kitchen. If you want to cook anything, you'll have to use the one in here."

She raised her delicate eyebrows, then followed him down the hall to the back of the house.

The kitchen was small and unremarkable, save for the large window box overlooking the side yard. It used to hold a mishmash of plants and potted flowers, but they were gone now. A lot of things were gone. Aside from a single coffeepot in the corner, the old Formica countertops were bare.

Jordan suddenly realized how drab it looked. He hadn't noticed before. But it didn't matter because it served its purpose, and it only needed to be functional for the time being. None of this would matter in a few months.

Kat walked into the kitchen, glancing around. "It's nice."

He felt a twinge of guilt. The house he'd grown up in was anything but nice. When his parents lived there, it was a perpetual mess and always in need of repairs. Sometimes there was no heat or electricity because they didn't pay the bills. It was always cold in winter, he remembered. Always chaotic. And now that they'd left the place, it was even more run-down. They'd been gone over a month before his mother thought to send him a hastily scrawled postcard from Malaysia with the news that they'd retired there.

A new adventure! she'd written. *The house is with your grandmother if you want it. We won't be returning.*

Jordan ran a hand over the sudden tension on the back of his neck. Once again, he'd have to clean up after their mess. But this would be the last time. All he had to do was fix up the place and make it look presentable enough to sell. That was the plan.

He watched Kat run her hand over the kitchen counter, as if deep in thought. She probably didn't like the idea of sharing a kitchen with strangers. He couldn't blame her. He didn't like it much, either. Back in Manhattan, he valued his hard-won privacy. The apartment, his driver, even his acquaintances and the women he dated, were all kept at a safe distance. Exactly where he liked them. Living here for the next couple of months with his grandmother, and potentially Kat, was going to be disturbing in more ways than he cared to admit.

"We don't do much cooking in here," he said. "But you're free to use anything you find."

Kat leaned against the counter and crossed her arms. "You don't cook at all?"

"Not if I can help it."

"So you're a cereal for dinner guy, huh?"

"Please, I'm not an amateur." He walked over to the fridge, opened the freezer, and pointed. Several frozen waffle boxes were stacked inside.

Her soft laugh did something to his insides, spreading over the hard places and seeping into cracks he didn't know were there. He didn't like it.

Jordan shut the freezer and quickly led her outside.

Weeds had taken over the lawn, and the grass was out of control and too long to mow. The rosebushes along the fence grew like wild things, all thorns and red blooms, no rhyme or reason to any of it.

"Beautiful," Kat said, stopping to touch one of the red roses.

Jordan squinted at the overgrown mess of flowers.

The bushes were exactly the same as he remembered, growing up. Ignored and abandoned. "No one's taken care of them in years. I'm surprised they're even still alive."

Kat shrugged. "They just need some pruning."

He frowned and kept walking, certain the rosebushes would need a bit more work than that. The entire yard looked like a scene from an apocalypse film. It shouldn't have bothered him, but for some reason now that she was there, it did.

He led her through the weeds to the garage, then up a narrow staircase to the room above it. The studio was large and spacious, which was the only decent thing about it. Everything else was dreary. It had a scratched table with a single chair pushed against the far wall. Above it was a bare window that overlooked the front yard. The only other piece of furniture in the room was an ancient, lumpy recliner chair.

Kat was quiet as she roamed the room and peeked into the small bathroom. Then she moved to the table and looked out the window.

She began shaking her head.

Jordan felt a sharp stab of disappointment. He took a deep breath and let it out quickly. So the room wasn't what she expected. He should've known. She was going to turn it down, and so be it. Could he blame her? The place was about as inviting as a jail cell. Utilitarian, drab, musty. Someone like her belonged in a place full of color and light.

Steeling himself, he walked to the door and pulled it open. It was no matter. He'd run the ad again for his grandmother. Someone else could tend to the animals for the time being.

She turned to him, biting her lip.

He gestured to the open door.

"It's nice," she said. "This will work great."

Jordan blinked as she passed him to head down the stairs. She'd surprised him again.

Back outside, he pointed to a small gray barn inside the fenced paddock beyond the garden.

"The animals?" Kat asked.

He nodded.

"What's in the red barn over there?" She pointed across the yard to the padlocked barn.

"Nothing important," he said dismissively. Certainly nothing he wanted to talk about. "Do you want to meet the animals or not?"

Kat lifted her delicate brows. "Sure." She charged ahead, calling over her shoulder, "You won't have to worry about a thing. Animals are my specialty. It'll be easy."

Jordan watched her go, distracted by the feminine curve of her hips and the sway in her gait as she marched toward the barn in those tiny black shorts and combat boots. He had the distinct feeling that nothing about Kat Davenport living there was going to be easy.

Chapter Three

The barn was dry and warm enough, but happiness didn't live there. Kat felt it the moment she stepped inside. An all-encompassing melancholy enveloped her, smothering her like a wet cloak.

She usually had no problem understanding what animals needed, and this was no exception. Even before she met them, she could tell they were neglected and needed attention.

The barn was about the size of a large toolshed. There was one stall and a pile of old hay in the corner. Three scrawny white chickens pecked at the ground, scattering when she stepped inside.

A scuffling noise came from the back stall, and Kat waited patiently. A few moments later, a small furry head peeked around the stall entrance.

"There you are," Kat murmured. "I'm so glad to meet you."

The miniature donkey blinked his long eyelashes and made a snuffling sound. He was fuzzy and gray, with a velvety nose and black tufts on his ears.

"Aren't you a beautiful one?" Kat crooned. She approached slowly, kneeling in front of him and murmuring things that made no sense. Things that weren't even part of a language. They were just the soothing noises she instinctively knew how to make to put the animal at ease.

The mini donkey approached her cautiously, then all at once, rubbing his head against her outstretched hands. The connection was instant. Glimpses of his daily life flashed through Kat's mind like scene snippets from a movie reel. Long, dull days in the pen. No one around to keep him company except the chickens. Boredom.

Kat smiled and scratched him lovingly behind the ears. "You're all right, aren't you? You just need a friend. We'll get you one, I promise. Things are going to get much better around here. Don't worry."

She rose from the ground and made her way to the chickens, only vaguely aware that Jordan was watching her from the doorway. The tiny donkey followed beside her.

Kat knelt close to the chickens and waited. They clucked and shifted nervously, ruffling feathers and strutting just out of reach. Soon they grew bolder, and within moments, Kat was petting them, searching for that thread of communication she always had with animals. A quick image flashed through her mind—the chickens, warm and snug in their old coop. Soon she understood exactly what they needed. "They're nervous," she said aloud. "They miss their old house, where they felt safe."

Jordan pushed off the wall where he'd been leaning, and came to stand next to her. The chickens scattered out of reach. "How did you know?" he asked. "The old chicken coop broke apart in a storm a while back."

"Chickens need a safe place to roost at night," Kat said carefully, making sure only to say things a normal person would know. "A place to keep them away from predators."

"I didn't even know we had chickens until a week ago. My grandmother said they'd all been lost in the storm, but she'd been leaving food out just in case. These three are the only ones left."

"Can you build them a coop today? I can help. They're very unhappy."

He gave her an odd look, but she was used to it. People had been giving her that look her whole life, but speaking up on behalf of animals was something Kat was compelled to do. Even if it meant making herself vulnerable to other people's scrutiny and judgment.

"I'll see what I can do," Jordan said.

"Good." Kat stood and slapped dust off her hands. "I'll have them all happy again in no time. I promise."

Jordan walked with her to the front yard. He was quiet on the way, and Kat wondered what he was thinking. Maybe he thought she was a weirdo with the animal stuff. But she was pretty sure she hadn't done anything too crazy. It's not like she hugged the chickens or anything. Which she totally planned on doing, as soon as she got the chance. Chickens were simple creatures, and they loved comfort. Some of them actually liked being held.

Near the porch steps, Jordan stopped. He studied her from beneath thick, sooty lashes. Why did men always get the best eyelashes? So unfair.

She fidgeted with the hem of her top, hoping she hadn't blown it with the animal whispering.

A small white bus pulled into the yard, and Kat was grateful for the distraction.

"My grandmother's back," Jordan said. "Come, and I'll introduce you."

She followed him across the yard as a tiny old woman in a purple velour jogging suit stepped off the bus and waved good-bye to the driver. Her white, wispy curls were so thin her pink scalp showed through, and her face was a road map of wrinkles, but her eyes were a sharp, clear blue. She saw Kat and broke into a grin.

"You must be Kat Davenport. I'm so sorry I was late to meet you." She bustled over to them, relying on a gray cane she gripped in one hand. "It's Milton Johnson's fault I'm late, as usual. He insists on calling out the bingo letters, but he takes forever. I think he does it on purpose. It's the only time he gets that kind of rapt attention from so many people."

She stopped in front of Kat, a little out of breath. "Well, look at you. You're just gorgeous. I wasn't expecting a beauty queen to answer my ad, but we'll just have to bear it as best we can, won't we, Jordan?" She jabbed him with her elbow and laughed.

A small crease formed between his brows.

"Well, isn't this fun?" Opal continued. "I'm looking forward to having another person around to talk to, I'll tell you that much. Has my grandson shown you around?"

"Yes," Kat said. "It's all very nice. I—"

"Oh, psh," Opal interrupted. "It's not nice here. It's abysmal. My cotton-headed son and his wife had no business trying to run a farm, which is why I moved in last year to help them out. But did they listen to me about anything? *No.* The only reason the lavender still thrives is because it's stubborn, like my grandson here." She tilted her head toward Jordan. "But his parents weren't any good at taking care of much. And now look." She pointed to the overgrown yard. "Everything's a mess. But Jordan's here now, and he's going to save everything. Won't you?" she asked him.

Jordan didn't answer, but Opal didn't seem to notice.

To Kat she said, "Jordan was always reliable like that. Even when he was a little boy, you could count on him."

Kat didn't miss the look of resignation that ghosted across Jordan's face.

"Is your room okay?" Opal asked as they walked toward the farmhouse. "I haven't been up to that room in years, on account of my leg trouble. But Jordan assures me it's all in working order." Her unhurried pace was slightly uneven, and Kat had to slow her steps to match.

"I like the room very much," Kat said. "And I'll take good care of the animals."

"Good," Opal said. "They'll be so much happier now."

They chatted for a few more minutes and Kat answered Opal's questions about where she came from, and what line of work she was in. Kat glossed over her answers with expert precision, like she always did. It was just easier than having to explain the real way she grew up. Anytime Kat said the words "foster kid," she got that look of pity she'd grown to hate.

The whole time Opal talked, Jordan remained quiet. Kat risked a glance at him and wished she hadn't. He was looking at her in mild amusement, as if he knew half her answers were contrived. As if he knew her secrets.

"Come in for some tea," Opal said. "We have molasses cookies."

Kat made a show of checking her phone. "I'd love to, but I have to get going. I have some packing to do, and then I'm meeting a friend later."

Jordan held his grandmother's elbow to help her up the steps.

Opal waved him away. "I can do it myself, boy. I'm not an invalid." Using her cane, she slowly and methodically ascended the steps.

On the porch, she turned back to Kat. "It's settled then. You'll stay. And I'll see you soon."

Kat watched as Opal disappeared into the house.

Jordan shook his head. "She does that a lot."

"What?"

"She says things like they're decided, even though they aren't. Pay no attention. Just let me know later today after you think it over."

"I don't need to think it over," Kat said quickly. "I'll take it." She jammed her hands into her pockets. "I mean . . . if you want me."

An odd expression flashed across his face. He cleared his throat. "Opal seems to think this arrangement is a good idea, but it's important that you know it's not permanent."

A familiar disappointment settled over her. Of course it wasn't going to be permanent. Nothing ever was. At least, not for her. But she'd hoped she could rent the place long enough to get on her feet.

"Um, did you think I was planning to live here forever?" she asked flippantly. "Of course it's not permanent. Although, now that you mention it, we didn't discuss terms of the lease."

"Month to month. I'll e-mail the paperwork."

Kat nodded with a sinking feeling. A month-to-month lease wasn't very promising. She'd hoped it would be a longer term. Then again, she had no other alternatives. If nothing else, she'd have a solid month to set some money aside, and if she was lucky, she'd have even longer.

After they said good-bye, she made her way to the car, determined to look on the bright side. Everything was falling into place. Maybe moving to the island was going to be the best decision she ever made. Maybe this would be a place she could fit in and just be herself.

When she neared her car, a dark shadow swooped past her head with a joyful *caw*!

Kat glanced up at the black crow making lazy circles in the clear blue sky. "Edgar," she called. "I've been wondering when you'd find me."

Edgar the crow fluttered down and landed on a low tree branch.

"I know what you want," she teased, reaching up to stroke his glossy feathers.

He preened, happy for the attention, then shifted on his

feet excitedly as she opened her car and dug through her tote bag on the passenger seat. She lifted an unshelled peanut from a small plastic bag. When she'd first arrived on the island, she'd absently tossed him one of her Cheetos, and for Edgar, it was love at first sight. Ever since that moment, he followed her around town. Kat usually kept treats in her bag, just for him.

When she walked back to the tree, Edgar flapped his wings, lifted off the branch, and settled on her shoulder.

She laughed. "You're such a sucker for a gourmet meal. We're two peas in a pod, you and I." She spoke quietly to him for a few moments, then handed him the peanut. He took it and launched into the sky.

She waved as he flew away, even though it was a silly gesture. Edgar was a wild bird, but she still thought of him as a friend. To any normal person, the whole exchange would probably seem odd. On impulse, she glanced back at the farmhouse and froze.

Jordan was standing on the porch watching her. He was far enough away that she couldn't see his expression, which was probably a good thing. Did he see her talking to Edgar? How weird did she look? Was it too much? The last thing she needed was to be rejected from her new living arrangement before she even had a chance to move in.

Kat got into her car, turned on the engine, and pulled onto the main road. She gripped the steering wheel and exhaled in frustration. If Jordan thought she was odd, he'd be one hundred and fifty percent correct. But she'd made the decision to just be herself from now on, and she wasn't going to try to fit into a mold. So yeah, she talked to birds. And other animals. That's who she was. She peered in her rearview mirror at the lavender farm as she drove away, then lifted her chin in resolve. "Like it or not, Jordan Prescott, this is who I am." She tossed her hair back. "Get used to it."

Chapter Four

At lunchtime the following day, Kat stepped into the local florist shop, Romeo & Juliette's, with Hank trotting beside her. She breathed in the mingling scents of fresh-cut greenery, flowers in bloom, and damp earth. The florist shop was one of her favorite spots on the island, mostly because of the manager.

Juliette Holloway emerged from the back room looking like spring incarnate. She wore a floral sundress that swirled around her legs when she walked, and a gardenia was pinned into her long dark hair. Layered over her dress was a flouncy green apron smudged with dirt. The whole effect made her look like a forest fairy. Juliette loved plants and nature, and anyone who knew her would agree that managing the shop was exactly where she belonged.

"Good," Juliette said, walking up to Kat and giving her a quick hug. "I've been waiting for you to get here. Ever since you ditched me in search of full-time employment, I've missed you. My plants miss you."

"Somehow I doubt that," Kat said with a grin. Juliette was Kat's first official friend on Pine Cove Island. For a few weeks, Kat had helped out by working part-time in the shop, even though she knew next to nothing about plants.

Since Kat had preferred to find a permanent job working with animals, she'd moved on once Juliette hired a full-time employee.

"Emma gets back from her honeymoon soon, so we all need to get together for a movie marathon at the house." Juliette lifted Hank off the floor and snuggled him up to her face. "And you and Hank are coming. That's not negotiable."

Kat felt a surge of warmth for her friend. From the moment they'd met at the beginning of the summer, she felt like they were kindred spirits. The rumor on the island was that Juliette Holloway had a magical green thumb, along with her cousin Emma, who baked wishes into her cupcakes. One of the reasons Kat wanted to stay on the island was her curiosity about these unusual women who seemed to have strange abilities like her. She hadn't discussed her connection to animals with them yet, but that was the beauty of their friendship. Both of the Holloway girls seemed willing to accept her exactly as she was, no questions asked.

Juliette set Hank on the floor and walked to the back counter. "How's the job hunt going?"

"I start at the Daisy Meadows Pet Rescue on Monday."

"Animals!" Juliette grinned. "That's perfect for you."

Kat beamed. It felt good to be able to share her progress with a friend. "I also found a place to live. I'm renting a room from Opal Prescott at Willowbrook Lavender Farm. Do you know her?"

"The lavender farm?" Juliette squinted for a moment, then gave a little gasp. "Hold on. Does she have a grandson?"

Did she ever. "Yes."

"Ooh." Juliette made a sound of approval in the back of her throat. "I've seen him at the farmer's market. Tall and swoony, with dark hair?"

"Are you girls talking about me again?" Romeo, Juliette's former boss, breezed in from the back room on a cloud of expensive men's cologne. He was a handsome man in his late sixties with silver streaks in his dark hair, and he had a smile that could charm the spots off a leopard. Romeo had recently agreed to sell the florist shop to Juliette, since he and his husband, Caleb, were retiring to Florida.

"We're talking about a guy Kat's moving in with," Juliette said with a laugh.

"And he's tall and swoony?" Romeo held up his coffee cup, toasting to Kat's success. "Good for you, honey."

"I'm not moving in with him," Kat said in exasperation. "It's not like that. He happens to live at Willowbrook Lavender Farm with his grandmother, and I'm just renting the place above their garage."

"Oh." Romeo chuckled. "That guy."

"Yes. Why?" Kat's brows drew together. "Is there something wrong with him? If he's a dangerous ex-con, tell me now because I plan to move in there after work tomorrow."

Romeo's coffee cup was halfway to his mouth, but he paused and lowered it. "Nothing like that. I was just getting my hair cut at Dazzle yesterday, and the ladies over there were complaining about him. They call him Mr. Mysterious because ever since he arrived a month ago, he's been keeping to himself."

"So?" Kat asked. "I keep to myself sometimes."

"But according to them, he's practically antisocial. And he's *single*," Romeo said with an exaggerated shudder. "That's why the ladies are bothered."

Kat wanted to laugh. She hadn't known Romeo long, but he had such an easygoing nature, and he was always quick to find humor in any situation. "Being single isn't exactly a crime, you know."

"Oh, honey," Romeo said. "In a small town like this, it is. If you're a hot-blooded American male, you have to at least try to be social. It's practically the law."

Juliette untied her apron and hung it on a hook behind the register. "Well, now Kat can get the scoop on Mr. Mysterious, and give us all the juicy details."

"What if I find out he's a serial killer?" Kat asked wryly. "What if that's the scoop?"

"Killer shmiller," Romeo teased. "Where's your sense of adventure?"

"I'm sure he's not a bad guy, Kat," Juliette said. "I've seen him selling lavender for his grandmother at the farmer's market. Some people are just really private."

"However," Romeo said, tossing his now empty coffee cup in the garbage can, "if he is a serial killer, can I have Hank when you're dead?" He grinned at the little dog and bent to scratch him under the chin. "You want to move to Florida with me and Caleb, little guy?"

Hank's tail wagged so fast, it was almost a blur.

Kat folded her arms and gave Romeo a look. "If I die, I'm going to haunt *you* first."

He let out a bark of laughter, then picked up the dog, bringing them nose-to-nose. "She can rattle her chains all she wants, right, Hank? We won't care, will we? No, we won't."

"Who said anything about rattling chains?" Kat sassed. "I'm talking *Poltergeist*, evil-clown-doll stuff."

Romeo's expression was a mixture of mock horror and glowing admiration. He glanced at Hank and whispered, "We'll talk later," before setting him back on the floor.

"Let's go grab lunch." Juliette pulled her purse out from under the register. "I'm starving and there's a veggie pizza at Zeek's with my name on it."

Kat thought about her empty apartment above the

garage, and her even emptier bank account. She'd have to wait until she got a few paychecks before she could indulge herself in going out to eat.

But before she had a chance to decline, Juliette pulled a slip of paper from her purse and waved it in the air as she marched out the door. "I have a coupon for buy one, get one free, so today's lunch is on me."

Kat waved good-bye to Romeo and followed Juliette outside with Hank trotting along at her heels. As they made their way toward the pizza parlor near Front Street, Kat thought of Jordan standing on the porch at the farmhouse. He just didn't seem to fit in there with his grandmother. Something felt off about it. He'd seemed restless and casually detached when he showed her around. Mr. Mysterious, indeed. She'd be moving in tomorrow. Whatever his story was, she was about to find out.

Chapter Five

"Here." Smitty dumped a pile of office supplies in front of Kat on Monday afternoon. They spilled across the receptionist desk in a jumble of visual white noise.

"Sort these into the desk drawers so they're organized." Smitty began pointing at drawers with a sparkly red fingernail. "The paper clips go there. The extra staples go here. And everything else goes inside individual boxes in the large file cabinet over there."

Kat feigned interest, mentally filing those instructions under "Things I'd Like to Do Never." She'd been working all day at the Daisy Meadows Pet Rescue, and she still hadn't had a chance to mingle with the animals. Smitty had insisted she learn how to answer the phones and file the paperwork, first.

The rescue office was a small, one-story building with an area in the back for animal crates. Most of the cats and dogs were assigned to volunteers' homes until they were adopted, so thankfully the place wasn't packed with orphaned animals unlike a shelter. One of the things Kat loved about her new job was the prospect of finding homes and pairing animals with the right volunteers.

As soon as Smitty left for lunch, Kat planned to go back

there and get to know the few who were still waiting for foster homes.

"And if anyone wants to drop off an animal, make sure they fill out these forms," Smitty said, pointing to the file divider on the desk. "We don't take any animals unless they fill out forms." She droned on and Kat took a quick peek at Hank under the desk. He was curled up on a pillow asleep, which is where Kat wished she could be.

"So that's it," Smitty finally said, grabbing her spangled denim purse. "I'm off to lunch, and then I have to run some errands. You should be fine here. Darla might come in to pick up the tabby cat. She's one of our foster volunteers." Smitty began digging in her purse, adding, "Just make sure she—"

"Fills out the forms?" Kat gestured to the file divider.

"You got it." Smitty pulled a silver lighter and a pack of cigarettes from her purse. "I'll see you around four o'clock. Call if you have any questions."

Without a backward glance, Smitty stepped outside, lit up a cigarette, and walked across the parking lot to her old Mustang convertible.

Kat watched her drive off, then groaned and laid her head on the desk. Smitty was one of those people who was okay in small doses. But because of all the new job training, today had been one giant overdose. She rose from the office chair and stretched, rolling her head to ease the tension in her neck.

The back room was bigger than the front office, with a wall of crates against the far wall. Larger crates were stacked on the bottom, with smaller crates on a ledge above. There was a dog-washing station in the corner, and shelves of pet food and cat litter near the back door. It wasn't exactly the Ritz-Carlton, but the accommodations were warm, clean, and dry. Sometimes, that was the best you could hope for.

A brown Labrador puppy began barking at Kat.

"Hey there." She opened the crate and helped him out. His whole body wiggled with excitement. Glimpses of long, dull days spent in the crate flashed through Kat's mind when she touched him. The puppy was bored. He wanted to run around. "Okay, you can do that."

She set him down to nose around the room with Hank, then checked out the other crate.

A fat orange tabby stared back at her. Kat read the tag on the crate. "Clementine. Female. Found on Eastlake highway. Estimated 4 years old. Pregnant."

Kat opened the crate, and Clementine laid her ears back. The orange tabby had been a stray for a long time. Kat could *feel* it, even before she touched her. When Kat reached out to stroke her soft fur, she was inundated with images and feelings. A tattered cardboard box left in an open field. Confusion. The shelter of a drainpipe during a rainstorm. Hunger. The roar of trucks speeding along the highway. Fear. Kat's heart squeezed. Clementine had been abandoned. Nothing was worse than being unwanted, but Kat was going to change that.

"You're safe here," Kat whispered, sending comforting messages to the tired cat. "I'm going to find you the best home in the world. I promise."

By the time Smitty returned, Kat was sitting at the reception desk poring over the volunteer list.

Smitty pushed through the front door with a grocery bag in one hand. "How'd it go?"

"Good," Kat said. "I found a volunteer to take care of the puppy, but the tabby cat still needs a place."

Smitty grumbled something and walked over to a small counter in the corner, which served as the makeshift kitchen. There was a mini-fridge, an ancient coffeepot, and some packets of powdered creamer. Her manager's office was right beside it, if you could call it an office.

It was so small, it looked like a closet with a desk and chair crammed inside.

"What about you?" Kat asked suddenly. "Can you keep Clementine at your place?"

Smitty let out a bark of laughter. "Honey, if you saw my place, you'd never ask. I've got three rambunctious dogs. Four, if you count Bobby."

"Bobby?"

"My scruffy dog of a nephew who lives on the other side of the island. He visits me on and off, though not nearly enough as he promises he will." Smitty's normally sour expression softened. "He can be a royal pain in the bee-hind. But family is family, right?"

"Mmm," Kat said. She wouldn't know, but it was easier than explaining she had no idea who her real family was. Foster care wasn't just for animals.

At five o'clock that evening, she scratched the tired tabby between the ears before leaving, vowing to find her a good home. Not everyone had the chance to start life in a happy place. Kat hadn't. She'd grown up in the system, moving every few years into different foster homes. It wasn't ideal, but she always believed she'd find the right place to belong. One of these days, she'd do it, too. But until that time came for herself, she'd help others like Clementine.

Ten minutes later, she pulled into Willowbrook Lavender Farm, parked her car, and headed toward the farmhouse. The front door swung open before she had the chance to knock.

Jordan stood in the doorway, his hair gloriously rumpled and his clothes covered in dust. He looked messy and tired but still too attractive for his own good. "So you came."

"Yes. I said I would." She self-consciously tried to smooth her hair, knowing it was futile. After driving over with the windows open, it probably looked like her head was on fire.

He studied her with a slight frown.

Kat felt a stab of nervousness, wondering if he was going to change his mind about the lease. Clearly, he wasn't thrilled with her presence there, which was beginning to bug her. She wasn't too thrilled with him either. "What's the matter?" she blustered. "Chickening out?"

Amusement flashed in his eyes. He withdrew a set of keys from his pocket and handed them over.

She gripped the key ring. "Why are there two keys?"

"One is for the main house so you can use the kitchen. Opal insisted."

Kat thanked him and turned to go. It had been a long day. The sooner she could unpack in her own private space, the sooner she could relax.

"Let me know if you need help carrying your furniture up."

"That won't be necessary," she said over her shoulder. "I've got it handled." She didn't want him to know there wasn't anything to carry up except a battered old suitcase and a tote bag. The last thing Kat wanted was anyone's pity. Years of practice had taught her just how to play it off when she was lacking something. "I'll see to the animals after I get settled," she said.

"I already took care of it today." He shut the door before she could respond.

"Then I'll just go say hi," Kat said under her breath. Jeez Louise, what the heck was up with him? The beast must've had a bad day at the castle. Or he just didn't like the fact that she was moving in. Whatever it was, she wasn't going to waste her time trying to figure it out. Jordan Prescott could brood all he wanted. Kat had plans for her future, and this time, she wasn't going to veer off course for anyone. Her friends were just going to have to live with the disappointment of not getting to know Mr. Mysterious, because Kat had no time to waste on him.

Twenty minutes later, she and Hank were officially moved in to their new home. Their new *temporary* home, she reminded herself. Eventually she'd need to find a more permanent solution, but for now, it worked. She dropped into the lumpy recliner chair as Hank nosed around the room. He didn't seem impressed.

"It isn't cozy yet, but we'll make it better," she assured him. "I'm going to go shopping as soon as we get our first paycheck."

The recliner chair was overstuffed and several decades out of fashion, but, it would work just fine until she got a bed. Hank jumped into her lap, and she snuggled him close. At least she wasn't alone. All in all, things were going to be okay.

It was past six o'clock by the time Kat made her way to the small gray barn beside the farmhouse. When she neared the gate, she slowed to a stop.

A brand new chicken coop had been erected against one side of the barn. It had nest boxes above the ground for roosting, and the whole structure was enclosed with sturdy wire mesh. The three scrawny chickens were pecking at a pan of corn in the corner. They clucked in contentment when she approached, and Kat could feel their relief at having a safe place to roost.

She thought of Jordan all covered in dust earlier. He must've spent the day building it. No wonder he was tired and grumpy.

Inside the barn, the mini donkey's ears perked up when she approached. He was happy to see her. Kat knelt down to pat his neck, and he pressed his head into her side. "It's good to see you, too," she said, rubbing her forehead against his. "What's your name, little guy? What do they call you?"

A shadow fell over the doorway. "He doesn't have a name."

She turned to find Jordan standing near the entrance. He'd changed his clothes, and his hair was damp, as if he'd just showered. Tall and broad-shouldered, he stood in the doorway limned in sunlight like some mythic warrior, watching her with those glittering golden eyes.

Kat felt her limbs go soft, and she bit her bottom lip. Jeez, the man could melt polar ice caps with that smolder.

"My grandmother wants you to come to dinner," he said.

Kat continued petting the donkey. "Waffles?"

"You want to name the donkey Waffles?"

"No," Kat said with a laugh. "I was talking about your freezer full of waffles. I figured that's what we were having for dinner since you guys rarely cook."

The corners of his mouth curved up. Finally, something other than a smolder. "I think she's making her cornflake casserole. Just lower your expectations and you should survive."

"I saw the new chicken coop," Kat said warmly. "You built it today, didn't you?"

Jordan ran a hand across the back of his neck. "Yes. But only because someone told me it had to happen right away because . . . What was it?" He made a show of searching the ceiling, trying to remember. "Oh, yes. The chickens felt sad and unsafe."

When he looked back at her, there was a mischievous glint in his eyes that made her whole body flush with heat. She had to glance away for a moment to gather up her scattered thoughts. Pressing her lips together, she tried not to smile. "You're teasing me just to get a rise out of me, aren't you?"

"Yes." He leaned his shoulder against the doorframe and grinned. "Is it working?"

Oh, it was working, all right. Just not in the way he meant. One look at Jordan's hard body and wicked smile made Kat want to rise up and follow wherever he wanted to lead. Even if it was flat on her back in the hay. Did he always have this effect on women? Maybe he did, and he was just born with it. She suddenly wondered what he was like as a child. "I bet you were a terror on the playground when you were younger, running around teasing girls."

He shrugged. "Not really. I was more of a quiet kid."

"And did your teachers buy into that whole quiet little angel act?"

He pushed off the doorframe and started walking toward her. "I never said anything about being an angel."

The mini donkey shied away, scrambling back into his stall.

"Hey," Kat called after him. "You're okay, little guy." She rose and followed him, bending down to run her hands over his back in long, comforting strokes. "What do you think of the name Waffles, huh? Does that work for you?"

He nuzzled her hand. Apparently, it did.

"He's afraid of me," Jordan said from a few feet away. "Most animals don't seem to like me."

She turned and stood. "Have you tried to make friends? Usually they're just wary of people who aren't interested. People hold the fate of animals in their hands. If a person has no interest, then they aren't invested in what happens to them. And that's a scary place to be, if you're an animal."

Jordan studied her from beneath dark, thick lashes. "I saw you with that crow the other day."

A nervous zip of energy shot through her. She wondered if he was going to bring that up. "That's Edgar. He's wild, but he's friendly."

"How did you manage to befriend a wild bird?"

"Magic," Kat said lightly. "And Cheetos. That's how it all began. I fed him Cheetos, and he followed me everywhere after that. It was insta-love. Sometimes that's just how it goes, you know what I mean?"

Jordan nodded. "No." That one word was rich with suppressed humor, but when his gaze lowered to her mouth, something in the air seemed to shift between them.

Kat grew very still. It was that same feeling she got when she stood near a wild animal. As if something strong and wild and free was hovering just beyond her reach, and if she was very careful, it might come close enough for her to touch.

She took a calming breath and tried to shake the feeling. "So, yeah. That's how I made friends with Edgar. You should try it sometime."

He lifted a brow. "Magic?"

"No," she said with a laugh. "Attention and treats." She pointed to Waffles, who was now peering around the corner of his stall. "You never know what kind of friendship will bloom if you just show a little interest. Some have lived their whole lives neglected and unwanted. It doesn't take much to win them over with a little bit of kindness."

All the easygoing humor fled from Jordan's expression until Kat could no longer detect anything but polite indifference. And she thought *she* was good at hiding her feelings.

"Dinner's in an hour." Without another word, he turned and walked away.

Kat watched him go, then glanced at Waffles, who'd stopped cowering in his stall once the coast was clear. "Was it something I said?"

The mini donkey stepped closer, rubbing his fuzzy head against her arm.

She scratched him behind the ears. "You know what? Who cares? I'm going to have cornflake casserole for dinner, and I'm determined to enjoy myself."

Waffles made a snuffling sound of encouragement.

"Thanks," Kat whispered. "I'm going to need it."

Chapter Six

Opal answered the door wearing an apron with an embroidered birdhouse on it. She would've looked like a typical storybook grandmother if it weren't for the glittery red fedora on her head. "You're here," she said happily. "But who is this?" She glanced down at Kat's feet.

Hank was sitting on the doormat, grinning up at Opal.

"Hank, I told you to stay outside." Kat pointed to the grassy yard.

"Nonsense!" Opal waved them in. "I've always loved dogs. Fabulous creatures, really. Bring him in and I'll give him a treat."

For a brief moment, Kat wondered how Jordan would react to her dog, but then decided she didn't care. It was Opal's house, too.

"I like your hat," Kat said, following her to the kitchen.

"Oh, I forgot." Opal pulled the fedora off her head. Her wispy hair feathered out in all directions. "It's part of my costume for casino night at the community center. I'm on the party planning committee, you know."

Kat eyed the red glittery hat with black feather plume, wondering what the rest of her costume looked like.

The kitchen table was set with blue and white melamine

plates, paper napkins, and cups. A plastic pitcher of lemonade sat in the middle of the table, along with a square Pyrex dish covered in tin foil. There was a tiny vase with a daisy and a few sprigs of lavender beside the pitcher. The whole effect was quaint and simple, and Kat loved it immediately. Opal had invited her into her home, and Kat was grateful to be included. It wouldn't have mattered if dinner was cold cereal or stale bread.

"Jordan won't be joining us," Opal said. "He had plans to go out."

Kat thought of Jordan out to dinner with Layla, the woman in the red dress, and brushed it aside. It was better if he wasn't there. At least she could relax and get to know Opal without feeling self-conscious. Jordan always made her feel like he could see the parts of herself she kept hidden away. The vulnerable parts. She didn't like it.

Opal went to the fridge and pulled out a covered plate, then chopped meat into tiny pieces, setting it on the floor for Hank. "Here you go, sweet boy." She glanced up at Kat. "Leftovers from yesterday. Dogs love beef."

"You're spoiling him," Kat said, taking a seat at the table. "If you're not careful, you're going to have a new best friend."

"I should be so lucky! I've always said this house needed more pets. A cat, at the very least. In my old house, I had five. But that was before my dear Gerald passed away and I moved in here. Now we've got the chickens and the donkey, but those are barn animals. It's not at all the same as a sweet dog or cat who can curl up next to you on the sofa." She sat in the chair opposite Kat. "Every house needs a good pet or two."

"Or ten," Kat said. "The more the merrier."

"I wholeheartedly agree. Dogs and cats are like potato chips. You can never have just one."

Kat suddenly sat up straighter. "Opal."

"Mmm?"

"Would you want a cat? Just for a little while? There's a pregnant feline at the animal shelter with no place to go. You could be a volunteer if you like, for just a few weeks until the kittens are ready for new homes. I don't think she'd be much trouble. She'd probably just hide and sleep a lot."

"A cat. Kittens." Opal paused, staring at the wall. She seemed far away, immersed in an old memory. But was it a good memory? Kat hoped so.

"Yes," Opal said. "I think that would be lovely. Bring her to me, and I'll take good care of her. I'm happy to be a volunteer at your shelter, too." She handed Kat a napkin. "Put my name on the list."

Kat felt a surge of gratitude for the old woman.

"Now. I hope you like Cheesy Potato Crunch Casserole."

"Sounds delicious." And even if it wasn't, Kat would eat it with enthusiasm. It was the least she could do, considering how much Opal was willing to help with Clementine.

A few minutes later, Kat found out that Cheesy Potato Crunch Casserole was sublime. It was the epitome of comfort food; like a cross between homemade mac 'n' cheese and scalloped potatoes. With cornflakes thrown in for extra crunch. *Cornflakes.* Who knew?

"Mmm," Kat said in bliss. "I think I need to get this recipe."

Opal dished another scoop onto Kat's plate. "I'm so happy you like it. It's impossible to get Jordan to sit still for dinner. He's always running out the door, preferring not to stay home unless absolutely necessary. But then, he was like that as a boy, too."

"He never liked staying home?" Kat would've killed to

have a home where she belonged. Especially if it came with a grandmother who cooked cornflake casseroles.

"I remember thinking he was too quiet. Always alone. Out wandering in the fields, staring off at the horizon. A boy needs more than just chickens to keep him company. But I blame his parents. My son was completely irresponsible in all things, and he found his match in Jordan's mother. Scatterbrained dreamers who preferred partying over the important stuff." She shook her head sadly. "Every pot has a lid, I guess."

Kat wondered what they must've been like. Or, rather, what kind of parents they were to Jordan, but she didn't want to pry. Instead she said, "How long have you lived here in this house?"

Opal poured more lemonade into their glasses. "Over one year now. Jordan's father asked me to come help out on the farm. I agreed because I was lonely after my husband died, but it was a dumb idea to move. At my age, I can't do much around the farm anymore. And I knew it was only a matter of time before they took off and left this all behind." She shook her head. "Never could stick to anything they started. I think they just invited me so there'd be someone to clean up after them when they took off."

"Where did they go?" Kat asked.

The back door to the kitchen suddenly opened before Opal could answer.

Jordan walked in with grocery bags.

"There you are," Opal said. "Come and have a seat, Jordan."

"I'm fine, Grandma." He set the bags on the kitchen counter and began putting the groceries away.

"We saved some of my signature casserole for you."

"I'm not hungry," he said without turning around.

"But it's still hot." Opal began to rise. "Let me get you a plate."

"No," Jordan said in annoyance. Then he seemed to check himself. "No," he repeated politely. "Thanks, but I'm just going to eat the leftovers I brought home yesterday."

Kat looked at Hank's empty dish with dismay. He was curled up under the table near her feet, snoozing.

"The dog ate it," Opal said brightly. "You'll have to eat casserole."

Jordan slowly turned from the cupboard. "What dog?"

Showtime. Kat pressed her lips together and pushed casserole around on her plate with her fork.

"The sweetest little dog you've ever seen," Opal said happily, pointing to Hank. "There he is, the angel."

Kat stole a glance at Jordan from under her lashes.

He was frowning down at Hank, who was oblivious. "You gave my leftover filet mignon to a dog?"

"Well, dogs love beef," Opal said. "Besides, I think—"

"Grandma," Jordan said flatly. "Why is there a dog in the house?"

"He's my dog," Kat said, lifting her chin. "If you don't want him in here I can take him outside."

"You never said anything about having a dog," Jordan accused. "You're here to take care of the animals. Bringing more animals here wasn't part of the deal."

Kat slowly rose from her chair. She'd expected to have more time before she introduced her dog to them, but it was too late now. Where she went, Hank followed. It was nonnegotiable. She arranged her features into a blank look of surprise. "I thought you knew I had a small dog."

"How would I know that?" Jordan's expression darkened. He was glowering. Yup, that was definitely a glower.

"I'm sorry," Kat blustered, knowing it was Hank's future on the line and, therefore, her own. "I could've sworn we discussed that."

"We didn't."

She gritted her teeth and stared him down. "It's not like

there isn't enough room for a tiny dog who barely weighs five pounds."

"A dog wasn't part of the agreement," Jordan continued. "It's not the size that matters."

Kat gave him a sideways glance. "You seem pretty knowledgeable on that subject."

There was a long pause. Uh-oh. Maybe she'd gone too far.

Jordan's mouth twitched. "*Any* dog, large or small, is unwanted here."

"I beg to differ, honey-boy," Opal said in a voice that brooked no argument. "I am pleased as punch to have Hank around the house. Kat and I both vote for Hank, which means you're outnumbered. Two to one."

With that, Opal picked up her plate and walked to the kitchen sink.

Jordan was still glowering at Kat.

She crossed her arms and mouthed, *Honey-boy?* It was deliberately sassy, but she didn't care. He deserved it. Hank was part of her family. If Jordan didn't approve of her dog, then he didn't approve of her.

Before she had a chance to say more, he stalked out of the kitchen.

Chapter Seven

"Can you please hold?" Kat asked for the third time. So far, her second day on the job was going over like a lead balloon. She switched the phone line to the next incoming call. "Hello?"

No one answered. Great. Another call she'd accidentally disconnected. When was she going to get the hang of the office phone? Probably never. Good thing her boss wasn't there to watch her crash and burn. Smitty had taken the morning off, mentioning that her grandson was supposed to stop by. Until that time, Kat was on her own.

She blew out a frustrated breath and switched back to the first caller. "Okay, Wanda, please bring them in." She held the phone away from her ear as the relieved woman on the other end shrieked in gratitude. "Yes, all of them. We'll figure it out."

When Kat finally hung up the phone, she slumped in her chair. "Hank," she said to her dog, who was sleeping under the desk. "Brace yourself for a whole lot of paperwork."

Thirty minutes later, a heavyset woman with ruddy cheeks and dark hair came through the door in a tangle of leashes, wagging tails, and excited barks. She looked exhausted, but the laughter and relief on her face was clear.

"You must be Wanda," Kat said as she came around the counter to take the leashes. Seven mixed Australian shepherd puppies zipped around her legs in a flurry of excitement.

"I might be," the woman said with a laugh. "I've been up for three nights straight and can't remember my name. My younger sister bought a dog without thinking things through. She just started college," Wanda said, as if that explained everything. "All those college kids get animals before they're settled. Next thing you know, my sister's dog has puppies and her landlord says they all have to go. So what does my sister do? She brings them to me." Wanda threw her hands in the air. "All seven puppies, plus the mama."

Wanda bent to pat one of the squirmy puppies on the head. "These little guys need homes with a lot of space where they can run around. I've kept them for almost a week, but at two and a half months old, they're going stir crazy and I'm a wreck. And so is my tiny house."

"What about the mama?" Kat asked. "Do you need a home for her, too?"

"Maisy?" Wanda looked startled. "No, never. She's staying with me for good. We're a family now."

Kat knew exactly how she felt.

"I'd keep them all if I could." Wanda's voice wobbled with emotion. "I really would."

Kat placed a hand on her shoulder. "You've come to the right place. We have a long list of volunteers who take in puppies until they can find good homes. And I'll make sure they only go to homes that are a perfect fit."

Wanda sniffed. "Do you promise?"

"I give you my word." Kat knelt on the floor as seven puppies came at her in a tornado of wet noses, snuffling sounds, and yips of glee. They were brimming over with jubilance and curiosity. Kat laughed. "I can promise you that they're happy and excited about their adventures ahead. You've done very well for them."

By the time Wanda filled out the paperwork and drove away, the new puppies were happily settled in the back room. Kat had already found a home for the other one, and had no doubt she could do the same for these.

"Don't worry," Kat whispered to Clementine, scratching the orange tabby behind the ears. "You're coming home with me today where it will be nice and quiet."

Slapping fur from her jeans and T-shirt, she returned to the front desk feeling pretty good. She was just pulling out the volunteer list to make some phone calls when the bells on the front door jangled.

A tall, handsome man in jeans and a plaid shirt stepped into the office. He was wearing an honest-to-God cowboy hat, cowboy boots, and a silver belt buckle. And it really worked for him. Kat wasn't used to seeing cowboys back in L.A., and she didn't think there were any in the Pacific Northwest, either. But his rugged good looks and warm, friendly expression made her glad to be wrong.

He tipped his hat and said, "Ma'am."

She almost giggled. Because of course he'd say "ma'am." "How can I help you?"

"I'm Bobby." He waited a beat, as if that was enough of an introduction. When Kat didn't respond, he said, "Bobby Bankston? I stopped by to take my aunt to lunch. She said she'd meet me here."

Kat's mouth fell open in surprise. "*You're* Smitty's nephew?"

He grinned, flashing a set of dimples that only added to his charm. "Surprised?"

"No," Kat said, shaking her head. "It's just . . . from the way Smitty talked, I was expecting someone different."

Bobby leaned his forearms on the counter. "Let me

guess. You were expecting a rambunctious, scruffy dog of a boy."

"Sort of?" Kat gave him an apologetic smile.

"If you'd caught me twenty years ago, that's exactly what you'd get. My aunt doesn't seem to realize I've grown up and I don't run around wreaking havoc like I used to. She still sees me as the kid who chopped up her good tablecloths to make a fort in the backyard."

Kat crossed her arms and considered him. "I think I like you better now, knowing you did that."

"If that's the case, I'll have to tell you more about my wild escapades."

Before Kat could answer, Smitty Bankston pushed through the front door on a cloud of nicotine. She took one look at Bobby, and her face splintered into a grin. "Bobby, you better not be hitting on my receptionist."

He walked up to Smitty and engulfed her in a bear hug. She let out a squawk of laughter, and Kat's mouth fell open. The woman could laugh? This Bobby Bankston had some magic in him.

Smitty slapped at his back. "Put me down, you big oaf. You don't want to break your poor aunt's bones. I'm old!"

Bobby gave her a spin and set her back down. "Nah, you're made of solid steel and everyone knows it."

Smitty patted her hair and rearranged her face into its normal sour expression. "Kat, this is Bobby, my no-good scruffy dog of a nephew."

"I like the name Kat," Bobby said, flashing his dimples again. "It suits you."

Kat flushed with pleasure.

Smitty swatted him on the arm. "What'd I tell you? No flirting with my receptionist."

Bobby winked at Kat, then turned to his aunt. "I'd never do that, Aunt Smitty. Scout's honor."

"You most certainly would. And the reason I know this

is because you were never a Boy Scout." She turned to Kat. "Don't believe a word he says." Even though Smitty was trying to look stern, Kat could tell she loved her nephew. It was a side of her boss Kat never expected to see. Crabby morning person? Check. Grouchy chain smoker? Check. Doting aunt? Mind-boggling.

"You taking me to lunch, or what?" Smitty asked, hoisting her denim handbag over her shoulder.

"Yes, but I also came for a legitimate reason. I'd like to adopt a dog."

Kat's admiration for Bobby Bankston jumped up a few more notches. A cute cowboy who also wanted to rescue an animal? That was solid gold in her book. "What kind of dog are you looking for?"

"I need a dog that can help with herding. Anything good for ranch life."

Kat's face lit up. "I just took in seven mixed Australian shepherd puppies. They're born for that kind of life. Once they've had their routine medical check, they should be ready to go. Would you like to see them?"

Bobby hesitated. "A puppy is a different thing altogether. I was hoping for a dog I could use right away. To help with the sheep."

"You'd be surprised how smart Australian shepherds are," Kat said, standing. "They're one of the smartest dog breeds I've ever worked with. I think you could be very happy with one if you gave it a chance."

Bobby hesitated, but Smitty elbowed him in the ribs. "Just go take a look, Bobby."

"All right. Show me your shepherd pups."

Kat felt a wave of triumph as she led Smitty's nephew to the back room where the puppies were frolicking. Another home for another puppy! Things were looking up.

By the time Bobby and Smitty left for lunch, Kat had a full set of paperwork filled out for a lively Australian shepherd puppy. She'd told him to call if he had any questions or concerns. She stapled the paperwork together, watching through the front window as Bobby opened the door of his truck for his aunt. Nice. Very gentlemanly.

She bent to pet Hank and whispered, "Who would've guessed someone like him would be related to Smitty? It's nice to know chivalry isn't dead."

The door swung open. "Ms. Davenport."

Jordan Prescott came through the front door looking tall, dark, and disgruntled—nothing new—and carrying a cylindrical green mesh container. He took a cursory glance at the small office and set the container on the reception desk. "From my grandmother."

Kat peered into the mesh cage. There was a small box on the bottom with a disk inserted into it. On the disk appeared to be several dark blobs. "What is this?"

"Uh . . . orphans?"

Kat frowned. "I don't understand."

He sighed and rubbed a hand across the back of his neck. Even though he seemed tired, humor lit his face and he looked like he was trying not to smile. "My grandmother went to the community center today for her quilting club . . . Or was it crochet?" He shook his head. "I can't keep it straight. Anyway, one of her friends was trying to give this away. It's from a preschool class, and the teacher wasn't able to continue the science lesson, or something."

Kat tried to follow, but she still didn't really understand why Jordan was bringing her what appeared to be cocoons. "So . . . your grandmother wanted me to have them?"

"No," he said. "Not you, specifically. She just wanted me to drop this off at the animal shelter. These cocoons are supposed to turn into butterflies but they haven't hatched, or whatever you call it."

"But why bring them here?" Kat asked.

"You guys take unwanted creatures, don't you?"

"Yes, but we—I can't," she sputtered, shaking her head. "We take *animals*. Like cats and dogs."

"Ah," Jordan said, and held up a finger. "And chickens, if I recall."

She rolled her eyes and pushed the cage toward him. "Don't give me butterflies. We can't take them."

"Sure you can." He backpedaled toward the door and pointed at the cage. "You just did."

Kat shot out of her chair, gripping the green handle. "What am I supposed to do with these? This is an animal shelter, not a bug shelter."

Jordan was grinning now as he pushed open the door. "Don't be so discriminatory. They're poor, sad orphans, remember? I'm sure you can think of something."

"We deal with *animals*," she called out in frustration. "The furry kind."

But he was already too far across the parking lot to hear her.

Kat blew out a breath and sat down hard in her chair. He was so . . . frustrating. Yeah. That was the word. And there was something about the way he walked that bugged her, too. All sexy and easy and confident, as if everything was going according to his grand plans.

She gritted her teeth in determination. Well, she had some plans of her own.

"Fine, Jordan Prescott," she said as he drove away. "I see your cage full of butterflies, and I raise you one very pregnant cat and a soon-to-be litter of kittens."

At six o'clock that evening, Kat carefully unloaded Clementine's plastic cat carrier from her car. She'd borrowed the carrier from the shelter's supply closet, promising Smitty to bring it back in the morning.

Clementine let out a long, low growl. She wasn't happy

with this new, unknown arrangement, but she would be. Kat would make sure of it. She ran up the steps to her apartment as quickly as she could. After the objections Jordan had made about Hank, she was certain he'd be against bringing a cat home. But that wasn't his decision to make. It was his grandmother's house too, and Opal was now an official rescue shelter volunteer. If Jordan had a problem with Clementine, too bad. For now, the poor feline just needed a safe, quiet place to rest, and Kat had found one.

While Kat was gathering the rest of the supplies from her car, Opal hobbled onto the porch with her cane. "I was wondering when you'd get home," she called. "Did you get the butterflies?"

"I did," Kat said.

"Oh, good. I knew it was the right thing to do. Jordan told me it was silly to drop off the cocoons at the shelter, but I knew you'd figure out what to do with them."

"Mmm," Kat said. "We'll take good care of them." How, she had no clue. What did an animal shelter do with cocoons? It wasn't exactly something you could take to the next adoption event. Kitten: Three months old, loves to cuddle. Puppy: Four months, likes to play fetch. Butterfly cocoons: Age unknown, low-maintenance, possibly dying or dead. Yeah. It just didn't have that "adopt me" vibe.

"I've brought the mama cat we talked about," Kat said.

Opal made a sound of delight. "Bring her over right now."

Kat went to get Clementine, and soon the cat supplies were tucked away in the downstairs bathroom of the farmhouse, and Clementine was tucked away underneath the couch. Hiding. Kat had tried to coax her out to meet Opal, but Clementine was having none of it.

"She's just a little nervous," Kat said, sitting up from

her crouching position on the living room floor. "But she'll come around once she figures out it's safe."

"Of course she will," Opal said. "She's a female, and therefore, brilliant. She can take all the time she needs."

Kat stood and slapped dust from her hands. The living room was small, with an overstuffed couch and two mismatched reading chairs. There was a steamer trunk in one corner and an outdated ottoman in front of the fireplace. Aside from the weak hall light, there were no other lamps in the living room. It should've been a cozy room, but there was an aura of neglect that seemed to permeate everything.

"Now," Opal announced. "These old bones are off to bed. I've got to be at my community center in the morning, bright and early."

"What do you have planned there?" Kat asked. She imagined Opal with her friends at the community center playing bridge, or painting with watercolors.

"Dance class."

"Dance?" Kat tried not to let the surprise show on her face.

"Sam Norton's going to lead tomorrow," Opal continued. "He's a great teacher. Much better than that granddaughter of Betty Lou's. Last week she tried to teach us hip-hop, and it was a disaster."

"I can just imagine," Kat managed. "Do you . . . do you dance often?"

Opal patted her hip. "On days when my leg acts up, I just help run the music. But on a good day?" She lifted her arms with a flourish. "Watch out, Ginger Rogers."

Kat laughed. She had a feeling Opal was just stubborn enough to do anything she set her mind to. "Thanks again for helping with Clementine."

"We have lots of space here. If there's any other special

cases, bring them to me." With a wave, Opal made her way down a short hallway to her bedroom on the first floor.

Later that night, Kat sat wearily at the kitchen table eating a sandwich. It had been a long day. After work, she'd managed to buy a few necessary groceries to last until her first paycheck, but beyond that she still had no furniture. She bit into her peanut butter and jelly sandwich, trying to look on the bright side. No furniture? No big deal. The overstuffed recliner chair wasn't the worst place she'd ever slept. At least it was soft and squishy. It was probably even more comfortable than some beds. Everything would work out. In just a few more weeks, she'd have everything she needed.

The front door opened, then closed. A few moments later, Jordan breezed into the kitchen, heading for the fridge.

Kat blinked. He looked so . . . different. Before, he'd always been wearing jeans and old flannels. Casual clothes. But tonight he was wearing slacks and a dress shirt. His hair wasn't as windblown as it usually was, either, and the faint scent of aftershave hung in the air. If she didn't know any better, she'd say he looked like he just came home from a meeting or dinner date.

He paused when he saw her. He seemed almost surprised, as if he'd forgotten that she would show up from time to time.

Get used to it, Mr. Mysterious. I live here now, too.

"How are the orphans?" he asked casually, opening the fridge.

She set her sandwich down and picked up her tea. "You mean the cocoons you forced on me?"

"Oh, come on, Ms. Davenport," he said, searching inside the fridge. "They're soon to be butterflies. Where's your sense of optimism?"

He selected a beer and a leftover deli sandwich.

"I'm plenty optimistic," Kat said, lifting her chin. "But I told you, the Daisy Meadows Pet Rescue doesn't take insects."

"What do you have against butterflies?" he asked.

"Nothing." She actually loved butterflies. They were especially important to the environment. In fact, she was already sort of enamored with her cocoons, and felt responsible for their well-being. What she didn't like was the way he'd breezed into her place of business, dumped them on her, and left without so much as a backward glance. Jordan Prescott was too arrogant for his own good.

"Wait, let me guess." He took a seat at the kitchen table. "You hate color, and butterflies are too colorful for you."

Kat frowned. "I don't hate color."

His gaze traveled over her black shirt. He even tipped his head sideways so he could see her black skirt and boots under the table. Then he gave her a look that drove his point home.

"I like colors just fine," Kat said, yanking on the hem of her shirt. She crossed her feet under the table and sat up straighter. Leave it to him to point out that all she ever wore was black.

He opened his beer. "If you say so."

She shook her head and took a sip of tea. Part of her wanted to explain why her entire wardrobe was black, but then he might wonder why she hadn't bought anything new. And if he came to the conclusion that she was broke, he might feel sorry for her. That was the worst. Kat would rather eat glass than have someone like Jordan Prescott pity her. She didn't need anyone's pity, least of all his.

Jordan took a bite of his sandwich and relaxed back into his chair. He seemed completely at ease in the quiet kitchen, which was the exact opposite of how Kat felt at the moment.

She glanced into her teacup. It was just easier not to look at him. A breeze swirled in through the open kitchen window, and the faint sound of crickets could be heard outside. She searched for something to fill the silence. "Why are you all dressed up?"

"Dinner date," he said, taking another bite of his sandwich.

Kat suddenly thought of the pretty woman named Layla she'd met the first day. The one with the tailored dresses and sleek stilettos. "And yet, here you sit. Eating dinner," she pointed out.

He shrugged. "Second dinner."

Kat studied him from beneath her lashes. "Must've been quite the date."

"Why do you say that?"

"Either it went very badly, or very well." She turned her attention back to her sandwich.

"And you think this because . . . ?"

"Because you either had such a terrible time that you left before dinner arrived, or . . ." She paused and searched for a delicate way to say what she was thinking. "Or you skipped dinner altogether and went straight to . . . dessert."

"*Dessert*?" His face lit with amusement, and something darker. Sexier.

Kat felt her cheeks grow hot.

"Is that what they're calling it these days?" he murmured.

She ate another bite of her sandwich, ignoring him.

"You have quite the imagination, Ms. Davenport."

"Will you please stop calling me that?" she asked irritably.

"Sure, Kat." He gave her that sensual half smile. The one that made the Queen of Impulsive Decisions grab a couple of butterflies and start doing a fan dance.

Kat concentrated on stirring her tea.

"Why did you move here?" he asked suddenly.

Kat gripped her teacup and took a slow breath. She hated personal questions like this. They always led to the inevitable questions about family. Usually she made up something vague and acceptable, but for some reason she didn't feel up to it. "My job ended, and I thought this seemed like a nice place."

"Really? This island?"

"Of course," Kat said, glad to speak the simple truth. "The moment I saw it, I fell in love. What's not to like? It's peaceful. It's beautiful. Life just seems quieter here. Less hectic than L.A., that's for sure."

"So you're from California?"

"Yup." She needed to think fast. In her experience, it was easy to deflect personal questions by asking her own. "Did you grow up here?"

"Yes." Jordan set his sandwich down and picked up his drink. "But I left as soon as I finished high school."

"Why?"

He stared at the far wall, his expression hard to read. Kat had the sudden feeling that he was a million miles away. "Why not?" he said, before taking a drink.

Okay, fine. They both had stories neither of them wanted to share. Even though she was genuinely curious, it was better this way. Keep things nice and light. She finished her sandwich and rose from her chair.

"There's no cable in your room," he said.

She paused, her plate in one hand. "What?"

"For television." He was looking at one of the condiment jars, not making eye contact.

"Oh. It's all right," Kat said. "I don't have a TV, anyway." She walked to the sink and began washing her dishes. After drying them and putting them away, she leaned against the counter and folded her arms. The silence stretched out between them.

"You can use the TV in the living room," he said. "If you want."

That was unexpected. If she didn't know any better, she'd say he was trying to be nice. "Thanks." Kat shifted on her feet, then gave up with the awkward silence. "Good night."

"You sure you don't want dessert before you go?" he asked.

She glanced sharply at him.

He pointed to the fridge, his expression carefully neutral. "The ice cream is in the freezer. Or maybe you don't like dessert?"

She almost missed the flash of laughter in his eyes. He was teasing her again.

Two could play at that game. "Oh, I love dessert. Lots and lots. Especially ice cream. I just lap it right up." She walked to the kitchen door and opened it. "But I like to save dessert for special occasions, and since there's nothing here worth celebrating . . ." She gave a little wave and stepped out the door, shutting it firmly behind her.

A deep, masculine laugh floated through the kitchen window, following her across the lawn. It was such a warm, pleasing sound that Kat slowed her steps to listen further. Later, after she'd stretched out on the recliner chair, she could still hear the warm echo of it in her mind as she drifted off to sleep.

Chapter Eight

Kat slouched in the lumpy recliner chair in her room on Wednesday night, staring glumly at the green mesh cage sitting on the foldout table. Smitty had tried to toss the thing in the dumpster out behind the shelter, but Kat had intercepted and decided to take it home. Whether or not the cocoons were going to morph into butterflies remained to be seen. If Kat concentrated very hard, she could sense life stirring in there, but that didn't mean the metamorphosis would be successful. She'd just have to keep a close eye on them and make sure they stayed safe.

As for her own place . . . Kat glanced around at the plain walls and empty room. "Just another week, Hank," she said to the little dog in her lap. "Payday is next Friday. And then we'll brighten this place up and make it feel like home."

Kat's phone rang and she dug for it in the recliner cushions. "Hello?"

"You're coming on Friday night, right?" Juliette's voice piped up on the other end. "Emma and Hunter are back from Hawaii, and we're going to celebrate with our official movie night."

"Of course I'll come," Kat said. She liked Emma as much as Juliette, and even though she knew very little of

Hunter, she liked him just on principle because he made Emma so happy. "Do you want me to bring anything?" She had to ask, but secretly hoped Juliette would say no. Money was going to be tight until payday, and even after that, she'd have to be extremely careful until she could replenish her savings account.

"Don't bring a thing. There's going to be enough food to feed an army. Logan's making my favorite vegetarian lasagna."

Kat didn't miss the note of happiness in Juliette's voice when she mentioned her fiancé. Juliette and her childhood crush, Logan O'Connor, had recently become engaged. And he was as smitten with Juliette as she was with him.

"Won't I be the fifth wheel?" Kat asked. "You sure you guys don't want to just have a couples' night?"

"Hells no," Juliette said. "First of all, you won't be a fifth wheel because you're bringing Hank. Second of all, we have movie night all the time, and it's totally casual. Emma insists that you come, and I agree one hundred percent. Besides, she usually makes a double batch of cupcakes, and if you don't come, I'm going to be forced to eat most of them myself."

"And that would be a problem because . . . ?"

"Good point," Juliette said. "But you're still coming, and that's final."

Once again, Kat felt a surge of warmth and gratitude for her friend. Something about the way Juliette and her cousin Emma included her into their circle of friends made Kat begin to hope. She'd never really felt like she belonged anywhere, but maybe this time . . . maybe for the first time, Kat would find a place she could truly call home.

After saying good-bye, she hung up and paced her apartment. Funny how just one phone call from Juliette had lifted her spirits and now she was filled with restless energy. She checked the time on her phone. It was past nine o'clock and the sun had already gone down, but she suddenly wanted to go outside. Breathe in the lavender-scented air. Stare up at the moon.

Kat stepped outside and quietly shut her apartment door, then headed down the steps and across the lawn toward the little barn. It was so dark, she used the flashlight on her phone to help navigate over the uneven ground. The heady scent of roses filled the night air, but the tangled bushes were cloaked in shadows, the red blooms invisible in the darkness.

When she reached the barn, she switched on the single light near the entrance. The chickens barely stirred, contentedly tucked away in their coop. But Waffles stuck his head around the stall to see who was visiting.

As soon as he saw Kat, he trotted over, butting his head against her. "I'm happy to see you, too," she said, scratching him between the ears.

She led him out of the gated paddock, across the yard with Hank following, and into a large, overgrown field. The donkey was happier than he'd been in a long time. Kat could feel it. He liked being with her. She made a mental note to find him a friend and to take him on more walks around the farm. Maybe she'd even find a way to move his stall to the larger field, so he could run around freely.

They wandered through the tall grass, in no particular direction. Kat shut off her phone and tilted her face up to the sky, taking in the countless stars overhead. The fresh scent of lavender wafted on the night air, melding with the rich scents of damp earth and the slightest hint of wood smoke. She glanced around, trying to find the source.

Beyond the field, near a small copse of trees, she could see a glowing fire. Like moths toward a flame, Kat and the animals wandered closer.

At the fence, Kat ducked through a slat and started forward. Hank let out a yip of disapproval, and Kat glanced down at her dog. He was staring at the donkey, wagging his tail.

"You'll have to wait with Waffles," she said. "He can't fit through the fence."

Hank trotted back under the fence and nosed around in the grass beside the donkey.

"I'll be back soon."

She made her way toward the small firepit. A long bench made from a fallen log sat in front of it. The fire glowed invitingly, and she crossed her arms, hugging herself. Closing her eyes, she let the warmth seep into her skin. It was blissful. Suddenly, everything she'd been worrying about seemed to slip away, and all seemed right with the world. Maybe if she stood there long enough, she'd start believing it.

Jordan opened the kitchen fridge, searching for the six-pack of beer he'd forgotten to take outside. After spending half the day dealing with the junk in the abandoned barn, and the other half making phone calls to line up help in the fields, he was in the mood for something easy. The campfire he'd started out back was waiting for him, and he intended to enjoy it with no distractions. Just like old times, he thought bitterly. No one around. Nobody to tell him what to do. Nobody to care.

"There you are, honey," his grandmother said, coming into the kitchen. The surprise of seeing her diminutive form, her thinning white hair, still hadn't worn off. She was so much older than he remembered. When he'd first arrived back on Pine Cove Island, he'd been shocked to realize just how much time had passed. Ever since he'd left for college on the East Coast, he'd never returned. In his memory, the place was exactly as he'd left it, and the people were the same. Now, looking at his grandmother, it was disconcerting to realize how much older she was.

He hadn't seen his grandparents very often when he was growing up. His own parents had a shaky relationship with them, so Jordan only saw them once in a while. But he remembered how kind his grandparents had been. They always seemed to remember the important things.

"I have something special, just for you." She headed toward the cupboard. He noticed she was favoring her leg a little more than usual. Some days she seemed okay, but he knew she struggled with a stiff hip and swollen joints.

"Grandma, how's your arthritis?"

"Same as it always is," she said over her shoulder. "Finicky. Has a mind of its own and sometimes it insists on taking the lead, but I won't give in that easily."

Jordan set the six-pack on the kitchen counter and watched her rummage through the cupboard. No, she wasn't the type to give up easily, which was one of the things he appreciated about her. He imagined he got his determination and drive from her. She was nothing like his parents.

"Here we go." She pulled out a paper bag. Her grin turned her face into a map of wrinkles, her pale blue eyes alight with happiness.

Jordan took the bag and peered inside. His chest tightened. "You remembered."

"Of course I did. I would never forget something so important. But I'm not going to make it out to the campfire this time, I'm afraid. My hip isn't up for that kind of a trek any longer. You'll have to go without me."

Jordan nodded, overcome with a bittersweet longing for days gone by. Years ago, his grandparents had started a tradition with him, and now that his grandfather was gone, Opal was carrying it on.

He suddenly wanted to hug her, which was crazy. They

didn't have that kind of relationship. Instead he patted her arm awkwardly. "Thanks, Grandma."

She laid a frail hand on his. "You know your grandfather and I were always so proud of you. We always wished to see you more. If your parents hadn't been so stubborn about living the way they did . . ." Her voice trailed off, and she wiped the corner of one eye with her hand.

Jordan patted her arm, then stepped back. He thanked her again, grabbed his six-pack and the brown paper bag, and set off toward the campfire. Now, more than ever, he just wanted to be alone. There was no use reminiscing about the past and what could've been. He'd learned that a long time ago.

He crossed the clearing in the far field and made his way toward the glowing campfire. Nearing the circle of warmth, he stopped and stared.

As though she'd been conjured from firelight, Kat stood in the center of the circle. Eyes closed. Face tilted toward the stars. Lips parted in pleasure. Arms outstretched, palms to the fire. She looked like a nature goddess, with her red hair swirling softly around her face.

Damn. Jordan's gut clenched. She was the kind of beautiful that could drive a man crazy. Good thing he'd had a lifetime of experience dealing with crazy, and he knew how to steel himself against it.

Jordan walked toward her until he was so close he could reach out an arm and touch her. Not that he would.

Kat opened her eyes and let out a startled gasp. She stumbled backward until the back of her knees hit the fallen log, and she sat down hard. "You scared me," she said in accusation.

Jordan set the beer and paper bag on the ground and stared down at her. "I'd apologize," he said. "But I'm not the one intruding." He sounded harsh, but he couldn't stop himself. Why was he always so confrontational around her? Maybe because it was easier to keep her at arm's length. She was the kind of woman a man could lose himself in, and that's the last thing he needed.

Kat tried to smooth her wild hair with both hands, but it was no use. The mop of curls sprang back as soon as she let go, surrounding her like a fiery halo. Jordan had the sudden urge to reach out and touch it. Instead he turned away and unhooked a can of beer from the six-pack.

"What are you doing out here?" she asked.

He sat on the ground with his back against the log. "Thinking." Without looking at her, he unhooked another can of beer and held it out.

She took it and sat on the fallen log. "I like the way you think."

They sat in silence for a while before he said, "What are you doing out here?"

"Taking Hank and Waffles for a walk."

As if she'd planned it, Hank trotted up to the campfire with Waffles trailing behind. The donkey took one look at Jordan and stayed just out of the circle of light.

"How did you guys get out of the paddock?" Kat asked her dog.

Hank touched his nose to her hand, then went over to investigate Jordan's shoe.

Jordan watched the tiny dog tug at his shoelace. "The latch on the fence is broken," he said, taking another swig of beer. "Do you always bring your four-legged friends with you on midnight strolls?"

Kat scoffed. "It's hardly midnight. And yes, as a matter of fact. I do take my animals with me wherever I can. I find their company to be a lot more pleasing than the alternative."

Jordan searched the shadows behind Kat. "Your donkey friend doesn't seem very pleased."

"He's scared of you because he thinks you don't care about him."

Jordan frowned. "I don't . . . *not* care about him. I never actually think about him that much."

Kat shook her head in resignation. "Apathy. That's even worse."

Jordan's lips twitched. She had the oddest way of simultaneously annoying and amusing him. "He's a donkey. What am I supposed to do? Read him bedtime stories and tie ribbons in his hair?"

She seemed to consider it for a moment. "I don't think he'd care about ribbons, but he'd be open to bedtime stories."

Jordan shook his head. "You're very—"

"Weird?" Kat slid off the log and sat cross-legged beside him, staring up at the stars. "I know. I also don't care. I've spent far too many years of my life caring about what other people think. This time, I'm just going to be me." She took another sip of her beer.

"I was going to say you're very imaginative." Jordan regarded her thoughtfully. The firelight cast a warm glow over her heart-shaped face, accentuating her high cheekbones and the sweet curve of her lips. She was like some beautiful mystery he very much wanted to solve. "What do you mean, 'this time' you're going to be yourself? When weren't you?"

Kat stared into the flames.

Jordan didn't press her. Instead he lifted a long, slender stick and pulled out a pocketknife. With slow, methodical strokes he began stripping the bark from the stick.

"What are you doing?" Kat asked.

"Something very important." He focused on the stick. "It's a tradition I started back when I was a kid. I could tell you . . ." He lifted the stick, considering it at all angles, then began scraping more bark. "Or I could just stare mysteriously into the fire. I haven't decided yet."

"I'm not trying to be mysterious," she said.

"And yet, I am mystified." He kept scraping the bark from the stick, not making eye contact.

"It's not all that interesting," she insisted.

Jordan felt a surge of triumph. "Tell me anyway."

"My life back in L.A. was a lot different. It was noisier, and there was always something going on." She paused. "And I had a boyfriend."

He studied the stick and continued scraping.

"I had a boyfriend," she repeated, "who was all wrong for me. He was really into partying, and he had lots of friends and connections. So we were always obligated to go places. Fancy places that required all sorts of preparation."

Jordan frowned. "What kind of preparation?"

"The kind you need for the L.A. party scene. You always had to worry about what to wear. What to say. What not to say. Where's the hottest place to be seen. And it all changed so fast. It was mercurial. One second you could be cooler than an iceberg in Alaska, and the next"—she snapped her fingers—"no one wants to know you." She took another sip of beer. "After a while I just went through the motions and forgot who I really was. I just got swept into this crowd I didn't even particularly like, and that became my life."

"Until . . . ?" He wondered what it took to bring her from that lifestyle to this one. It was a big change.

She set her beer down and held her hands toward the fire. "Until one day, I was supposed to go to this fancy event, so I borrowed a dress from one of my friends. The night of the party, we were getting ready to leave, and he found out it was borrowed. So he got mad and said I would embarrass him if I wore recycled clothing to a photographed event. And I said I didn't care. And then we argued." She acted like it was no big deal. But Jordan could tell it was a memory she didn't want to think about. He had a lot of those.

"He told me to go change, but something snapped inside me. I refused. And then he said he'd be better off going without me. And that was it."

"So then you left him," Jordan said conversationally, trying to keep his tone light, for her sake. "But not before grabbing him by the throat and choking him with his own bow tie."

Kat gave a weak smile.

"So what happened?" Jordan asked.

"Timing was on my side," she said. "I'd just got offered a summer job on a houseboat reality show, taking care of that little guy." She pointed a finger at Hank, who was now sniffing at the brown paper bag. "So I took the job and never looked back. A woman on the show used Hank as an arm charm, but she didn't really care about him. When my job ended, so did her interest in Hank, so I took him with me."

Hank heard his name and zipped over to Kat, wagging his tail.

She picked him up and snuggled him close, staring into the fire.

"And that's when you decided to stay here?" Jordan asked.

"I thought this was as good a place as any to start over. And I'd been wanting to leave the L.A. scene behind for a long time; I just didn't have the opportunity, I guess."

Jordan waited for her to say more, but she didn't. "It sounds like you did the right thing," he said quietly. "For yourself, and for Hank."

The way she looked at him with the firelight glancing off her brilliant hair, highlighting her delicate heart-shaped face—she was so damn alluring, any man would be an idiot to let her go. Her ex-boyfriend was a fool.

A snuffling grunt came from behind Kat's right shoulder. The donkey had grown a little bolder, moving closer to Kat.

"Waffles, Jordan wants to be your friend," Kat said. "Don't you want to come and say hello?"

The donkey brayed and trotted away.

She turned back to Jordan. "I guess he's being cautious. You should make the first move. Next time, give him a treat."

Jordan gave her a dubious look. "I'm not in the habit of carrying treats around for barn animals."

"Maybe you should try it," Kat said.

He finished whittling the stick and set it beside him.

"So?" Kat asked. "Are you going to tell me what you're doing with that stick?"

Jordan opened the paper bag his grandmother had given him, then pulled out a bag of marshmallows and opened it.

Kat's jaw dropped. "You're kidding me."

Jordan speared two marshmallows on the end of the stick, then leaned forward and held them over the fire.

"You're roasting marshmallows out here, by yourself," Kat said, incredulous. It was the type of thing a person did at summer camp. With a group of friends. When you were twelve.

"I'm not by myself." Jordan glanced sideways at her. "You're here. And so are two of your closest friends."

Jordan handed her the stick, then pulled out a package of graham crackers and a bar of chocolate.

"Oh, *what*?" Kat blurted. "You're making s'mores

now?" She couldn't believe it. What guy did that by himself? No guy she ever knew.

"You don't have to have one, if you don't want one," he said, pulling out a graham cracker and breaking off a piece of chocolate.

She looked at him like he was crazy. "Of course I want one. But this is just so weird."

"Not any weirder than talking to wild crows," he said pointedly.

Heat crept up the back of her neck. He had a point, but still. "I don't know a single person who builds a campfire and makes s'mores by themselves. It just doesn't seem right."

He gave her a level stare. "S'mores are always right." Then he scooped melted marshmallow onto a graham cracker square, added chocolate, and handed it to her.

She took it mechanically, staring at him. "Shouldn't you be doing this with sleeping bags and friends and singing 'Kumbaya,' or something?"

"I wasn't planning on spending the night out here." He paused and gave her a sideways look that sent a shiver of excitement through her. In the firelight, his eyes were more golden than ever, reminding her of a wolf. The thin, silvery scar on his cheek just added to the wildness. "But if you really want to, I could go grab camping gear and get my guitar."

"You play the guitar?" A ripple of pleasure washed over her at the idea of him strumming away in front of the fire. She shoved it aside, focusing instead on another bite of chocolatey melted marshmallow heaven. Sure, the whole scenario tonight was a little surprising, but so what? Nothing special about a guy who played guitar and roasted marshmallows over secret campfires. Nothing sexy, either. Nope.

"I do," he admitted. "But it's been a while."

Kat's fascination with Mr. Mysterious was beginning to escalate, and that was not good. So he had some hidden talents. Lots of guys did. She fought to ignore the warmth blooming inside her at the nearness of him.

For long moments, they ate in companionable silence, staring into the flames.

Waffles eventually grew bolder and wandered closer to the campfire. The faint sound of crickets melded with the sound of the breeze whispering through the tall grass. Kat was lulled into a deep sense of contentment. The warm fire. The s'mores. The stars overhead. The odd feeling of companionship with a person she barely knew.

"I've never done this," she mused.

"Had s'mores and beer with a donkey in the middle of the night?" He speared another marshmallow with the stick and held it over the fire. "Me neither."

"No, this." She gestured to the campfire. "The whole camping thing. I mean, I know we're not camping, but still."

He studied her for a moment. "You grew up in California and never went camping?"

A twinge of alarm gripped her. She didn't usually talk about her past. "I grew up in a big city with a lot of things to do . . . but I just never got around to camping, I guess." She searched for something to say to steer the conversation in another direction. "But it does seem odd to me. You out here by yourself, making s'mores. I mean, who does that?"

"My grandmother's idea," he said.

"Still—"

"When I was a kid, she and my grandfather would sneak over late at night and we'd come out here on my birthday."

Kat suddenly didn't feel like teasing him anymore. "It's your birthday?"

Jordan gave a half shrug. "Just a dumb tradition."

An odd sense of melancholy washed over her. "I don't think it's dumb. I think it's pretty wonderful you had grandparents like that."

He didn't respond.

"Why'd they have to sneak out late at night?" Kat asked.

He stared into the fire for long moments. "My parents didn't get along with them. So I rarely saw them."

"Oh." Kat didn't know what to say. Usually it was *her* story that rendered people at a loss. "Well," she said as brightly as possible. "I like your family's tradition."

"Not my family's. Just mine. My grandparents started it when I was a kid, but over the years they stopped coming because my grandfather couldn't drive at night."

Some of the warmth from the firelight seemed to ebb away. "So you celebrated your birthday out here . . . by yourself?"

He took another sip of beer and gave her a quizzical look. "Don't look so distraught. It wasn't that big of a deal. My parents were what they liked to call 'free spirits.' They didn't celebrate birthdays or holidays very often."

"But, why?" Kat asked. "Was it a religious thing, or something?" It didn't make any sense. If Kat had a family, she'd make birthdays the most important thing in the world.

"Because that would've required them to be responsible and dependable," Jordan said casually. He appeared not to care, but Kat wasn't fooled. "It would've required them to pay attention to calendar dates and conform to societal rules, which they shunned. This farm was their grand, hippie idea to live off the land. Except they never actually worked the land, so things were always falling apart."

Kat's heart squeezed at the thought of Jordan as a small boy, living in such neglect. She finally understood a little about why he was so closed off. Growing up with such uncertainty made a person cautious. They had more in common than she realized.

"How long have you lived here?" she asked.

"I don't live here, thank God," he said firmly. "I live in Manhattan. I've taken a couple months off from my business to help my grandmother and to fix up the house. But I'm heading back as soon as that's done."

Now it all made sense. "I knew you didn't look like a lavender farmer. So that's your plan. Fix up your family's house, sell it, and then go back to New York?"

"I'm not staying out here one moment longer than necessary." The marshmallows fell into the fire, and he tossed the stick in after them. A muscle clenched in his jaw, as if he were steeling himself with resolve.

Kat knew that look, because she'd felt it herself. She rallied for his sake. "Well, I'm happy I stumbled upon you and your secret birthday tradition."

Waffles snuffled her hair, and she laughed, swatting him away.

The miniature donkey eyed Jordan. Or more precisely, he eyed the graham crackers. He took a tentative step toward him.

"Now's your chance," Kat said in a stage whisper. "Just give him one, and you'll make a friend for life."

Jordan shook his head, but he dug into the box and pulled out a broken square.

Waffles tilted his nose up and sniffed the air, but he didn't step closer.

"Just ask him to come closer," Kat urged.

Jordan shot her a skeptical look. "*Ask* him? Just like that?"

"Sure. Ask him. I talk to animals all the time. It's the best way to befriend them."

"I'll pass."

Kat didn't know who was more stubborn, Jordan or the

donkey. "Okay, then. Maybe put the graham cracker in between us, since he's more comfortable with me."

Jordan surprised her by scooting closer.

Her cheeks grew warm, and it had nothing to do with the fire and everything to do with Jordan Prescott sitting close enough that their shoulders were almost touching.

Waffles backed away, standing just out of the circle of light.

Kat crooned to the skittish animal, then called him closer. She was peering into the dark, but she could feel Jordan watching her.

Waffles slowly moved forward until he was within an arm's length of them.

"That's it," Kat said. "Look what Jordan has for you. He brought them all the way out here just for you, because he wants to be friends."

She stole a quick glance at Jordan.

He gave her a skeptical look.

She almost laughed, but she didn't want to startle the little donkey.

Waffles waited a few more moments, then finally stretched his neck, plucked the graham cracker from Jordan's hand, and trotted away. The sound of contented crunching could be heard beyond the circle of light.

"That's a win," Kat said happily. "I think there's hope for you yet."

He seemed pleased, in spite of himself. When his warm gaze lowered to her mouth, Kat suddenly felt as though everything slowed to a halt. She tried to remember all that stuff about living her own life and focusing on what she wanted, except the only thing she wanted right now was to lean closer and see what happened next. Would it be so bad? Just a simple, no-big-deal kiss? Maybe she should just go for it. Inside her, the Queen of Impulsive Decisions sat bolt upright amid her bed of stirring butterflies and nodded her head emphatically.

Jordan shifted slightly, his broad shoulder touching hers.

Awareness washed over her, and she took a shaky breath. Maybe they could just kiss this one time, and then it would be out of the way. Done. A funny moment she could laugh about later.

Jordan's expression grew more serious. Neither of them were smiling anymore. Kat knew with sudden certainty that no part of kissing him would be a laughing matter.

Very slowly, he began to lean closer.

Her mouth opened on a tiny inhale. Was this kiss actually happening? She exhaled softly as she tilted her face up. Maybe just this once—

Suddenly, Jordan stiffened and bumped into her. Their faces mashed together awkwardly and he cursed, bracing a hand against the log. He spun around. "What the . . . ?"

Waffles brayed once, then nudged Jordan's back again with his nose.

Kat stared wide-eyed at the donkey, who was now wedging his head between them, searching for more treats. The tension building inside her released in the form of a giggle. Then another. She took one look at Jordan's disgruntled expression and couldn't stop.

He leaned back against the fallen log with a heavy sigh.

"I think you have a new best friend," Kat managed. "He's not scared of you anymore."

"Lucky me."

"It's a good thing," she insisted.

"Right." He reached into the box of graham crackers and pulled one out. "Here, you greedy beast."

Waffles took the treat and, instead of leaving, stayed right where he was, crunching the snack in Jordan's face, dropping crumbs into his lap.

"Admit it," Kat said in a voice tinged with laughter. "You're glad we showed up to help celebrate your birthday."

"It's debatable." He gently pushed Waffles to the side and rose to throw another log on the fire.

"Oh, come on," Kat teased. "At least we're not boring. Think of us as a fabulous, unexpected birthday surprise."

A smile tugged at the corners of his mouth. "You're unexpected. I'll say that." He rose to throw another log on the fire. When he finished, he settled back on the ground a few feet away, like before.

Okay. Kat took a sip of her beer. So the kissing window of opportunity was now firmly slammed shut. She felt a stab of disappointment, but she refused to let it linger. What the heck was wrong with her? She should be sighing with relief that they didn't kiss. It would've just made things awkward. He'd be heading back to New York City soon, and she'd be settling into her new home here, and that was that. It was better this way.

Jordan was sitting with his back propped against the log, one leg drawn up, a forearm resting on his knee as he stared into the fire. Even relaxed as he was, he exuded a sort of wild, tightly coiled energy that made her want to crawl over there and lay her hands on him just to see if it would resonate through her bones.

She tore her gaze away and gave herself a quick mental shake. *Get a grip.* She knew better than to get all dreamy-eyed over someone like him. Most of her past relationships with men were tumultuous, whirlwind affairs, burning hot and bright in the beginning, then dying out faster than a candle in a windstorm. That's probably all this was—a frivolous interest in him because he was new and mysterious. Better to recognize it now, before she let herself get swept away.

Hugging her knees to her chest, she tipped her head back and let out a heavy sigh. Somehow, as much as she wanted to believe Jordan Prescott was no big deal, she couldn't quite make the stretch. There were a lot of uncertainties in her life since she moved to Pine Cove Island, but one thing was as clear as the starry sky above. If she had kissed Jordan, it would not have been something she could easily forget. A person doesn't just slide up and kiss a wild animal without losing a piece of themselves in the process. And as alluring as this beast was, she couldn't risk it.

Chapter Nine

Kat stepped out of the shower feeling restless and a little off-center. Ever since the campfire moment with Jordan, she'd had a hard time keeping him out of her head. It would've been easier to forget about him if he'd just remained "Opal's grandson" or Mr. Mysterious or even just Tall, Dark, and Broody. Sure, he was sexy as sin, but hey. She could've ignored that. Maybe. The problem was, she'd seen a different side of him last night. He'd been more easy and relaxed. When he told her a little about his childhood, it was like a door in her heart opened just a crack. He'd been easy to talk to. A great listener. Sweet to her animals, even when one of them greedily demanded graham crackers and derailed that kiss before it had a chance to happen.

Muttering under her breath, Kat ran a comb through her damp hair, then walked out of the bathroom. Now things just felt all jumbled up inside. Jordan was a complication. That was the problem. Lord knew she'd always been attracted to complicated men.

"But not this time, Hank," she told her dog as she flopped onto the recliner.

Hank jumped into her lap.

"This time I'm staying on track. No complications."

A text message popped up on her phone. She didn't recognize the number.

Hey, it's Bobby. Are you free for dinner tonight?

Kat stared at the message, considering. Nothing complicated about Bobby Bankston, and his cowboy charm wasn't lost on her, either. He even lived on the island, which was a big plus. But he was Smitty's nephew, and it was probably better not to date her boss's relatives. Besides, she'd already sworn off men until she established her new life on her own terms. She started to text a polite reply when another message popped up.

This dinner invitation is strictly for the purpose of learning more about the puppy I adopted. Not because I think you're cute, or anything. Scout's honor.

Kat grinned, then texted back. I have it on good authority that you were never a Boy Scout.
A long pause.

Come to dinner with me anyway. I'll tell you stories about how I drove my aunt crazy when I was a kid.

That sounded entertaining. And she was kind of hungry . . .
Okay, Kat texted back. That won me over.

Not my charm and ridiculous good looks?
Nope.
I can live with it. Pick you up at seven?

Kat agreed and tossed her phone on the recliner, then went in search of something to wear.

Jordan sat across from Layla Gentry at the Silver Coho Grill. The small restaurant was a renovated house with modern décor and low, intimate lighting. They'd just spent the last hour going over the details of his property, comparable pricing, and the right time to sell.

Layla was on another one of her rants about the market, and Jordan just let her talk. They'd been friends for a long time, and he knew how passionate she was about her business. After all, that was why he'd chosen her. Of all the Realtors on the island, Layla Gentry knew the market better than anyone. If he was going to turn the property around and make a decent profit, Layla was the one who'd help him do it.

He signaled the waiter for the check, then stopped when he saw the couple coming through the front entrance.

"But enough about all that drama," Layla said with a throaty laugh. "What about you? What's going on with your business back home?"

Jordan murmured something in response, distracted by the petite, curvy redhead in the fitted black dress. *Kat.* She was smiling up at some guy in a ridiculous cowboy hat as the hostess led them to a table . . . right next to his. Of course.

Kat sat down and scanned the restaurant. When their eyes met, she looked startled, then she glanced at Layla, who was reading a menu.

The waiter stopped to refill Jordan's glass.

"Mmm, let's have dessert," Layla announced. "What looks good?"

It would have taken a herculean effort not to look at Kat in that moment.

"Ooh, this one has homemade French vanilla whipped cream. Yum," Layla said with enthusiasm.

Kat raised her brows, her bright green eyes dancing with humor.

He suddenly wanted to laugh. She had the oddest way of doing that to him.

Kat's date said something, and she turned toward him.

Disappointment and something sharper twisted in Jordan's gut. Something he wasn't accustomed to feeling. Jealousy? Surely not.

He finished off his wine and forced his attention back to Layla. He'd agreed to meet with her so they could discuss the property, but Layla had drawn out the dinner with talk of people they both knew from high school. If there was one thing he remembered most about her, it was her knowledge of all the latest gossip. It didn't bother him because he knew the level of importance she placed on her position in the community, and he understood why.

Layla had once been dirt poor like him, and she'd clawed her way to the top through sheer force of will. She was smart. Pretty. Determined. All things he admired. They'd once tried dating back in high school, but that had been a total flop. Both of them quickly realized there was no spark, and they'd even laughed about it later. Layla was like the sister he never had. All he felt was a brotherly affection for her and an admiration for how far she'd come. Being around her was comfortable and easy.

Kat laughed at something her date said, and Jordan flicked a glance in her direction. She was reading the menu, her hair a riot of bright curls around her delicate face.

He frowned. Nothing comfortable about Kat. Everything about her bothered him, especially the sassy way she tilted her chin, and the lush fullness of her mouth, and the soft curves of her body in that form-fitting black dress. Yeah, he was bothered, all right, but he didn't care to examine why.

Forcing his attention back to the menu, he pretended to read the dessert choices.

"What're you going to have?" Layla asked. "I think the crème brûlée sounds good."

Kat said something to her date in a low, throaty murmur that made Jordan's skin prickle in awareness and blood flow in a heated rush through his torso . . . and lower. *Christ.* Just the low pitch of her silky voice made his body jerk to attention like a horny teenager.

Jordan grimaced and set the menu aside. He needed to get out of there. "I'm not having any."

Layla looked surprised. "Really? But you love dessert."

Kat stifled a laugh. It might've been because of something her date was saying, but Jordan had the distinct feeling she was laughing at him.

Her date reached across the table, pointing to a small scar on his hand.

Kat studied it, tracing the pad of the man's thumb with the tip of her finger.

A sharp pang twisted inside him again, making him feel hot and irritable. What the hell was wrong with him? It couldn't be jealousy, except it damn well felt like it. He shifted uncomfortably on his chair. "Why don't we go to the pie bar over on Seventh Avenue?"

Layla brightened. "Sure. I love that place."

Jordan signaled for the waiter. He had absolutely no desire for pie or for prolonging their dinner meeting, but he'd do anything to get out of the restaurant. The last thing he wanted to do was sit beside Kat Davenport while she fawned over some other man. Not because he was jealous, of course. It just wasn't any of his business. That was all.

Chapter Ten

It was seven o'clock by the time Kat pulled her car into the driveway of Emma's house for movie night on Friday. She'd dressed in her usual black clothes, carefully applied her makeup, and wove her hair into two thick braids down her back. Everything about the scenario should've felt normal, but as Kat neared the house, she had the oddest jittery feeling in her limbs. Like she was hovering at the top of a roller coaster, about to plunge into strange and unknown territory.

She pulled into the driveway and parked, staring at the yellow Queen Anne house with the turret and cheerful white porch. It was a beautiful house. The kind of house that made a person ache for a place just like it to call home. A lump formed in her throat, and she blinked at the sudden rush of emotions. What the heck? It wasn't like her to get so nostalgic about a place. Especially a place she'd never been. It must be all the stress over finding new living arrangements and trying to make a new life for herself.

Hank, who'd been sitting on her lap, hopped to the ground as soon as she opened the driver's-side door. He immediately began nosing around the rosebushes near the fence. Kat slowly stepped out of the car.

For several moments she just stared wistfully at the

house. Warm light glowed through all the windows, and
Kat knew with sudden certainty that happiness lived there.
She was glad for Juliette and her cousin Emma. Both
women had found the perfect balance in their lives. Juliette
with her flower shop, and Emma with her bakery. How
wonderful it must be to know exactly where you belonged.

"What must that be like?" Kat mused under her breath.
It wasn't until a sudden breeze swirled into the yard, pushing at her back, that she shut the car door, gave a shaky
laugh, and marched across the lawn to the front porch steps.

"Hank, let's go," she called.

Hank ran out from under the rosebush, and she picked
him up, then climbed the porch steps.

At the door, she tucked a loose curl behind her ear and
prepared to knock.

The doorknob turned, and the door swung open.

Kat grinned, expecting to see Juliette on the threshold.
Instead she saw . . . no one.

She shifted on her feet, waiting for someone to appear.
Who had opened the door? Voices in conversation came
from down the hall. Kat could hear Juliette laughing at
something her fiancé, Logan, said. Still, no one came to
greet her.

Kat took a tentative step over the threshold. "Um,
hello?"

The foyer was small, with a table and vase of flowers
against the wall, and a row of hooks for coats and car keys.
There was a colorful round area rug on the gleaming hardwood floor, and the walls were painted a soft yellow—the
exact color of sunshine. Everything about it was warm and
inviting, just like the Holloway women.

Hank tried to wriggle out of her grasp, but Kat held on.
It would be impolite to let him run around the house before
she'd made her presence known.

A huge dog with fleece the color of brown sugar came

scrambling into the foyer. He looked like a Muppet from *Sesame Street*, with floppy ears and paws the size of dinner plates.

Hank wriggled harder in her arms.

Kat crouched down to greet Emma's dog. She'd only met him a few times, but he was a gentle giant and Kat was already half in love with him. "Hi, Buddy," she said. "I've brought Hank to visit."

Setting Hank on the floor, she stepped farther into the foyer while the dogs greeted each other with bounces and loud snuffling.

The door swung firmly shut. Kat startled, glancing behind her. It must've been the wind. Remnants of the cool night air still lingered in the entry room.

The voices down the hall suddenly stopped talking.

"Hello?" Kat slowly walked toward the direction of the voices. She stopped at the entrance to a cozy living room with well-worn furniture and a shabby chic vibe.

Juliette and her fiancé, Logan, were sprawled beside each other on an overstuffed couch with a quilt and a bowl of popcorn between them. Logan's tawny hair was mussed, and he had his arm slung around Juliette's shoulders.

Emma was sitting cross-legged on the floor with her blond hair piled in a messy bun. Her husband, Hunter, sat behind her in an armchair, his hands resting on her shoulders as though he were in the process of giving her a neck massage.

All four people were looking at Kat in shocked surprise.

She shifted nervously on her feet. "Um, I'm sorry the door slammed." She gestured behind her. "I think the wind blew it shut. Someone opened it, but I didn't see anybody, so . . ."

Still, nobody spoke.

Juliette looked incredulous.

Emma's mouth was open.

The men glanced at each other.

Kat jerked a thumb behind her nervously. "Sh-should I go back outside and knock again?" Something was up, but she had no idea what. For several moments, she could hear the clock on the mantel ticking loudly in the silence.

Then everyone began talking at once.

"—How did you get inside?" Emma asked, coming to her feet.

"—Did the door open on its own?" Juliette leapt from the couch, tossing aside the patchwork quilt.

Logan's arm shot out to steady the bowl of popcorn.

"This is interesting," Hunter said to Kat.

"Somehow, I'm not surprised," Logan said with a laugh, setting the popcorn bowl on the coffee table.

Juliette reached Kat first. She gripped her by the shoulders with excitement. "How did you get inside?"

Emma came up behind Juliette. "Did the door open for you? Like, did the handle turn?"

Both women were staring at her like she was about to reveal the secret to the lost city of gold.

Kat began to frown. "Yes. But I figured—"

Juliette let out a *whoop* of delight and Emma clasped her hands together.

"Let's check, just to make sure." Juliette grabbed Kat's hand and pulled her toward the front door. "The house never makes mistakes."

Before Kat knew what was happening, Emma and Juliette pulled her back out the front door and down the steps. What was going on?

"Stay right here," Juliette commanded.

Then they disappeared back inside and shut the door. Kat could hear them sliding a deadbolt home.

She stared down at Hank and Buddy, who had followed them outside. "What the heck is going on?"

Both dogs grinned up at her, tails wagging furiously.

A few seconds later, one of the living room windows slid open and Emma and Juliette stuck their heads out.

"Okay," Emma called. "You can come in again."

"Just walk up to the door," Juliette said.

Kat hesitated. "Why am I doing this again?"

"Just try knocking, like before," Juliette called.

Kat started up the front porch steps. Again.

This time, she heard the deadbolt slide. Then the doorknob turned, and the front door swung wide.

She slowly stepped over the threshold. "Okay, I'm in."

Both Juliette and Emma came barreling down the hall toward her. They enveloped her in a jumble of hugs and giggles and the scent of popcorn and vanilla shampoo.

Kat started to laugh, then fought against the lump that formed in her throat. Not for the first time, she had the distinct feeling of connection with these two women. "Can someone please tell me what the heck is going on?" Kat asked.

Emma pulled away and said, "This is the Holloway house. *The* Holloway house. It's been in our family for generations, and it knows things."

Juliette grinned. "It recognizes family, or people who belong. And if you belong, it lets you in."

Kat blinked. "What?"

"The house is . . ." Emma looked as if she were searching for the right words.

"It's opinionated," Juliette said simply. "It always has been. So it's kind of magic, I guess you could say. It has a mind of its own."

Hunter walked into the foyer. "It opened for me, too, when I fell in love with Emma."

"And Logan," Juliette added. "After we got engaged, I brought him over and the door swung wide. The house just knows things."

Logan came up behind Juliette and put his arms around her. He nodded at Kat. "It's true."

The dogs were running circles around the foyer, as if they could sense the excitement.

Kat searched the faces of her friends. They all seemed sincere. A normal person would assume they were playing a joke on her, but she wasn't a normal person. She communicated with animals and knew what they were feeling. She'd never been normal.

"Okay." Kat drew the word out slowly, trying to grasp what they were telling her. "So this house is magic. And it has decided to let me in, which means . . . it likes me?" She felt silly saying it, but both Emma and Juliette nodded.

"It doesn't just like you," Hunter said, crossing his arms. "It's saying you belong here. With us. You're part of the family, somehow."

Kat felt suddenly lightheaded. An overwhelming mixture of disbelief and sadness and bittersweet hope flooded through her. What were the odds? "I don't understand what you're saying."

"Come into the living room and let's talk." Juliette wrapped an arm around Kat's shoulders.

They led her into the cozy room and helped her settle into the corner of the couch. Juliette set a bowl of popcorn in her lap, and Emma made her a cup of hot chocolate. Kat felt as if she were in a strange, alternate universe. Like she'd driven up to the house and somehow fallen down a rabbit hole into a world where she had family connections and people who were genuinely interested in her. She gripped her cup of cocoa as Juliette and Emma explained the Holloway history.

"We've always been different," Juliette said. "You know those rumors about us having special abilities? Well, it's all true. The Holloway women each have a special gift.

I've been connected to Mother Nature since the day I was born."

"And I have kitchen magic, like our grandmother did," Emma said gently. "She taught me everything I know about baking and sweet charms. And my mother has wanderlust, which is why we never see her. She travels the world, moving from place to place, helping people in need. All of us women are born with something we can't deny. It's like a calling."

Kat took a sip of hot cocoa, comforted by the sweet, rich taste of chocolate and melted marshmallows. She knew what they were going to ask next.

"Do you . . . Can you do anything special like us?" Juliette asked.

Kat gathered her courage. "I can communicate with animals," she said quietly. "For as long as I can remember, I've had the ability to understand them. Relating to them . . . helping them . . . It's just what I do."

"I knew it!" Juliette said.

Both women were grinning like kids on Christmas morning.

The men exchanged glances, and Hunter cleared his throat. "You guys probably have a lot to talk about."

Logan pulled car keys from his pocket. "We're going to the store. You want ice cream?"

Juliette batted her eyelashes at him. "Um, have we met?"

"Right." Logan chuckled and dropped a kiss on top of her head. "I'll buy extra."

Kat watched them leave, still stunned by what was happening. Before coming to the island, she'd never in a million years expected to find people who were like her. Her whole life seemed to be a series of moments where she was always searching, and now, finally, she'd found people telling her she belonged. It was almost too good to be true.

"My grandmother's sister had animal magic," Emma said. "But we don't know much about her because she left home when she was young, and my grandmother never saw her again."

"Let's figure this out," Juliette said. "What about your family? What's your mom like?"

Kat braced herself for the empty ache that always accompanied that question. For some reason, it wasn't so bad this time. Maybe it was because she didn't feel entirely alone. "I don't know," she finally said. "She died when I was born and I grew up in foster care."

"I'm sorry," Emma said softly. "That can't have been easy."

Kat shrugged. "I was fine." It was a lie, but she'd been saying it for so long that it just slipped off the tongue. Growing up the way she did had not been fine at all. It had been hard, and lonely, and sometimes heartbreaking. Why did people always say they were fine when they really weren't? Maybe it was because it was just easier than telling the truth.

"Then that settles it," Juliette said firmly. "The Holloway house already claimed you as family. So you belong with us."

Emma placed her hand on Kat's. "Our family might seem a little crazy, but we're loyal."

"There's got to be a way to figure out where you came from," Juliette added. "We have about a million dusty trunks up in the attic we can go through, to start. Maybe there'll be a clue."

There was a sudden ache in Kat's throat she couldn't speak around. These women were so ready to accept her into their lives, and they barely knew her. A long time ago,

Kat had decided that animals were her only family, since she didn't have the luxury of having anyone else. But now, sitting between these two amazing women, Kat felt as though the world as she knew it had begun to shift, and she had no idea how to navigate around it.

Chapter Eleven

Bright morning light spilled through Jordan's bedroom window as he sat at his desk, sifting through e-mails from Prescott Enterprises.

His partner, Chad Newland, had been keeping him updated on the latest developments. Prescott Enterprises had been doing exceptionally well since Jordan had landed the LM Development account three years ago. It had been his big coup. He'd gone through months of tough negotiations, while having to stave off the competition from other, far larger firms like Archer Anders.

Jordan's negotiating had gone on for so long, the owner of LM Development—old Leo Morgan, himself—had finally come into the city to meet Jordan in person. Leo Morgan was an ambitious man who came from humble beginnings, too, and that was how he and Jordan bonded. When they finally sealed the deal, he'd remarked that Jordan reminded him of himself forty years earlier.

With small-time Prescott Enterprises suddenly in charge of two hundred million dollars in retirement funds, municipal bonds, and other assets, Jordan had gone from subletting a place in Bedford Park to a comfortable apartment in SoHo virtually overnight. It was everything he'd worked so hard for. Even after Leo Morgan passed away the following year, his nephew Morgan Jr. had stayed with Prescott Enterprises out of loyalty. Now, other companies were coming to Jordan for asset management, too. Things were looking up.

Jordan leaned back in his chair and stretched his arms overhead, yawning. A warm breeze swirled in through the window, bringing with it the scent of rich earth and lavender. He'd almost forgotten it, after being gone for so many years. His life in Manhattan was nothing like this, which is exactly what he'd wanted. But as much as he fought to get away from the Pacific Northwest, a part of him missed the simplicity of the island life. Every day in the city seemed jam-packed with activity; something was always happening. On Pine Cove Island, entire days could go by with nothing happening at all.

When he'd first arrived back on the island, it was hard to adjust. There were no blaring car horns or garbled snippets of conversations or police sirens in the distance. He'd grown used to those things. In New York, everything was constantly moving and changing, from the rivers of people on the city streets to the billboards and the scents of car exhaust and perfume and restaurants. Now that he'd been on the island for a few weeks, he realized just how peaceful it was to be close to nature again. Difficult as it was to believe, he'd missed it.

Birds chirped in the tree outside his bedroom window, and aside from that, the only other sound was the leaves rustling in the wind. No . . . there was another sound. Jordan cocked his head and sat up. A softly singing voice. It was sweet and clear, and he knew it was Kat. Unable to help himself, he rose from his chair and walked to the window, peering through the screen.

Kat was sitting cross-legged in the animal pen, hugging one of the chickens. She stopped singing and bent her head to whisper something to it. Her fiery hair was in a messy bun on top of her head, exposing her slender neck, and her faded tank top revealed pale arms smudged with dirt. When she started singing again, her voice hit him like a metal spike through the heart. It wasn't a fancy, powerful singing voice. It was sweet and soft and melodious. The kind of voice that got under your skin and made you want things.

Jordan clenched his hands and turned away from the window. She was too alluring for her own good. At the campfire the other night, he'd wanted to haul her into his lap and devour her. He'd wanted to hear her breath catch in surprise and watch her brilliant eyes go all smoky with desire. He couldn't stop thinking about it, which was becoming a problem. *She* was a problem. Kat Davenport was a distraction he didn't need, and he'd do well to remember it. He was here to do work, tie up loose ends, and go back to his real life. End of story.

Sitting back at his desk, he started scrolling through e-mails with an odd sense of detachment. Work seemed so far away. He hadn't realized coming back to the farm would be so easy; like stepping into an old pair of shoes. Too bad those shoes were so damned full of holes.

Jordan scrubbed his face with both hands and sighed heavily. He'd told Chad he was taking a sabbatical and that he'd return in a couple of months. But there would be no rest here. This was a final cleanup of the mess his parents left behind. Sure, he could have paid someone to come out here and take care of it all. Make the problems go away. But Jordan didn't need a psychiatrist to spell out that he needed closure. This was to be his last visit to Pine Cove Island. He was going to put all these memories behind him, once and for all.

He clicked on the most recent e-mail, flagged urgent. It was from Chad.

Morgan Jr. is talking about stepping away from the day-to-day and handing everything over to the board. Yesterday I ran into a guy from Archer Anders at the bar. He was drunk, and started spewing some nonsense about them planning to swoop in and take over the account. Do you know anything about this? Shit's about to go down here, man. When are you coming back?

Jordan sent a quick reply. I've got it covered. Call you later today.

He picked up his phone and began to dial Morgan Jr.'s number. He wasn't concerned about the snakes at Archer Anders. Leo Morgan had been a straight shooter, and so was his nephew. They were decent people, and they knew Jordan did business aboveboard. They were trustworthy, which was more than Jordan could say for a lot of people he'd worked with in the financial industry. His own up-bringing was so lacking in direction and stability, he'd learned that trust was a rare, precious thing. And once you had it, you did everything you could not to break it.

Chapter Twelve

Kat scattered corn for the chickens as the late afternoon breeze ruffled her hair. She was still in a daze about her visit to Emma's house the night before. Everything that had happened seemed almost like a dream. Her insides thrummed with the possibility that she might finally discover her roots. She turned the idea over and over in her head. Really, what were the odds? To come all the way to this tiny island town in the Pacific Northwest, and discover . . . her real family? It seemed impossible. It was too much like a fairy tale. That kind of stuff didn't happen in real life, and she'd do well to remember it. It was safer to stay practical. Then she wouldn't be devastated when things went wrong.

She used to wonder about her real parents when she was younger. Did they ever love each other? Did her mother have the ability to communicate with animals, too? Kat used to pretend her mother had been just like her, so she'd feel less like a freak of nature. But as she grew older, she'd stopped thinking about who her parents might have been. Why bother? Pretending and wishing for that kind of stuff never changed anything. She'd decided to create the life she wanted, without them.

And yet . . . The image of Juliette's and Emma's joyful, smiling faces sprang into her mind. They'd seemed so sure she was part of their family. Their happiness made Kat wish it were true.

As if sensing her heavy mood, Waffles ambled over and nudged her leg. Then Hank trotted into the pen and sat beside her, while the chickens pecked at the corn. All the animals seemed comfortable with one another, which lifted Kat's spirits.

She lowered herself to the ground, petting Hank and scratching Waffles behind the ears. The wonderful thing about animals was that they didn't judge. They simply accepted. Animals were her family. She could always count on them.

The old farm pickup truck came barreling down the gravel driveway, and Kat turned to see Jordan pulling up to the house.

The truck windows were rolled down, and an old song about Jack and Diane was blasting on the radio. Jordan's left hand was tapping the side of the door in time to the music. In sunglasses, with his windblown hair all mussed up, Kat couldn't help but stare. It wasn't just that he looked ridiculously sexy in that rusted old truck; he seemed carefree and content. No matter how many times he said he wasn't going to stay, Kat couldn't help but wonder why he wanted to leave. If she'd had ties to a place like this, she'd never want to be anywhere else.

Jordan cut the engine and got out of the truck.

Opal was at one of her community center events, so this afternoon they were alone on the farm. Together. Kat ignored the shiver of awareness that skittered up her spine.

They hadn't spoken to each other since that almost-kiss at the campfire a few nights ago, and as far as Kat was concerned, that was a good thing. If enough time lapsed between that craziness, they could both pretend nothing was between them.

She sat very still, grateful that he didn't notice her before he went into the farmhouse. When the turquoise door closed behind him, she exhaled in relief. It was so stupid for her to be tiptoeing around him as if she'd done something crazy. She *hadn't*. Neither of them had. Sure, the idea of throwing caution to the wind and jumping his bones, licking melted marshmallow off his lips, running her hands over his muscular back, had crossed her mind a time or twenty, but that was all safely tucked away in her mind. No harm, no foul.

In fact, Kat decided as she stood and smacked dust off her black jeans, they might even get along eventually, as normal roommates.

"What the ever-living hell?" Jordan's voice boomed from the open window on the second floor.

Kat stood up quickly and went toward the gate.

Jordan came storming out of the front door, glowering like the god of fire and brimstone. He started toward Kat's apartment.

"I'm over here," she called, striding across the grass from the barn. Hank and Waffles followed behind her.

Jordan whirled, his whiskey-colored eyes flashing. Dark, unruly hair framed his suntanned face, and he so perfectly fit Kat's initial impression of an enchanted beast, she almost smiled. Almost.

"What's wrong?" Kat asked. He clearly had a bone to pick with her. An entire carcass, from the looks of it. She braced for it.

"There is a *cat* in my house," he said with a grimace.

"Yes." She shrugged, like it was no big deal. Because it wasn't. What guy would get so worked up about a cat? "Opal said I could bring her to the house, so I did."

"Come with me." Jordan waved her over and stalked back toward the house.

She followed, because as grumpy as he was, she was worried about Clementine. The poor thing needed peace and quiet and as few disruptions as possible.

He left the front door wide open and took the stairs.

Kat hurried after him. When she reached the top of the landing, he was already standing at the far end of the hall, holding a door and waiting for her.

"In here." His voice was low and controlled, but there was a thread of frustration in it that she didn't miss.

"Is that your bedroom?"

"Yes. And that," he said, pointing to the large bed in the middle of the room, "is my bed." It was a mahogany four-poster with a gray comforter and a blue fleece throw piled in the center. And in the middle of that rumpled blanket was Clementine . . . and kittens.

Kat gasped with delight and pushed past Jordan.

Five brand-new kittens nestled next to their mother. Clementine was tired, but Kat could sense her pride and contentment.

"Oh, Clementine, look at your sweet babies." Kat climbed onto the bed and reached out to stroke a finger between Clementine's ears. "I'm so happy for you."

Clementine started to purr.

Jordan cleared his throat from the doorway. "I don't know how this happened, but they have to go. Now."

Kat spun around, gaping. "She's just had her kittens. You can't move her yet. They're all in a very delicate condition."

"This is my room," he said evenly. "I'm *allergic* to cats."

Before she could respond, Hank came flying into the bedroom, running in joyful circles around them.

Jordan crossed his arms, sighing. "And now your dog has joined us."

She gave him an apologetic smile. "I must've left the door open when I followed you into the house."

Suddenly they heard footsteps clattering on the hardwood floors downstairs. No . . . Kat realized with a dawning sense of alarm. *Hoof* steps.

Loud, pitiful braying began echoing through the house.

"*No.*" Jordan's voice was thick with incredulity. "If that animal—"

"He won't come upstairs," Kat assured him. "Donkeys aren't able to navigate long flights of stairs. That's why he's so upset. He wants to be up here where the party is."

"This is no party."

Hank began to bark.

Ear-piercing *hee-haws* punctuated the air.

Clementine began meowling her disapproval.

Kat took one look at Jordan's face and said, "I'll take care of it." She scooped up Hank, raced down the stairs, and shooed Waffles out the front door. Then she sent Hank after him into the yard, firmly shut the door, and ran back to Jordan's room.

She leaned against the doorframe, slightly out of breath. "I'm sorry about that."

He was standing over the bed, hands on hips, looking at the cats like a disgruntled king surveying disloyal subjects. "Your cats have to go. Now."

"Technically they're your grandmother's cats. Opal's a volunteer for the shelter now." Kat knew she was treading on thin ice, but she couldn't move Clementine and the kittens yet, and she needed to make him understand. "They just need a little bit more time," she said calmly. "Can't you sleep somewhere else? It would just be for a couple of days."

Jordan's back went rigid. "You don't seem to realize what you're asking me. I work in here." He gestured to the laptop computer on the simple wooden desk near the window. "This is my private space. In twenty minutes I'll be coughing and sneezing and miserable. If you won't move them, I will." He brushed past Kat and walked toward the stairs.

"Where are you going?"

"To get a box."

"No!" She ran after him. "The kittens are barely hours old. Would it be so hard just to give them a little extra time? Can't you take your laptop and work in another room for just a couple of days?"

He ignored her, charging down the stairs. When he came to a door in the hall, he swung it open to reveal a broom closet with supply shelves on either side. He began rummaging around, shoving aside baskets and cleaning bottles. Finally he lifted a box full of towels and turned it upside down, emptying the towels onto the floor.

Kat's concern for Clementine and the kittens quickly escalated to frustration. Then annoyance. She stepped into the broom closet and gripped the edge of the box he was holding. "You have an entire house at your disposal. There are other rooms upstairs. Can't you just show a little patience?"

"Patience?" He gave her an incredulous look, tugged the box out of her hand, and set it on a shelf out of her reach. "Ever since you moved in here, you've been testing my patience. You weren't even living here before you insisted I build a new coop for the chickens. Then you bring your dog without asking. You sneak a pregnant cat into the house and sign my grandmother up as a pet volunteer. You intrude on my campfire—"

"Oh, I *intruded*?" Kat jammed her hands on her hips, angry heat flooding her face. "You didn't seem so eager to have me leave when you handed me a beer and we made s'mores together."

For several heated seconds they stared at each other, as

if both were remembering the moment in front of the fire where they'd almost kissed.

Jordan leaned toward her, his broad shoulders blocking her view of the shelves behind him. "And now today," he said silkily, "you and your animals have taken over my bedroom."

He was standing so close. Kat could practically feel her heart thumping against her rib cage. "It's just one cat and a few kittens," she managed. "I'm sure you can survive a couple of days."

He cocked his head, studying her as if he were trying to decide what to do with her. "I shouldn't have to survive. I should be able to sleep in my bed tonight. This is your fault."

"It's not like I planned for this to happen," Kat said in exasperation. "I'm not the one who chose your bed."

Something changed in the air between them, a languid, sensual shift that prickled the hairs on the back of her neck.

"If you had chosen my bed," he murmured, a wicked glint in his eyes, "we wouldn't be having this conversation."

Kat swallowed hard. The closet suddenly seemed to grow smaller . . . and warmer. Or was that heat coming from him? He was so big, looming over her like some gorgeous, avenging angel about to demand surrender. And he smelled divine—woodsy and fresh, like evergreens in sunlight. She wanted to grab fistfuls of his shirt, yank him closer, and breathe him in. The Queen of Impulsive Decisions let out a tinkling laugh.

Kat licked her lips nervously.

Jordan's heavy-lidded gaze dropped to her mouth.

"Forget it," she whispered.

His mouth kicked up at one corner. "I didn't say anything."

"I'm not kissing you, so just forget it." Kat was trying to act calm and cool, but her voice sounded too breathy.

He lifted a brow in sensual amusement. "I was going to say something else, but now that you mention kissing . . ."

Kat's face flushed with heat. She lowered her head and feigned a sudden interest in the floor tiles. Fascinating shade of beige, those. "Never mind. What were you going to say?"

"No more animals."

Her head snapped up. "What?"

His expression was stern, which should've done something to alleviate the crazy, animal attraction she was feeling, but it just seemed to enhance it. "I'll let the cats stay where they are for two days, but don't bring anything else home. I'm trying to fix this house up and get it ready to sell. I can't keep tripping over your animals. There's no room."

"There's plenty of room." She tilted her head back to glare at him, but it was hard to look down on someone when the top of your head barely reached their shoulders. "We're on a farm with hardly any animals, if you haven't noticed. Even the paddock is empty."

"Don't bring any more pets home, Kat. I mean it."

She thought of all the unwanted animals that would be coming through the shelter and all the unused space on the farm. Why was he being so difficult? He was leaving soon, anyway. It shouldn't matter to him if there were some extra animals around.

She gathered her courage. "No."

He jerked his chin back slightly in surprise. "*No*?"

"You heard me. I can't promise that." She tried to appear nonchalant, but it was almost impossible when he was standing so close. All she had to do was rise up on her tiptoes and it would be so easy to press her lips against the hollow at the base of his neck to find out if it was as warm and smooth as it looked. *Focus!*

Kat swallowed hard. "Opal said she'd volunteer for any

other animals who might need homes. And this is her house, too."

He lazily braced his hands on the shelf behind her head. "You're telling me that you're willfully going to ignore my request?"

"Yup."

"I am so glad you said that." His voice was deeply satisfied, like the purr of a jungle cat. All Kat's nerve endings went on high alert.

She glanced up sharply. "Why?"

"Because it's settled. And now we can go with your idea." In one swift move, Jordan leaned down and brushed his lips over hers.

Kat stood frozen in the moment, aware of nothing but the warm, soft caress of his mouth. The rasp of his flannel shirt against her bare arms. The crisp scent of pine soap and warm, male skin. His kiss was subtle, yet insistent. Coaxing. Intoxicating. Heat bloomed inside her, spiraling out in every direction like a sensual drug too powerful to resist. She slid her hands around his neck and pressed closer.

A low growl came from Jordan's throat. He drew her against his hard, muscular body, molding her to him as he deepened the kiss.

Kat dug her fingers through his hair, glorying in the rich, silky feel of it and the slow, sweet glide of his tongue. An ongoing wave of pure, delicious sensation rippled over her, one kiss barely over before the next one began.

When Jordan slid a large, warm hand under the back of her T-shirt to caress her bare skin, she let out a tiny gasp of pleasure. He pulled back slightly, the tip of his tongue darting out to lick her lower lip as if he could taste the pleasure on her mouth. Kat's knees went weak. This was madness; she knew it. But she just couldn't bring herself to care. All rational thoughts seemed to slip away like wispy clouds on a stiff breeze, until the only things left were the hot, bright taste of him and the feel of his powerful arms around her and the thudding beat of her heart. In that moment, only one thing was achingly clear.

Jordan Prescott knew how to kiss.

Chapter Thirteen

By the time Kat stumbled out of the broom closet, she'd felt as dazed and wobbly as a newborn colt. Who could blame her? She'd just been kissed to kingdom come by an enchanted beast who somehow managed to make her forget reason. She felt like he'd woven some kind of spell over her with those drugging, sensual kisses that were so addicting they should be illegal.

Her breath came in little pants. His chest rose and fell. They stared at each other as if coming out of some kind of dream.

Kat was the first to take action. Without a word, she turned and walked out of the house. Across the lawn. Up the stairs to her apartment. When she finally closed the door behind her, she leaned against it and slid to the floor.

What in the holy heart attack had just happened? *You kissed a man and he knocked your socks off,* the Queen of Impulsive Decisions sighed dreamily. Kat squeezed her eyes shut and tried to pretend it didn't happen, but her lips felt swollen and her limbs were shaky.

Someone knocked at the door, and she jumped.

There was no peephole to see who it was, so she waited.

The knock came again. Was it Jordan? Had he followed

her to her apartment? A bolt of alarm shot through her. She didn't want him to see that the apartment was still empty.

"Kat?" Juliette's voice called.

Kat scrambled for the doorknob. She cracked the door a few inches and peered out.

Juliette stood on the other side with a box in her arms. She wasn't covered in leaves and dirt yet, which meant she was probably on her way to work.

Great. Kat didn't want Juliette to see her apartment, either. The last thing she needed was someone's pity. Maybe she could just have a conversation with Juliette outside. "Oh, hey, Juliette," Kat said. "How's it going?"

"Good . . ." Juliette eyed her suspiciously. "How are you?"

"Great," Kat said brightly. "I'm doing great."

"Uh-huh. Then why are you on your knees, hiding behind your door?"

"Oh." Kat scrambled to her feet. "I thought you were Jordan. I thought he might have followed me from the house."

"Why?" Juliette glanced back at the farmhouse. "Is he stalking you?"

"No. Nothing like that." Kat let out a heavy sigh. "It's complicated."

Juliette nudged the door open with her shoulder.

Kat gave up and let her in.

"Wow, I love what you've done with the place," Juliette said, plunking the box on the floor in front of the recliner. "It's so . . . minimalist chic."

"I have furniture coming tomorrow," Kat lied. "This is just temporary." It was just a tiny white lie. Technically, in a few days she'd have a futon or something, once she picked up a few things from the local thrift store. No matter what, she didn't want Juliette feeling sorry for her. Kat hated that. She was a grown woman who had always relied on herself, and this time was no exception. "But for now," Kat said, gesturing grandly to the recliner chair, "would you care to have a seat on my chair-slash-bed?"

Juliette tightened her ponytail and glanced around the room. "Really minimalist. What's that on your table?"

Kat glanced at the green mesh cage sitting on the table under the window. "Butterfly cocoons." She rolled her eyes. "Don't ask."

Juliette settled on the floor, tucking her long boho skirt around her. Then she opened the box to reveal a jumble of colorful clothes and a few paperback romance novels.

Kat joined her on the floor. "What's all this?"

"Last night you mentioned only having black clothes from your last gig, and that you were planning to buy more when you got paid."

Kat watched as Juliette pulled out a few summer sundresses and colorful tops. "So Emma and I decided you should have these for the time being."

Juliette held up a flowy sundress in brilliant shades of turquoise. "I think this would look gorgeous with your hair."

Once again, Kat felt overwhelmed by Juliette and Emma's kindness. "You guys didn't have to do this." She ran a hand over the soft fabric. It was always hard for her to accept handouts from people. It usually made her feel uncomfortable. But for some reason, coming from Juliette, it was okay.

"We wanted to," Juliette said. "It's no big deal. Emma and I share clothes all the time, and even though I'm taller than both of you, these stretchy dresses fit all of us. And the books are from Emma. She says they're some of her favorites."

"Thank you." As grateful as Kat was for their kindness, she couldn't help feeling a twinge of worry. They were so eager to accept her into their family, but how could she possibly be related to them? Her mother was from L.A.

Kat didn't know much, but at least she knew that. The odds of her being related to the Holloways were slim to none, and as much as she loved being welcomed into their lives, she hated to disappoint them.

Juliette grinned and leaned back on her hands. "So, tell me all about Mr. Mysterious."

Kat rubbed her face with a groan. "I'm avoiding him."

"Clearly," Juliette said. "But why? Is living here that bad?"

"No, it's fine. The barn animals are easy to care for, Hank enjoys all the space to run around, and Opal's been great. She's even become a volunteer at the rescue shelter."

"It's Jordan, then." Juliette studied Kat closely. "He's your problem."

"Yes," Kat said with a sigh. She ran her hands through her hair, shaking out the mass of curls. "We got into a big argument today because I brought a pregnant cat home, and she just had kittens."

Juliette's face lit up. "How sweet! I want to see them. I love cats."

"It's not sweet to him." Kat had a flashback of Jordan's face when he pointed to Clementine. "She had kittens in his bed. And apparently, he's allergic to cats."

"Psh," Juliette said, waving a hand. "That's an easy fix."

Kat wrinkled her nose. "I don't know. He's pretty upset."

"No, I mean the allergies. I just made a fresh batch of herbal remedies to bring to the florist shop, and I have one specifically for allergies. They're in my car. I'll give you a vial for him."

Kat looked hopefully at Juliette. "Will it work?"

"Of course. All my herbal potions work, but they're even more powerful if the person has the desire for it to work. For example, if Jordan really likes the cat and wants it to stick around, the remedy will work even better. Does he like her?"

"Not from the looks of it," Kat said glumly. Jordan

didn't seem interested in Clementine at all. "But it could be worth a try."

"Is that the only reason you're avoiding him? Because he's unhappy about the cat having kittens in his bed?"

"Not exactly." Kat's gaze slid away. She plucked at a loose thread on the hem of her T-shirt. "He annoys me other times. We sort of rub each other the wrong way, but for the most part, it's been working out okay."

"So . . . ?" Juliette tucked a strand of hair behind her ear. "You get him to take my allergy remedy, and problem solved."

"The problem isn't him; it's me," Kat said in resignation. "I'm the Queen of Impulsive Decisions."

Juliette laughed and drew her knees up, hugging herself. "Yet another reason for me to love you. We have a lot in common."

Kat sighed. "When I made the decision to move here, I promised myself I would stick to the plan. Make a life here that's on my own terms. Figure out what makes me happy and not get sidetracked. . . ."

"And you're getting sidetracked?" Juliette asked with the barest hint of a smile.

"All right, here's the thing," Kat said in a rush. "Jordan just kissed me, and I kissed him back."

Juliette grinned. "I'd call that sidetracked. How did that happen?"

Kat filled her in on Clementine, and Jordan's order not to bring any more animals home.

"So then I told him 'no,'" Kat said. "And then he said okay and kissed me in the broom closet. And now I'm all weirded out because, what's up? That was not part of my plan. How am I supposed to go on like nothing happened?"

"Well, did you like it? Did kissing him make you happy?"

For a scant few seconds, Kat considered it. "I'm not sure

'happy' is the right way to describe it." Scorching hot kisses in a dark broom closet with an enchanted prince made her feel all sorts of things. Wild. Uninhibited. Sexy as sin. "Happy" was not high on the list. But still, she felt a little giddy when she thought about it. The heat of his hands on her back as he pulled her against him. The way she'd melted into him and kissed him back, completely uninhibited. The walls could've crumbled down around them and she wouldn't have noticed. Kissing Jordan Prescott had taken all her focus, and she'd liked it. Way too much.

"If you didn't like it, then that's easy," Juliette said. "All you have to do is—"

"I never said I didn't like it." Kat stood and paced to the little window. "I'm just not sure what to do now."

"I say you go on about your own business, and just let things unfold as they will," Juliette said, standing. "You've got the upper hand here. You get to decide where you want this to go."

"Nowhere," Kat said firmly. "It's not going anywhere because I'm not going to kiss him again. Besides, he's heading back to New York as soon as possible. He's not even planning on staying here, and I am."

"Okay, you aren't going to kiss him again. So that's that. Now all you have to do is be civil when you run into each other."

A memory flashed through Kat's mind. Jordan's teeth tugging gently at her bottom lip while his large hand slid up her thigh. Nothing civil about that.

Juliette took in the empty room again. "I hate to break it to you, but you've got bigger problems. This room has lost its will to live. You need to decorate, stat."

"It's fine." Kat leaned against the small table. "I get paid on Friday so I'm going shopping."

"Good," Juliette said. "But I'm still going to help you

with this"—she waved her hands in the air—"jail cell of yours."

"I won't be here for long, anyway," Kat insisted. "It's only a month-to-month thing, so I'm not planning on doing a lot of decorating."

"Are you planning on doing a lot of sleep? You need a bed at the very least. Unless there's a bed in the farmhouse you're thinking about hijacking." Juliette gave Kat a sly grin.

Kat rolled her eyes. "Clementine the cat has already taken Jordan's bed, remember?"

"Who said anything about Jordan's bed?" Juliette said innocently. "I was thinking they might have a spare room, but I see where your mind is going with this."

Kat wanted to contradict her, but everything she said was true. She was going to be thinking a lot about him, whether she wanted to or not. The big test would be whether or not she could keep him at arm's length. The old Kat would've had no problem getting all wild and crazy with him, but she wasn't going to be that person. Not anymore. This time she was going to do things on her own terms, without the distraction of someone else influencing her choices. She owed it to herself to at least try.

Chapter Fourteen

By Sunday evening, Kat was a tightly wound bundle of nerves. It had been over twenty-four hours since she'd seen Jordan—kissed Jordan—and she still didn't know how she was going to pull off acting normal around him. Seriously, what had she been thinking? Kissing in a broom closet? With her landlord?

Groaning, Kat rose from the chair and stretched to ease the tension in her neck. A hot shower was exactly what she needed to scrub all thoughts of that heated encounter from her mind. Trudging into the bathroom, she started the shower and began to undress. The small bathroom was stark and white, with a pedestal sink and shower stall barely big enough to turn around in. She adjusted the showerhead, then stepped under the warm spray with a grateful sigh.

Okay, fine. Fact number one: Jordan Prescott was hot.

Understatement.

Fact number two: He was good at kissing.

Understatement of the century.

She scowled as she poured shampoo into her hand. None of that mattered. She'd promised herself she wasn't going to fall into any more relationships that were going nowhere. Jordan made it clear he was leaving soon, so he was just about the fastest train to nowhere on the island. And Kat knew better than to take that ride.

She lathered the strawberry-scented shampoo into her hair, massaging her scalp to ease tension. Her last boyfriend had been like a shiny Tilt-O-Whirl at the county fair. He'd seemed like fun at first, but after a while she began questioning her choices. And by the end, all she wanted to do was hurl. They'd had nothing in common, but she'd still pretended it could work. She'd been pretty dazzled by him, but that's the way it always was. Kat got dazzled. Kat got caught up trying to make it work. And in the end, Kat got disappointed.

But not this time. She grit her teeth and rinsed her hair. Because fact number three: Kat was in charge. *You hear that, Queen of Impulsive Decisions?* This time, Kat had everything under control.

The shower spray suddenly sputtered, and a shock of icy water hit her in the face.

She gasped, fumbling for the showerhead. She tilted it to the wall as quickly as she could, but the old thing just slid back, spraying her with another icy blast of water.

With a muffled shriek, Kat knocked the showerhead sideways and grabbed the nozzle to turn the water off. She pulled it down, and the whole thing popped off in her hand. Then the showerhead fell off, spraying icy water everywhere.

Kat scrambled out of the shower, dripping water onto the floor. She yanked the shower curtain closed so water wouldn't spray all over the bathroom, but the flimsy curtain couldn't stop the strong blast of water from spewing onto the tiled floor. What now? She wasn't about to go running for Jordan. For one thing, she still wasn't ready to face him and for another, she didn't want him to see the state of her living arrangements. It was bad enough that Juliette saw her empty room, but if Jordan saw it? No flipping way.

Think! A pair of pliers. That's what she needed. If she could just find a toolbox in the garage, maybe she could grab pliers or a wrench and manually turn off the water. Quickly, Kat toweled her hair and dug through the box of clothes Juliette had dropped off. She threw on a loose blue sundress and raced down the stairs.

Jordan stood in the garage, surveying the piles of debris, the rusted tools strewn everywhere, and the cardboard boxes shoved along one wall that held only God knows what. There was no rhyme or reason to any of it, but why would there be? His parents had never been the type to organize or clean. Things usually stayed wherever they fell. As a kid it didn't bother him because he didn't know any better. But once he got older, he saw how other kids lived and realized his parents' lifestyle wasn't typical.

He stopped in front of a pile of messy canvases splashed with color. Dried tubes of paint and ruined brushes were scattered on the floor near a broken easel. Something inside him clenched at the site of the misused, forgotten art supplies. He remembered spending a summer in the front yard, watching his mother at her newest obsession. She was brilliant and artistic and determined. He remembered thinking she was the most talented person in the world. That was before he realized that all her obsessions were just passing fancies. She never stayed interested in anything for that long. Not even him.

Bending to lift a rusted toolbox, he heard a quick intake of breath behind him.

He turned and almost dropped the box. *Holy hell.* Kat Davenport stood in the middle of his garage, looking like she'd just been yanked out of one of his secret fantasies. She was wearing some kind of flimsy blue dress. A very *wet* blue dress. He swallowed hard, his gaze traveling over the delicious curves of her body. She was wet all over. Even her hair. It streamed down her shoulders and over the intriguing swell of her breasts. Heat blasted through him faster than he could blink, and he was rock hard. Ever since their wild moment in that damn broom closet, he couldn't get her out of his mind. Her soft sighs. The feel of her body molded to his. The subtle strawberry scent of her hair and the taste of her lips. He didn't think anything could be hotter than that memory, yet here she was now, standing in front of him dripping wet, eclipsing all of it.

Kat bit her bottom lip, then lifted her chin and said coolly, "I need to borrow your toolbox."

Humor tangled with arousal inside him, and he suddenly wanted to laugh. Only Kat could pull off sounding like an imperious queen while she stood barefoot, barely clothed in a puddle of water. Were those soapsuds on her feet?

"What for?" he asked, noting the way she clenched her hands. Jordan frowned. Something was wrong. If he hadn't been so blindsided by her appearance, he'd have noticed sooner. "What happened?"

"Nothing. I just need to borrow a toolbox. Is that it?" She pointed to the thing in his hand.

Jordan looked down at the ancient toolbox he'd been holding. No telling what was inside.

She launched toward him, reaching for it. He inhaled sharply. She smelled like strawberries and vanilla, and he fought against the urge to toss the toolbox aside and reach for her.

She tried to grab it, but he held it away.

"This isn't what you want," he said. "This is just an old piece of junk. My tools are over there." He jerked his chin to the workbench at the back of the garage. The tools he'd recently purchased at the hardware store were neatly arranged inside a shiny new box.

Kat charged toward it.

"What's going on? Tell me," he demanded.

She stubbornly shook her head and opened the box. "I just need to borrow a pair of pliers. That's all."

He cocked his head, listening . . . The sound of running water could be heard above them. "It's the shower, isn't it?"

She didn't answer. Instead she started rummaging through the box, pulling out containers of nails, a hammer, a screwdriver . . .

"Stop." Jordan brushed past her, trying to ignore the warmth of her wet skin sliding across his forearm. God, she made him crazy. He closed the toolbox and started toward her apartment growling, "I'll take care of it."

"No!" Kat followed behind him, frantically grabbing at his hand.

He paused, staring at her small hands circling his wrist. Her fingers were slender and pale against his darker skin.

She seemed to realize she was touching him, and she let go quickly. "It's just the pipe in the bathroom. I can do it myself."

Cursing, Jordan turned and hurried up the stairs. He knew that showerhead was old. He should've fixed it before his grandmother started looking for a tenant. If water got into the walls, there'd be more problems than just the showerhead.

"You can't just barge into my place," she cried.

"I'm sorry if it inconveniences you." He pushed open the door. "But I can't risk water getting in the—" He took in the empty apartment. "Walls." Something sharp twisted inside him, but he didn't have time to address it. For now, he had to stop the water from flooding.

"I told you," Kat said angrily. "I can do it myself." She came up behind him in the bathroom, a little out of breath from running up the stairs. Her chest rose and fell, and her green eyes seemed darker. Stormier. She was glaring at him like some fantasy game sorceress about to cast a spell. "You don't just get to barge in here like you own the place."

He could've mentioned that he did, in fact, own the place, but he didn't dare. Instead he set his toolbox down, kneeled on the wet floor, and opened it up. He could feel her hot emerald eyes on him, and he knew she was about three seconds away from either knocking him over the head with the toolbox, or conjuring up a fireball from thin air and hurling it at him. Neither of those things would've surprised him, but he didn't have time to worry about saving his skin.

Water spewed from the broken showerhead. The handle had fallen off, and the bathroom floor was a mess. He yanked out a wrench and a pair of pliers, then got to work.

An icy blast of water hit him square in the chest. Swearing, Jordan tried to twist the nozzle. The wrench was useless, but with the pliers he was finally able to clamp onto the metal pin. He turned it clockwise until the water pressure decreased, and the spray eventually slowed to a trickle, then nothing.

He sat back and assessed the damage. Luckily, the pipe wasn't broken, so water hadn't leaked into the walls.

"The fixtures will need to be replaced," he said, standing. "But it's not too bad. I'll get them in tomorrow while you're at work."

Kat had her arms crossed like she was hugging herself. She still looked bothered, but she seemed to have lost some steam while he was working. "Thank you," she said quietly.

"Don't worry about it. This stuff is old, and should've been replaced a long time ago." His clothes were dripping wet and he headed to the front door. "I'll bring some towels to mop this up."

"I can do it myself," she insisted.

He turned back and fixed his gaze on hers. "Do you have towels?"

Kat flushed a lovely shade of pink and rubbed one foot on top of the other. "No."

He nodded and went to the house. After gathering an armload of towels, he walked back to her apartment with a nagging sense of unease. It bothered him that she didn't have furniture. He needed to change that.

Kat opened the door and reached for the towels.

"No," he said. "I'll do it."

She looked like she was going to protest, then rolled her eyes. "Fine." She swung the door wide.

In the bathroom, Jordan set the towels on the floor and began mopping up the water.

Kat took another towel and joined him.

They worked together, tossing each soaked towel into the sink and wringing them out until, at last, the floor was just slippery.

Kat sat back on her heels. Her dark red hair hung in loose waves around her face. Her cheeks were pink from exertion, the blush extending down her neck and across her chest.

Jordan felt his throat go dry. She was so damn beautiful, and she probably didn't even know it.

"I'm still mad at you for barging in here," she said, even though her mouth curved into a tired smile.

"I know."

She looked like she was going to say more but changed her mind. Shivering, she crossed her arms over her chest.

He stood quickly. "You should put on some dry clothes."

"I will as soon as you leave." She jumped up fast and slipped, stumbling forward.

Jordan reflexively caught her against him. Heat spiked through his veins, hot and fast. She was warm and wet and her strawberry scent was intoxicating. "Be careful," he said huskily.

"Will you stop telling me what to do?" She thumped him on the chest. "I can take care of myself."

"I know you can," he said. "But that doesn't stop me from wanting to help." He was still holding her, and she didn't pull away. He could feel her body melting against him.

Bright green eyes fringed with dark lashes studied him. Jordan held very still, reveling in the feel of her in his arms. What he really wanted to do was devour her. Throw her over his shoulder and take her to bed. He wanted to finish what they'd barely started in the broom closet the day before. Instead he waited.

Very slowly she lifted up on her toes and whispered against his mouth, "Thank you." Every muscle in his body went taut and he gripped her tighter.

She brushed her lips sweetly against his, then pulled away.

He blinked, his body straining with desire. "What was that?"

"A thank-you kiss," she said with a shrug. "You know, for helping me even though I didn't need it."

"A *thank-you* kiss?" he asked, unimpressed.

"Sure." Her face lit with amusement. The little minx was teasing him. "People sometimes do that. Don't they?"

"Oh, hell yes," Jordan said with a wicked smile. "All the time."

She let out a little squeak as he pulled her closer and "thanked her" right back.

The kiss was meant to be quick. Playful. She was smiling

at first and hell, so was he. But when she wrapped her arms around his neck, dug her fingers into his hair, and made a little *mmm* sound in the back of her throat, he wasn't feeling playful anymore. Hot arrows of lust shot through him. All his focus was on her. The sweet cinnamon taste of her mouth. The heat of their wet bodies, pressed together. There was so many things he wanted to do with this woman. If she had any idea, she'd probably run for the hills.

When he finally pulled away, they were both breathing a little unsteady.

"Um." She stepped back. "I think you should go now."

He fought for a casualness he didn't feel. "Now that we've both properly thanked each other?"

"Oh! I almost forgot." She turned away, and it was all he could do not to drag her right back.

Opening the medicine cabinet above the sink, she handed him a cobalt bottle of liquid. "This is from my friend Juliette Holloway. It's a remedy for your cat allergies."

Jordan took the vial and held it up to the light. "A Holloway potion," he mused. "I'd forgotten about these."

"You're familiar with them?"

He closed his hand over the small vial. "My parents didn't believe in conventional doctors, so they were all about natural, homeopathic remedies. My mom always kept some of the Holloway stuff around when I was a kid. She bought it from the old lady who lived in the house. Herbal teas to bring down fevers, sprays to help with poison ivy, that sort of thing. The lady said Holloways were healers, and she kept gallons of their family's remedies in the attic."

"So you believe in it, then? The Holloway magic?"

"Magic?" He let out a huff of amusement. "My mom was the believer. All I know is the remedies seemed to work. But then, I was a kid so I had nothing to compare it to." He slid the vial into his pocket. "Thanks."

She seemed bothered. Jordan had the distinct feeling he'd just disappointed her, somehow.

"I'm sure it will help," he added, not quite knowing what else to say.

"Great." She walked out of the bathroom with her head high. She was such a bundle of contradictions. One moment she was kissing him like a fiery hot vixen, the next she was walking away like an ice queen. As alluring as she was, she also frustrated the hell out of him.

When he gathered the wet towels and followed, she was standing near the door of her apartment. One bare foot rubbed the top of the other, and if it weren't for that nervous movement, she'd have looked perfectly composed.

Jordan glanced around the apartment, noticing everything. The small suitcase pushed against one wall. The cardboard box of clothes beside the suitcase. The table near the window with the butterfly cage on top. There was a single loaf of bread and a small jar of peanut butter on the table, and aside from those things, there was nothing else.

She has nothing else.

Guilt roiled inside him. He was living in a house full of furniture. The upstairs rooms were crammed with things nobody used, and here she was living like this. He should've known. He should've thought to check.

"Why don't you have a bed?" he asked, aware of the rough edge to his voice. The woman turned him upside down and inside out.

"Because I like to live spartan. I'm a minimalist."

Jordan took a last look around the room as she ushered him out. *Spartan, my ass.* She was broke, and he knew it. If there was one thing he understood, it was bravado. He'd mastered it a long time ago. Always pretending things weren't that bad. Pretending he wore outdated, ill-fitting clothing as a kid because he wanted to, not because he had to. Pretending he wasn't hungry at lunchtime because there was no food in the fridge that week. Growing up hadn't been easy, and he'd learned how to build walls around himself for protection. He knew walls when he saw them, and Kat had the rock-solid, steel-beamed, impenetrable kind. The kind that kept most people conveniently at a distance.

But he wasn't most people.

Chapter Fifteen

Kat leaned back in her chair at the Daisy Meadows Pet Rescue, stretching her arms above her head. It was only ten o'clock in the morning and already she'd begun making arrangements for their annual Pet Adoption Day on Saturday. Volunteers who took care of homeless animals would bring them to the waterfront for a meet-and-greet with the public. If all went well, they'd find homes for many of the cats and dogs.

"Not bad for a newbie on the job, right, Hank?" She reached under the desk to pet the snoozing dog.

Hank scooted out and licked her hand, tail spinning happily as she settled him in her lap. That morning, she'd opted to finally wear something other than her old work clothes. After the shower fiasco the night before, she'd busied herself sorting through Juliette's box of clothes. Anything to keep her mind off Jordan. Not that it helped.

She adjusted the bodice of the sundress she'd chosen. It was bright and lovely, in shades of lavender and deeper purple. When she pulled it over her head that morning, it had instantly lifted her spirits, though she'd have to do something about her black combat boots soon.

"Well, I've gone and kissed him again, Hank," she murmured, stroking the dog's silky ears. "But it's nothing."

Hank made a snuffling noise.

"No, I mean it. It's not going to be a big thing with him. He's just . . . around, you know? He's just around, and so I happened to kiss him, that's all."

Smitty Bankston bustled through the front door with a bag of dog food. Today she was wearing acid-wash jeans with a lime green top, and her hair seemed bigger than usual. "Hardly working, eh?"

Kat gave her a cheery wave. She was beginning to suspect that even though Smitty's default expression was sour, she might actually have a sweet side. Maybe.

Smitty had called earlier to say Bobby was picking her up for brunch. Kat could hear the thread of pride in the older woman's voice when she announced it. Clearly, Smitty loved her nephew, and why wouldn't she? He was charming and easygoing, and Kat had enjoyed having dinner with him the other night. They may not have had a whole lot in common, but that was okay. It had been easy. Comfortable. Bobby was one of those nice, gentlemanly types. Unlike a certain unruly beast who bothered her more than she cared to admit.

"Where are you guys going for brunch?" Kat asked.

"Ask him yourself." Smitty jerked a thumb behind her. "Some hoity-toity place on the waterfront." She disappeared into the back room with the bag of dog food.

Bobby came through the door holding a bouquet of daisies. With the cowboy hat and dimples, he looked like the perfect gentleman. He set the flowers on the reception desk. "These are for you."

"Are you sure Smitty won't mind?" Kat teased. "She might accuse you of flirting with the hired help."

"Nah, she won't care." He lowered his voice in a stage whisper. "She'll think they're for the office, but you'll know the truth."

"Killing two birds with one stone, huh?" Kat took the

flowers and went to the corner cupboard to search for a vase. "How's the puppy doing?"

"Already running around the ranch like he owns the place. We're a good match."

"Did you tell her about the dog?" Smitty called from the back room.

"Oh, yeah," Bobby said. "My friend has a dog he's thinking about putting down."

Kat spun around from the cupboard, heart thumping. "Why? Is the dog dying?"

"I don't know, but I think it's old. Only has three legs. It belonged to my friend's ex-wife. She left the dog behind when they split, so he's planning to take it to the pound."

"Tell him to bring it here," Kat blurted. She hated the idea that someone was considering putting a dog to sleep just because it was inconvenient for them. "I'll take him. I love three-legged dogs. They're my favorite. The older the better. Can he bring him in today?"

Bobby chuckled. "I'll see what I can do."

"Or I can pick him up at your friend's house, if it's easier," Kat said quickly. "I just don't want him to do anything rash."

"I'll bring it in myself," Bobby said. "If it'll make you happy."

"It would," Kat assured him.

He gave her a warm smile. Kat was once again struck by what a good-looking guy he was. And the fact that he was willing to bring the dog himself was nice, too. Everything about Bobby was nice. A girl could get used to that.

Smitty came out of the back room. "Move your caboose, Bobby, or we'll be late for our reservation."

"Yes, ma'am."

On the way out the door, he turned and winked at Kat. "See you soon."

After they left, Kat swept the front office, sanitized the

empty crates in the back room, and did inventory on the cat and dog food. She made coffee and let it grow cold. She drummed her fingers on the desk, willing the phone to ring. By four o'clock, she'd resorted to folding Post-it notes into tiny paper airplanes. And all the while, she fought not to think of Jordan. His sinful kisses. His hard body pressed against hers. His large, warm hands on her wet skin.

She dropped her head onto the desk and groaned. What she needed was a diversion. Somebody who would distract her from sexy thoughts.

The front door opened and a right jolly old elf walked in. The old man had a comb-over of sparse, white hair, bushy eyebrows, and a ruddy complexion. He wore a faded polo shirt, khaki pants, and a good-natured grin that made him look exactly like Santa Claus. All sexy thoughts flew straight out the window. He was *perfect*.

"Good afternoon," Kat said brightly.

"You must be Opal's new tenant." He ambled into the office. "She told me you worked here."

Kat stood and gave him her best meet-the-parents smile. She genuinely liked Opal, so it was important to make a good impression. "Yes, I'm Kat Davenport."

"Sam Norton," he said in a jovial voice that really cemented the whole Santa Claus impression. "I've been on this island for about a hundred years, so if you have any questions at all, just ask."

Who takes care of your reindeer? Do elves get paid vacation? Am I on the naughty list? "How can I help you today?"

"Well now, I have a friend who's in a bit of a pickle. He's a farmer on the other side of the island, and he's got a goat who needs a home."

"We don't really take barn animals," Kat said gently. "The crates aren't big enough, and most of the volunteers on our list only foster cats and dogs."

The old man looked resigned. "That's what I told Wally, except he wanted me to try."

"Why can't he keep the goat on his farm?"

"He says it's bad luck, on account of Wally being superstitious and the goat being born with only one eye."

For the second time that day, Kat responded on impulse. "I might be able to take it. Opal has a lot of space on her farm. Let me ask her and see if she's okay with it. Our miniature donkey needs a friend."

Sam eyed her thoughtfully. "You know, Opal said there was something special about you, and I have to agree. You're good people, Kat Davenport."

She could think of a certain someone who'd beg to differ, especially once he found out about the new goat and dog. But she'd worry about that later. When it came to animals in need, they had to come first. Kat clearly remembered what it was like to feel different—flawed—growing up. That bone-deep belief that she wasn't good enough and nobody really wanted her . . . It wasn't something that just went away. Heck, even now that she was an adult, the wounded feeling remained. It was just buried over years and experience like a piece of shrapnel in the body, surrounded by layers of scar tissue. Life went on, and sure, it hurt occasionally, but it just became part of who she was. But her love for animals was more than bone-deep; it was part of her soul. She'd do everything she could to help them, especially the needy ones nobody wanted. This was her calling, and she wasn't going to let them down.

Chapter Sixteen

Later that evening, Kat pulled into the driveway of Willowbrook Lavender Farm and parked, scanning the front yard and fields for any sign of Jordan.

His truck was there, but as far as she could tell, he wasn't outside. That was a good thing. As much as she planned to pretend nothing had happened between them, she wasn't quite ready to face him yet. Especially since in the space of one day, she'd agreed to take responsibility for two more animals. He wasn't going to like it, but if Opal said it was okay, that's all that mattered.

The moment she opened the driver's-side door, Hank hopped off her lap and ran across the yard toward Waffles. The mini donkey was grazing in the large paddock. He took one look at them and brayed.

"Hello to you, too," Kat said as she approached him. How had he gotten out of his pen? She scanned the field, but there was no one outside.

Waffles ran along the paddock fence, tossing what looked like an old rubber bicycle tire. It seemed he'd found a new toy and wanted to show it off. He flung it side to side, then up and down, kicking his hind legs out in happiness.

Laughing, Kat rested her arms on the fence, filled with

a sense of contentment. Waffles was doing so much better than when she'd first arrived. She could feel that he was happier, and that was the best feeling in the world.

She walked across the lawn to feed the chickens and find out how Waffles had gotten out. Maybe she'd left the fence unlatched.

As she neared the barn, she slowed to a stop.

Jordan was standing with his back to her, his hand resting on the handle of a shovel. He was breathing heavily and, from the looks of it, he'd been cleaning out the pen. Sweat dampened his T-shirt, making it cling to the defined muscles of his back. In a swift, unexpected move, he tugged the hem of his shirt up and over his head, then used it to rub his face and damp hair. Now he was standing with his very *naked* back to her.

Kat had the sudden urge to reach out and touch him. Jordan Prescott was truly a gorgeous specimen of a man. Broad, muscular shoulders and back. Dark, tanned skin. Narrow waist, lean hips, and a backside that . . . Kat wanted to move closer. For precisely this reason, she took a giant step back. She really needed to get it together. It's not like she'd never seen a half-naked hot guy before. A twig snapped under the heel of her left boot.

He turned toward her. His gaze swept slowly down her body, sending all kinds of delicious shivers over her skin. Jeez, the man didn't even have to touch her, and she reacted. She was definitely going to have to be on guard with him around. Kissing him in that stupid broom closet had been a bad move. And then again in her apartment yesterday? Even worse. Because now it was all she could think about. Sure, she'd kissed other men before, but none of them had ever wound her up so hard and so fast. Jordan didn't just kiss with his body, it was like he wrapped his mind around hers, and he knew exactly what she wanted even before she did. Exactly what she needed. It was deeply erotic and more than a little unsettling. She suddenly wondered if he was thinking about kissing her, too.

"Special occasion today?" he drawled, gesturing to her dress.

She folded her arms over the bodice of her sundress, trying to channel a calm she didn't feel. It was hard to act iceberg cool when he was standing there like some half-dressed god of washboard abs. "I told you I don't always wear black." *Quick! Set the tone. Say something normal.* "Did you let Waffles out of his pen? I saw him over in the large paddock."

"He's an escape artist," Jordan said. "I found him wandering around the yard so I put him in there."

Kat wrinkled her brow. "How did he get out? I know I closed the gate."

"The latch was rusted, and it broke."

Kat turned to go and inspect the gate.

"Don't bother," he said. "I fixed it this afternoon. I just left him in the larger pen because I thought he might like it better."

"You did?" Kat asked, pretending not to feel the jolt of pleasure. He thought of Waffles! That meant he cared. At least a little bit.

Jordan ran the back of his hand across his face. "Seemed like he wanted to run around, so . . ." he trailed off with a shrug.

"That's nice." Kat tried very hard not to check out his naked torso for the twelfth time. Would he notice if she just took one more peek? Probably not. *There.* Last one. She was done now. No big.

Jordan's lips curved up at the corners.

She tossed her hair and stared straight into his eyes. See? She wasn't fazed. She could just look at his face and not the six-pack abs and sinewy muscles that ran along his torso to that intriguing V that dipped below his hip bones. Easy peasy. She forced herself to focus on the hollow beneath his throat and the dark stubble on his unshaved jaw. The corner of his perfect mouth twitched.

She licked her lips and glanced away. Even she had her limits. Staring at him was too dangerous. The kiss they'd shared the day before hung in the air between them. She shifted uncomfortably on her feet. Maybe she should just mention it, so they could get it out in the open and not make it a big deal. She opened her mouth to say just that, but instead said, "I'd like to go check on Clementine, if you don't mind. And the kittens?"

He propped the shovel against the barn wall and grabbed another shirt hanging on a nail. "They're fine, last I saw. Opal put the cat food and water dish in my room, too. She said you requested it."

"I did. Clementine isn't going to want to go far from her kittens. It only made sense to move everything up to your room."

"I need my room back, Kat." Jordan's voice brooked no argument. "I've had a very demanding day, and I have work to do." He walked toward her, pulling the shirt over his head. She took one last peek at his rippling abs while his face was obscured. "You said to give your cat two days, and this is day two." He was standing right in front of her now, towering over her in a way that should've been intimidating, but instead it made her stomach swoop and her knees feel like melted marshmallows.

"Fine," she said as calmly as she could. "I'll move them downstairs so you can have your precious room back."

Jordan held his hand out in an "after you" gesture that was so gallant, he'd never looked more like the disheveled, enchanted prince she'd imagined when they'd first met.

Except he wasn't being gallant at all, the beast. He was being annoying.

She strode toward the house. How was it possible to be lusting after him one minute, and irritated with him the next? Would it kill him to be displaced from his room for a few more days? It's not like he didn't have a couch to sleep on. She only had a stupid recliner chair, and she was surviving just fine. And there were even other rooms upstairs for him. They probably had desks and beds. He could just take his business calls in another bedroom for a day or two. What was the big deal?

Kat stomped up the porch steps, completely aware that Jordan was following behind her, glowering and sweaty and covered in dust. He'd probably need to take a shower soon just to wash all that dust off his body. With soap and shampoo . . . Her mind began to expand on the glorious image of him in the shower. *No.* She shut it down fast. He wasn't allowed to be hot right now because she was annoyed at him.

Once inside the house, she ran up the staircase and veered down the hall to his bedroom. This time, when she entered, she took more time to look around.

It was a spacious corner room, with dark wood floors and an exposed wooden beam across the vaulted ceiling. A large picture window overlooked the front yard. There was a desk with a laptop, a computer monitor, and a sweatshirt thrown casually over the desk chair. Aside from that one article of clothing, the room was spotless. Apparently, Jordan was a neat freak. Figured. Controlling types usually were. He'd probably lose it if he saw the places she'd lived. Not that he ever would. Those places were tucked firmly away in the past, where they belonged.

She took in the gleaming chest of drawers and the pair of dress shoes lined neatly against the wall. A place for everything, and everything in its place. Except for Clementine.

Kat approached the mama cat and her kittens. She couldn't help grinning when she saw the sweet tiny bodies nestled close to their mother. Two of the kittens were gray, two were orange and white, and one was a calico.

"How's everyone doing today?" Kat asked.

Clementine began to purr.

"I'm glad to hear it." She stroked the cat between the ears. The kittens were so new, she didn't want to handle them too much yet. In another week or so, their eyes would open and they'd begin to see things around them. For now, Kat wanted to be sure to disturb them as little as possible. It was probably better to get them out of his room, anyway. Up here, they were so far away from the kitchen and downstairs bathroom. At least down there, she'd be able to check on them frequently without having to go up to Jordan's bedroom.

When he came into the room, she wouldn't look at him. "Please bring that box from the closet downstairs." *You know, the closet where we made out like it was the Kissing Olympics and we were going for the gold?* She didn't say it out loud, but she didn't have to.

He paused as if he wanted to say something, then just grabbed the sweatshirt from the chair and left.

Kat continued to pet Clementine, sending her reassuring vibes. "He's making me move you and your babies downstairs," she whispered.

Clementine's ear twitched. "I know, but he's a guy. I guess he wants his man cave back."

Clementine stopped purring for a second.

"My feelings exactly," Kat said. "But you're probably better off down near Opal, where I can check on you more often. Jordan would end up driving you crazy. He'd probably make you listen to bad rock music and watch MMA fights on TV and only feed you beer and potato chips."

"Don't be ridiculous," Jordan said from the doorway. "I'd offer her pizza, too. I'm not a complete monster."

Kat pretended not to hear him and continued talking to Clementine. "Besides, do you really want to share a room with someone like him? I bet if we checked his Internet search history right now, you'd change your mind." She looked at Jordan from beneath her lashes. "You just never know what guys like him are up to behind closed doors."

"You're welcome to come join me tonight to find out," he said, his voice lowering to send a jolt of physical awareness rippling over Kat's skin. "I'd be happy to pick up where we left off."

She tried not to look at him but failed. What was he thinking, saying things like that? Was he being serious?

Jordan was smiling just a little.

"If you're referring to that thank-you kiss in my apartment yesterday, don't bother," she said casually. Or at least, she tried for casual. Her heart began thumping madly in her chest because they were talking about it, and just talking about it brought the whole incident back into her mind, front and center. "I have no intention of repeating it," she said as firmly as she could.

He set a large, shallow box on the bed. Kat was surprised to see he'd already lined it with his faded sweatshirt. All things considered, it did look rather cozy.

"Are you sure you don't want to repeat anything?" he asked softly.

"One hundred thousand percent," she lied.

He looked amused, as if he knew all her secrets. She didn't like it.

"Okay," he said simply. Too simply. Kat had the distinct feeling he had other plans, but she didn't want to ask.

She bent to murmur to Clementine, then slowly lifted each kitten, placing them in the box. Clementine immediately stood and gave a *mrreow!* of protest.

"I know," Kat said. "But this grumbly beast is forcing you to leave, and I think he's right. You'll be much better off downstairs." Clementine climbed into the box after her kittens.

"I've got it," Jordan said, reaching for the box.

"What about your cat allergies?"

"Gone," he said. "I still can't believe it. One drop of that allergy remedy, and I haven't had a problem. Did she say how long it will last?"

"I'm not sure," Kat said.

"No matter. It works now, and that's all I care about." Before Kat could protest, he lifted the box and walked out of the room.

She followed him down the stairs to the small guest bathroom, watching as he carefully placed the box in the corner, out of the draft. Clementine was disgruntled. She hopped out of the box and began to nose around the bathroom.

Kat sat on the floor, gently encouraging Clementine, until eventually the cat rejoined her kittens in the box. "There, that wasn't so bad, was it?" Kat whispered. After a while, Clementine started to purr again, nudging Kat's hand with her head.

When Jordan left the room, Kat took a deep breath and let it out slowly. Being near him was a lot harder than she'd thought it would be. He didn't even have to do anything. All he had to do was stand next to her, and she felt like every part of her body was tuned to his. Why did she have to go and kiss him again? At least before, he was just a guy she'd kissed once. Now that they'd done it twice, it was like a floodgate had cracked open between them and all sorts of things could come spilling out.

A few moments later, Jordan returned with the water and food dishes. She watched as he laid out a folded towel and arranged the dishes.

"You seem pretty fond of Clementine," Kat said.

Jordan looked bored. "No, I'm not."

"Says the guy who tucked his sweatshirt into the cardboard box for her."

"To make it more comfortable for the kittens. I'm not heartless. But it doesn't mean I have feelings for your cat."

Says the guy who was now taking a seat beside the box to check on the purring Clementine. Kat smiled.

"What?" Jordan asked.

She shook her head, her smile widening. "Nothing."

"Don't read into something that's not there," he warned. "I was going to throw the sweatshirt out, anyway."

"Okay," Kat agreed, not believing him for one second. She could tell he liked the kittens, and she could tell Clementine liked him. "Did you know that your sweatshirt was the best thing you could've given them?"

"Why?"

"Because it smells familiar to them. Clementine's kittens were in your bed, so lining the box with something that smells like you makes them feel safe."

Jordan didn't say anything. He just stroked the cat between the ears.

Clementine's loud purr seemed to echo off the bathroom walls.

"Uh-huh," Kat said. "I thought so. She's your cat."

Jordan drew his hand away. "No. She's your cat. And in case you're forgetting, I'm allergic. You're the one who foisted her on my grandmother."

"First of all," Kat said, "I never foisted her on your grandmother. Opal officially volunteered. And second of all, you're not allergic anymore. Juliette's potion fixed that. And third of all, Clementine is not my cat. She's clearly chosen you. Ask her."

Jordan threw her a look. "No thanks."

"I'm telling you," Kat insisted. "Felines are funny like

that. People don't really get a choice in the matter. If a cat chooses you, that's it. You're theirs forever."

He cocked his head, studying her. "And you know this for a fact."

"Look, there are a lot of things in this world I don't know, but I know about animals. And this cat," she said, pointing at Clementine, "wants you."

His expression grew darkly sensual, and Kat was suddenly aware of how close they were sitting, with just the box between them. He slowly reached out and lifted a lock of hair from her cheek, sliding it between his thumb and forefinger, watching the silky strands fall from his fingertips. "What about this Kat? What does she want?"

She opened her mouth, then closed it. He was giving her that sinful look that said he knew what she wanted, and he could give it to her. For a few crazy seconds, she almost lost her resolve to keep him at arm's length. Would it be so bad? Maybe just one more kiss, and then she'd be finished with him for good. Sort of like a good-bye kiss. Third time's a charm, and all that. The Queen of Impulsive Decisions thought it was a great idea.

Jordan was still giving her that intense hungry-wolf look, waiting for her answer.

The front door opened, and Kat heard Opal bustling through the door.

Kat stood quickly. "I have to go." She walked through the kitchen and out the back door so she wouldn't have to make small talk with Opal. It would've been impossible to focus on a conversation when her mind was in turmoil.

Striding across the yard to the garage, she scolded herself the entire way. For a person who swore they were going to do things right this time, she was really making a mess of it. She had a good job, good friends, and the island felt like the kind of place she could really be happy. So why was she letting herself get all fluttery over Jordan, who clearly didn't belong in her world? Here she was, fighting an attraction that seemed to grow stronger every time they crossed paths.

She marched up the stairs to her apartment, vowing to put him out of her mind. He wasn't even that big of a deal, she told herself. Yesterday had just been another stupid slip-up. He'd fixed her bathroom and she'd kissed him again, but could she really blame herself? He'd had a tool-box. And he was soaking wet. Soaking wet, tool-wielding hot guys who fixed stuff were irresistible. Everyone knew that. And sure, he was nice to Clementine today, but so what? That didn't mean anything. Lots of guys were nice to animals.

Kat pulled her keys from her pocket, unlocking her door. Let's face it, Jordan Prescott was just a passing fancy. He did nothing for her. He did not enhance her life in any way.

She pushed the door open and stopped, staring in shock.

Chapter Seventeen

Her apartment had been vandalized.

Hank trotted up the steps with a happy bark.

She gripped her keys in one hand, heart thumping in her chest. No. Her apartment had been . . . *reverse*-vandalized.

She stepped inside and slowly took in the new room. What the hell was going on?

In the corner of the far wall was a twin bed with a patchwork quilt. Two fluffy pillows were propped against the wooden headboard, and an old nightstand sat beside the bed.

Frowning, Kat shut the door behind her and leaned against it for support. There was a small love seat in the center of the room with a coffee table, and a narrow chest of drawers pushed against the other wall.

She slowly walked into the room, almost afraid to touch anything. Everything looked so homey and inviting. And none of it belonged to her. Kat frantically searched the room for her suitcase, spotting it under the table near the window. Relief washed over her. Good. At least she still had her own things. The vandal hadn't taken her stuff. He'd just left his own. And she knew exactly who the vandal was. Jordan. Of that, she was certain. He'd seen her apartment the day before and took it upon himself to come in, uninvited, and change things.

Kat clenched and unclenched her hands, emotions warring inside her. A spark of anger at having her private environment changed without her consent. The flush of shame at being pitied by him, of all people. The soothing balm of gratitude. Annoyance for appearing needy—for *being* needy. Relief at having some actual furniture, even if it wasn't permanent. Confusion. Why would he go to all this trouble? A part of her wanted to be happy, but none of it was actually hers. It was borrowed, or rather, a gift that came with some kind of strings attached, surely. Kat knew from experience there was no such thing as a free handout. People always wanted something, and their motives usually weren't to be trusted.

She walked to the bed. The patchwork quilt was faded from years of use. Lifting a pillow, she brought it to her face and breathed in the scent of cedarwood and lavender. Very carefully, she lay on the bed and stared at the ceiling until the tiles blurred. Why did he have to go and do something like this? How could she keep her dignity if she owed him? It would take her weeks to furnish her apartment with her own things, but that's what she planned to do. They wouldn't be as good as these, but at least they'd be *hers*.

She sat up and scrubbed her face with her hands, then walked to the bathroom to splash cold water on her face. The old shower fixtures were gone, replaced with shiny new hardware. There was even a fancy rain can showerhead and a stack of extra towels.

An uncomfortable, sinking feeling settled over her. It was all too much. She couldn't accept it.

Kat flung open her door and set out in search of the vandal.

She knocked firmly on the front door of the farmhouse. Even though she could easily go in the back door to the kitchen, she wanted to make a point that she was not part of their lives. She was a tenant. Completely self-sufficient.

Opal answered the door in a robin's-egg blue sweater. Was she wearing blue eye shadow? Kat hadn't noticed her wearing makeup before. "Hi, Opal. Is Jordan here?"

"He's out in the field, I believe. He wanted to speak with two of the workers he hired to help with harvesting." Her face lit up. "How did you like your surprise?"

"You mean the furniture?" *That's not mine. That I didn't pay for.*

"Yes. Jordan was working on your apartment for most of the day." She looked so pleased, Kat hated to disappoint her.

"It's very nice," she said carefully. "But I can't accept it, Opal. It's too much."

"Nonsense! The rental should have been furnished. I can't get up those stairs, but Jordan told me it was empty, and that was unacceptable. He was on a mission today." She laughed. "You should've seen him hauling stuff around. No stopping him when he gets like that."

"I see," Kat said, even though she didn't. Why would he do something like that? If he thought that buttering her up would earn him more escapades in broom closets, then he was in for a big letdown. "He's in the field, did you say?"

"I believe so. But come inside and have a cup of tea." Opal stood back to let her in. "Clementine and the kittens would love to see you."

"I will," Kat promised, backing away. "I just need to go talk to him first."

She was down the steps and across the yard before Opal had a chance to protest. Most of the lavender plants were already cropped, but some of the later-blooming varieties still needed harvesting. There was one more farmer's market the following Friday, so the workers were probably gathering the last of it.

Kat searched the field for signs of Jordan. Two men were rolling a cart piled with freshly cut lavender to the barn. Kat greeted them with a wave. "Is Jordan out here?"

One of the men pointed behind them, down the hill.

She thanked them and made her way past the field and down a small hill, where large willow trees grew beside a babbling brook. It was quiet and secluded, with a shady bank of grass near the water's edge. The breeze ruffled the leaves of the willow trees, and the air smelled fresh and sweet from green things growing. A secret oasis. Even in her state of turmoil, it was hard not to appreciate the beauty of the place.

Jordan was stretched out under a tree, hands behind his head, eyes closed. He looked so peaceful, she almost felt bad disturbing him. Almost.

Kat cleared her throat and marched toward him, stopping just a few feet away. "I just saw what you did to my apartment."

When he didn't answer, she noted the rhythmic rise and fall of his chest. How could he sleep out in the open so easily? Must be nice to feel that safe and secure in your surroundings. There was a sort of careless freedom in that she'd never had. But of course, he'd grown up here with his parents, surrounded by all this natural beauty. Yet another thing she'd never had. Kat jammed her hands on her hips. "Hello?"

Jordan cracked open one eye. Kat stood on the bank by the stream, her long dress billowing in the breeze. Her fiery red hair was a riot of waves around a heart-shaped face that was so delicately lovely, it was completely at odds with her stormy expression.

Some survival instinct kicked in and he sat up slowly,

brushing aside the cobwebs of sleep. When he focused more clearly on her, a bright memory flashed in his mind. *La Belle Dame sans Merci.* She reminded him of the Beautiful Woman Without Mercy. It was a painting in one of his college literature books—a woman on a horse, leaning over a knight who stood transfixed with awe. There'd been some poem with it, but hell if he could remember the details. Something about the enchanted woman leading the poor knight astray, then later abandoning him on a hillside to die.

Kat tossed her hair over her shoulder and cocked a hip, her green eyes flashing fire.

God, she was beautiful. One crook of her finger and he'd follow her anywhere. What man wouldn't?

She placed her hands on her hips and fixed him with a heated glare. Even in fight mode, she was alluring.

Yup. He'd be dying on a hillside in no time flat.

"My apartment," she said carefully, as if that was all that needed saying.

Right. All that work he'd spent helping her out with the furniture. He smiled sleepily. Clearly, she was unhappy about something, but he couldn't stop himself from teasing. "Did you come to give me another thank-you kiss? Because I'm on board with that."

Kat's gasp of outrage clued him in that there'd be no thank-you kisses anytime soon. Damn.

Jordan rubbed a hand over his face, then mussed his hair. How long had he slept? The sun was setting low on the horizon. Soon it would be twilight. He loved that time of day. When he was younger, he used to sit outside and watch the shadows soften everything. The sky would grow darker until eventually, his house looked like any other normal house. No peeling paint or neglected yard. Just a regular home where a regular family might have lived.

"Sorry to wake you from your nap." Kat's voice snapped

him back to the moment. "No doubt your exertions in my apartment wore you out earlier."

He glanced up at her, trying to gauge her emotions. High color on her cheeks. Mouth pressed tightly together. What now? "Is your shower broken again?"

"No," she said impatiently. "The shower's fine."

"Then what's wrong?"

Kat threw her hands up. "There's a bunch of furniture in my apartment that doesn't belong to me. That's what's wrong."

"I know," he said through a yawn. "I put it there."

"But I didn't ask for it. None of it's mine."

"You needed it," he said simply. "I saw your apartment yesterday."

"No, you *assumed* I needed it, and you didn't bother to find out. You don't know enough about me to assume things." She began to pace. "Maybe I've already ordered furniture. Maybe I have a whole set of Chippendale antiques on the way from California as we speak. The point is, you put that stuff there without asking me. And that's my private apartment. That's my personal space."

"Wait." The truth finally dawned on him. "You're *mad* at me for furnishing the rental space?"

"Yes, because you didn't even ask me if I wanted it."

He frowned. "Look, when I went in to repair the shower this morning, it just seemed like a good idea. It's not that big a deal. There are three empty rooms upstairs in the farmhouse, filled with mismatched furniture no one's using. So I brought some up."

She came to stand above him, eyes glittering with some emotion he couldn't catch. "Why would you do something like that?"

"What do you mean, why? I thought it would make you more comfortable."

"Like lining Clementine's box with your sweatshirt,

right?" Her voice was tinged with bitterness. "Like I'm an orphan who needs a handout."

Ah. So that was the way of it. Jordan leaned his head back and studied her carefully. He needed to be very careful how he responded. "No. That's not at all why I did it. Clearly, you don't need anyone's help."

The tightness in Kat's expression eased. She straightened her spine. "I don't."

"I know," he said, meaning it. From the moment they'd first met at the farmer's market, he'd known she was strong and independent. A survivor like him.

"Why, then?" she asked in frustration. "Why would you go through all that trouble? I can't pay you back."

He shook his head. "I don't want your money."

Kat's expression hardened. "I'm not paying you back in *any* way. So if you think for one second that I'll—"

"Hold on," he interrupted. "Are you suggesting that I gave you that stuff so . . . you'd sleep with me?" Surely, she couldn't possibly think that. The idea of it was too ridiculous to even contemplate. And yet, as he watched the emotions flicker across her face, it seemed she did.

She looked away and muttered, "Maybe."

Jordan's eyebrows shot up, and he started to laugh. Deep, curling laughter that rose up from his chest and made his shoulders shake. "Well?"

She glared at him. "Well, what?"

"How'm I doing so far? Is it working? Because usually my thrift store reject furniture really gets the ladies excited."

She wasn't amused.

His humor died away, and he studied her closer. Mouth tight, arms crossed, hugging herself. *Well, hell.* She really was bothered by what he'd done. What kind of a world did she come from? He'd heard the Hollywood crowd harbored a lot of shallow individuals, but for her to jump to the conclusion that he'd expect payment—of any kind—was just wrong.

"Look, Kat," he said softly. "It's just some old stuff that was gathering dust. I'm glad it's finally getting some use."

"Even so, it just makes me feel . . . indebted. I don't like it. I don't need anyone's help. People don't just give stuff unless they expect something in return. That's how it's always been. That's how the world works."

"Not always," Jordan said. "Sometimes people give stuff to others because they just want to help. You do it all the time. I see you do it when you care for the animals. Do you expect anything from them?"

She swallowed visibly. "No, but this is different."

"Why?"

"Because . . . Because I like them, and I care about what happens to them."

"And is it so hard to believe that I might like you and care about you, too?"

Her swift inhale wasn't lost on him. He'd surprised her. "It's different," she blurted. "I don't want to owe you anything, don't you get that? It just complicates things between us."

"Kat." Jordan took a deep breath and ran a hand through his hair. "Things are complicated between us already. We both know it. And none of these feelings have anything to do with dusty old furniture."

Her eyes grew glossy, and she glanced away quickly, wringing her hands.

"Hey." Jordan's chest clenched. He hated seeing her upset. He started to stand.

She surprised him by dropping onto the grass, hugging her knees up to her chest, and staring at the stream.

"Hey," he repeated softly, moving to sit close enough that their shoulders were almost touching. "If you don't want the furniture, it's okay. My grandmother always meant for that to be a furnished rental. It's my fault for not paying closer attention and making sure it was furnished before you moved in. Can you just use the stuff until you find things you like better? Or when your shipment of Chippendale furniture comes in from California?"

She threw him a look that said they both knew there was no shipment.

"I mean, you're going to have to weigh the pros and cons," he continued. "And I don't envy you that hard decision. Are you going to want fancy meticulously crafted antique furniture, or Goodwill rejects from a broken-down old farmhouse? Tough choice, I know."

A reluctant smile tugged at the corner of her mouth.

Jordan felt the tightness in his chest ease, like heavy bands of rope loosening with each breath. He nudged her with his shoulder. "Just help me out and keep the stuff, for now, all right? If you don't, I'll never hear the end of it from my grandmother."

"All right." The strain slowly eased from her face. "Fine."

Relief washed over him. He felt as if he'd been hanging from a branch and just managed to hook his leg over it so he could regain balance. The strength of his reaction surprised him, but he didn't try to analyze it. He just wanted her to be happy. He liked it when she was happy.

"I'll keep it until I get my own stuff," she said. "But promise me something."

He'd promise her anything if she'd keep smiling like that. "What?"

She shoved him with both hands until they toppled onto the grass in a tangle of legs and arms. Kat pressed her hands into his chest and stared at him with those mesmerizing eyes. *La Belle Dame sans Merci, indeed.* "Never go into my apartment again without my permission, or I'll . . ." She paused as if searching for a dire consequence.

Abandon me on a hillside and leave me to die? Jordan

smiled softly at her, trying to ignore the delicious curve of her hips pressed against him. "Or you'll what?"

"I'll . . ." She gasped in delight. "I'll round up every pregnant cat I can find and release them into your bedroom."

"Easy there, wildcat." He chuckled softly. "I don't plan on going into your apartment again."

She seemed to accept that answer because she started to pull away, pushing off his chest.

"Unless." He lightly circled his hands around her wrists to keep her close.

She paused, narrowing her eyes.

He tried to think fast. "Unless there's a fire, and Hank is in there and needs rescuing."

She considered it for a moment. "Fine." She started to pull away again, but he held on.

What else could he say to keep her exactly like this—on top of him? He wasn't ready to give her up. "Or, unless there's an earthquake, and you're trapped under that treacherous lump of a recliner, and you need rescuing."

Kat rolled her eyes. "I think I could manage that on my own, thanks."

"True, but you'd need to conserve your strength because of the flood outside."

She arched a brow and began to smile. It made his heart flatline in his chest. God, he wanted her. "Oh, there's a flood now?"

"Yes." He rubbed his thumbs lightly over the delicate skin of her inner wrists, wondering if she was this soft all over. He wanted—needed—to find out.

"I'll be fine," she said impishly. "I'm a good swimmer. I won't need your help." She started to jump up but he caught her around the waist and pulled her back down on top of him.

Kat let out a little shriek of laughter.

"But who will steer the ark?" he murmured against her ear. "You know, the one I built? To save all the animals?"

He could feel her chest vibrating with laughter. She slid her knees on either side of his hips until she was straddling him.

Jordan's throat went dry, and heat spiked through his veins. He suddenly knew exactly how the poor knight in the painting felt. Helpless to resist.

"Now you're just trying to sweet-talk me." Her voice was like warm silk sliding over his skin.

"I might be," he said huskily. "Is it working?"

She pushed against his chest and rose up slowly. "It might be."

A bolt of lust shot through him, and he reflexively reached up to grip her hips.

"You still haven't promised," she breathed. "Promise you'll never enter my apartment again."

Jordan had to work to find his voice. "I promise. I won't unless you ask me."

"And that I never will. So, problem solved."

He wanted to say her problem was far from solved, because he had every intention of chipping away at her carefully constructed walls until she begged him to come inside, but how could he form coherent words when she was on top of him? Very slowly, she leaned forward until her hair fell in a soft curtain around them, and he could feel the warmth of her breath against his mouth. It was everything he could do just to hold still and let her go at her own pace.

"I think I might need to kiss you again," she whispered.

Thank Christ. All systems were *go*. No argument there. Except she'd better hurry or he'd kiss her first.

She melted over him like warm honey until every delicious curve of her body wrapped around him. "Oh, and also, I'm bringing home a friend for Waffles this week."

Somewhere deep down, Jordan knew he should care. But holy hell, she could bring home the entire San Diego Zoo if she'd just—

She brushed her lips over his. Once. Twice. The tip of her tongue darted out and she licked his mouth, like a cat lapping cream.

And that was it. A mortal man could only take so much.

Jordan gripped the small of her back with one hand, anchoring her tightly against him. Then he slid his other arm around her and, in one swift move, rolled until she was exactly where he needed her to be.

Kat's eyes widened in surprise, hair fanning out on the grass as she lay beneath him. Then she reached up and wound her fingers around his neck, pulling him closer with a tiny exhale. He captured her mouth with his, swallowing her sigh.

Sweet. Hot. Damn. Her soft murmur of surrender just about blew every shred of decency and control he had left. All the blood in his brain rushed lower, leaving him with only one coherent thought. *Mine.* He wanted her, and he wasn't going to waste any time trying to analyze that. Kat Davenport drove him crazy, but he'd go there with an idiot smile on his face because there was no place he'd rather be.

They kissed until he lost track of time. Minutes, hours, days, he didn't care. When he slid his hand up her thigh, dropped kisses along her neck, and sucked on the pulse at the base of her throat, she made a soft, mewling sound that almost killed him. She smelled like strawberries and vanilla, tasted like wild, sweet abandon, and he wanted all of her. Every breath. Every sigh. Every whimper of need. He couldn't get enough. Somewhere in the back of his mind, Jordan recognized just how screwed he was, because this woman was dangerous. She blasted past all his barriers and made him forget reason and common sense. Yes, they were outside in the open field. Yes, he should have more control. But did he care? Not even a little. One word—one tiny whisper—from her and he'd give her everything he had. If she'd let him.

A lone seagull cried overhead, jerking Kat out of the erotic haze surrounding her and Jordan. Heart thumping a staccato inside her, she pulled back, staring at his beautiful face in the waning light. His expression was molten hot, burning a path all the way through her body, turning her insides into a liquid pool of desire. She wanted to jump right back in and bathe in it. Maybe drown in it. Their faces were so close, their breaths mingled, and it was all she could do not to lay her mouth on his again. Why had she ever decided he was a bad idea?

She swallowed hard, clutching at his open shirt, wondering when she'd unbuttoned it. She took in the rigid muscles on his torso and the smooth, tanned skin of his chest, her gaze sliding up to his sinfully seductive face. God, he was gorgeous. He looked like a really, really good idea. She couldn't seem to remember why he wasn't. The Queen of Impulsive Decisions certainly wasn't going to remind her. Kat forced herself to focus. Breathe in. Breathe out. Ah, yes. Jordan was moving away and not planning to come back. Something sharp gripped her insides. He was leaving, and he'd made it very clear. That was it. Taking a shaky breath, Kat shut her eyes and used her last ounce of self-control to push against him.

Jordan's arms tightened around her in reflex. He was so strong, he could've been carved from granite. She shivered with need, refusing to meet his eyes. If she did, there was no way she'd be able to resist him. She'd be jumping his bones like a wild animal right outside under the open sky.

"I think . . ." She cleared her throat and tried again.

He's not planning to stick around, remember? "I think we should stop."

Jordan dropped his forehead against hers for a moment. Both of them were panting hard. She could feel his body shudder, and then he nodded and pulled away. Kat watched him rise to stand above her. His gaze never left her face as he began buttoning his shirt. In a daze, she glanced down at her dress, the skirt bunched up around her thighs, both straps hanging off her shoulders. With shaky hands, she pulled her skirt down, fixed her dress, and started to stand.

Her legs felt like warm Jell-O, and he reached out to steady her. She leaned against him as she regained her balance. He tucked a lock of her hair behind her ear in a gesture that felt both intimate and familiar. Then he cupped her cheek with his large, rough hand, his expression far too serious. Kat pressed her cheek into his palm and closed her eyes, as if she could commit the feeling to memory and take it out later to relive it again and again.

All too soon, he pulled his hand away, and they started heading back.

It was deep twilight when they neared the farmhouse. Shadows pooled across the uneven ground, and a cool breeze swirled through Kat's hair. She turned her face up to the sky, breathing in the night. She couldn't believe they'd just made out like horny teenagers. Like the sky was falling and the world was coming to an end. She should've been worried, but something about the moment had felt so incredibly right, even though she knew it wasn't going anywhere.

Jordan reached out and gently pulled her to a stop. They were standing at the edge of the field behind the house. It was quiet and peaceful, with only the sound of the wind through the tall grass. His expression was still serious, and it suddenly made her nervous.

"Don't tell me I have to kiss you again so soon," Kat

teased. If she could somehow keep things light between them, then she wouldn't be in danger of falling head over heart into the raging river of lust that was Jordan Prescott. It was probably already too late, but she had to at least try to paddle toward the shore.

"Would it be so bad?" he murmured, drawing her closer.

She brought her hands up to rest on his chest. No, it wouldn't be so bad. It would be so *good.* It was a miracle she'd been able to stop before going all the way. The spark between them had been nothing short of combustible. Kat felt as though every single sublime moment under the willow trees was branded into her memory for life. If she was very, very careful, she could stay grounded enough to get out of this with minimal damage. *Keep it light.*

She tilted her head as if considering his question. "No, it wouldn't be bad. But I don't think it would be wise." Pulling away, she started walking toward the house again. She was afraid if he saw her face, he'd know she wasn't feeling as nonchalant as she wanted him to believe.

"You're probably right." He fell into step beside her.

A sharp pang of disappointment twisted in her chest. "Of course I am," she said brightly. "That whole thing back there." She waved her hand. "I'm not saying it wasn't fun, but maybe we shouldn't repeat it, you know?"

Jordan didn't say anything, and she was too chicken to look at him. They were nearing the farmhouse. Just a few more steps, and they could go their separate ways. He'd go up to his room and do whatever it was he did at night. And she could go back to her apartment, make a peanut butter sandwich for dinner, and promptly freak out. In private.

When they reached the overgrown backyard, Kat started to turn left to go around the house. She was just about to give him a flippant, cheerful good night when Opal's warbly voice called from the kitchen window.

"There you two are! I was wondering when you'd show

up. Come inside and tell me all about the lavender. Kat, I made your favorite casserole."

Kat turned to Jordan. She waited for him to make excuses, but he didn't. Instead he surprised her. "Come have dinner with us."

"I can't," she whispered. "Look at me. My hair's full of twigs and grass, and my dress is a wrinkled mess. She's going to know we were up to no good."

"Up to no good?" he teased. "Is that what you kids are calling it these days?"

"Please. I'm twenty-six. If I'm a kid, then so are you."

"Not true. I'm much older. And therefore, wiser. You should listen to me." Jordan pressed his hand to her lower back and gave her a gentle nudge toward the farmhouse.

Kat let him, because secretly, she did want some of Opal's casserole. And, if she was being perfectly honest with herself, she didn't want to say good-bye to him yet. "How old are you, then?"

"Thirty-one," he said. "Far more mature."

"Says the man who just celebrated his birthday with a mini donkey and campfire s'mores."

"And beer. Don't forget there was beer."

At the kitchen door, Kat stopped and took a calming breath. Okay. She tried to smooth the wrinkles from her dress.

"Hold on." Jordan backed her up against the door. He pressed close—closer than was necessary, not that Kat would complain—and he ran his hands through her hair, lifting the heavy weight of it and letting it fall softly around her face.

"Is it gone?" Kat whispered.

Jordan dipped his face into her neck and murmured, "What?"

"The leaves, or grass, or whatever." She shivered as his lips brushed along her collarbone. "Is my hair okay now?"

He lifted his head and smiled down at her. "There wasn't anything wrong with it. You're perfect. I just wanted a reason to touch you again."

She tried to push him away, but it was a half-hearted attempt and they both knew it. By the time Opal came to the door, they were both grinning like fools.

Opal stood in the doorway wearing a Hawaiian print apron. There was a hot pink, plastic hibiscus flower in her hair. "I just covered the casserole and set it on the stove because I wasn't sure when you were getting in. Oh, Kat! What a lovely dress. Purple is really your color."

Kat felt her cheeks grow warm under the woman's praise. She self-consciously tugged at the skirt of her dress.

Jordan headed to the sink to wash up. "What's with the Hawaiian theme, Grandma?"

"I'm preparing for another costume party," Opal said proudly.

Was she blushing? Kat studied the old woman. Her cheeks were pink, and she was wearing a bright shade of pink lipstick.

"What's the party?" Kat asked.

"We're having a luau on Saturday, and it's going to be the biggest barbecue of the summer. Everyone's dressing in tropical attire, and we'll have live music and dancing."

Jordan took the casserole and set it on the kitchen table. "Grandma, you have a better social life than anyone I know."

"And well I should," Opal said firmly. "Lord knows I work at it. I'm not going to be one of those old ladies who sits around in a rocker all day." She grinned at Kat, her blue eyes crinkling at the corners. "You two should get out more and do something fun. Jordan, you're always working on the house or on conference calls. You two could come to the luau."

"Sounds nice, but I can't," Jordan said. "I have plans on Saturday."

Opal made a face. "What kind of plans? What's more fun than a luau?"

Jordan uncovered the casserole. "I have a date."

Kat felt a sharp, twisting sensation in her chest. Of course he'd have a date. Why wouldn't he? Besides, they weren't together. They weren't even really anything. Sure, they'd just had a rock star make-out session under the willow trees, but that's all. She bit the insides of her cheeks and went into the kitchen. She'd chosen it. She'd wanted it. And she'd gotten it. *Don't make this more than it is, Kat.* She clenched her teeth and turned on the faucet, scrubbing her hands with soap. This is how the Queen of Impulsive Decisions got into trouble.

"Oh, psh!" Opal said, taking off her apron. "What date? Is it that woman with the spiky shoes? Never trust a woman with painful-looking shoes, I always say. She'll walk all over you."

"Thanks for the advice," Jordan said.

Kat thought about making an excuse to leave. Suddenly, all she really wanted to do was go back to her apartment and curl up with Hank. But if she did, it would seem too obvious. She didn't want to give Jordan any clue that his going on a date bothered her. It shouldn't bother her. They weren't a thing. Instead she dried her hands and sat at the table like everything was totally normal.

"I wish I could come, Opal, but I have plans, too," Kat said. "Pet Adoption Day is this Saturday."

"Oh!" Her face lit up. "Well, it's always nice to see animals get proper homes."

Kat decided now was as good a time as any. "Speaking of animals getting homes, Sam Norton came in to see me recently. He has a buddy who needs to find a home for a goat."

Opal's hands fluttered with excitement. Was she blushing again? Kat stared in fascination as the older woman giggled. "Yes, Sam told me all about it. You bring it here. We have plenty of room."

Kat refused to look at Jordan. "I think Waffles would love to have a friend."

"Wonderful!" Opal said, patting her hair. "Sam will be so pleased."

Jordan opened his mouth to say something, but Kat didn't give him a chance. "And I already told Jordan about it earlier this evening," she said. "He was totally on board."

He raised a brow. "Was I?"

"Oh, yes," Kat said sweetly. "Remember when I told you outside? Near the willow trees? You were all over the idea."

Amusement flashed across his face.

"Very enthusiastic," Kat added. To Opal, she said, "Thanks for cooking dinner. This might just be my favorite meal anyone has ever made me."

"You're welcome anytime, dear. And now I am off to bed. You two enjoy." She turned to go.

"You're not going to eat with us?" Jordan asked.

"I'm all tuckered out," Opal said over her shoulder. "Besides, I ate dinner at the community center." She started down the hall, then called, "And Jordan, do reconsider your Saturday plans. We could really use your help at the limbo pole."

A few moments later, her door shut firmly down the hall.

Kat started mechanically spooning casserole onto her plate, focusing on the idea of Opal and her friends doing the limbo. It wasn't a pretty picture. It actually seemed like a disaster waiting to happen, but it was much easier than thinking about Jordan's Saturday date.

The kitchen was quiet and the silence stretched out between them.

Jordan was watching her. She could feel it, but she refused to look at him. Because everything was totally normal and fine, and she just needed to get the last bit of casserole onto the spoon. The toasted, cheesy parts in the corner. Those were the best parts.

"Kat," he said.

"Mm-hmm?"

"It's not a big deal, the date. It's a business thing."

She glanced up, all systems in order. She totally knew how to play this off. How many times in her life had she pretended things didn't faze her? About a jillion. This was nothing. "Oh, I don't care. That's totally your business."

"It is," he said, "about my business."

"Okay." Fine. Even if it was a business date, it was probably best to clear the air between them. "But look, you're free and I'm free. Let's keep it that way, okay? Let's not make that"—she waved in the direction of the field—"a thing."

His expression was unreadable.

"What I'm trying to say is, you don't have to make excuses to me. We're both adults," she said with a laugh. It was a good laugh. It sounded completely genuine. Extra points for her! She busied herself eating casserole. If she was eating a little faster than necessary, well, it's because she was hungry. Not because she was trying to get the hell out of there as fast as possible. "Mmm, this is good. Did you have this a lot when you were a kid?"

Something in his expression shifted. "No."

"Then what? Frozen waffles?" She spooned in another mouthful of cheesy potatoey goodness.

He rubbed at a spot on the Formica tabletop. "I ate a lot of cereal when I was a kid."

"Your parents didn't like to cook?"

"They were very . . ." He paused as though searching for the right word. "Busy. I was more of a 'free-range' kid. They weren't very interested in mundane, household stuff."

That explained a lot. No wonder the house was in such disrepair. "What did they do?"

Jordan shrugged. "Whatever they were into at the time. They weren't big on conforming to societal norms."

Kat tilted her head. "What do you mean?"

He took a bite of casserole. Chewed. Swallowed. His expression was shuttered, and difficult to read. She recognized it because she slammed those same shutters on her own emotions all the time. "They liked to call themselves free spirits."

"Okay," Kat said slowly. "Free spirits as in . . . ?"

"As in, they couldn't be bothered with trivial things like caring for a child. Whenever I complained about the lack of food in the house, or the electricity getting turned off, or the holes in my shoes, they spouted off about societal expectations and the importance of being free spirits. But really it just meant free to get high and free to embrace bad parenting."

Whoa. This was Jordan Prescott's childhood. He'd been a free-range hippie kid? It was hard to imagine. He just seemed so grounded and set in his ways. She had so many questions, she didn't even know where to begin. "That's so fascinating," she said, meaning it.

"Fascinating?" Jordan let out a huff of laughter. "That's putting a spin on it."

Kat bit her bottom lip. "I just mean . . . People's relationships with their parents, family dynamics, and all that? I've always found it interesting."

"What about you?" he asked.

She gripped her fork tightly and moved food around on her plate. Usually she just gave people the old song and dance—a made-up story about parents in L.A., no siblings, a boring suburban life. But for some reason, she didn't want to lie to Jordan. She took another bite of casserole to buy some time.

"Let's see." Maybe she could just steer the conversation back into easy territory. "I think my favorite dish growing up was grilled cheese sandwiches with tomato soup. The cheaper, the better." Not a lie.

"Really?" The sheer amusement on Jordan's face made her feel like a soap bubble floating on the breeze on a warm summer day.

"Yup." She grinned, relaxing back in her chair. "Cheap American cheese, soft white bread, and Campbell's soup from a can. Sublime."

"Fancy," he teased. "Were your parents chefs?"

She lifted her glass and shrugged. "I have no idea. My mom died when I was a baby, and I never knew my dad." Kat casually took a sip of water, then almost choked when she realized what she'd said. She had to force herself to swallow. Breathe normally. Because people breathed. That was a normal thing to do. What had made her tell him that? She never blurted out stuff about her past.

"I'm sorry to hear that," he said quietly. His expression was filled with compassion, and it settled over her shoulders, heavy and uncomfortable, like a blanket of scratchy wool. She'd seen that look on other people before, and she didn't like it. She didn't need pity. She was totally fine. He seemed to be waiting for her to elaborate but she wasn't going to.

Suddenly very tired, Kat scraped her chair back. "It's getting late. I should go."

Jordan stood, too.

She brushed past him and walked to the sink to rinse off her plate. Even just that subtle touch made her body thrum with delicious energy.

Jordan came up behind her as she was washing dishes.

Their eyes met in the reflection of the kitchen window above the sink.

"I'm not going to pretend nothing happened," he said quietly. "Because even right now, I want to drag you up to my room and finish what we started."

Kat's knees grew weak at the low timbre of his voice and the intensity of his gaze. She had absolutely zero doubt in her mind that if she stood there for another minute, she'd be the one dragging him up those stairs.

She turned off the faucet and dried her hands.

"Come upstairs with me." He stepped closer and she could feel the heat of his body behind her.

They were still staring at each other through the reflection in the window. She bit the insides of her cheeks, grounding herself in case she decided to blurt "Sure! Race you to the bed!" With careful determination, she gathered herself together and said, "I can't. I have to get to bed."

"Agreed."

"I have to get to *my* bed," she said with a laugh, stepping around him. *Keep it light.* "And we have to forget about this." She backed away, gesturing between them with her finger.

His expression was unreadable, so she continued before she lost her nerve. "I just really want to focus on work right now, and settling in here with friends. I don't want any complications so I think we should just carry on like before, okay?"

To her surprise, he started to smile. But it wasn't an "okay-sure-no-prob" type of smile. It was the kind that held all sorts of secrets. The naughty kind. "Yeah, Kat. We can try that."

"Good," she said brightly.

Before Jordan had a chance to say anything more, she gave him a quick wave and bolted out the door. She walked briskly to her apartment, chin held high, back straight.

Well, the Queen of Impulsive Decisions had derailed her plan to stay away from him, but she wasn't so far gone that she couldn't jump right back on track. And that's exactly what she'd do. A couple of kisses and a crazy make-out session didn't amount to much. As long as she kept her focus on work and practical things, she'd be totally fine.

Later that night, she lay in her new bed with Hank curled up on the quilt beside her. Every time she tried not to think of Jordan, the memory of them together came roaring back to life.

She rolled onto her back and stared at the tiled ceiling, thinking hard about work. She needed to go over the details about the Pet Adoption Day.

Jordan's hard, lean body pressing against hers as he rolled her onto the grass.

She flopped onto her stomach. She needed to make some more calls tomorrow. Remind the volunteers what time to bring their foster pets.

Jordan's mouth at the sensitive spot near the nape of her neck, trailing lower, and lower still.

She turned sideways and curled into a ball. Lots to do. Lots to do.

Jordan's hand sliding under her dress, the fabric bunching between them. His fingers caressing her until the pleasure burned so hot and bright, she felt as if she was coming apart at the seams.

Kat sat up fast, swinging her legs over the side of the bed. She refused to think about it. Instead she walked to the small table and stared at the mesh butterfly cage. It was easy to sense life in the cocoons now. She had a feeling it wouldn't be long before they broke free and spread their wings. She almost envied them. Soon they would be something completely different, something better and bolder and brighter than ever before.

She sat at the table, leaning her chin on her hands.

Maybe, if she was really careful and followed the plan, her life could be better, too. All she had to do was stay the course and focus on what was good for her. She was smart. She could totally do that. No problem.

Jordan's hands tightly gripping her waist, his mouth hot and insistent on her bare skin.

No problem at all.

Chapter Eighteen

Kat stood in the middle of Emma's attic, surrounded by a sea of dusty boxes, steamer trunks, and various odds and ends from the Holloway family's past. Emma and Juliette had invited her over to spend Tuesday night participating in what they called "Operation Family Tree," a project they'd been working on for the past two hours. Kat had agreed, hoping it would help her focus on something other than her tumble down Lusty Lane with Jordan Prescott yesterday evening.

"So, what exactly are we looking for again?" Kat asked, edging around a dusty carousel horse.

To say the attic was odd would've been a vast understatement. It was crammed to the brim with Holloway heirlooms, and it had a strange way of changing and shifting, depending on where Kat was standing. The changes were so subtle, she didn't notice them at first. When she passed the old carousel horse, the air smelled of candy apples and popcorn, and when she ran her hand over the wooden horse's side, she swore she heard the faint sound of laughter and carnival music.

A dainty floral chair smelled like fresh roses, and when Kat brushed past an oil painting of a leopard, she thought she heard it purr. There was a cuckoo clock with a mechanical bird that popped out whenever she passed by, and a sun hat that sounded like the ocean when she placed it on her head.

It was as though each item in the attic was individually hand-dipped in Holloway memories, and those memories rippled outward, melding together, when touched. Kat was fascinated. She felt as if she could spend an entire month in the attic and never grow bored.

Emma and Juliette were much more blasé about it. Tonight they had only one goal: to find a missing link somewhere in their ancestors' belongings that would connect Kat to the Holloways.

"We're looking for a family album. Or family photos. Or anything remotely family-ish." Juliette's muffled voice came from behind a dressing screen in the far corner. She emerged with an armful of clothing heaped so high, it obscured her face. "I can't believe how much the Holloways have accumulated over the years." She dumped the pile of clothes on top of several boxes. "I mean, look at this stuff, Em. It's like the Queen of Sheba left her wardrobe here." She held up a white gauzy dress with a gold snake for a collar and Egyptian-style hieroglyphics around the border.

Emma was kneeling under one of the attic windows, going through a cardboard box of what appeared to be dishes. "I think that's from one of the aunts. Grandma once told me we had a relative who was all into stage acting and opera."

Kat navigated her way around stacks of boxes, toward Juliette's clothing pile. Beautiful gowns in rich shades of emerald, sapphire and amber twisted around sparkling skirts, embroidered scarves, and elaborate headdresses. She lifted a blue velvet gown and held it up. Even in the weak attic light, the dress glowed like a crown jewel.

"Okay, it's official," Kat announced. "You guys have the coolest family, ever."

Juliette, who had gone back behind the dressing screen, let out a laugh. "Cool is one way to describe it. You could also say crazy, odd, loony—"

"Bizarre, unconventional, deranged," Emma added.

Juliette hefted another pile of clothes from behind the screen and said, "Peculiar."

"Freakish," Emma called back.

"And don't forget . . ." Juliette grabbed a theater hat off the floor and shoved it on her head. It was black satin, with a huge swath of black tulle cascading over the edge. She flashed a devious smile. "*Witchy.*"

"You look really good in witchy," Kat said. "And even if people called you those things, the whole mystery behind your family is kind of romantic, you know?" She held the blue dress up to her shoulders and turned this way and that. Really, it was too beautiful to hide in the shadows.

"Try it on," Emma said.

Kat started to say "no," but the dress suddenly clung to her body like it was charged with static electricity. "What the—?"

"That," Juliette said with a laugh, "is the house. Remember when we told you it was opinionated?"

Kat nodded, wide-eyed. Goose bumps rose on her arms, but it was from excitement, more than anything else. She wasn't afraid. She was just surprised.

"Well, the house thinks you should try on the dress," Juliette said. "And so do I."

"Me too," Emma called. "Just have fun with it. Juliette and I used to play dress-up here when we were kids. We played pirate kings and fairy queens and what was that one you liked, Jules?"

"Sasquatch hunters."

"Oh, that's right." Emma gave her cousin a long-suffering look. "I always had to be Bigfoot in the ratty fur coat."

"Because you were better at lumbering about," Juliette said with a laugh. "And I was better at sneaking. We were playing to our strengths."

Emma rolled her eyes.

Juliette nodded to the blue dress that was still clinging to Kat. "Go ahead and give it a whirl. You should do it now, because we might not see it again."

"It's true," Emma said, stepping over a rolled-up rug to join them. "The hardest thing about all this"—she swept her hand wide—"is that it's ever-changing. We're constantly finding things we've never seen before."

"Or losing things we swear we left up here," Juliette said. "One time I found a slingshot, and I was so excited because I spent the whole afternoon gathering stones for it. I was going to try it out on Mean Mikey Matthews because I overheard him saying he was going to toilet paper our house. Remember that, Em?"

Emma nodded. "So Mean Mikey came in the middle of the night with his cronies, and Juliette went running up to the attic to get her slingshot, but it was gone."

Juliette made a sound of disgust. "Just disappeared right out of the box I put it in."

"But in its place was a Polaroid camera," Emma said. "Which worked out better, anyway. Juliette snuck into the garden and took pictures of them. Then she left the pictures on the principal's desk with an anonymous note."

"And Mean Mikey got detention for a week," Juliette said with pride. "His parents grounded him and made him clean it up, too. But I still think it would've been more fun to sling pebbles at him."

Emma glanced at Kat. "You've probably figured out by now that she's the bloodthirsty one."

"But didn't they see the Polaroid camera flash when you took the pictures?" Kat asked.

"Nope," Juliette said smugly. "It didn't have a flash."

"But . . . Then how did the pictures turn out?" Kat asked. "That doesn't make sense."

"Who knows?" Emma said breezily. "If it's from the Holloway house, it rarely makes sense."

"So now's your chance," Juliette said. "Go try on the dress and make the house happy. There's a mirror behind the screen."

Kat picked her way through the boxes until she got to the red dressing screen with Japanese flowers. She quickly undressed and pulled the sleeveless gown over her head. Miraculously, the static electricity was gone. It slipped on in a whisper of silk velvet, sliding over her curves like it was made just for her. The neckline came up high in a halter style, but when she turned around and looked in the mirror, she couldn't help saying, "Whoa."

The back dipped into a low V that accentuated Kat's small waist, and the skirt of the gown fell to the floor in soft, elegant folds.

"Let's see," Emma called from across the room.

Kat emerged from behind the screen, feeling a little shy and a whole lot glamorous. She slowly turned in a circle.

"Holy Hollywood pinup girl!" Juliette said. "You look like a million bucks."

"Gorgeous," Emma agreed. "And it fits you like a glove. It's perfect on you. I think you should keep it."

Kat gasped. "No."

"You're keeping it," Juliette said with finality.

Kat looked at them like they were crazy. "Heck no, I'm not taking this dress. It probably cost a fortune."

"It didn't cost *us* anything," Juliette said. "Besides,

every girl needs a gown to misbehave in, and that's yours. The house thinks so, too."

The overhead light flickered.

"See?" Emma said.

"Thanks, all of you. But, no." Kat walked behind the screen again. "Besides, where would I wear it? It's a little too dressy for feeding chickens and cleaning animal kennels."

"If you like it, it's yours," Emma said. She pulled an emerald green enamel box off a pile of clothes. "Hey, I remember this jewelry box. It was my grandmother's." When she opened the lid, a lovely melody began to play. Emma started humming along.

"Ooh! I think I found something," Juliette exclaimed.

Kat emerged from behind the screen in her old denim shorts and T-shirt. She made her way over to Juliette, who was rummaging inside a brown steamer trunk.

Emma joined them as Juliette pulled out a large, thick photo album.

"This could be one of the family albums we've been searching for," Juliette said excitedly. She plopped onto the floor and opened the album.

A couple of postcards were tucked into the front page. One was a glossy image of the great pyramids of Giza in Egypt. Another was a tropical beach.

"I think these are from your mom," Juliette said, handing them to Emma.

Emma held the postcards and murmured, "Yes, I remember these. She sent a few when I was little." She turned to Kat, handing her the postcards. "My mom's gift is wanderlust. She travels the word, helping people in need, and can't ever rest unless she's on the move. I was raised here by my grandmother, who had kitchen magic, like me."

Kat studied the glossy images in her hand. She turned

the tropical beach card over. *Having fun in the sun. Hope all is well.* That was it. The message wasn't even signed. It seemed so . . . impersonal.

"Do you ever see her anymore?" Kat asked.

"No," Emma said. "She belongs out there. It's her calling." She seemed resigned, as if she'd come to peace with her mother's absence a long time ago. Kat felt an unexpected wave of sadness for what Emma must've gone through.

Kat handed the cards back to Juliette, who was browsing through an old photo album.

"See anything useful?" Emma asked.

Juliette turned the page. "I don't know yet."

Kat peered over Juliette's shoulder. The page held small black-and-white photos. Most of them were landscape images of grassy hills and cottages in the distance. A couple photos showed two women in dresses with aprons and work boots.

Juliette closed the album and stood. "I'll take this one home with me and report back. Let's all get together at O'Malley's pub on Friday night. Gertie and Molly are going to be there. Kat, you want to come?"

"Sure," Kat said. Gertie and Molly were Emma's and Juliette's friends who worked at the local hair salon, and they were always vivacious and full of chatter. It had been a long time since Kat had gone out just for fun, mostly because she was broke. But Friday was payday, so she'd have money for the first time in what felt like ages.

"Good." Juliette slapped dust from her broomstick skirt. "I have to go now. Logan's parents are flying in from Florida to meet me. Ever since he told them we were engaged, they've been riddling him with questions about me. Now they're coming out and there's nothing I can do except light a few of those Peace and Acceptance candles I make, and hope for the best."

Emma placed a hand on Juliette's shoulder. "You're not going to need the candles. They're going to love you."

Kat murmured her agreement, unable to imagine anyone *not* loving these women. They were so open and generous and kind. They were special, and not just because they both had a gift like her. They were unusual because they accepted her completely and without judgment. Even if Kat never found out who her parents were, she would always be grateful for Emma's and Juliette's friendship.

It was dark by the time Kat pulled in to Willowbrook Lavender Farm. Jordan's truck was parked on the side of the yard. Just thinking about him made heat rise up the back of her neck and her limbs go weak. She wasn't sure it was possible to pretend things were normal between them, but she had to try. Luckily, it was too late to run into him.

She hopped out of her car and set Hank on the grass. He immediately took off to see Waffles. Kat leaned against the garage wall and looked up at the stars. It was dark outside, except for the single floodlight near the animal pen.

A fluttering sound came from overhead. She held her hand out, instinctively knowing her friend was close by.

Edgar the crow landed on her outstretched hand, carefully wrapping his talons around her wrist.

"And where've you been?" Kat asked in a soft voice. "I haven't seen you in a while."

Edgar tilted his head and rose into the air, then settled on her shoulder. He rubbed his head against her cheek.

She reached up to pet him, grateful for his presence. Making her way across the grass, she came to a stop at the fence where Hank was snuffling around the ground beside the sleepy donkey.

"You guys are my family," Kat whispered. Edgar pressed his head to her cheek one more time, then disappeared into the night sky.

She may not have a family like Juliette and Emma, but she had her animals, and that was more than enough. It had to be.

Chapter Nineteen

"You're the handsomest three-legged dog I've ever met," Kat assured the shivering animal who was cowering under her desk. She'd arrived to work on Wednesday morning to find the dog's crate dropped outside the front door of Daisy Meadows Pet Rescue before they even opened. He was alone and afraid, and the only paperwork that came with him—much to Smitty's annoyance—was a note taped to the top of the crate that read:

Thanks for taking Lucky off my hands. Joe.

There were a couple of things Kat realized immediately. The first being that Joe was a total dillhole. The second thing she realized was that Lucky wasn't old. He couldn't have been more than three, and he buzzed with a youthful, nervous energy that was only contained because he was scared of people.

She could tell right away the dog was anxious, so she spent the first hour taking calls from the floor near her desk.

At first, Lucky was uninterested in Hank's encouragement to come out and sniff around the office. But after a while, the dog warmed up to Kat, calmed by her voice and the waves of reassurance she sent him. She felt a jolt of triumph when he crawled out from under her desk and laid his head in her lap. His back right leg was missing, and he had an odd, loping gait when he walked, but Kat could tell it didn't bother him anymore, which was a huge relief.

Kat scratched Lucky behind the ears, and he let out a contented snuffle. Her mind was suddenly filled with images of Lucky's former life. A car accident in the driveway of an old trailer home. An angry, screaming lady and a drunken, yelling man. The cold, white walls of a veterinarian clinic. An overgrown backyard as he learned to walk again.

Lucky licked her hand, and Kat's heart filled with happiness. This was the best part of her gift: being able to bring comfort to innocent animals who couldn't speak for themselves.

"We're going to be just fine," Kat murmured. "Things may not have been so great before, but you're with me now, so that's all about to change. Just wait and see."

By the time Kat left work that day, she felt happier than she had in days. She'd lined up all the cats and dogs for the Pet Adoption Day on Saturday. Their foster parents would be dropping them off ahead of time, and Kat would be overseeing all potential adoptions. With her ability to read animals' emotions, she'd know right away what each one needed. Just the idea of finding permanent homes for unwanted pets made her heart feel light.

Not only that, Lucky had already warmed up to her and Hank, and she couldn't wait to get him settled in her apartment. If a tiny part of her was nervous about Jordan's reaction to another pet, she refused to think about it. He didn't have to know right away. She'd be keeping Lucky with her and Hank at work during the days, so maybe it wouldn't come up.

When they arrived at the farm, Kat was relieved to see that Jordan's truck wasn't there. She wasn't quite ready to face him yet. Sure, the plan was to act normal and go on like before, but it would be easier said than done. She was just introducing Lucky to the barn animals when a vehicle with a small covered trailer pulled into the driveway.

Sam Norton slowly opened the door, greeting Kat with a wave. Today he wore a red polo shirt that made him look more like Santa Claus than ever. When he opened the back door of the trailer, Kat half expected reindeer to come flying out. Instead a tiny black-and-white goat came prancing out on a rope leash.

"Oh, she's lovely!" Kat said with delight.

"Yes, her name is Lulabelle. She's a bit feisty, but I think she just needs attention." Sam handed Kat the leash. Lulabelle peered at her with one bright yellow eye.

"Aren't you a beauty?" Kat crooned, laughing when the goat tried to nibble her jeans. "Come and meet your new friends."

Sam looked at the farmhouse, patting the hair on his mostly bald head. "Well now, is Opal in? I promised her I'd pay her a visit when I came by."

"Yes, she's inside."

"You go on ahead, then." He waved a hand. "I'll just go have a chat with her."

Kat took Lulabelle to meet Waffles while the dogs stayed behind to nose around the yard. Once inside the pen, Kat slipped the rope over Lulabelle's head.

Waffles came trotting out, and the tiny goat began bouncing around the perimeter of the pen, joyfully kicking up her hind legs in excitement. An overturned barrel sat in the corner and Lulabelle jumped onto it, dancing around in a circle. Then she jumped off. Then on. Then off.

Waffles wasn't impressed.

"Come on," Kat said, coaxing Waffles closer to the tempest in a teacup. "This is your new friend, Lulabelle."

Waffles stood his ground while Lulabelle ran circles around him. Clearly, he wasn't sure what to make of the tiny goat.

Kat spoke quietly to them, doing her best to make them feel comfortable. Not all donkeys got along with goats. It depended on the animal's character. But with Kat's ability to put animals at ease, she felt certain they'd be friends in no time. For now, Lulabelle was romping around the pen with enough energy to power a small city, and Waffles wasn't having any of it.

"I understand," Kat murmured as Waffles pressed close to her side. "She is quite a little firecracker, isn't she?" Waffles turned around and trotted back into the barn.

Great. This might take a little more time than she expected.

When Jordan's truck rolled into the driveway, Kat's whole body flushed with excitement. Now that they'd gone from zero to sixty underneath the willow trees, the thrum of delicious anticipation seemed even more amplified.

Jordan came strolling up, shoulders back, head high, like a man who knew what he wanted and was used to getting it. When he reached the gate, he leaned his forearms on the fence and eyed the dancing Lulabelle. "Looks like trouble."

"She's no trouble at all." Kat patted Lulabelle on the head.

"I wasn't talking about the goat."

She glanced sideways at him. "She just needs time to settle in. She's actually pretty excited to be here. Back at her farm she was kept on her own, so she didn't have a lot of interaction with other animals. She was lonely a lot."

"How do you know?" Jordan asked.

"I just . . . know." She straightened, filled with the sudden desire to tell him the truth. "Animals and I have an understanding."

Jordan hooked his thumbs into the pockets of his jeans. "What do you mean?"

Kat gathered her courage. Would he believe her? Would he laugh and think she was ridiculous? Only one way to find out. "I know how she's feeling, and I can communicate my feelings to her. It's hard to explain." She watched him carefully, trying to gauge his reaction. "It's just the way it's always been."

He looked at her with equal parts humor and skepticism. "Are you telling me you can somehow magically talk to animals, and they can talk to you?"

Kat took a deep breath and let it out fast, displacing a wisp of hair that had fallen in her eyes. How did she even begin to explain it? "I mean . . . yeah. That's pretty much it. Call it magic, if you want. There sure as hell isn't any other explanation for it. Nothing that I've been able to come up with."

"All right." Jordan's voice was tinged with amusement. He jerked his chin up in challenge. "Prove it."

Kat crossed her arms. "What do you want to see?"

He shrugged. "I don't know . . . Order one of the animals to do something."

"I don't just *order* them to do stuff," she said in exasperation. "They're individuals with their own feelings. But I can ask."

His mouth curved up at one corner. "Let's see it, then."

Edgar suddenly swooped down from the sky above her. His timing could not have been more perfect.

"Okay." Kat held out her hand dramatically. "Edgar, will you please come here?"

The large black crow fluttered down, settling onto her wrist.

"How are you?" Kat asked him.

Edgar crowed once.

She turned to Jordan. "He's looking for snacks."

If Jordan was surprised, he did a good job of hiding it. He ducked through the fence slats and walked over to them. "This is the pet crow you were telling me about?"

"Not a pet. I told you." Kat smoothed Edgar's sleek black feathers. "He's a wild bird. Now Edgar, Jordan here doesn't believe we're friends. How are we going to prove it?"

Edgar tilted his head and fixed Jordan with a beady eye.

"I know," Kat said. "Why don't you wait here with him, and I'll go to my purse and get you a treat?"

Edgar cawed loudly, rose into the air, and landed on Kat's shoulder.

"He's not sure you're trustworthy," Kat said to Jordan.

Frowning, Jordan watched Edgar inch closer to Kat's face, his long claws curving over her shoulder. "Is that safe?"

She ignored him and said, "Edgar, if you want a treat, you need to let Jordan hold you. He'll be very gentle, I promise."

Edgar shook his head.

Jordan looked mildly surprised.

"Hold your hand out, like this." Kat showed Jordan how to hold his hand sideways so his fingers were straight. "Now just ask him to come."

Jordan laughed. "Just *ask*?"

Kat nodded.

Jordan sighed and held out his hand. "Here, bird."

Nothing happened.

Kat rolled her eyes. "You call that asking?"

Edgar tipped his head back and made a chuffing sound.

"He's laughing at you," Kat told Jordan. "But I'll accept that you're a work in progress." She turned to Edgar. "Now, if you want that treat I promised, you'll have to wait with Jordan over there. He's a friend, too, even though he hasn't learned how to ask nicely. He won't hurt you."

Edgar seemed to think it over for a few moments. Then, in a flurry of feathers, he rose off her shoulder and settled onto Jordan's hand.

Jordan let out a huff of surprise.

Kat grinned and ran to fetch a snack from her purse. When she returned, Jordan and the bird were still sizing each other up.

"Here." Kat handed the cracker to Jordan. "You can feed him."

Jordan held it out, and Edgar took it quickly, then launched into the air. They watched him fly away until he was just a dark speck against the cerulean blue sky.

Kat slapped crumbs off her hands, grinning triumphantly at Jordan. "How's that for proof?"

"You do have a way with animals," he said with a smile. "I'll give you that."

She pursed her lips to the side. He still didn't seem convinced. She turned to Lulabelle, who was busy munching on a patch of tall grass near the fence. "Lulabelle, will you please come here?"

The little goat raised her head reluctantly, still chewing on a weed.

"Jordan still doesn't think we can talk to each other. Can you go say hi to Jordan to help me prove it?" She pointed to where Jordan was standing.

Lulabelle bounded over to Jordan, did a quick circle around him, and butted her head against his leg. Then she went back to the grass and resumed eating.

Jordan stared at the tiny goat, then at Kat. He wasn't smiling anymore.

Kat held Jordan's gaze and called, "Waffles!"

The donkey poked his head out of the barn.

"Waffles, Jordan doesn't believe we can communicate. Can you go over and give him a nudge to help me prove it?"

Waffles trotted over and nudged Jordan with his velvety nose. Then he did it again.

Jordan stood there with his hands slightly raised, blinking down at the donkey.

"Now do you believe me?" Kat asked, daring him to say something. Anything. Hoping he wouldn't say she was a freak.

There was an odd expression on his face. "That's . . . crazy."

Kat felt her heart sink. He was going to turn on her. Treat her like a weirdo. That's what usually happened when she tried to reveal her connection with animals. At first, people thought it was novel; a funny trick. They were fine with the idea of it until they saw it in action. Then it just made them uncomfortable or scared.

"It's pretty fantastic," he continued, staring at her in amazement. "It really is."

Kat flushed with relief. Jordan was surprised, but there was no judgment or fear on his face. He *admired* her ability.

"You're pretty fantastic, Kat Davenport," he said quietly.

Her skin tingled with pleasure. She waved a hand self-consciously. "It's just a thing. Some people are really good at math. Or engineering. I'm good with animals."

Before he had a chance to say anything else, a sleek white sedan pulled to a stop in the driveway, and Layla Gentry emerged. She was wearing shiny black stiletto pumps, a black shift dress, and the same bright red lipstick. This time, her brown hair was pulled into a low bun. She was the epitome of understated elegance.

"I'll talk to you later, okay? I have an appointment." Jordan walked over to greet Layla and they strolled toward the house. As they neared the porch, she placed a hand on Jordan's forearm and let out a throaty, melodious laugh.

Kat scowled and kicked at a clump of dirt. Even the woman's laugh was fancy-pants. She glanced down at herself. Her jeans and T-shirt were splattered with mud from the water spigot when she fed the animals, and she was pretty sure her hair was now a scrambled mess around her head. Whatever. It's not like it mattered. Nobody there to care. She took another peek at Jordan. He was now deep in conversation with the lovely Layla.

Lulabelle butted Kat's leg.

She glanced down and laughed. "What's the matter? You're not getting enough attention?"

Without a second thought, she plopped down in the muddy grass and gave Lulabelle a hug.

Waffles quickly trotted over, because if hugs and attention were happening, he needed in on that.

Pretty soon, Hank showed up for his fair share.

"Where's Lucky?" Kat asked him.

Hank gave a little whine. Apparently, Lucky wasn't happy.

Kat jumped up, slapping dust from her jeans. "Where is he?"

Hank started off toward the farmhouse, and Kat followed. When Hank reached the porch, he nosed underneath it and whined again.

Layla and Jordan were sitting on the porch chairs. Kat knew they were watching her, but she didn't have time to feel self-conscious. Lucky needed her, and that was more important.

She gave them a cheery wave. "Sorry, carry on. I'm just getting one of the animals."

She crouched low and saw Lucky shivering under the porch. "Hey there," she said softly. "Want to come out and play with the others?"

Lucky looked away.

Kat scooted under the porch on her stomach until they were face-to-face. "You don't need to hide here," she whispered, reaching out to gently pet him. "This place is safe."

Lucky nudged her hand with his wet nose, but he wasn't convinced. She could feel nervous energy pouring off him, so she did her best to calm him down. "I know all this is new, but everyone's so happy that you're here. You have friends now." She inched closer until she could snuggle up beside him. For a few minutes, Kat continued to pet him until he stopped shivering. Even though he was calmer than before, he still seemed very jumpy.

"How about this," Kat said gently. "You come out from under the porch, and I'll pick you up and carry you back to my apartment, where it's safe. It will be just you, me, and Hank. How's that?"

"What's going on down there?" Jordan called.

Lucky startled and backed away.

Kat heard footsteps on the porch above her. "Nothing!" she said quickly. "I'm just talking to—" Maybe it wasn't such a good idea to say she was talking to animals in front of Layla. "I'm just getting my dog."

"Hank is right out here," Jordan said, coming up to stand behind her.

Kat cringed. Now she was in for it. She glanced back and saw his work boots and a pair of spiky stilettos. Great. Both of them were there to witness her awkward sprawl under the porch. At least Jordan had seen her scroungy before, but Layla's presence just made the moment a zillion times worse. Layla was like an origami swan, all lovely and sleek with perfectly pressed edges. And Kat felt more like an origami boulder—a lumpy, wadded-up piece of paper.

"I wasn't talking about Hank," Kat said as calmly as possible. "I was talking about my other dog."

There was silence for a few seconds. She could just

imagine Jordan processing this information, and how he'd react. She held her breath.

"What other dog?" Jordan's tone was deceptively mild.

She exhaled fast. Now was as good a time as any. "My dog Lucky. The one I rescued."

Kat looked at Lucky and said very low, "I'll be right back."

She shimmied out backward on her stomach, fully aware of how she must appear to Jordan and Layla. Her jeans were filthy from sitting in the animal pen, her T-shirt rode up to expose bare skin on her lower back, and her hair probably looked like a bright red tumbleweed. When she finally rolled out from underneath the porch, she was even muddier than she'd been before. Origami boulder, ladies and gentlemen. Here for your viewing pleasure.

Jordan looked deeply suspicious. "Who's Lucky?"

Layla's head was tilted in polite observation.

"You remember," Kat bluffed. She latched onto Layla's presence like a shield. "The three-legged dog that nobody wanted. Remember I told you I was rescuing him because they were going to put him to sleep?"

Jordan began shaking his head "no."

Kat nodded. "And then you said it was a good idea. And I should save him from such a sad fate, because you couldn't imagine anyone doing that to a poor, innocent animal."

Layla's face softened, and she turned to Jordan. She pressed her hand on his arm again. Why did she always do that? Like she was afraid if she didn't touch him, he'd run away. "Oh, that is the sweetest thing I've heard all day. You always were a champion for others. You have a good heart, Jordan Prescott."

"He does." Kat eyed him carefully. "He really does."

Jordan seemed to be searching for a way to respond.

Kat held his gaze, daring him to contradict her. It wouldn't be wise. Not with the lovely Layla so enamored of his good heart.

Jordan's mouth twitched. "Right," he finally said. "Do you need help with your poor, innocent dog?"

"Nope," Kat said brightly, beaming at both him and Layla. "I've got it all under control. We'll only be a minute."

When Jordan and Layla wandered toward her car, Kat seized the moment. She ducked back under the porch and army-crawled to Lucky. Then she used all her good energy to coax him out. Once they were free of the porch, she gathered him up, called to Hank, and made her way to her apartment above the garage.

When she reached the door, she glanced back at Jordan.

Layla was still talking to him, but he was staring straight at Kat with a calculating look on his face. Clearly, he wasn't finished with her.

Yeah? Well maybe she wasn't finished with him, either. She threw him a sassy grin, tossed her hair off her shoulder, and closed her apartment door.

Chapter Twenty

On Friday evening, Kat flopped onto her bed, sorting through the treasures she'd bought at the thrift store that afternoon. She'd purchased a pair of sandals that looked like they'd never been worn, a couple of colorful tops, and a shiny gray hair dryer. Those things, plus the bags of groceries she'd bought, made her feel like she was back in the saddle again. She even had some extra money in the bank, so yeehaw. Things were looking up.

On impulse, she picked up her phone and dialed Juliette.

"Hey," Juliette said, somewhat out of breath. "The girls are meeting at O'Malley's at eight. Are you coming?"

"I'm not sure," Kat said, trying to weigh exactly how much money she could spend on expensive drinks. "Did you find anything in that photo album?"

"Maybe." Juliette's voice sounded strained. "Hold on."

Kat heard a loud crash, and Juliette's frustrated groan.

"What was that?" Kat asked.

"That," Juliette said, breathing heavily, "was the sound of our great-aunt's stage wigs falling all over the place. And for the record, Marie Antoinette must've had a neck made of tempered steel. This wig weighs a ton."

"Where are you?"

"In the attic looking for something. Gotta go. Text me if you're coming!"

Kat said good-bye and jumped off the love seat with renewed energy. Maybe getting out and doing something fun with the girls was just what she needed. She grabbed her hair dryer and the new can of shine serum she'd picked up at the grocery store, then trooped into the bathroom to do battle.

Less than an hour later, she stared in the mirror feeling chic and polished for the first time in weeks. Her hair was now as straight as glass, hanging in a sheet down her back. It was thick and shiny, with not a frizz in sight.

"I remember you," Kat said to her reflection.

Back in L.A., her ex-boyfriend had always urged her to straighten her hair. He'd said frizzy hair was tacky. So for weeks after she left him, she just let her hair go wild. It was her way of embracing her true self. But tonight, this was *her* choice. She ran her fingers through the sleek red strands and stared at her face. Her eyes seemed larger and her cheekbones more pronounced. It was definitely an elegant, understated look. Layla would probably approve.

Kat glanced at Hank and Lucky. "What do you guys think?"

Hank thumped his tail. Lucky gave her a huge grin, his pink tongue lolling to one side. That was the wonderful thing about dogs. A truck could run over you, back up again, and a dog would still think you looked perfect.

"Okay, then," she said. "I'll leave it for tonight."

She pulled on a green sundress with a flowy skirt. Then she added her new sandals and checked the time. Great. It was only seven. She still had an hour to kill before texting Juliette.

Kat flopped on the love seat and had started scrolling through her phone when she felt an odd, stirring sensation inside. She rose and paced her apartment, trying to pinpoint

the feeling. It was as if something big was about to happen—
some major shift in the order of things. She slowly walked
toward the mesh cage near the window and peered inside.

One cocoon had opened and a butterfly was starting to
emerge, its black and orange wings still wet and crumpled.

Kat beamed with delight. "There you are. I knew you
guys were going to make it."

The other butterflies hadn't emerged yet, but Kat felt
confident that they soon would. She had already done
some research on how to take care of them. By tomorrow,
she'd scatter some flowers sprinkled with sugar water on
the floor of the cage. In just a few days, they'd be ready to
go free.

She studied the emerging butterfly with a glowing sense
of optimism. A bold new life. A new beginning where they
could spread their wings and fly. What could be more exciting than that?

A loud crash came from outside, startling her. Seeing
nothing out the window, she flew to the door and swung it
open. Another sound—like pots and pans toppling over—
came from the large red barn on the other side of the yard.
The door was cracked open, which was odd. Ever since
she'd moved in, the red barn had been sealed with a padlock. Filled with curiosity, Kat made her way across the
yard toward all the commotion.

When she peeked through the door, she saw Jordan
standing in what appeared to be an episode of *Hoarders*.

Kat stepped inside, staring around the barn in fascination. It made Emma and Juliette's attic look like a sunny
walk in the park.

It was stuffed with . . . well, *stuff*. Rusted bicycles with
no wheels were propped against a kayak and decaying
cardboard boxes. There were piles of dried flower wreaths
and moldy beanbag chairs and a crushed tent that hadn't

been properly dismantled. Native American dream catchers hung from the rafters along with Hawaiian print shawls and a broken beach umbrella and snarled sets of Christmas lights. A harp with no strings stood in one corner, and an entire back seat of a car with rips in the vinyl upholstery leaned against a wall.

Things were tossed in heaps, piled so high that in some places, Kat couldn't see what was on the other side.

She skirted around a stack of paint-splashed canvases, then tiptoed over broken flowerpots and garden tools. The barn was so crammed with junk that the floor was barely visible. It looked like the place forgotten things go to die. And in the middle of it all stood Jordan.

He was facing away from her, muttering as he lifted a rusted birdcage from a pile of blankets.

"Um, is everything okay?" Kat asked.

Jordan spun around. His gaze touched on her hair, her clothing, her shoes, and back up to her face. "You shouldn't be in here," he said in a low voice.

"I heard a loud crash so I came to see if someone was murdered." She made her way toward him, avoiding a dismembered mannequin. "Looks like I didn't make it in time."

Jordan tossed the birdcage aside. "It's not really safe in here. You should go."

Kat walked to the fallen birdcage and lifted it. There were two small toys inside. One was a rubber duck, and the other was a plastic Superman figure. "What is all this stuff?"

Jordan's face was unreadable. "Nothing."

She ignored his non-answer and held up the birdcage. "Was this yours?"

"Never mind that," he said, reaching for it.

A hot streak of annoyance spiked through her. She held the cage away. It was a simple question. It wasn't like she was asking him to reveal personal secrets. The least he could do was answer her. After making out under the willow trees, it wasn't like they were total strangers. Besides, she'd shown him her ability to communicate with animals. This was nothing, compared to that.

"Did you have a bird when you were little?" she pressed.

A muscle ticked in his jaw. "Sure, Kat. I had two canaries."

"Oh." Her grip on the birdcage relaxed a little.

"They were a birthday present from my grandparents when I turned six. A few days later my parents got rid of them because they were 'too much work.' Those," he said, pointing to the toys in the cage, "I put in afterward. So I could pretend they were still around."

Kat felt something twist in her chest. A sadness welled up inside her, making her nose tingle. She turned away with the pretense of setting the cage down. She knew how much she hated others to pity her, so she carefully controlled her voice when she said, "I'm sorry that happened."

"Why should you be?" he said dismissively. "It wasn't your fault."

She wanted to say she understood. That even though she wasn't there, she'd been in situations like that in her own life, and she understood. But before she had a chance, something behind him caught her eye.

A caravan wagon was parked in the far corner of the barn. It was hidden in shadows and impossible to see from the front entrance. The sides of the caravan were painted in bright colors with sparkly scarves tied together to form a cheerful garland around the roof. Shawls with mirrored embroidery hung in the windows, the beaded fabric glinting in the low light.

Kat let out a tiny gasp. The bohemian-style wagon looked like something straight out of a fairy tale. She loved it immediately. The fact that it was so colorful, but shrouded in shadows, made it all the more mysterious. "What is *that*?"

Jordan glanced behind him. "A caravan."

"Yes, but what's it doing here?" She started climbing over boxes and scattered junk to get closer.

"Watch out for the broken chair," Jordan warned as she jumped over a rusted set of lawn furniture.

She moved toward the caravan until she was close enough to see the letters painted on the side: WINDS OF CHANGE. She repeated the words out loud.

Jordan came up behind her. "My parents' folk band. They had this made when they were planning to tour and go to festivals. The farthest they ever got was the front driveway." His voice grew pensive. "Such a waste. All that planning and talking. Castles in the air, my grandma used to call it. My parents were excellent at dreaming and setting their sights on the next big thing."

She turned to face him. "What do you mean?"

"They were constantly flitting from one plan to the next. That huge painting in the house? The one you noticed when you first arrived? My mom made that back during her artist phase. It was the only thing she made before she got bored and abandoned that for something else."

"It's a beautiful painting," Kat said, remembering the brilliant colors and abstract design. "She was very talented. I'm surprised she didn't continue."

Jordan shrugged. "I'd have been more surprised if she had. My parents never followed through on anything."

"But how could they afford any of this?" Kat took in the caravan and all the junk filling the barn. "I mean, if they weren't big on responsibility, who worked to buy this stuff?"

Jordan gave a dry chuckle, rubbing a hand over the back of his neck. "Neither of them. My mother inherited a large sum of money after her parents passed away. She and my dad had plans to become wildly successful entrepreneurs. Of what, they had no clue. They managed to buy this farm before the money dried up. They had some romantic notion that living close to nature would be good for us. What little money was left, they squandered on whatever whim came their way." He slapped the side of the caravan. "This one lasted about six months."

Kat walked along the caravan, running her hands over the colorful letters with glass jewels inlaid in the wood. "It's so beautiful."

"Yes," Jordan said, watching her. "After my parents' folk band fell apart, they parked this in here and forgot about it. And for a while, I made it mine."

"Can I see inside?" Kat laid her hand on a small red door painted with colorful flowers.

When he pushed it open, she felt like she was stepping into a dream. This was a piece of Jordan's past she hadn't expected. The more she got to know him, the more he surprised her. It smelled faintly of lavender oil and cedar, with a hint of some spicy, earthier fragrance that reminded her of sandalwood.

"Hold on." Jordan left to retrieve a small camping lantern. He switched it on, illuminating the room in a soft, warm glow.

Colorful shawls with mirrored embroidery lined the walls. There was a red patterned area rug and a pile of pillows in every color of the rainbow. In the back of the caravan was a platform bed covered with a fleece Seahawks blanket. An NFL poster was taped to the wall, and a stuffed, plush orca toy was tossed in the corner. There was also a deck of cards, a jar of marbles, and a stack of books.

"You used to hang out in here when you were a kid?" Kat asked.

Jordan leaned a broad shoulder against the wall. "For a while."

She roamed the caravan, trailing her fingers over the embroidered wall hangings. It was like being inside a strange jewel box. Near the bed, she lifted a book from the stack. "*Conan the Barbarian.*" Her mouth twitched. "Interesting."

Jordan came to stand beside her. "If by interesting, you mean an awesome classic that everyone should read because it's a perfect example of fantasy escapism? Then yes."

She raised her brows. "I might have to pass on that. Barbarian books aren't really my thing."

He scoffed. "Give me some credit. I didn't *only* read barbarian stories." With one hand, he pushed the stack of books and sent them fanning over the bedspread. Most of them were science fiction and fantasy books. He lifted one and held it out. "Take *Attack of the Killer Space Slugs,* for example. Another great classic."

"Mmm, yes. I see what you mean." Kat picked up a book with a curvy female warrior on the cover. The woman was battling a horde of giant bugs. "*Goddess of the Fire Sword?*"

"Now that book was an all-time favorite," he deadpanned.

She studied the cover. The woman was wearing nothing but a pair of fur boots and a tiny bikini. "I'm sure it was."

He gave her a crocodile grin. "She was just really good with that sword."

"Uh-huh." Kat rolled her eyes. "With her lack of protective armor, she'd have to be."

His laughter was warm and uninhibited, and it made Kat's entire body hum with pleasure. She wished he'd laugh more often.

He gathered the books and placed them next to a guitar buried under some of the throw pillows.

The instrument gleamed warmly in the low light. Kat reached out and dragged the guitar across the bed. "Will you play something?"

He jammed his hands into his pockets. "Nah."

"Come on," Kat pleaded. "Just one song. Anything."

"I haven't played in a really long time."

"It's okay. If you mess up, I won't even know." She held the guitar out. "I've never been good with instruments. I even failed at the recorder in grade school. The music teacher made me play the triangle in the class concert instead."

Jordan's easy grin made her toes curl.

He took the guitar and settled it on his lap. She was suddenly aware of how close he was. She could reach out and touch him, if she wanted. And she did want. Memories of them locked in a heated embrace, rolling in the grass together, flashed through her mind. Heat throbbed deep and low inside her, fanning up through her chest and prickling across her cheeks. Could he tell what she was thinking?

Thankfully, he wasn't looking at her. He propped his back against the wall and started tuning the guitar.

Kat had the oddest sense of déjà vu. The seclusion of the caravan and the image of Jordan in the dim light surrounded by sparkling embroidery seemed almost dreamlike.

He strummed a few chords of "Stairway to Heaven" she recognized, then he stopped and shook his head.

"What is it?"

He glanced at her thoughtfully, the vibrations of music fading until the room was silent again.

"That song's too typical for you." He began to strum the chords lightly, watching her with those lazy wolf eyes. "You need something unique."

Kat felt her cheeks heat, and she was glad for the low light.

When he finally began to play, she felt as though the entire world fell away and the only thing left on the planet was the two of them. She pretended she was watching him play the guitar, but really she was just watching him. The way his glossy hair fell over his forehead. His sensual mouth. The hollows beneath his cheekbones. The dark stubble on his jaw. His large hands expertly strumming the chords.

The music was sweet and haunting and unusual, yet achingly familiar. The melody seemed to unfurl in the air, winding around them until they were both joined together by some invisible bond.

When it was over, they sat in silence for a few moments as if neither wanted to break the spell.

"That," she whispered, "was beautiful. What was it?"

"An old Irish lullaby. This old Irish man from my parents' folk band taught it to me before they split up." He propped the guitar against the wall, rising to stand in front of her. Tilting his head, he studied her for several long moments without saying anything.

Kat shifted uneasily. It was disconcerting to be on the other end of such deep scrutiny. "What?" she demanded.

A slight shake of his head. "Nothing. I just haven't seen you with your hair straight like that."

She tucked a shiny lock behind her ear, wondering if he liked it.

"It suits you better when it's wild," he said.

An odd mixture of disappointment and pleasure knocked around inside her, and she glanced away. "If you don't like it, then don't look at it."

"I never said I didn't like it. I only meant if I had a choice, I'd choose your natural hair."

"Well, it's not your choice, is it? It's mine." She bristled, tossing the length of hair over her shoulder.

"See? Wild and feisty, just like your hair. It suits you better." In the dim light, he looked exactly like the charming, enchanted prince he reminded her of when they first met. "I like it wild," he said with a wink.

Of course he did. So did she.

His teasing expression began to fade, replaced with a powerful, masculine intensity that Kat couldn't ignore. The desire between them was palpable. She felt like they'd been orbiting around each other for days, and the gravitational pull had finally become too strong to resist. They were going to collide into each other, and she didn't even care. She wanted to slide her hands around his back, drag him up against her, and throw caution out the sparkly caravan window.

Here, with him, the rest of the world seemed far away. Like they were hidden inside some fairy tale place where time stood still and there was nothing beyond the pages of this story, this moment. With him standing in front of her, watching her like a hungry wolf, every instinct she had was the opposite of what she should have. Because she didn't want to run from the wolf. She wanted to embrace him.

Very slowly, he reached out and lifted a lock of her hair, sliding his fingers over the silky length. When it fell back to her shoulder, he did it again. She shivered at the nearness of him, remembering just how good his hands had felt on other parts of her body.

When he cupped the nape of her neck under her hair, cradling the back of her head, she closed her eyes and shivered, knowing exactly where this was going to lead, and struggling to remember why she shouldn't let it.

"Kat. Do you want this?" His voice was low and hushed, but there was a velvety rough edge to it that felt like a physical caress.

They both already knew the answer to that. But how could she even begin to explain all the reasons she needed to avoid him? Maybe it was time to just tell him the truth.

She took a shaky breath. "I promised myself when I

moved here that I wouldn't get caught up in something that wasn't good for me."

He pulled his hand away and sat beside her on the bed, not quite near enough to touch, but close enough for her to feel the delicious heat of him through the thin layer of her dress. It took all her effort not to lean into him. "So you think I'm not good for you."

"No, it's not you, exactly." She licked her lips and tried to sound calm and reasonable, but it was impossible. That's not at all how she felt. Unless the calm, reasonable thing to do was to rip her clothes off and jump his bones. Clearing her throat, she tried again. "It's just that you don't live here. You're going to leave, and I . . . It wouldn't be a smart move, that's all. It would just end in disappointment."

"Why do you think that?" he murmured.

"Because I'll be sad when you go." There. She said it, and it made perfect sense. No one could argue that.

"How can you be sure?" Oh God, he was playing with her hair again. Kat gave up and melted into his touch, reveling in the warmth of his body against hers.

"Maybe you'll decide I annoy you," he said huskily. "And you'll be relieved when I go."

She almost laughed. "It's a high possibility."

"Maybe we won't even be compatible." There was a gleam of mischief in his eyes. "In bed, I mean. Maybe it'll be a huge disappointment."

She glanced at him from beneath her lashes. "Something tells me that won't be an issue."

A sensual curl of his mouth. "But how can we be sure? I could surprise you in all the worst ways."

She pressed her lips together, trying not to smile. "Maybe."

"Maybe we should find out? Fine, I give in. Let's."

Now Kat did smile. She smiled when he reached for her.

She smiled when they tumbled back onto the coverlet. And she smiled when he slid his hand from nape to hip in one long, sensual stroke as he gathered her closer.

After that, Kat's smile faded and her body gave in to every deep, pleasurable sensation. Because Jordan did surprise her. In all the very best ways.

Chapter Twenty-One

Kat made her way across the lawn near the waterfront at ten o'clock the next morning. It was one of those Pacific Northwest days at the end of the summer where the sun shone bright, the sky was a clear blue, but the breeze coming in off the ocean was chilly. She shivered, wishing she'd worn a jacket instead of just a hoodie, but her mind hadn't been on the weather that morning. Her mind had been on Jordan Prescott.

She smiled, this time shivering for a much different reason. The caravan escapade with him the night before had been like some erotic fantasy dream. She'd woken before dawn feeling deliciously languid and drowsy with Jordan beside her, the blanket twisted around them. Hushed whispers. Quiet laughter. A good-morning kiss that quickly turned from sweet to incendiary. They'd spent hours in that secret hideout, and by the time she'd returned to her apartment, the sun was already creeping over the horizon.

Now, as she walked toward the Daisy Meadows Pet Rescue tents on the waterfront lawn, she rubbed her bleary eyes, grateful for the extra cup of coffee she'd brought with her in a travel mug. She may have been sleepy, but she was grinning like a fool. *Because you are a fool,* the Queen of Impulsive Decisions whispered. *Everyone's a fool in love.*

"No," Kat said under her breath. It wasn't love. Every single time she'd been involved with someone in the past, she'd tried to pretend it was love for a while, until she realized it was just that. Pretend. With Jordan, she already knew things weren't going to work out because he was going back home to New York. The giddy, squee-tastic feeling she was experiencing right now was a direct result of the secret caravan fling they'd had the night before. That was all.

"Good of you to make it," Smitty groused as she attached a label to one of the cat crates.

The entire event consisted of two tent canopies, divided into a cat section and a dog section. Each space had a small gated area with a chair so people could get to know the pets they were considering. The tents were set up right on the waterfront lawn, where foot traffic was expected, especially on a Saturday.

Darla, one of Smitty's on-again, off-again volunteers, was organizing pet adoption forms.

"We've already done most of the hard work," Smitty added as she set the last of the crates on the table. "All the foster volunteers dropped their animals off thirty minutes ago."

Kat checked her watch. "It's only just ten o'clock. You said come at ten."

Smitty grumbled and shoved a stack of flyers at her. "Here, you can arrange the table. I'm going for some fresh air."

Kat watched her make a beeline for the parking lot, pulling a lighter and pack of cigarettes from her purse. Smitty seemed even more grumpy than usual this morning.

"Hey, Kat," Darla called. She was a cheerful woman with gray hair and an obvious love of cats, if the fur covering her

T-shirt was any indication. "Smitty says you've been doing good work over at the office."

"She said that?"

"Don't look so surprised." Darla laughed. "She seems grouchy most of the time, but she's actually pretty cool."

Kat glanced at the scowling Smitty, who was pacing back and forth near her car, puffing on a cigarette. "She doesn't seem very cool right now."

"That's because she's been trying to get a remodel going at the shelter, and it's not looking good. She wants to build a kennel area outside for the bigger dogs who need more space to run. And a special cat room with carpeted cat trees for them to climb around. But it's hard to get funding, and the building owner is a real piece of work." Darla made a face. "Some hotshot who lives in Seattle and has no vested interest in the shelter. It was his ex-wife's pet project, but now she's moved on and he doesn't care about it. The place barely makes enough money to break even."

Kat could see Smitty still pacing, mumbling to herself. She had no idea the shelter was barely hanging on. "So what's going to happen?"

"If we're lucky?" Darla flipped through a stack of crate labels. "Nothing. And we can continue on with everything status quo. No remodel, but at least the rescue office will still be there. If we're unlucky, the guy will probably sell the property and we'll have to disband the operation. That's what's so frustrating. For everyone who actually cares about the animals, it's a huge unknown."

No wonder Smitty was always in a foul mood. She actually cared about the animals, and there was no way of knowing how long the Daisy Meadows Pet Rescue would last. This worried Kat not because of job security, but because she hated the idea that the homeless animals were at risk. In a world where so many animals went unloved and unwanted, it meant everything to her to be able to help, even in a small way. Not for the first time, Kat wished she had a truckload of money so she could truly make a difference for them.

Darla picked up a name tag and latched it to another crate. There was a small white cat inside, curled up in the corner. It had green eyes and a red collar with a tiny bell. "This here's Princess Leia. She's small, but sassy, so make sure you call her by her title."

Kat opened the crate and reached in to pet her. The cat meowed and twitched her tail. Kat instantly felt a connection and began sorting through Princess Leia's emotions to make sense of what she needed. "She's not big on crowds. She wants a home where it's quiet and peaceful. No kids. Preferably someone older. An apartment would be just fine. She'd like to be the only pet in a home where she could spend quiet nights on someone's lap in front of the TV."

"Wow," Darla said in surprise. "You really nailed it." She held out Princess Leia's chart. "It says here she came from a large family where she was constantly bothered by two rowdy dogs and a toddler. Her owners gave her up, saying she needed to be in a quieter place."

"Then that's what we're going to do, Princess," Kat said to the feline, who was now purring. "We're going to find you a nice quiet place to live."

"You really have a way with them, don't you?" Darla mused. "Smitty said that about you."

Kat felt a surge of gratitude as she continued visiting each animal crate, helping Darla make notes on their charts. It wasn't often Kat was in a position where her abilities could be truly appreciated, and she was glad Smitty noticed and accepted her. By the time the adoption event started, they had a solid plan of action for each animal.

Kat took up her post near the dog tent, hoping a good

number of people would show up. A brisk gust of cold air swirled over the lawn and she bounced on her toes, rubbing her arms to keep warm.

"You should've worn your chicken costume." Jordan walked up behind her. His voice was light with amusement, but Kat's body instantly flushed with heat as she turned to see him.

He was dressed in dark blue jeans and a charcoal gray T-shirt. With his windblown hair and tanned face, she'd once thought he looked like a thundercloud, but not anymore. To Kat, he was as bright as the sunlight glancing off the distant waves. She wanted to act nonchalant and cool, unfazed by his presence. But it was impossible. After the night they'd shared, she doubted she'd ever be able to pretend around him again.

A thrill shot through her as he came to stand a little closer than usual. He smelled like fresh-cut grass and damp earth and that woodsy pine soap. He must've been working outside at the farm. She wanted to bury her face in his chest and breathe him in. Instead she cleared her throat and said, "Have you come to adopt a pet?"

"I'm already up to my ears in animals." He reached out to tug lightly on the string of her hoodie. "One Kat in particular is giving me all kinds of trouble. Very demanding. She kept me up all night."

"Oh, is that right?" A warm blush spread across her face. "I wonder what you did to bother her. Maybe it's what you deserve."

"Lucky me." He leaned a little closer, and Kat had to struggle not to step right into his arms. It would've felt like the most natural thing in the world. Everything had shifted between them. But maybe that wasn't so bad. Some changes were good, weren't they?

"I forgot to tell you," she said. "The butterflies started to emerge yesterday."

He gave her a warm smile. "Did they?"

"Yes, and they're beautiful."

"I'm sure."

Kat's skin tingled with pleasure. She had the distinct feeling he was thinking about all the things they'd done the night before. She rubbed one foot on top of the other, feeling suddenly shy.

"Come out with me tonight," he said.

"Where?"

"Does it matter?" He bent to whisper in her ear. "Let's get into some more trouble."

Her breath caught in her throat. Somewhere in the back of her mind, she knew she wasn't supposed to let herself get carried away, but that ship had already sailed. She was far out to sea, by now. Not even caring that these were dangerous waters and he could break her heart. *Just go with the flow*, the Queen of Impulsive Decisions whispered. *See where it leads.*

Kat shivered with delicious anticipation. She knew exactly where it would lead, and a big part of her wanted to swan dive right in.

He gently took her hands, warming them between his own. It was a simple gesture, but the intimacy of it set her blood on fire. Jordan Prescott was like a drug. The more she got, the more she craved. She was just wondering if he was going to try to kiss her right there out in the open, when a cheery voice interrupted them.

"There you are," Juliette called from across the lawn. "I thought you'd be here."

Jordan let go of Kat's hands as Emma and Juliette approached.

"We have to talk." Juliette brushed a lock of hair off her face, sending a couple of loose leaves floating to the ground.

She'd been working at the florist shop, which was evident from the soil smudge on the knee of her overalls and the sprig of greenery tucked into her pocket. "I wanted to tell you last night at the bar, but since you didn't make it—"

"We found something in the attic you need to see," Emma finished, cheeks pink with excitement. Next to Juliette, Emma looked squeaky clean and sweet in a peach-colored sundress and white cardigan.

Both women were stealing glances at Jordan like he was some rare, exotic breed they'd never seen before.

Kat quickly introduced them. Jordan was standing so close to her, their arms were touching, but he made no move to step away. It sparked a warm glow inside her that seemed to flicker and grow.

"So you're Kat's new landlord," Emma mused, tilting her head thoughtfully.

"Yes," he said with an easy smile. "For now."

For now. The temporary nature of that doused the glow inside her like a splash of cold water. For the umpteenth time, Kat had to remind herself Jordan wasn't sticking around. He wasn't going to be in the picture. Not even at the edge of the frame.

"I think I've seen you at the farmer's market," Juliette said to him, stuffing her hands into the pockets of her overalls.

"Yeah, it's where I first met Kat, actually." Jordan gave Kat's elbow a playful nudge. "She was doing some . . . interesting work for the animal shelter."

Kat groaned at the memory of that ridiculous chicken costume.

"I can't believe I missed the farmer's market that day," Juliette said, giggling. "I'd have paid good money to see you in that costume."

"It was nightmare fuel," Kat said. "Be glad you were spared. Those feathers still haunt me."

"You were glorious." Jordan's voice was tinged with warmth and admiration.

Kat rolled her eyes, trying to pretend his praise didn't affect her.

"We came to see if you wanted to come to lunch," Emma said.

Kat glanced back at the tents. "I'd love to, but I have to stay here and help with crowd control."

Juliette scrunched up her nose and peeked over Kat's shoulder. "I don't see a crowd."

"Are you expecting a lot of people?" Emma asked. There was only one person browsing the puppy tent.

"I hope so," Kat said glumly. "But we didn't have a huge advertising budget, so I'm not sure what will happen."

"Come over tonight, then," Emma said. "We can have dinner and fill you in on the stuff we found."

Kat glanced at Jordan. She really wanted to jump into some of that trouble he'd mentioned earlier, but she didn't want to turn down Emma and Juliette, either. She loved the camaraderie they shared whenever they were all together, and she suddenly felt torn.

"You should go." Jordan placed a warm hand on her lower back. "Rain check."

"Wait," Emma said. "Did you guys already have plans?"

"Not at all," he assured her.

It was the truth, yet Kat felt a twinge of disappointment.

"I've got to run," he said. "It was good to meet you both." He flashed Juliette and Emma a devastatingly handsome smile. Then he winked at Kat and took off across the lawn in long, purposeful strides.

She watched him go, because it was impossible not to. The way he moved—all smooth, masculine grace—did warm, melty things to her insides.

"Soo," Juliette sang in a voice full of delightful innuendo. "Mr. Mysterious seems rather taken with you."

Kat felt her face grow hot. "We're just friends."

"Uh-huh," Emma teased. "That's why you're blushing like my favorite champagne."

"She's right," Juliette agreed. "I saw the way you looked at each other. I think you two blew past the friend zone several miles back."

Kat tried not to smile, but couldn't help herself. "Is it that obvious?"

"Clear as vodka shots," Juliette declared.

Emma clapped her hands. "So when did you start dating?"

"We're not dating," Kat said quickly. "We're . . ." What could she say? We're just kissing in broom closets, making out in the open fields, and having hot, wild sex in the back of bohemian caravans? "We're just . . ."

"Hooking up?" Emma said, grinning.

"Ooh!" Juliette's eyes widened in scandalized glee. "Wait until the girls at the salon find out he's taken. Hearts are going to be breaking all over the island."

"He's not *taken*," Kat insisted.

"I'm so proud of you," Juliette teased. "Getting busy with Mr. Mysterious!" She raised her hand for a high five.

Kat left her hanging. "That's not what this is, you guys. You make it sound like I'm just a big floozy. Out there all"—she flapped her hands around—"floozying it up."

"Of course you're not," Emma said kindly.

"And the reason we know this is because it's not the early nineteen hundreds," Juliette added. "No one says 'floozy' anymore."

"Old Mrs. Mooney does," Emma declared. "That's what she calls the French poodle who bothers her dog, Bonbon."

"You know what? I like it," Juliette announced. "Let's bring floozy back. I say we make it happen."

Kat rolled her eyes. "Are you guys done here?"

Juliette slung an arm around Kat and kissed her on

the head while Emma patted her on the back. "We're just teasing you because we love you."

The girls continued their usual chatter, but Kat stood rooted to the spot. Stunned. Their kindness, their casual acceptance of her was almost overwhelming. They treated her as if she were a best friend or a sister. It made her wish, more than anything, that her connection to Juliette and Emma's family was real. Even though she kept telling herself it couldn't possibly be true, a tiny voice inside her whispered, *What if?*

Chapter Twenty-Two

When Kat returned home, the first thing she did was check on the butterflies. All seven had emerged, and every time she saw them she felt optimistic about the future. They were a constant reminder that change could be wonderful. After feeding them some sugar water, she walked over to the farmhouse kitchen, put a kettle on the stove to boil, and slumped into a chair, exhausted.

It had been a long day, and she wanted nothing more than to crawl into bed and sleep for the next forty-eight hours. But since she wasn't going to get that before heading over to dinner at Emma's house tonight, a double hit of Earl Grey tea would have to do.

The teapot whistled, and she dragged herself over to turn off the stove.

Opal entered the kitchen wearing a pink housedress and terry cloth slippers. She was relying heavily on her cane today and moving slower than usual. "My dear, you look like you've been through a blender."

Kat chuckled. "I'm beat. But we found homes for three dogs and two cats, so it was worth it."

Opal took a seat at the kitchen table. "Did you have a mad rush of people?"

"Hardly." Kat pulled two cups from the cupboard. "But

trying to facilitate good homes for the pets in such a short amount of time drains me of energy."

Opal tilted her head. "How so?"

"Sometimes people decide they want an animal, but it's not right for them. So I have to step in, and it's not always easy." Kat poured the tea and set one in front of Opal. Then she sank into the chair opposite her. "For example, today a young woman wanted to adopt a cat of ours named Princess Leia. The woman already lived with three roommates, a large dog, and a parrot. Princess Leia would have been miserable. She needed a quiet home with no other animals."

"Is that what her former owners told you?" Opal asked.

"No . . ." Kat hesitated. It would've been so easy to just say "yes," but she cared about Opal. She wanted to tell her the truth. "It's what the cat told me."

"Really?" Opal lifted her teacup, completely unfazed. In her pastel housedress she looked fragile and unassuming, but Kat had a feeling the old woman was strong as tempered steel on the inside, where it counted most. Would she be able to take the truth? Only one way to find out.

Kat took a bracing sip of tea. "The thing is, Opal, I was born with this ability to understand how animals feel, and I can communicate with them. I know it sounds crazy, but it's true. That's why I work so well with them."

"Mmm. That makes sense," Opal said mildly. "You're not the first person I've heard of with that ability."

Kat sat up straighter. All her previous feelings of fatigue flew out the window. "Who else has it?"

Opal's forehead wrinkled. "Well now . . . I can't remember exactly, but my friend Sam was close with the Holloway family way back before your time. He said they had special talents, and I seem to remember one of them was a horse whisperer, or some such thing."

A bolt of hope struck through Kat like lightning. It was

so sharp and pure, it almost hurt. She'd told herself for so long that she didn't need to know where she came from, but that tiny voice inside her whispered a little louder. *What if?* What if she did truly belong on this island? The intense, desperate desire to figure out her roots rocketed through her. She'd forgotten what it felt like because she'd kept it buried for so long.

"I'll have to ask Sam," Opal said vaguely. "He has a very good memory with these sorts of things."

"That would be nice." Kat concentrated on spooning sugar into her tea to give herself something to do. She didn't want to show Opal how much her statement affected her.

"So you communicate with animals," Opal said, like she'd just remarked on the weather. "And that's what you had to do today, which is why you're tired?"

"Yes. And the young woman was very adamant about adopting Princess Leia. I had to explain that they wouldn't be compatible. The woman got annoyed and demanded to speak with Smitty, my boss."

Opal pursed her lips. "And what did Smitty say?"

"She told the woman to forget it." Kat felt a rush of gratitude at the memory. "Her exact words were, 'If Kat says you're not compatible with that animal, then you're not compatible. End of story. Move along, chickadee.'" A wide grin stretched across Kat's face. Watching Smitty Bankston go to bat for her had been the greatest thing Kat had experienced since she began working at the Daisy Meadows Pet Rescue. As grumpy as Smitty was, she clearly believed in Kat's talent, and that meant a lot.

"Good for her," Opal said, beaming. "It sounds like you're in the right profession, trying to find homes for those poor animals. It must be hard for you to see so many with no place to live."

"It is," Kat admitted. "My whole life, I've always wished I could have a big enough place to house all the animals who were unwanted. Especially the needy ones, like Lucky and Lulabelle."

"Well, until that time comes," Opal said, reaching out to pat her hand, "you bring them here."

Kat's heart filled with warmth, but she knew it wouldn't be a real solution. "Thanks, but Jordan's made it pretty clear he doesn't want more animals roaming around. I know he's trying to fix the place up to sell it."

"So he says," Opal said smugly. "But I do wonder."

Kat gripped her teacup with both hands. "What do you mean?"

"I've watched that boy grow up, and I know his parents were irresponsible. He didn't have the easiest time of it, but he just seems genuinely happier here now, as the days go by. You should have seen him when he first arrived. All sharp edges and clipped words and slicked back hair. He roamed around the place like a caged tiger, restless and broody. But the longer he stays here and the more he does—sorting, and cleaning, and fixing up the farm—the more relaxed and comfortable he seems. I just can't help but feel like this is where he belongs."

Kat wanted so badly for it to be true. She took a sip of tea, letting the sharp, bright taste of bergamot ground her. Yes, she liked Jordan a lot. More than a lot. Every time she thought of him, her heart felt lighter. But she had to stay focused and stick to her plan. She couldn't afford to get carried away hoping for things that were beyond her control.

The clock on the wall chimed and Kat suddenly remembered her plans with Emma and Juliette. She rose from the table and gave Opal an apologetic smile. "I wish I could stay, but I promised my friends I'd meet them for dinner."

Opal set down her teacup. "First, I have a favor to ask. Next Saturday the seniors are hosting the annual Summer's End Charity Gala at the country club. It's a black tie affair and a great big hullaballoo." Her hands began to flutter with excitement. "There'll be live music and dancing, and all proceeds will help fund our future activities. I want you to come."

"A black tie affair?" Kat glanced down at her thrift store sandals. "It sounds wonderful but, unfortunately, I just don't have the clothes for something that fancy. Maybe another time."

"It's still a week away," Opal reasoned. "A pretty girl like you should have no problem finding something to wear. You look lovely in everything. If you change your mind, I'd be so proud to introduce you to my friends."

Kat thanked her and promised to give it some thought, even though she already knew it was out of the question. She highly doubted she'd make Opal proud if she showed up in shorts and a tank top, or a tie-dyed sundress. Still, Kat felt a warm glow of happiness that Opal had thought to invite her. The more Kat got to know Opal, the more she liked her. How could Jordan want to leave when he had a grandmother like her? If Opal was her grandmother, Kat would hang on tight and never let go. But then, she'd always observed that people who had a family usually didn't realize how precious it was until it was gone.

Chapter Twenty-Three

Kat pulled her car into Emma's driveway, excited to find out what they'd discovered. The Holloway house stood like a bright sentinel in the waning light. Its yellow paint with white trim seemed to glow with welcome, and once again Kat was struck by how much it felt like home.

Hank had already jumped out of the car to investigate the lawn, and he was now circling back to her in excitement.

"Even you feel it," Kat said as she lifted him into her arms. Hank's warm presence comforted her like a security blanket. She snuggled her face into his fur. "Come on, trusty sidekick. Let's go see what all the fuss is about, shall we?"

Kat glanced up to see Juliette's head poke out of an upstairs window. "We're up in the attic."

Gathering her courage, Kat approached the porch steps, suddenly overcome with nervousness. What if the house didn't let her in this time? What if it had been a fluke? Kat was glad the other women were up in the attic, so they wouldn't have to witness her failure if the house changed its mind about her.

"Hi again," she said tentatively.

The porch light grew very bright for a moment, as if the house was saying "hi" back. Or maybe it was just a power surge. Maybe she was being ridiculous and all of this was just a bad joke.

She drew in a deep breath, lifted her chin, and began climbing the steps. Before her boot hit the top step, she heard the door unlatch. It swung wide to let her in, and she exhaled a shaky breath. So it wasn't just a fluke.

"Thanks, house," she murmured under her breath.

The door closed gently behind her.

Kat set Hank on the floor as Buddy came bounding around the corner. She instantly felt the Labradoodle's intense joy at having company. He greeted them both with slobbery licks and occasional *thwacks* of his tail.

By the time Kat made her way to the attic, her trusty sidekick had abandoned her for a game of tug-of-war with Buddy in the living room. She pushed open the attic door to find Emma and Juliette sitting cross-legged on an old Persian rug. They were surrounded by trunks and stacks of books, and they were both scrutinizing something in an album.

"Hey," Kat said. "What's going on?"

Juliette waved her over without looking up. "Come and see this."

Kat joined them on the rug and peered at the album. The pages were yellowed, and the black-and-white photos were very small. She was looking at the album upside down, so it was hard for her to make anything of it.

"Look here." Emma turned the album to Kat. "These are old photos of our grandmother's family."

Kat looked at the series of farm pictures. A dog in a field. A copse of trees. Two girls sitting on the hood of an old tractor. One of them appeared to be twelve or thirteen, with curly hair and a floral dress. She was holding a fluffy white chicken in her arms. The younger girl couldn't have been more than three years old, with the same hair and a shorter version of the same dress. Behind them in the distance stood the Holloway house. It looked exactly the same as it did now, only the trees surrounding it were much smaller.

"This little girl," Juliette said, pointing to the toddler in the blurry photograph, "was our grandmother."

"And the older girl," Emma said, "was her sister Caroline. She ran off to join the circus when she was only sixteen, so we never knew much about her. My grandmother was still very young when Caroline left the island. They didn't grow up together, and what little my grandmother knew was from an occasional postcard. I remember her saying that Caroline married someone in the circus and never came back."

"So . . . you think your great-aunt who ran away might be related to me?" Kat asked.

"We aren't sure yet," Juliette said. "But look at the rest of the photos."

Kat turned the page. Several images of birds. A crow standing on a pumpkin. Some chickens. A cat on the front porch of the Holloway house. "All animals . . ."

"Exactly," Emma said, bubbling over with excitement. "We thought maybe this great-aunt of ours had animal magic. If you look through the photos, almost every picture of her has an animal in it. And she ran off to join the circus, right? What better place to go, if you like being around animals?"

Disappointment began to settle over Kat. The photos were a nice depiction of Emma and Juliette's relatives, but they proved nothing. "There's still no way to be sure."

"Just keep looking," Juliette said, placing the album in her hands.

Kat flipped through the rest of the pages. Many of the photos were just random farm images of scenery. But the photos of the young teenager always showed her with animals. Sitting in the grass with a dog. Standing on the stairs holding a black cat. Even an image of her posing next to a cow. The most unusual photo showed her sitting against a tree trunk, laughing, with her arms extended. Birds were perched along both arms, and there was even a bird standing on her head.

"It's true, she's always with animals," Kat mused. "But making the leap from her to me is quite a stretch."

"Take a look at this," Juliette said. She thumped her hand on a small steamer trunk behind her. It was dark brown, with scratched sides and worn leather straps. There were three brass latches on the front, and handles on either end. Juliette grabbed a handle and dragged it onto the rug. "Emma and I found it this afternoon. I swear it wasn't here the last twenty times we looked, so it has to be important."

She unlatched the trunk and pushed it toward Kat. It appeared to be full of scarves and old knickknacks.

Both Emma and Juliette watched her expectantly.

Kat glanced back and forth between them. "What do you want me to do?"

Emma moved her hand in a swishy motion. "Just rummage through it."

Kat looked at the pile of things in the trunk. "Rummage?"

"Yeah, dig around in there," Juliette said. "That's how it works. Sometimes new things pop up in this attic, depending on who's doing the looking, or who needs something."

Kat took a deep breath and dug her hands in the box. She pulled out a turquoise silk scarf with butterflies on it. It was so light and delicate, it almost seemed to flutter in the air.

"See? That wasn't there before," Juliette said triumphantly. "Not when I looked."

"Nope," Emma agreed, grinning.

Kat reached in again and pulled out more odds and ends. There was a sparkly white shawl that shed tiny snowflakes when she shook it. There were beaded neck-laces that sounded like wind chimes when they clinked together, and a pair of long white gloves that smelled like champagne and roses. Near the bottom of the trunk, some-thing flashed brightly. Kat reached in and pulled out a tarnished silver key with a three-leaf clover design.

"Ooh!" Emma squealed. "What is that?" She reached for the key, turning it over and over in her hands. It was old, but the clovers sparkled like polished emeralds.

"Never seen it before," Juliette murmured. She nodded to Kat. "Keep going."

Kat pushed aside a satin top hat and pulled out a small cigar box. When she opened it, a few postcards and old newspaper clippings slid out. She looked at Juliette and Emma.

Both women gave her an encouraging nod.

Kat opened the first newspaper clipping. It was an ad for the Bellamy Brothers' Circus, promising "Earthly Delights Beyond Compare and Exotic Creatures from the Unknown." Another clipping was a short biography about David Bellamy, the circus owner, with a picture of him standing proudly with his wife and baby beside a striped circus tent.

Kat gasped. His wife was the teenager in Emma and Juliette's family album. "This must be your great-aunt." She handed the newspaper clipping to them and continued sift-ing through the rest of the postcards. One showed a beach scene with a short message on the back. Kat read aloud. "We're here on the coast for a few weeks. Darling Evange-line has grown like a weed. She's wild and free and full of wanderlust, I'm afraid. XOXO Caroline." Kat glanced up from the postcard and said, "Darling Evangeline?" The name seemed to echo off the walls.

A soft gust of wind swirled through the attic, surrounding the three of them, stirring their hair and kissing their eyelashes. It felt like a typical summer breeze, except no windows in the attic were open.

Kat shivered.

Emma and Juliette were staring at her, wide-eyed.

No one said anything.

Kat was suddenly aware of the deep silence that surrounded them. It was so quiet, she felt as though the house was holding its breath. "Evangeline," she whispered. Could that be her mother? She started rummaging through the box, in earnest. The last postcard was from Ireland, written in the same looping script as before. Kat read, "We've retired home to Ireland. Evangeline left us a year ago to follow her own path. She goes wherever the wind blows her, but such is the way of things in our family, is it not? Still, a mother's heart will always yearn for her child. Live well, dearest sister. XOXO Caroline."

A hollow ache settled inside Kat. There was such a melancholy sense of finality to that last postcard. She cleared her throat. "What happened to Evangeline?"

Juliette took the postcard from her and studied it. "We don't know yet, but we're going to do everything we can to find out."

"Is there anything else?" Emma asked, pointing to the steamer trunk.

Kat reached in to draw out the last item in the box. It was the sapphire blue gown she'd tried on before.

She clutched it in surprise. "Did you guys put this in here?"

"No," Juliette said.

"Sometimes things show up in odd places," Emma explained. "It's the house."

Kat slid a hand over the luxurious velvet gown, marveling at everything they'd discovered. She placed the dress carefully back in the box, along with the other objects. Her mind was spinning, and she was suddenly overcome with an equal mixture of frustration and elation.

"This is driving me crazy!" she said in a shaky voice. "What if we never find out for sure?"

Juliette laid a hand on Kat's shoulder. "Don't worry. The house already knows you're part of the family. We'll figure this out."

"We will," Emma said gently. "Trust us. In the meantime"—she stood and stretched—"I think we all need food. The lasagna should be ready in about a half hour. Let's go downstairs and discuss what we found over tea and cupcakes."

"Dessert before dinner?" Kat asked with a lightness she didn't feel. "That's my kind of plan."

As they headed downstairs, Kat considered the possibilities of what they'd discovered. Could Evangeline be her mother? There was so much uncertainty surrounding it, she had to shove down the feeling of desperate hope that kept bubbling up. The only thing she knew for sure was that she now felt more connected with Emma and Juliette than ever. And even if they could never prove they were related, Kat didn't care. To her, Emma and Juliette already felt like family.

Chapter Twenty-Four

Kat scattered corn for the chickens the following afternoon, seeking comfort from the simple act of caring for the animals. A deep yearning to know about Evangeline had settled inside her—one that she couldn't shake. Emma's husband, Hunter, was going to reach out to his friend from the police department who specialized in cold cases. If they could just find out any information on Evangeline Bellamy, since she likely took her father's last name, maybe they'd know where she went and what might've happened to her. Then maybe they could find out how Kat fit into the Holloway family tree. *If* she fit in. Until then, there was nothing Kat could do but wait. She hated limbo.

The chickens clucked around her, pecking corn from her hand.

Edgar swooped down from a tree and landed on the fence. He greeted her with a loud *caw!*

"Of course I have some for you," Kat said, tossing a handful to the ground in front of him. "You're like a bottomless pit, you know that?"

She gave the last of the food to the chickens, then turned to the mesh butterfly cage sitting beside her. "And as for you,

Painted Ladies, today is the day. It's time to spread your wings."

Kat carried them to the other side of the yard where the wildflowers and lavender grew along the fence.

Jordan's truck pulled into the driveway just as Kat was getting ready to release them.

She raised a hand to shield her eyes from the sun, a sweet rush of pleasure flowing through her at the sight of him getting out of his truck. He was deliciously rumpled in worn jeans and work boots, an old flannel shirt, and messy hair. Opal was right. Jordan did seem more carefree and content as the days passed.

He saw her, and his face lit up. "There you are."

She grinned like a fool. "Here I am."

He sauntered toward her, noticing the butterfly cage. "Setting them free?"

"I am. You're just in time," she said, unzipping the mesh cage.

The brilliant orange-and-black butterflies floated out into the breeze, spreading their wings to land on the flowering shrubs.

Kat watched them with a deep sense of contentment, knowing that this was where they belonged. She sighed. "Home sweet home."

"It's pretty amazing."

"They are, aren't they?"

"I meant you." Jordan turned to face her. "You're amazing. The way you help things find homes."

A blissful warmth spread through her body. Jordan's unexpected praise made her feel like she'd swallowed the sun. Kat knew she was blushing, but she couldn't help it.

"I mean it," he said. "Not a lot of people have the patience or the desire to care for others the way you do." The way he looked at her—with so much warmth and admiration—was almost too much.

Kat had to look away before she did something foolish. Like jump his bones. He was standing so close, she wouldn't even have to jump very far.

"Come to lunch with me," he said suddenly.

She laughed. "I already ate lunch. It's almost three o'clock."

"Dinner, then. Afternoon tea. Hell, I don't care." He reached out and hooked a finger in the pocket of her jeans, gently pulling her closer. "Just come with me."

Kat's breath hitched. "Where?"

"Anywhere," he murmured.

She felt a swooping sensation in the pit of her stomach, like she was falling and there was nothing to hold on to, and she didn't even care. Jordan Prescott was too alluring for his own good, with his pirate smile and wild hair and intoxicating whiskey-colored eyes. Just one glance and she could go from stone-cold sober to drunk on him in three seconds flat. Did he have any idea how much his nearness affected her? Especially now that she knew how good it could be between them?

She bit her bottom lip and tried to sound casual. "I was just heading back to my apartment to change out of these clothes."

"Good idea," he said. "Let's go."

Yes, let's! the Queen of Impulsive Decisions cried. Kat tried to remember all the reasons she shouldn't get involved with him. She could have told him she'd meet him later. She could've reminded him that her apartment was her private space. It wasn't too late to try to keep her distance. But after the night she'd had at the Holloway house, Kat wasn't in the mood to be cautious anymore. Who knew what the future held? One day you could be all alone, and the next you could find out you're related to a family of magical women. Life was unpredictable. Maybe she should just enjoy each moment while she could and quit worrying too much about what came next.

He watched her intently, with that same hungry-wolf look she remembered from back in the caravan, as if he was thinking of all the things they'd done together. All the things he still wanted to do. But he said nothing further to persuade her. Kat knew that if she wanted the wolf to pounce, it was entirely her choice.

She sucked in a breath and exhaled quickly. It wasn't a hard choice. "Okay."

He blinked. If he was surprised, he didn't show it. Instead he dipped his head in acknowledgment. It was an oddly noble gesture, like a king who'd just been given a precious gift. "Lead the way."

By the time they reached the door of her apartment, Kat knew one thing with perfect diamond clarity. She wanted Jordan Prescott, and he wanted her. There was no question. There was only the answering thrum of desire that seemed to ricochet between them.

They stepped inside, and Kat closed and locked the door. Then she turned to face him, leaning against it. "So." A flutter of nervous anticipation.

"So." He braced a hand on the door above her head with a hint of amusement. "You've invited me in." His voice rolled softly over her skin. It was deep and low. Confident and unhurried. Like he was aware she'd just invited the wolf into her house, and there was no turning back for her. Did she care? Not even a teensy bit. "Now what should we do?"

She looked up at him from beneath dark lashes. "Any ideas?"

He chuckled, a low rumble in his chest that curled its way through her insides in a sweet, throbbing ache. "I've got all kinds of ideas." Then he reached up to cradle her face with his large hand, running the pad of his thumb lightly over her bottom lip. "The question is, where to start?"

"How about here?" She pulled his head down and brushed her lips lightly over his. It was meant to be playful, but in less than a heartbeat, the game ended and something much better began.

Jordan gripped her waist, pulling her against the hard length of his body. He kissed her slowly. Thoroughly. Until the yearning inside her grew fierce and demanding, and she trembled with the desire for more of him. More of everything.

When he pulled away and rested his forehead against hers, they were both breathing hard. Kat's hands were fisted tightly in his shirt, holding on as if she were in danger of falling. And maybe she was. But she couldn't find it within herself to care. A tremor went through Jordan's body like he was holding himself back. She didn't want him to hold back. She wanted every wild part of him.

"More," she whispered, twining her fingers through his hair and rising up on her tiptoes to taste him again.

Jordan let out a harsh breath and lifted her up against him. She wrapped her legs around his waist as he carried her over to the bed. Then they were both falling onto the faded patchwork quilt. And all Kat's previous thoughts of keeping him at arm's length dissolved into the sweetest of surrenders.

Chapter Twenty-Five

Evening light pooled through Kat's window, lending a dreamlike quality to her room. She snuggled farther under the quilt and rolled over to study the sleeping beast beside her.

Jordan lay on his back with one arm slung over his head. With his eyes closed, he looked much younger and more vulnerable. She loved how dark and thick his eyelashes were. She loved the curve of his lips and the hollows under his cheekbones. She wanted to rub her hand against the slight stubble on his jaw and trace the silvery, thin scar on the side of his face.

"If you're going to stare, I think it's only fair I get to do the same." He opened his eyes and rolled to face her, propping his head on his hand.

Kat blushed, feeling like a kid caught stealing candy. "How did you know I was awake?"

He blinked like a sleepy owl. "I could hear you."

Her voice filled with humor. "I didn't say anything."

"But you were thinking very loudly." He reached out and pulled her closer so her head rested on his shoulder. "And your breathing changes when you're not sleeping."

"How very perceptive." She snuggled against him.

He trailed the back of his fingers over her naked shoulder. "I notice a lot of things about you."

"Like what?" Kat rubbed her feet together under the covers.

"Like, you rub your feet together when I say something that makes you nervous."

"I'm not—" She immediately stopped moving her feet.

He chuckled. "It's one of your tells."

"Oh, yeah? What else you got?" Kat couldn't decide if she was nervous at being so transparent, or pleased that he saw her so clearly.

He toyed with a lock of her hair. "You sing to the animals when you think no one's listening."

She gasped and buried her face in his chest. "You've been spying on me."

Jordan smoothed the back of her head with his large hand. "Not 'spying,' but I can hear you sometimes when my bedroom window's open. I especially like the lullaby you sang to Lucky when you first brought him home."

Kat remembered the song, and how scared the poor dog had been. She pulled the quilt around her shoulders. "'Baby Mine.' It's a song from a scene in the movie *Dumbo*."

"The elephant cartoon? Never saw it."

"Well, you're not missing anything. Parts of it are pretty depressing."

"It's a kids' movie," he said through a yawn. "How bad can it be?"

Kat lifted her head off his shoulder to face him. "Dumbo's mom gets locked in a cage away from her baby. They can't reach each other through the iron bars, but she can stretch her trunk out just enough to hold him and rock him while he cries."

Jordan frowned. "This is a kids' movie?"

"At least he's reunited with his mom in the end." Kat

laid her head back on his shoulder. "It's not like what happened to Bambi's mom."

"Do I even want to know?"

Kat pulled away and stared at him like he was one of the space aliens from his childhood books. "You've never seen *Bambi*?"

He shook his head, clearly amused. "My parents didn't believe in television. I didn't get one until I was much older."

"God, and I thought I had a tough childhood," Kat blurted.

His golden eyes lit with interest. "Why? What was it like?"

Kat shrugged it off. "Nothing worth talking about." She began rubbing her feet together, then forced herself to stop. "I have a question for you."

"You do that a lot." He took her hand and linked their fingers together.

"Do what?"

"Change the subject to avoid talking about your past."

Kat ignored him, tracing the tip of her finger across the silvery scar on his left cheekbone. "How did you get this scar?"

"Running with scissors," he said smoothly. Kat got the feeling he used that explanation a lot. He took her hand and kissed her open palm. Then he dipped his head to nuzzle her neck. She shivered in delicious anticipation as he brushed a kiss on her bare shoulder.

She pulled away, though it wasn't easy. "How did you really get it?"

Jordan rolled onto his back with a sigh. Several moments passed in silence, and Kat started to think he wasn't going to answer. Could she blame him? She never talked about her past, either.

"I got into a fight in high school with a kid named Sebastian Harrington and some of his buddies," Jordan finally said. "It was me against the four of them, and I was winning. Until Sebastian shoved me backward and I fell against a broken chain-link fence. Sliced my face to the bone. The principal came rushing out, broke things up, and I got suspended."

Kat frowned. "Just you? Nobody else?"

He stared up at the ceiling like he was a million miles away. "By the time the principal came out, Sebastian's buddies had run off. He couldn't run because I had my fist in his hair. I was the one bleeding, but it didn't matter. Sebastian's parents were on the board and donated a lot of money to the school, so he was pretty much a golden child on campus. I, on the other hand, was the scrappy kid from the wrong side of the tracks with no support network. It was just easier for them to pin it on me and call it a day."

Kat laid a hand on his chest. "Why were you fighting?"

A muscle clenched in his jaw. "Sebastian was harassing a younger girl who was poor. Making fun of her shoes. Laughing at her hand-me-down backpack. Then his buddies took her backpack and threw it in the garbage, saying it belonged there. Saying *she* belonged there. She looked like she was trying so hard not to cry. And Sebastian just stood there in his fancy clothes with that trust-fund smirk on his face."

"That's awful." Kat grew up in hand-me-down clothes, and she knew what it was like to be the butt of other people's jokes. "So you figured his face needed punching?"

Jordan smiled. "At first, I just shoved him away and retrieved her backpack. I may have also made some comments about Sebastian's lack of masculinity because he felt the need to pick on vulnerable girls." Jordan paused for a long moment. "Then things just got ugly. He came at me from behind, kicking and punching. Yelling that I was in no position to play the hero because I was just a trashy mutt with drugged-up hippie parents. He said I should be embarrassed to be alive because nobody cared whether I lived or died, not even them."

Kat felt a sharp, painful ache in her chest for the boy he'd been. "And then you punched him?"

"Yeah, then I punched him." He gave a self-deprecating laugh. "And his buddies joined in to help take me down."

"It was good of you to champion that girl," Kat said. "She wasn't strong like you."

The tension in Jordan's face eased. "Layla's a power-house now, though."

"Layla of the Fancy Shoes?" Kat asked in surprise. It was hard to imagine her as a poor little girl in hand-me-downs.

Jordan smiled. "We've known each other a long time. We even dated for a brief time in high school."

Jealousy reared its ugly head but Kat refused to look it in the eye. Everyone had a past, and it was only normal for Jordan to have had relationships with other women. It was high school, for God's sake. What was wrong with her, anyway? She shouldn't even care.

"Layla had it tough at home. We were both dead set on changing our lives the moment we got the chance. I did it by going off to college, and she started her own business. She's now a successful real estate agent." His tone grew lighter and Kat could tell he was happy for Layla. "She has a house by the water now, which was her dream."

As much as Kat wanted to dislike her, she just couldn't. She was glad Layla ended up successful. It wasn't easy to find a place when you didn't have a good support network to begin with. "What happened to Sebastian?"

"He moved away during our senior year because of his dad's job. We never saw him again."

"Well, I'm glad your story has a happy ending."

Jordan laughed. "That one does, anyway."

"So . . . You and Layla, huh?" she asked with a lightness she didn't feel.

"We're just friends." Jordan gave her a brief squeeze. "The brief thing we had years ago was exactly that. Years ago. We weren't even together for very long before we realized we didn't have much in common. She's just helping me put the house on the market when it's ready."

"Is it ready?" Kat's heart suddenly began thumping hard against her rib cage. "You're going to give me some notice, right? I mean, if you're going to sell the place I'll need to look for a new apartment." She worked hard to appear nonchalant, because she didn't want Jordan to know just how attached she'd become to the farm. It wasn't just the beauty of the place, it was the animals and the people that came with it. The people who fit so seamlessly into the life she'd begun to weave there. Opal. Jordan. *Especially* Jordan. Oh, crap. She was falling, wasn't she? Now what? The Queen of Impulsive Decisions let out a tinkling laugh. *No use trying to plot your course now, sugar. This train has left the station, so buckle up and try to enjoy it.*

Kat took a shaky breath. Try to enjoy it. She could do that. Who knew what would happen? Maybe a bunch of miracles were in store and things would work out for her. Yeah, because stuff like that happened all the time. She bit the insides of her cheeks and fiddled with the corner of the quilt.

Jordan shifted onto his side to face her, his expression very serious. "It's not ready to sell yet, Kat. I still have some work to do, and the red barn needs to be cleared of all the junk. So it'll be a while."

Kat nodded. A while was good. She could live with that.

"What about you?" Jordan nudged her foot with his. "Tell me your story."

"My story?" Kat suddenly noticed a loose thread on the

quilt. She started working at it with her fingernail. "I came here several weeks ago—"

"—No. I don't mean what you're doing here. I mean before." He fixed her with a steady gaze. "Where did you grow up?"

She continued pulling at the thread until he laid a warm hand on hers.

"California," she said, steeling herself. "My mother died when I was a baby, and I had no other relatives. So I went into the system. Foster homes." There. She said it. And it wasn't even that hard. She waited for the usual prick of shame that came with the telling—that ever-present feeling of being "less than" other people—but this time it didn't come. Maybe it was because she knew he'd had a difficult childhood, too. Telling him had been much easier than telling other people, which was strange. He was just easy to talk to.

Jordan was quiet for a while, which was a relief. The usual pity or surprise wasn't there on his face, which she'd half expected. He just seemed accepting.

"And what was that like?" he asked softly.

Kat gave him a look. "What do you mean, what was it like? It was foster care. Foster homes. Some better than others. None of them great."

"But I thought babies usually got adopted by couples. At least that's how I thought it worked."

Kat scoffed. Maybe that's how it worked on TV. In real life there were no guarantees. There certainly hadn't been for her. "The system doesn't always work that way. It might if you're very lucky, and if you're a normal kid. But when you don't bond with people, and you talk to animals? Not exactly ideal circumstances."

Jordan sat up to lean against the headboard. "What happened?"

Kat pulled the quilt around her. "I was very young when

I was placed in what was supposed to be a permanent home. I think the couple genuinely wanted me, and it might've worked out, except . . ." She trailed off. She barely remembered any of it, except what she was told later by the social workers. "By the time I was four, I'd started to show signs of my affinity toward animals, and it bothered them."

"Bothered them how?" Jordan asked. "I mean, you were just a tiny kid."

"A tiny kid with the ability to communicate with the family dog."

"So?"

"So . . . I never spoke to them and mostly only spoke to the dog. They thought there was something wrong with my brain, so they put me in child therapy until I was in first grade. I had a standing weekly appointment, and every Tuesday night when my foster mom went off to her book club and I went off to bed, my foster dad had a little weekly appointment of his own. He was having an affair with Millie, the lady next door."

"So what happened?"

"I told my foster mom all about it," Kat said with a shrug. "I was too young to know any better, and I was only relaying what I understood from the dog. I kept telling her that Millie came over on Tuesday nights to put Dad to bed. Anyway, it all went downhill from there. My foster mom freaked out. They fought all the time, after that. They used to argue about what to do with me sometimes, but then they separated, and I was put into another home."

Jordan took her hand. He didn't say anything, but he didn't have to. It was comforting just to have him there, listening without judgment. And it was so easy to talk to him. Kat had never felt this way around anyone.

"My last memory of them was the dog whining on the porch when I left," she continued. "I think I missed him the most. There *was* something wrong with me. I communicated better with animals than my own foster parents. No wonder they thought I was broken. It wasn't until later that I started connecting more with people. But even that was hard, because by then I'd learned not to get attached. Things could just change at any moment, and most of it was beyond my control. Animals were a great comfort to me, but I couldn't really share that part of myself when I was younger. I learned to pretend it didn't exist, because I needed to fit in. Nobody wants a freak show."

He squeezed her hand. "Don't say that."

Kat glanced at him from beneath her lashes. "You have to admit it's kind of freaky."

"No," he said firmly. "I was surprised when you first showed me how you talked to that crow, and then the other animals. But it's not freaky. It's cool. My mom used to believe in all the Holloway magic, so why the hell not?" He said it like it was no big deal, and his easy acceptance warmed her in all the right places.

"Where are your parents?" Kat asked.

He shook his head. "They went to join a hippie commune in Malaysia, last I heard."

"Wow. Talk about leaving it all behind." It seemed impossible to contemplate. Even though Kat hadn't been there that long, Willowbrook Lavender Farm was the best place she'd ever lived. She couldn't imagine wanting to abandon it. "When did you last see them?"

"The day I left for college. So, thirteen years ago, give or take."

Kat stared at him, but his expression was hard to read. She drew her knees up and hugged them to her chest under the blanket, wondering how his parents could be okay with that. Wouldn't they want to know their son? To be in his life? "Are they happy there?"

Jordan gave a hollow laugh. "The last message I got from my mom was to tell me they loved it and were never coming back. They mortgaged this place to the hilt. I think the money just ran out, so they split. They were just going to let the bank foreclose on it, right under my grandmother. So yes, I think moving to Malaysia appealed to their 'free-spirited' ideals. No bills to worry about and nobody to take care of except themselves." If there was a tiny edge of bitterness to his voice, Kat couldn't blame him. Jordan had had to grow up fending for himself, and he'd become an amazing person. And the tragedy of it was that his parents would never know just how amazing he was.

They were quiet for a long time, but it was a comfortable silence. He wrapped an arm around her and drew her closer. She leaned her head on his chest, listening to the steady thump of his heart.

"Thank you," Kat said before she could stop herself. "For what you said earlier about my animal magic. I'm glad you don't think I'm whackadoo."

His chest shook with silent laughter, and he tightened his arm around her. "Believe me, Kat. I grew up with 'whackadoo.' You are nothing like that. You're perfect."

Her face flushed with heat at his unexpected praise. "Emma and Juliette seem to think I'm related to them, but I have no idea. We're trying to track down who my mother was, and they think they found a lead in one of their relatives."

He looked genuinely pleased. "That's great."

Kat felt a twinge of anxiety. "It's only great if it's true. What if it's not? What if they think I'm related, and then I turn out to be just Kat. Just Kat, by herself, like before. Like always . . ." She trailed off.

"Would that be so bad?" Jordan asked gently.

"Yes." She frowned. "I mean, no. I don't know."

"Look." He shifted to face her. "If it turns out that your mom was a Holloway, great. Then you'll know you're related to your friends. But if it turns out you're not"—he shrugged—"it doesn't matter."

"How can you say that?" She rubbed her feet together under the covers. "Family matters more than anything. No one knows that better than a person without one."

"But you're still *you*, regardless of who they are."

Kat squeezed her eyes shut. He didn't get it.

"Listen to me," Jordan said fiercely. "You can *make* your family." Kat had the sudden feeling he wasn't only talking about her. "Not everyone gets the right start. But you learn and you grow, and you learn to gather the people around who you can trust. The people who support you and lift you up. The people you can rely on. That's the family that matters."

"Is that what you did?" Kat asked, searching his face. "Is that why you want to go back to New York? Because you have people you trust, and a life that's everything you ever wanted?" She didn't want him to go, but she wasn't going to fault him if that's really what he had back there. To find true happiness and be living the life you've always dreamed about—that must be something.

Jordan ran a hand over his face and glanced away. "I have a pretty sweet deal going on back there. A great place, a successful business, absolutely no family drama. It truly is the city that never sleeps. There's always something going on. Things to see and do. It's never quiet, like it is here."

"That sounds like fun." *For you.* She'd already done the party scene in California, and she knew it wasn't for her.

"It is fun," he said earnestly. "You can never get bored there."

Kat smiled. "When you surround yourself with needy animals, trust me. Boredom doesn't often factor in."

"You should visit me in New York," Jordan said suddenly.

"Maybe." Except she was pretty sure she never would. New York was nice, but she wouldn't be visiting him there. It would just be too hard. She already knew she was going to hurt when he left.

With a heavy sigh, Kat ran her hands through her hair, massaging her scalp.

"What's the matter?" Jordan asked.

"Nothing." She searched for a diversion. "Except I'm starving! You know what we need? Chocolate chip cookie dough ice cream. The really good kind where you can taste the grainy brown sugar in the cookie dough, you know? With the extra-large chocolate chunks mixed in?" The idea was almost enough to distract her from the sobering thought of Jordan going back to New York City.

"No, thanks. I've got my favorite dessert right here." He leaned over and kissed her. "Besides, I need real food. Let's order pizza. I'm too lazy to get out of bed." He yawned and stretched his arms up, drawing attention to the defined muscles of his shoulders and biceps.

"You don't look lazy." Kat was momentarily riveted by the way his ab muscles flexed and bunched when he stretched. "Not with all *that* going on." She waved her hand at his torso and arms.

A wicked smile. "You make me lazy. I should be out there working, but for some reason I get around you and all I want to do is fall into bed." He gripped the edges of the quilt and yanked it away. Then he lunged for her, wrapping his arms around her in a bear hug, tickling her ribs with his fingertips. Kat giggled, then laughed, then all-out shrieked, squirming under him until their humor evaporated into something far more delicious and satisfying than even the best cookie dough ice cream.

Chapter Twenty-Six

"That girl doesn't deserve a scorching hot kiss in the rain like that," Juliette said, propping her feet up on the coffee table in Emma's living room. "It's wasted on her. She's flighty and can't make up her mind, and Ryan Gosling's been pining away for her for years."

Kat scooped another handful of popcorn as Emma and Juliette argued over *The Notebook*. They had invited her over for Chick Flick Movie Night, and they were deep in a discussion about the pros and cons of the film.

"But they truly love each other," Emma insisted. "She's just confused because her parents didn't approve of him."

"See? She's spineless!" Juliette said with conviction. "Yet another reason she doesn't deserve his devotion."

"Kat, what do you think?" Emma asked from the corner of the couch. She was curled under a knitted throw the exact color of a summer sky. Juliette was on the overstuffed chair, with Hank and Buddy asleep at her feet.

Kat was trying to think of something diplomatic to say when an object on the coffee table caught her eye. It was the silver key with the clover design. "Hey, isn't that the old key I found in the attic a few days ago?"

Emma glanced at it. "Yeah. It keeps showing up in the house. Every time I turn around, it's there." She set her cup of cocoa on the coffee table. "This morning I found it in my makeup drawer. And when I went to bed last night, it showed up under my pillow. The house is trying to tell us something, but we can't figure it out."

Kat picked up the key, turning it over and over in her hand. The green crystals sparkled in the dim light. "I wonder what it's for?"

A door shut firmly upstairs.

Juliette sat up fast, startling the snoozing dogs at her feet. "Shh! The house is talking."

Another door shut upstairs. Then another.

"That's how the house talks?" Kat wrinkled her nose. "By slamming doors?"

Suddenly all the lights in the living room turned off, plunging them into darkness.

Hank ran to the couch and jumped into Kat's lap. She laid a comforting hand on his back. "Um, does this happen often?"

"Pretty much," Emma said. "It's got lots of opinions, and it has no problem letting us know."

Buddy let out a soft whine.

A light in the hallway turned on.

"Well, that's our cue," Juliette said, standing. "We need to follow where the house leads."

Kat followed Juliette and Emma down the hall, the dogs trailing close behind her. As soon as they reached the end of the hall, another light turned on in the kitchen. They moved into the kitchen, then all the lights blinked out again.

"Now what?" Emma asked.

Moonlight pooled in through the kitchen window, but it was still too dark to see much.

"Maybe the house is confused," Juliette said.

A kitchen cupboard opened, then snapped shut.

"No," Emma laughed. "It's definitely not confused, thank you very much."

An outside light by the kitchen door clicked on.

"It wants us to go outside?" Juliette asked. "That's different."

Kat walked toward the door with Hank close at her heels. She peered through the window into the dark garden. The light flickered, as if it was impatient. Turning the knob, she stepped outside, followed by Emma and Juliette. When the outside light shut off, the three women were left standing in the yard in the moonlight.

Kat thought she heard whispers in the wind. She had the sudden feeling that something monumental was about to take place.

"What now?" she asked quietly.

The house seemed to settle in a frustrated *hmph*.

"We can't very well go any further if you don't tell us where," Emma said half in amusement, half in exasperation.

Suddenly there was a loud *caw* and Edgar swooped out of the sky to land on Kat's shoulder.

"Hey there." She reached up to pet his glossy feathers. "Where've you been?"

Edgar rose into the air and circled overhead, then flew to an overgrown area of bushes and weeds at the base of the house. He landed on a dead branch and let out another loud *caw!*

The house lights flickered.

Kat watched Edgar intently. "He's calling us over there."

They followed the black bird until they were standing near the far corner of the house. Weeds had grown in a riot all over the ground, and vines had snaked up over the roots of dead bushes. Edgar hopped to a lower root near the weeds and damp earth. He tilted his head and waited for Kat expectantly.

Kat pointed. "He wants us to go there, but that doesn't make any sense." She was certain he was trying to show her something, but all she could see were bushes and weeds.

Emma gasped. "I think I know what we're looking at." She began scraping at the ground. "This house has a root cellar. Remember, Jules? Grams mentioned it a time or two, but we never used it." She started yanking at the roots, trying to clear away the overgrowth.

Juliette laid her hand on Emma's shoulder, and Emma stood back to let her through.

"Do your thing, Jules," Emma said.

Juliette stepped directly into the brambles and waited. The gnarled mass of roots seemed to loosen, then slowly slide away, one by one. It was entrancing, watching the way they swayed as though they were moving underwater, making way for Juliette. Soon she was standing on an old metal hatch. The area around her had cleared.

"Wow," Kat breathed. "That was . . ."

"Amazeballs?" Juliette grinned. "Mother Nature and I go way back."

Emma bent to lift the hatch. "It's too heavy."

Kat and Juliette grabbed on, and together they all pulled. With an echoing groan, the metal hatch opened, revealing a stone staircase that led down into the root cellar.

Kat followed them into the darkness with a shiver of unease. She wasn't really afraid; she was just deeply curious. What could the house be trying to show them? Hank had picked up a small twig and was following close at Kat's heels.

When they reached the bottom of the stairs, Kat noticed the oddest thing. The room wasn't shrouded in darkness. It should've been, but the faint glow from outside stretched across the walls and floor, pooling over the stones, allowing them to see. It was as if the moonlight had followed them inside.

The root cellar was musty and small, with a floor constructed of loose, flat stones. It had a low ceiling and a couple of empty barrels in the corner. Nothing else.

Kat turned in a circle. "Huh."

"Exactly," Juliette agreed. She tipped her head back and spoke to the ceiling. "What are we doing down here, house?"

Buddy started snuffling around one of the corners. He made a little whining sound as he scratched at the stone floor.

"He's done that before," Emma said. "When the house wanted me to find something."

One of the stones wobbled under Buddy's foot.

Juliette went over and lifted it with both hands. All three women stared down at what looked like . . .

"A keyhole?" Kat asked.

Hank scampered to the hole and dropped something beside it. Earlier, Kat thought it was a twig, but she now saw that he'd been holding the clover key.

"Hank, you are brilliant," Kat said with admiration. She took the key, placed it in the lock, and turned it.

Nothing happened.

"Turn it the other way," Juliette urged.

Kat tried again, twisting the key in the other direction, but still nothing happened.

Emma took the key and tried, then Juliette. For several minutes they worked at the lock.

"Obviously the key fits," Emma said with frustration. "Why isn't it working?"

"Maybe it's rusted shut or something," Juliette said, bending down to blow into the keyhole. Then she took the key and tried again. But no matter how many times they worked at the lock, it wouldn't budge.

"Well, this is craptacular." Juliette sat back on the stone floor. "I feel like we're so close, but—"

"We're missing something," Emma finished.

Kat felt the same way. "Is there anything you guys can think of? Maybe something you read or heard about growing up?"

"Nothing about the cellar," Emma said. "All my grandmother ever said was that the house knew a lot of things better than we did. We certainly never learned anything about keys and hidden locks."

Juliette groaned and rubbed her face. "All I remember was her telling us to wash our hands before dinner, and not to play in the road, and to always stick together."

"And support each other," Emma said softly. "Grams was good about stuff like that."

"Good at reminding us that we were special," Juliette said wistfully. "And that being special was a good thing."

Kat felt a sudden sense of melancholy. Like she'd lost out on knowing the woman Emma and Juliette remembered fondly. She wondered what it would be like to have someone in her corner like that, growing up. "Sounds like she was an amazing person."

"She really was." Emma pushed to her feet. "I think she'd have loved you."

Juliette stood and slapped her hands together. "Let's call it a day. This was good progress, people. We can try again tomorrow. Maybe look through the attic again. There has to be something we're missing."

By the time they made their way back into the house, the lights were on and the pizza delivery car was just pulling into the driveway. For the rest of the evening, they rehashed what they'd found, discussing possibilities over bites of cheesy pizza and frozen margaritas and occasional input from the house. Every once in a while, the clover key would appear. Once when Juliette opened a kitchen drawer for napkins. And again when Emma reached her hand into the popcorn bowl. Later, when Kat was putting on her shoes to leave, the key showed up in the left toe of her boot.

"Okay, this key is very persistent." Kat set it on the hall table.

"It's the house." Emma blew a curl off her forehead and tilted her face to the ceiling. "Give it a rest, okay? We're doing the best we can."

As Kat turned to leave, she could've sworn the house settled in a *hmph*.

Chapter Twenty-Seven

"You lied." Kat propped her chin in her hands. She was seated in the farmhouse kitchen across from Jordan while his grandmother put away the teakettle. They'd just finished washing dishes after a delicious dinner of lasagna and Caesar salad. "You're not doomed to live a life full of frozen waffles for dinner. You, Mr. Prescott, can cook."

Jordan relaxed back in his chair. "I can when I want to. I just don't usually take the time because it's no fun cooking for one."

"Well you're here with us now," Opal said, lifting her teacup. "You are no longer 'one,' you are 'three.' Five, if you count the dogs. I know for a fact they'd love some more of your leftovers."

Jordan glanced at Kat and winked, which made her body flush with heat. Every time he gave her that look, it reminded her of all the secret, sexy things they'd been doing together. She dragged her gaze away and stared into her teacup so Opal wouldn't catch her getting all googly-eyed over him.

Opal began filling them in on her preparations for the Summer's End Gala. She told them about the auction baskets and the hired musicians and the photographer. "And who doesn't like a black tie affair, once in a while?" she asked, drawing her apron over her head and hanging it on a hook. "It's not often a person has a chance to get all gussied up. So I say both of you need to take advantage of it."

"I'm sure it'll be fun, Grandma, but I didn't exactly pack my tuxedo when I came out here," Jordan said.

"Do you have your own tuxedo?" Kat asked. She wouldn't mind seeing him all "gussied" up, as Opal put it. Lord knew Jordan could make a pair of old jeans and a ratty T-shirt look like a million bucks. She liked the idea of him in formal attire, all James Bond–style.

"He doesn't need his own tuxedo," Opal said firmly. "I already scheduled you a fitting for a rental tux, Jordan. It's at Belle of the Ball. You know the shop near the water-front?"

Jordan made a face. "The *prom* shop?"

"It's not just for proms," Opal assured him. "Vivian handles weddings and funerals and other fancy events, too."

"Great," he said without enthusiasm.

Opal pursed her lips. "Now listen. I don't ask much, but I expect you to be there. Everyone's bringing their friends and families, so I need you." She stared him down with an expression that could only be described as "grandma power."

"Of course," Jordan said. "If it means that much to you, I'll come."

"And as for you." Opal turned her "grandma power" on Kat. "I know you say you don't have a dress, but you can rent something from Belle of the Ball, too. There's no reason why a beautiful girl like you should stay home from the biggest event of the year. I want you to come. You live here with us, so as far as I'm concerned, you're family, too."

Kat opened her mouth, then shut it. Happiness bubbled up from inside her until she felt her nose tingle with emotion. Opal just included her in the family, and for that kindness, Kat would fly to the moon and back for her. "I'll do my best, Opal."

"Good." Opal gave a satisfied nod. "Then that's settled. Now I'm off to bed. So long, you two night owls."

They said good night and waited until they heard Opal's door shut down the hall.

"Night owls?" Kat whispered. "Do you think she's onto us?"

"I doubt it," Jordan said.

For the past few nights, they'd been having secret get-togethers. On Monday, Jordan had stayed over at her apartment and sneaked back into the house before the sun came up. The night after that, they'd met in the kitchen for midnight ice cream sundaes, after which Kat followed Jordan back to his room for a second "dessert." Last night, they'd gone out to make campfire s'mores, much to Waffles's delight. And the more time Kat spent with Jordan, the more she wanted more. There was a part of her that wished she could just back away. Break it off now, before she got in too deep. But it was much too late for that. She was in way over her head this time, and there was nothing she could do but ride it out. In a perfect world, Jordan would decide to stay, but the world wasn't perfect. Kat shook off those thoughts and forced herself to remain in the moment.

"I think I'd enjoy seeing you dressed for prom," she teased. "All gussied up from *Belle of the Ball*." She'd drawn the name out for emphasis, then bit her lower lip to keep from laughing.

Jordan narrowed his eyes and shot out of his chair.

She backed away, unable to contain her laughter.

He scooped her up, carrying her down the hall toward the stairs. "If I have to gussy myself up, so do you."

"I told Opal I'd do my best," Kat said. "But I'm not big on gussying."

"It doesn't matter what you wear. You'd look gorgeous

in anything. A burlap sack. An empty barrel. A bedsheet." He set her down at the foot of the stairs. "Actually, come up to my room so I can double-check about the bedsheet."

"No way. I can't sleep over tonight."

"Is that what you thought I was planning?" he murmured against her neck. "Sleep?"

Kat shivered, so tempted to follow him up to his room. "I know exactly what you were planning, and that's why I can't. If I don't get some actual sleep, I'll be sleepwalking through the day tomorrow, and I have to visit Emma and Juliette after work."

"Did you find out anything new at their house?"

Kat took a seat on the bottom step, and he joined her. She filled him in on the odd night she'd had at Emma's house, with the key and the hidden root cellar.

While she was talking, Clementine padded up to them with a soft meow.

"Oh, really?" Kat said to the orange tabby. To Jordan, she said, "Clementine needs more attention from you."

"Me?" He looked offended.

"Yup. You."

The cat climbed into Jordan's lap and began to purr.

"She would like you to visit her kittens more often," Kat said.

Jordan smoothed his hand over Clementine, whose rumbling purr grew even louder. "I've checked on them twice today, already."

"But you're the surrogate dad. You need to be more involved."

He made a face. "No, thanks. She can have full custody."

Clementine meowed, and Jordan leaned toward her. "Trust me, I'd be a terrible role model. Your kittens would be knocking back beers and hanging with the alley cats in no time flat."

The purring cat butted her head against Jordan's chest.

"Ooh, that's a head mash!" Kat said. "Those are hard to come by. You should just give in to her demands. It's futile to resist. She has you wrapped around her little paw, like it or not."

He gently set Clementine aside, pulled Kat to her feet, and whispered, "Like it." Then he drew her in for a long, slow kiss that eventually led to her sleepwalking through the following day, after all. But it was so worth it.

Chapter Twenty-Eight

"Can you make a 'Get Rich Quick' cupcake?" Kat asked as she stirred her third cappuccino a little too fast. Some of it sloshed onto the wrought iron bistro table. "If so, I'd like a baker's dozen of those."

Kat was sitting with the Holloways at Fairy Cakes near the waterfront. They'd all agreed to get together at Emma's bakery for coffee. But even with the cozy atmosphere and great company, Kat felt oddly unsettled. Things between her and Jordan were so good, it was making her nervous. She was falling for him, and that meant she was in danger of losing control of her goals. Maybe if she could at least control her finances and gain some security there, it would make her feel better prepared for whatever happened next.

Emma leaned across the table and handed Kat a napkin. "Even if I could make that kind of cupcake, I doubt it would work for you."

"Why? Did you read my tea leaves, or something?" Kat dropped her chin into her hands. "I'm destined to be poor forever, aren't I? Just give it to me straight. I can take it."

"No, it's not that," Emma said.

Kat took a sip of her drink. "Then how about a 'Winning Lotto Numbers' cupcake? I'd be on board with that one, too. I'm not picky."

"Holloway magic doesn't work on us." Juliette bit into her cupcake with an expression of utter bliss.

"It only works on other people," Emma explained. "And since you're somehow linked to us, you're probably immune to the charms."

"Let's conduct an experiment." Juliette set a delicately frosted blackberry and vanilla cupcake on Kat's plate. "Try this."

Kat lifted the fluffy cupcake and took a bite, suddenly understanding Juliette's blissed-out expression. It was utterly delicious. She sucked the sweet, tart frosting off her fingertip, marveling at the heavenly concoction Emma had whipped up. "Wow. This one tastes like . . ." It was hard to describe. The French vanilla was rich and decadent, and the addition of fresh blackberries reminded her of sweet, lazy days spent outside. "It reminds me of walking in the warm sunshine picking berries."

"But does it make you *feel* anything?" Juliette asked quizzically.

"I feel . . ." Kat glanced back and forth between the two women. "Good, I guess."

"You sure you don't have the sudden desire to run and tell someone you love them?" Emma asked.

"What? Of course not!" Kat gave her a "now you're talking crazy" look, even though Jordan's face flashed across her mind. She cleared her throat. "Why would I?"

"Because that," Juliette said, pointing to the cupcake, "is called 'Summer Loving.' It's supposed to make you feel open to sharing your feelings with the one you love."

Again, Jordan's face appeared in Kat's mind, but that was ridiculous. She ignored it. *Hard.* Regardless of her growing infatuation with him, she definitely had no desire to run home and tell him anything. God, the idea was mortifying even to contemplate. "No sudden desires," Kat said firmly.

"Not even just a teensy urge?" Emma asked with a soft smile.

"Like, a *mysteriously* teensy urge?" Juliette teased.

Kat rolled her eyes. These women were not subtle. "I can promise you, I have no urges to profess my undying love to anyone. Except Emma, for creating these heavenly treats." She took another bite, chewing forcefully.

Juliette sat back in her chair. "Told you," she said to Emma. "I knew your cupcake charms weren't going to work on her. My 'Be Chill' soap never worked for her, either. We're definitely related, somehow. We just have to figure out how."

"Tomorrow we'll all hit the attic again," Emma said. "There's got to be something we're missing."

Kat sipped her coffee, channeling all her focus into the task ahead.

"I'm telling you, there has to be a clue in here." Emma's muffled voice came from the corner of her attic.

Today the carousel horse was smack in the center of the room, so the air smelled sweet and cheerful, like popcorn and cotton candy and peanuts. At least there was that aspect of the search to make the Sunday afternoon a little brighter.

She settled near a trunk of photo albums and started going through them again, looking for clues. But what? They were searching for a way to open a lock, with no idea what they'd even find. Not for the first time, frustration gripped her because it all seemed so futile. The more she started to believe she might be related to these amazing women, the harder it seemed to prove.

"What about a locksmith?" Juliette grumbled from a beanbag chair against the wall. She lifted a music box off a pile of old books and turned it over in her hands. "Or maybe we could blast the lock open with some dynamite, like in the movies."

"Right." Emma emerged from behind an old wardrobe. "I'm sure the house would love that."

A pile of clothes beside Juliette bucked into the air, landing all over her.

"Fine," Juliette said to the ceiling. "No dynamite." She brushed the clothes away and opened the green enamel jewelry box in her lap.

A tinkling melody began to play, filling the attic with a lovely song.

"But why does it have to be so difficult?" Juliette complained. "I mean, we have a key. We have a lock. What more do we need?"

Emma started to hum to the melody.

Kat was on the other side of the room, but she could hear the music clearly. The blue velvet dress lay in her lap. Not because she'd been looking for it, but because it kept showing up in every box she opened. She'd finally stopped trying to pack it away.

Kat began humming along with Emma. "I know that song from somewhere. What is it?"

Juliette turned the music box and looked at the bottom. "There's no title."

"I think it's a song Grams used to sing," Emma said.

Juliette shut the lid and tossed it into a box of clothes.

Kat lifted the last stack of albums from her box across the room. Her hand brushed against a small, rectangular box with hard, sleek edges. Very slowly, she lifted out the exact same music box Juliette had just set aside. "Um . . . you guys?"

Juliette saw the music box in Kat's hands and scrambled off the beanbag chair.

Both cousins hurried over to where Kat was sitting.

Kat opened the music box, letting the soft melody fill the attic room again. It was heartbreakingly sweet, and strangely familiar. "What song is this?" She searched the box, but there was no indication of the name or place it originated. There wasn't even a key to wind it. "How does this work?"

"No clue," Juliette said.

Kat looked for a hidden compartment. "Batteries?"

"No," Emma said. "It's an antique, so no batteries. It's just one of the house's things. They don't always make sense."

Kat cocked her head, listening to the lovely music. "I know I've heard this song before." But where? She wracked her brain, trying to remember. The melody continued to play, and the longer it played, the more powerful it seemed, until Kat felt as though it wove a spell around the three of them.

Somewhere over by the carousel horse, an object clattered to the floor.

Kat jumped.

"It's just that banjo," Emma said.

Kat stared at the banjo on the floor a few feet away. The strings. The glossy wood.

The music box continued its melody.

A fragment of a memory flashed in her mind. Colorful scarves. An enchanted prince playing a guitar. A jolt of recognition shot through her. Kat gasped. "I know where I've heard this! It's an old Irish lullaby."

Juliette took the music box and stared at it, as if she could find answers in the emerald green, velvet-lined interior. "How do you know?"

"Jordan played it for me on his guitar," Kat said.

"*Jordan*?" Juliette looked incredulous.

Kat nodded.

"Wait." Juliette held up a hand. "He's mysterious and handsome *and* he plays the guitar? No wonder you've been floozying it up in Floozyville with him. Who wouldn't?"

"Does the song have words?" Emma pressed. "Did he sing it?"

"No," Kat said. "But he played it beautifully. He said he learned it from someone in his parents' folk band."

"And now he's the son of musicians?" Juliette threw her hands in the air. "You've been holding back on us, Kat. Your Mr. Mysterious is much more than just another pretty face."

Kat stuck her tongue between her teeth and grinned like a Cheshire cat. "He's a lot of things." A lot of wonderful, amazing things.

"What if this song has lyrics?" Emma continued with growing excitement. "What if there's a clue in the song? What if—"

"It helps us open the lock?" Kat considered it. "But how? I mean, seriously. What are the odds that some old man from Ireland just happened to teach Jordan a song that just happens to hold a clue to help us unlock a spell for the Holloway house all these years later?"

"Never ask the odds," Juliette said, jumping to her feet. "Not in this house. What are the odds that any of this"—she gestured to the entire attic—"would exist? Magical coincidences happen every day in the world, but most people just don't recognize them. Just because they can't be explained, doesn't make them any less real. The three of us should know that better than anyone. Come on." She walked toward the attic door. "Let's go."

Kat set the music box aside and rose to her feet. "Where?"

"To talk to Jordan."

"Maybe he'll be able to help us," Emma agreed.

Kat followed them down the stairs. "But what if he doesn't help us? What if it's just a regular song?"

"Then the trip will still be worth it," Juliette said. "Any time a super-hot guy serenades you with a guitar? That's a win."

Chapter Twenty-Nine

Jordan heard a knock at the front door and hoped it was Kat. The likelihood was low because she normally entered through the kitchen, but he hadn't seen her all day and he missed her. Hell, he missed her all the time. Even when they spent hours together, it never seemed to be enough. It was entirely possible that he'd been bewitched by *La Belle Dame sans Merci*, but he wasn't sure he cared. At least he'd die a happy man.

He opened the door, swinging it wide when he saw Kat.

"Jordan!" Kat's eyes were bright, and her cheeks were flushed. He liked seeing her like this, only usually it was under different, more intimate circumstances. He wanted to haul her off somewhere private and give her more reasons to blush, but he had to pull himself together because she wasn't alone.

"You remember Emma and Juliette Holloway?" She gestured to her two friends standing behind her on the porch.

Jordan nodded. "Hi."

"We came to ask you something." Kat shifted restlessly on her feet. Almost like she was nervous.

He leaned a shoulder against the doorframe. "Why do I

get the feeling you're about to ask me to foster a herd of needy giraffes?"

"I'm not," Kat assured him.

He crossed his arms. "A flock of rhinos? A gaggle of whales?"

Kat stamped her foot impatiently, and he fought not to smile. Even frustrated, she was so damned adorable.

"It's a crash of rhinos. A pod of whales," she said quickly. "But never mind that. I need you to do something very important for me." Kat glanced at the other two women, then back at him with her pleading, fallen-angel face. "For us."

He started to wave them into the house because he already knew he was going to be suckered into whatever it was Kat wanted. It was impossible for him to deny her anything when she looked at him like that. Whatever she needed, he'd give it to her. *Damn,* he had it bad for this woman.

Kat reached out and touched him lightly on the hand. "No, what we need is over there." She pointed in the direction of the red barn. Whatever she was going to ask, he had a feeling he wasn't going to like it.

"Jordan," Kat said, squaring her shoulders. "I need you to play us a song on your guitar."

What the hell? "Sorry, ladies. I'm not in the business of playing my guitar for anyone." He gave Kat a pointed look. That song he'd played for her in the caravan was private. "It's been a really long time, and I'm out of practice."

"It's not so much the delivery that's important," Kat said. "It's the song itself. Remember the old Irish lullaby you played for me in the caravan?" So much for privacy. "Does it have lyrics?"

"Yes, but just a few and they don't make much sense."

"Who taught it to you?" Emma asked. "My grandmother used to hum the same tune, and she had a jewelry box with that melody."

"One of the old men from my parents' folk band taught it to me," Jordan said. It was odd to talk about his parents with strangers, let alone admitting they had a folk band. But something about these women made it seem okay. "He was a musician from Ireland, but he didn't stay for very long. He disappeared after they split up."

"Can you sing it to us?" Juliette asked. "Please?"

Jordan noticed the way Emma was wringing her hands and how anxious her cousin Juliette looked. Kat seemed as though she were holding her breath. She looked somehow fragile. Like her life depended on this moment.

He crossed his arms. "Why?"

They filled him in on what they knew, until Jordan's mind spun with possibilities. Magic house. Magic women. Magic key. To anyone else, it might sound crazy, but he knew Kat now. He'd seen the way she worked with animals—how she communicated with them. If that wasn't magic, then what was? He'd never been one to place much belief in his mother's flights of fancy, but she always said the Holloway magic was real. Maybe it was. Who was he to disagree?

Ten minutes later, Jordan found himself sitting on the front porch with Kat beside him. Juliette and Emma sat on the steps and waited. If anyone had told him a month ago he'd be back at the farm, serenading women with old folk music, he'd have said they were crazy. But life was crazy. He'd always known that.

Kat gave him a sweet, encouraging smile.

What he hadn't known was that sometimes life could be crazy *good*. He strummed the guitar until he found the tune, then began to sing in a low, deep voice:

*"Fae lovers met in a wild wood to bid farewell to
     their children three.
 They left the north, they traveled south, then west
     across the sea.*

*And over years the children changed, and forgot
   the wild wood,
Forgot the tales of other realms and spells that
   worked for good.
But for a whisper of a song, the youngest child did
   sing:
Together is the answer, love. Together you have
   everything."*

Jordan kept strumming, but stole a glance at the three women. "And that's all. It's just that verse, and then the rest of the song is a repetition of,

*"The secret to the hearth and home:
Do together what you cannot do alone."*

When the song ended, Kat looked at Emma and Juliette. "Any idea what it means?"

No one said anything for a while, and disappointment began to settle over him. As far-fetched as their hopes were, he'd really wanted to help them.

Emma suddenly gasped. She jumped up and whirled to face them. "We have to get back to the house. I think I know how to open that lock!"

Jordan set his guitar aside. "How?"

Emma looked fiercely determined. "*Together.*"

After the women dashed back to the house, Jordan sat on the porch with the guitar, absently strumming the melody. Something warm and sweet and too powerful to name flooded through him when he thought of Kat's beautiful face and how it glowed with hope as she thanked him before they left. He wanted to see her light up like that every day. He wanted her for all sorts of reasons. For a long time, he stayed on the porch, his mind spinning with thoughts of Kat, and how he could make her happy.

* * *

Back at the Holloway house, Kat followed Emma and Juliette down into the root cellar. The three of them knelt beside the lock.

Emma withdrew the clover key from her pocket. "I think we're meant to do this together."

"You mean like, hold the key together?" Juliette asked. "It can't be that simple."

"Let's try it." Kat reached out to lay her hand on Emma's.

Juliette did the same, and Emma inserted the key into the lock with a loud *click*.

Kat's hand began to buzz with a strange, tingling energy.

A cool breeze swirled into the room, surrounding all three of them. It kissed Kat's eyelashes and ruffled the hair on the nape of her neck. She thought she heard whispers in the air around them.

"Do you feel that?" Juliette's face glowed with triumph.

"Yes," Emma breathed. She turned to Kat. "That's Holloway magic."

Kat stared at the lock, wondering what was about to happen. Whatever it was, she had a feeling her life was about to change in a huge way.

"They left the north and traveled south." Emma whispered the lyrics as they turned the key south.

Another clicking sound in the mechanism.

They all exchanged excited glances.

"Then west across the sea," Juliette said. They turned the key to the west, and this time, the click sounded like the chime of a grandfather clock.

"Together is the answer," Kat whispered.

The lock sprang free, revealing a wooden box carved with flowers and vines and strange, Celtic-looking symbols. It was long and narrow, with a fitted lid.

Juliette opened the lid to reveal a rolled-up piece of parchment.

Emma pulled it out, and Kat helped her unroll it. The paper was surprisingly sturdy, considering how old it looked, and the comforting scent of sweet herbs and spices seemed to waft in the air around them.

They all peered down at the faded words.

"It's a spell," Juliette breathed.

"Hearth and Home," Emma read aloud. "To create a true home. A sentinel to guide and protect."

"A sentinel," Kat repeated. "Like this house?"

"Yes." Emma scanned the words quickly. "I think this spell only works if the three of us do it together. It's for making a home that recognizes and protects our family."

"*Wow*," Juliette said in awe. "And to think it's been here all along. Why are we just finding it now?"

Emma slowly turned and looked at Kat. "I think it was waiting for the right Holloway to arrive."

Back in the kitchen, Emma put the kettle on while Kat poured over the "Hearth and Home" spell on the marble island. Her head ached with the monumental significance of what they'd just discovered.

"So let me get this straight," Juliette said between bites of a white chocolate macadamia nut cookie. "That spell is from our ancestors, but it could only be discovered and used when three Holloways were present."

"Yes," Emma said, pulling three teacups from the cupboard. "And once Kat came along, I guess it was finally ready to be found. So whenever we're ready, it looks like we can bring the spirit of this house into both of your homes, too. A sentinel to guide and protect."

The lights flickered joyfully, and all three women laughed.

Kat shook her head, still floored by the newfound proof

that she was part of the Holloway family. "I wish I knew for sure how I fit in to all this."

"We'll figure it out," Emma assured her. "But we don't need more proof. You belong with us."

Kat looked at the two women who had come to mean so much. The kitchen curtains billowed out by an unseen breeze.

"That's the house chiming in," Emma said, handing her a cup of tea. "It agrees."

"Yup," Juliette said. "We're keeping you, so you're just going to have to get comfortable with that. Now come eat these cookies. They're insane."

Kat felt a sudden burst of joy. No matter what they found out about her past, these women had accepted her into their lives, and Kat had never had that before. She wasn't sure what she'd ever done to deserve something this special, but she was going to treasure it always.

"Wanna stay for dinner?" Emma asked. "Hunter will be home soon. I can ask him to go get ice cream, and we can all watch *Sherlock* to celebrate solving the case!"

"I want to, but I've sort of promised Opal I'd show up to her Summer's End Gala. It's a black tie event her assisted living community puts on every year."

"Sounds fancy," Juliette said. "What are you wearing?"

Kat pulled out a kitchen chair to sit down. Draped neatly across the seat was the blue velvet dress. She let out a tiny gasp.

Juliette leaned sideways to get a better look. "Yeah," she said, chewing thoughtfully. "That's a good choice." To the ceiling she said, "Nice one, house."

Kat lifted the blue dress, hugging it to her chest, and the house settled in what sounded like a satisfied *hmph*.

Chapter Thirty

The Pine Cove Island Country Club was situated on the edge of a beautiful golf course on the north side of the island. A tree-lined driveway filled with twinkling lights lit the way to the main building, a huge manor house with old-world-style columns and a three-tiered fountain out front. By the time Kat's Uber pulled into the circular drive, she was buzzing with excitement. She'd been to black tie events back in L.A., but this was different. Jordan was here. He'd gone ahead to take Opal, and Kat couldn't wait to see him all "gussied up."

Kat thanked the driver, got out of the car, and slowly climbed the grand staircase to the entrance. She'd dressed at Emma's house in the blue velvet gown. Juliette had gone hunting in the attic and, of course, found a pair of shoes that fit Kat perfectly, and a lovely beaded clutch. Together they'd helped Kat with her hair and makeup, and by the time they were finished, Kat felt like Cinderella going to the ball.

Now, as she stepped into the grand foyer of the country club, all she needed was to find her prince. If it crossed her mind that Cinderella's night didn't end very well, Kat wasn't going to worry about it. Tonight was her fantasy, and she was going to spin it how she wanted. In her fairy tale, Cinderella and the prince would dance, drink, have a scorching hot make-out session in some secluded alcove, and then catch a ride on the first pumpkin home so the real party could begin. In her bedroom. Now *that* was a happy ending.

Kat joined the partygoers, searching for Jordan or Opal. People mingled in the grand hall while servers wove through the crowd with trays of sparkling champagne. There was laughter and conversation, and Kat suddenly felt very alone.

She stopped beside a marble column and pretended to check her phone. It gave her something to do while she gathered her courage to enter the grand ballroom by herself.

"Look what the cat dragged in," said a familiar, raspy voice.

Kat glanced up and grinned. "Smitty! I didn't know you were going to be here." She'd never been so glad to see her crotchety boss.

"All us older folks come to the Summer's End Gala. It's one of the only times of the year we get to dress classy." Smitty's hair was supersized tonight, as were the shoulder pads in her gold sequined, V-necked cocktail dress. She stuck a hand on her hip and eyed Kat thoughtfully. "The real question is, what are *you* doing here?"

"Opal Prescott invited us. She's on the committee, and I'm renting a room from her, so she extended the invitation."

"Us?"

"Hmm?" Kat searched the foyer behind Smitty for any sign of Jordan.

"You said Opal asked 'us.'"

"Oh, yes. She invited her grandson Jordan to come, too."

"Uh-huh." Smitty snorted. "That explains it." She finished off her champagne in one gulp.

"What do you mean?"

Smitty pointed to Kat's gown with a gold sparkly nail.

"This Miss America thing you've got going on here. It looks good on you, kiddo. Just let my nephew down easy, will you?"

"What?" Kat asked. "We never—"

Bobby Bankston came walking up with two flutes of champagne. He was dressed in a black tuxedo with a bolero tie. Somehow, it suited him. Even without the hat, he still looked like a cowboy.

Bobby's eyes grew wide when he saw Kat. "Hot damn."

Kat beamed. "Hey, Bobby."

"I'm going out for some fresh air." Smitty pulled a pack of cigarettes from her spangly purse and walked away.

"You look . . ." Bobby seemed at a loss for words.

"Thanks." Kat felt suddenly guilty for not returning Bobby's calls. He'd called her a few times, but she'd ignored him. Anyone in their right mind would love to have a nice guy like Bobby, but Kat had to be honest with herself. And him. He deserved honesty. "I'm sorry I haven't called you back."

"Nah," he said, waving a hand and glancing away. "I understand."

But did he? Kat felt it only fair to tell him the truth. "The thing is, Bobby, I think you're a really great guy."

He chuckled. "Oh, man. Kiss of death, those words."

"No, I mean it," Kat insisted. "I really enjoyed going to dinner with you. You're charming and entertaining and handsome and all those things. But . . . I'm kind of hung up on someone else."

"Yeah, I hoped that was it," Bobby said easily.

"You did?" Kat asked in surprise.

He flashed his boyish dimples. "It's a much easier setdown if I know there's someone else in the picture. If I thought a gorgeous girl like you was ignoring my calls just because of me, well. That'd sting a hell of a lot more, you know what I mean?" He took a drink of champagne, only it was more like a swig.

"I hope we can be good friends." Kat wished she could say something less cliché.

"Oh! The trifecta." He tipped his head back and laughed. "You're a great guy. It's not you, it's me. I hope we can still be friends."

Kat rolled her eyes. "I really mean it."

He gave her a firm nod. "Damn straight we'll be friends. I'm still going to need your input with the puppy training."

"I'll be happy to help." She said good-bye, suspecting that deep down, even Bobby knew they weren't right for each other. As enjoyable as their dinner date was, there just hadn't been much of a spark between them. If he had truly felt it—that all-encompassing, fever-inducing, lust-filled attraction that swept you up like a hurricane and eclipsed all rational thought—he probably would've tried harder. Kat knew.

"Excuse me." The deep voice swept over her like a hurricane.

Kat turned to find Jordan smiling down at her. Her heart did a sudden backflip. He was gloriously handsome in his tuxedo. His normally windblown hair was swept back, but there was a slight stubble on his jaw which, paired with the silvery scar across his cheekbone, made him look just a little dangerous. Like every fantasy she'd ever dreamed up. Every dark hero she'd pined for in books. Every deep desire personified.

She took a small step back, as if that could distance her from the truth, but it was too late for pretending. She didn't have any defenses left around this man because . . . she *loved* him. She'd probably started falling the day Clementine had kittens in his room and he'd lined the box with his sweatshirt. Or it could've been the day he'd begrudgingly fed graham crackers to Waffles. Or the day he witnessed her magical gift of communicating with animals and accepted it. Accepted her. Every time something funny happened at work, she couldn't wait to get home and tell him. Every hour they'd spent together over the past few weeks had been leading up to this realization. She was in love with Jordan Prescott. There it was. A trickle of apprehension slid down her spine, but she straightened her back, steeling herself against doubt. Maybe this time, falling for someone didn't have to end badly. Maybe it would work out because he loved her, too. If Opal was right all along and Jordan was happier here . . . Maybe he would stay. Kat suddenly hoped with all her heart he wouldn't go. She held on to that hope like a lifeline.

"Do I know you?" he teased, taking her hand.

She brushed aside her whirlwind thoughts and forced herself to focus on the moment. "I think I met you in a caravan once."

Jordan's gaze darkened with desire, his whiskey-gold eyes sweeping over her in open appreciation. He gave her a look so charged with heat, Kat had the sudden urge to climb him like a tree, wrap her legs around his waist, and kiss him and not stop kissing him until the gala was over and the band packed up and the country club concierge kicked them out.

"La Belle Dame sans Merci." He took her hand to kiss the tips of her fingers.

"What's that?" Kat asked, distracted by the feel of his lips on her skin.

"A poem about an enchanting woman whose beauty captured a mortal man."

"How very lyrical of you," Kat said, laying a hand lightly on his chest. "What did she do with that man, after she captured him?"

"Whisked him away to paradise, for a while," Jordan said. "Then left him on a hillside to die."

She burst out laughing. "Be careful then. I could spell your doom."

"I don't want to be careful. I want to throw you over my shoulder and steal you away right now." From the way he was looking at her, Kat believed he might just do it.

"But I haven't even seen Opal yet," Kat said. "And I promised her I'd come. Have you seen her?"

Jordan tilted his head in the direction of the ballroom. "She's dancing."

He tucked Kat's hand on his arm and led her through the grand double doors. A sea of people dipped and swirled to a waltz in the center of the ballroom where a huge, glittering chandelier hung suspended from the coffered ceiling. Smaller chandeliers hung at varying intervals throughout the rest of the room, casting a warm glow on the party below. Those who weren't dancing sat at round tables covered in crisp white tablecloths, and in the center of each stood vases of flowers surrounded by twinkling fairy lights.

"It's so beautiful," Kat said, as Jordan led her to one of the tables. "I had no idea it would be such a big deal."

"My grandmother warned us it was going to be the event of the year," he said. "I meant it when I said she has a bigger social life than anyone I know."

The live orchestra began a new waltz, and Jordan held out his hand. "Dance with me?"

Now this, she'd like to see. Jordan Prescott of the beat-up truck and old-school rock music was leading her into a waltz? Inquiring minds needed to know. . . . She placed her hand in his.

They walked into the colorful swirl of dancing couples. Then he swung her toward him, placed his free hand on her lower back, and stepped easily into the waltz.

Kat didn't know what surprised her more—the fact that

he could dance, or the sudden skin-on-skin contact of his large, warm hand on her naked back.

"Your dress is going to be the death of me," he said huskily.

"Where did you learn to dance?" Kat managed. It was difficult to concentrate on the steps when he was touching her like that.

"My mother. When I was in fourth grade she went through a ballroom dance phase. Swore that no man was complete unless he knew how to dance."

"Did you like it?" She tried to imagine him as a little boy dancing with his mother. It wasn't easy.

"I was okay with it." His amber eyes lit with humor. "But her ballroom phase eventually fizzled out, which is why this is the only dance I know."

An older couple careened toward them and Jordan pulled Kat against him, expertly spinning her in a circle to avoid them. "Where did you learn to dance?" he asked.

"I used to date a dancer," Kat said. It seemed like a lifetime ago. She'd been barely twenty and so starry-eyed back then. She'd tried so hard to be whatever he needed, and when it didn't work out, she'd been crushed. With Jordan, she didn't have to try hard at all. It was the first time in her life she could just be her true self. All the more reason to want it to last. Plus, she had Emma and Juliette now. There was something so liberating about knowing you had backup—people who would be there for you if the whole world fell apart.

He spun her in another circle, shielding her from a teetering couple who'd had a few too many cocktails.

"Kat!" Opal's sweet, warbly voice called. "Oh my dear, just look at you."

Opal and Sam Norton weren't moving fast across the dance floor—they were hardly moving at all—but Kat had never seen Opal look happier. She was wearing a forest green evening dress with long glittery sleeves, and someone had given her a wrist corsage with white roses.

When Sam glanced over at them, he stutter-stepped, then came to a complete stop.

Opal looked questioningly at him. "Sam?"

The old man blinked a few times, muttering under his breath.

"Sam, you remember Kat Davenport?" Opal asked.

He cleared his throat. "I do. I do. Only I didn't quite realize the resemblance until I saw you in the dress."

"What resemblance?" Jordan asked.

"You look exactly like Caroline Holloway," Sam exclaimed, his voice trembling with emotion. "The older Holloway sister. You're the spitting image of her, especially in that dress."

Kat bit her bottom lip, hope swelling inside her. "Did you know her?"

"Not well," Sam admitted. "She was a bit older than me, but she was the talk of the town back in the day, right before she ran off to join the circus. A young, beautiful girl with roses in her cheeks and stars in her eyes and always surrounded by animals." He chuckled at an old memory. "Right before she left town, there was a big fancy party and she wore *that* dress. If I recall correctly, she had a white dove on her shoulder and it caused quite a commotion."

"Emma and Juliette think she might have been my grandmother," Kat said. "I never knew my parents, but I've always had a connection to animals. How do you know so much about the Holloways?"

"I was a friend of their grandmother's when I was a young man," Sam said. "Seems like another lifetime ago." He reached out to take Opal's hand. "Life never ceases to amaze, does it?"

"Never," Opal said, smiling up at him.

Kat glanced away because she didn't want to intrude on what clearly was a tender moment between the older couple. She could tell just by the way he and Opal looked at each other they were in love.

As the night carried on, Opal introduced them to all her friends from the community center, which turned out to be a group of lively older people who seemed to adopt Jordan and Kat instantly into the fold. They were already invited to bingo night, Sunday movies on the lawn, and Sam Norton's fishing party. Jordan was asked if he played golf, if he could troubleshoot the assisted living home's computer network, and when he and Kat were getting married. Kat was asked if she wanted to attend water aerobics, if she could bring therapy animals to visit the home, and if she and Jordan planned to have a lot of children. They'd both expertly dodged the uncomfortable questions, secretly grinning at each other.

A short while later, giggling from a bit too much champagne, Kat escaped the ballroom with Jordan to walk in the gardens and—since this was her fairy tale—hopefully find a secluded alcove to be naughty in. The air was warm and balmy, and the rich scent of jasmine floated around them. The twinkling white lights woven through the trees and shrubs made everything appear magical.

Kat held Jordan's hand as they strolled. She felt as if they were in a dream. Everything about the moment felt perfect, and she suddenly wanted to tell him she loved him. It could work between them, she decided. He just had to want it as much as she did. She stole a glance at him from beneath her lashes.

Jordan's expression startled her. He looked so serious, she felt a tiny prickle of anxiety. She stopped walking. "What's wrong?"

He pulled her to a secluded spot beside a fountain. "Nothing's wrong. I want everything to be right." But his face was so solemn, her anxiety began to escalate.

"Everything is right," she said carefully. "Isn't it?"

He took both her hands. "You grew up differently than me, but I think we both had to become survivors, in our own way."

Now she was really worried. "Okay."

"We adapt easily, don't we?"

"Sure." Kat couldn't read his expression. What was he getting at?

"I want us to be together," he said firmly. "I don't want to lose you."

Kat felt a tidal wave of relief. If a choir of angels had sung the words, they couldn't have sounded better. She was so filled with warmth and happiness, she might've lit up the sky like a firework. "I feel the same way, Jordan. I want us to be together, too." It felt good to finally say it out loud.

Jordan looked like he wanted to say more, but a group of people walked up to the fountain.

"Let's get out of here," he said suddenly.

"Where do you want to go?" Kat asked.

He didn't even hesitate. "Home."

Home. Yes. She'd go anywhere with this man, but home sounded like the best place in the world.

Chapter Thirty-One

On Sunday morning, Kat woke to the sound of rain outside. Thunder rumbled in the distance, which yanked her right out of a delicious dream she'd been having. She shifted onto her side, coming face-to-face with the dream.

Jordan was still fast asleep. Waking up with him seemed like the most natural thing in the world. She rose carefully, padding over to the window to look outside. The summer rain made the yard look like a faded watercolor painting. Still, the farm had gone through remarkable changes in the few weeks since she'd been there. Jordan had fixed the front yard, reseeding the grass and trimming the overgrown hedges. He'd even planted a row of bright flowers underneath the farmhouse porch. As for the porch itself, he'd fixed the sagging steps and repainted everything—even the front door had a fresh coat of bright turquoise paint. The red rosebushes along the fence were still overgrown, but it did nothing to mar the quaint beauty of the property. Now, through the gauzy haze of rain, it almost looked like the ideal farmhouse she'd expected when she'd first answered the ad.

She boiled water in an electric teapot on her table, then pulled out a canister of English Breakfast tea. So much had changed since she'd arrived on Pine Cove Island. She'd made friends. She'd found a connection to family, and she'd found *him*.

After making tea, Kat stood at the window watching the rain. A blue jay landed on the windowsill outside.

"Hey there," Kat whispered. "What's your name?"

A soft chuckle from the bed. "Talking to the birds again?"

She propped her hip on the windowsill. "Just making new friends."

Jordan rose to a sitting position and leaned against the headboard, his broad shoulders taking up most of the space. "We need to do something about this bed. It's barely big enough to roll over in."

"I'm perfectly comfortable with it. But that's only when a certain beast isn't hogging all the space."

"Tonight you need to come to my bed," he said.

"Oh, is that how it's going to be now?"

"Yes, my bed is huge. It's big enough for me and you *and* the cats, if they decide to invade."

Kat flushed with pleasure. He'd included the cats, which meant he'd accepted them as part of his life. It was as if he was accepting everything about *her*, and it made her love him even more. Somehow over the course of the past few weeks, the animals had wound their way into his life too. Even Hank had become part of their family. He'd spent the night curled up on the sofa with Lucky in the main house.

"Come back to bed," Jordan said sleepily. "Let's pretend we have nothing to do all day except lounge, even though it isn't true."

"Why? What do you have going on today?" She set her teacup down and moved to the bed.

Jordan pulled back the quilt, and she snuggled in beside him.

"I've got to start emptying out the red barn today," he

said. "It's going to be a hell of a lot of work. My parents stored decades worth of junk in there. There's a truck arriving this afternoon to haul stuff away."

"I can help," Kat said. "I mean, I was planning to lie here all day and listen to the rain, but if you need me . . ."

He drew her up against him. "I definitely need you. But I'm not going to make you dig through all that junk. It's a safety hazard."

He kissed the top of her head, and once again she was overcome with the intense *rightness* of the two of them together. It was time to tell him her true feelings. He'd told her last night he didn't want to lose her. Kat started to gather her courage, but Jordan's phone rang.

He picked it up off the nightstand and checked it, then set it aside.

She snuggled closer. "Who was it?"

"My business partner, Chad. He called three times last night. I should call him back."

"Mmm." She yawned and stretched like a cat, sliding her bare legs over his.

He watched her through half-closed eyes, but she wasn't fooled. She knew that look on him by now. Jordan wasn't sleepy at all. He had other plans.

"You have the softest skin." He lowered his head to kiss the hollow at the base of her throat, making her pulse race.

"What about your business partner?" she whispered.

"No idea." Jordan slid over her. "Not really interested in his skin."

It was hard to kiss while laughing, but somehow they muddled through.

Later that morning, Kat finished taking care of the animals while Jordan went to make phone calls. Lulabelle and Waffles seemed restless because of the rain, so she spent extra time with them, talking and singing as she fed the chickens.

She stopped and leaned against the fence to watch the goat and donkey together. They were practically inseparable now that they'd become friends.

Lucky came ambling over to the fence, his three-legged gait not stopping him from making a beeline toward her with a ratty tennis ball. He dropped it at her feet, tongue lolling happily, head cocked to one side.

"You don't mind the rain, huh?" Kat asked.

Lucky gave an excited *yip,* and Kat laughed. "There'll be plenty of mud puddles around here, so you're in luck."

She picked up the muddy ball and tossed it across the yard.

He bounded after it, splashing through a puddle, then backtracking to splash through it again, doing a quick roll through the mud. It was clear that Lucky was one of those dogs who lived for water. Hank, on the other hand, wasn't thrilled with it. He dozed comfortably on the front porch, which made Kat happy. All in all, things were looking up and life was good. *Really* good.

She put her hands on her hips and surveyed the yard, the farmhouse, and the fields beyond. The air smelled of damp earth and fresh rain and new beginnings. She couldn't think of a single thing she'd want to change, now that Jordan felt the same way she did. If he truly meant what he'd said last night—that he didn't want to lose her—then they could actually have a life together here. Warmth flooded through her, filling her with a giddy sense of optimism she'd never felt before. Things were finally falling into place.

Her phone rang, and she pulled it from her pocket. "Hey, Juliette."

"Hey, yourself." Juliette's voice bubbled over with excitement. Kat could hear Emma in the background talking to someone. "Can you come to the house? Like, right now? Hunter called Emma from Seattle. Apparently, he met up with his friend who specializes in missing persons, and he got some information about Evangeline!"

Yes, things were falling into place. "I'll be right over."

Fifteen minutes later, Kat had changed into clean clothes and made her way to Emma's house. She parked her car and jumped out, eager to see her friends and find out what Hunter knew about the mysterious Evangeline.

The house's lights glowed just a tad brighter in greeting, and the door swung wide.

"We're in here," Emma called from the living room.

Kat hung her rain jacket on a peg as the front door closed behind her. In the living room, Emma was sprawled on the couch, and Juliette was on the floor with Buddy. She sprang up when Kat entered.

"Here," Juliette said excitedly, leading Kat to the overstuffed chair. "You'll want to sit down for this."

"What did you find out?" Kat asked, looking back and forth between them. Both Emma and Juliette looked like kids on Christmas morning.

"Apparently, Evangeline Bellamy moved from place to place, after she left her parents," Juliette said. "She was young and wild and full of wanderlust, determined to make it to the West Coast where she could see Hollywood. She rarely kept in contact with her parents, which is the way of that particular Holloway gift. Those with wanderlust are always out there blowing in the wind. Now get ready for this."

Juliette opened her mouth to continue, but it was Emma who blurted, "Evangeline Bellamy was a theater actress for a little while in California, and she changed her name to Kate Davenport!"

"You are the daughter of Kate Davenport," Juliette said triumphantly. "That makes you our second cousin!"

Kat felt no surprise, only relief. Somehow, she'd already begun to believe it. It was good to finally get proof. "But, how?"

"Hunter's contact into missing persons had to dig deep," Emma said. "But twenty-six years ago, an infant with no known relatives was taken into a police station in L.A. That same night, Kate Davenport, a single mother, left her apartment complex to go out with friends. She left her infant daughter with a babysitter and never returned."

Kat felt an odd, swooshing sensation in her head, as if all the years of unanswered questions about her family were now funneling down through a narrow tunnel into this exact moment. A moment she'd been waiting for her entire life. "What happened to her?"

"There was a multicar pileup on the freeway that night." Emma's face was etched with sympathy. "An overturned truck. Several people died, including your mother."

Juliette reached out and laid a hand on Kat's shoulder.

"They said she died," Kat whispered. "But I never knew how."

"The babysitter was only a teenager," Juliette continued. "So when your mom never returned, the babysitter and her parents took you to the police and told them everything they could, but they didn't know much about your mother. Not even her real name. Only that she was a waitress who lived in the same apartment complex. So you went into foster care, and we never knew you were out there. Even Evangeline's parents in Ireland didn't know about you. Hunter's contact said he tracked down the babysitter and interviewed her. All she remembered was that your mother had a boyfriend in the military who'd died. She said your mother was always talking about moving up north to the islands in the Pacific Northwest. I think she was planning to bring you here."

"Just like my mom did with me," Emma said softly. "I think the three of us were meant to grow up together, but your mother died before she could bring you to the island."

Kat felt an odd swell of sadness mixed with joy. She'd always wanted to know what happened to her mother, and who her family might have been. And now she knew.

Emma and Juliette were beaming at her like she hung the moon.

"So there you have it," Juliette said. "You're a Holloway, and you belong here."

"But we knew that already," Emma said, rising from the couch. "The house never gets it wrong."

The window curtains billowed out, as if the house was agreeing.

Kat let out a shaky laugh. Then they were all hugging and talking and teasing one another in that comfortable way that family does. And in that moment, a large missing puzzle piece of Kat's life fell into place. With these women who'd come to mean so much to her, she felt as if she could do anything. Brave anything.

She suddenly needed to see Jordan. She wanted to tell him about her past, about her relation to the Holloway family, and most of all, about her feelings for him. The memory of what he'd told her last night only amplified her feelings more. *I want us to be together. I don't want to lose you.* Kat took a deep breath, filled with determination. She loved Jordan Prescott, and it was time to let him know.

Chapter Thirty-Two

Jordan leaned back in his chair and propped his feet on his desk. Chad Newland's voice sounded anxious on the other end of the phone. Jordan could tell he was on speaker because of the slight echo in their conversation. He could just picture his business partner back in Manhattan, pacing in his corner office, stress ball in one hand, glass of scotch in the other, tie crooked from tugging on it.

"Where've you been?" Chad asked. "Did you get my messages?"

"I wasn't home last night," Jordan said, staring up at the ceiling. Kat had so enthralled him that he hadn't wanted to waste a single moment on work. The second he saw her in that blue velvet dress, he'd been thunderstruck. She was so damn gorgeous, and not just because of the dress. Hell, Kat could be standing in the animal pen covered in mud, and she'd still be the most beautiful woman he'd ever seen. Everything about her was irresistible. Her sweet and sassy nature, her genuine kindness, her ability to laugh in the face of hardship. She was—

"Morgan's selling the business."

Jordan's train of thought came screeching to a halt. "What?"

"You gotta get back here, man." Chad paused and Jordan

could hear the ice clinking in Chad's glass as he took a drink of scotch. "The board announced that he has to move all our accounts to a larger firm." He paused for a fraction of a second. "They're going with *Archer Anders.*"

Jordan sat bolt upright in his chair. "Like hell they are."

"But wait, it's not bad news. Morgan agreed to the board's demands *only* if Archer Anders agrees to buy us out. You and me." More ice clinked. "We're getting executive positions. Equity. Golden parachutes—the whole nine yards. And if Archer doesn't comply, Morgan's going to go with the first firm that will." Chad hooted in triumph. "Get this. Morgan said he wants to honor the relationship he has with you, and the relationship you had with his grandfather. Said you had integrity that's hard to find these days." Chad's voice grew louder with excitement. "This is *it*, man. Everything we've talked about. Archer has already agreed. We've got them by the balls. You gotta get back here so we can firm up the details."

Jordan listened as Chad filled him in on the plans. Everything sounded perfect. This was the dream. The lifestyle. The crazy stock options. The Upper East Side penthouse with the view. It was exactly what he'd always wanted. Wasn't it?

As Chad droned on, Jordan stared out his bedroom window feeling an odd sense of melancholy. Before meeting Kat, he would've been elated. He'd have jumped on the first plane back to JFK without a backward glance. But now there was her, and everything felt different. His mind began to spin with possibilities, searching for a way to hold on to it all.

By the time Jordan made his way to the red barn to begin tossing out the refuse of his former life, he'd come up with a plan.

* * *

Kat drove up to Willowbrook Lavender Farm, her whole body a roiling mixture of excitement and nerves. There was so much she wanted to tell Jordan.

The doors of the red barn were thrown wide open for the first time, and a huge pile of junk had formed out in the yard. She could hear Jordan banging around inside and knew he was in the process of hauling everything out.

She poked her head into the doorway just as a giant stuffed carnival bear sailed onto the junk heap. "You sure you don't want to keep that purple panda?"

Jordan took one look at her and covered the distance between them. Then he scooped her up, spun her in a circle, and kissed her before setting her back down.

"Careful," Kat laughed, glancing back at the farmhouse. "Opal might see you."

"Oh, no. She might think we like each other." He kissed her again. "I want to talk to you, but first I have to get all this crap out of here by three o'clock when the truck comes."

Kat walked into the barn. "It looks like you've got most of it already." It was mostly empty, save for some junk stacked along the walls, a broken lawn mower, and the beautiful caravan.

She lifted a deflated plastic kiddie pool. "Did you swim in this when you were little?"

"No." He tossed a broken lawn chair outside. "They used it to hold ice and beer during outdoor parties."

Kat threw the inflatable pool onto the growing pile outside, then continued chatting as they gathered the rest of the junk. She was in the middle of asking him if he'd ever used the sparkly pink Hula-Hoop, when he began to chuckle.

He was leaning against the barn entrance, watching her. His chest heaved from tossing another box onto the junk heap outside, and he had a crooked grin on his face.

"What is it?" she asked, gripping the Hula-Hoop.

"You," he said. "Talking so much."

Kat jammed her hand on her hip. "Well, when something interests me, I have a lot of questions."

"I like it. I love hearing you talk."

"Oh." Sunlight bloomed inside her. He said "love." "Then I'll keep talking. Because I actually wanted to know about the broken skateboard back there. It's missing a wheel, and I was wondering if you used to skate. When I was twelve, I wanted to be a skater. Mostly because it sounded cool, and I had a crush on a neighborhood boy who used to skate on this half-pipe by the house where I lived. Anyway, I tried to learn to skateboard, but—"

"Kat," Jordan interrupted. His expression grew very serious. "Kat, I want to ask you something."

She gripped the pink Hula-Hoop, wondering if now would be a good time to tell him she loved him. He seemed . . . excited, actually. Like he was about to say something really important. She had important things to say, too.

"Come to New York with me." He said it with so much conviction, it almost sounded like a demand.

Kat blinked, swallowing the declaration of love that had been on the tip of her tongue. "What?" She exhaled on a nervous laugh. "I can't go on a trip right now." For one thing, she didn't have the money. And for another, she'd only just found out she was a Holloway. There were things she wanted to do here with Emma and Juliette. And she had to take care of the animals.

Jordan walked over to her, gently took the Hula-Hoop, and tossed it aside. "I'm not talking about a trip, Kat. I told you last night I don't want to lose you. I want us to stay together. Come back to New York with me. I've been giving it a lot of thought, and I think you'll love it there." He reached for her hands, holding them tightly. "I'll do everything I can to make you happy."

She kept her hands limp, because she was too confused to do anything else. "You want me to go *live* there?"

"Yes." His expression was dead serious. "With me."

Kat pulled her hands away with the pretense of pushing her hair back. Her heart thudded painfully in her chest. She tried to focus on what was happening. Leave Pine Cove Island? *Never.* Not when she'd just discovered her real family. Not when she had people and animals relying on her. Didn't he know her at all?

"It'll be just you and me," he continued. "We won't have to deal with any of this." He gestured around them. As if that was a plus. As if that was everything he'd ever wanted. A life far away from here.

"You aren't . . ." She cleared her throat, hating that her voice sounded small. "You aren't going to stay?"

Jordan jerked his chin back. "*Here?*" He looked like he'd just discovered a litter of tigers on his bed. "No. That was never my plan. Something big just came up at work. A job offer of a lifetime, really. I want you to come with me. Things would be much easier there, and you wouldn't even have to work if you didn't want to. Say yes." He seemed so sincere and hopeful, it hurt.

The dawning realization that they both wanted such different things made her suddenly ill. A dull, painful ache stole over her, the steady pressure of it tipping her off balance. She felt like she was teetering on the razor edge of some dark place she'd been before. Disappointment. Emptiness. Loss. The place didn't really have a name, but she knew it well. Only this time it felt much worse.

He'd said he wanted to ask her something, and now she knew. Except he hadn't really asked, had he? *Come back to New York with me. I want you to come with me. Say yes.* None of them were questions. Just demands. But then, he'd never been very good at *asking* things. Maybe it was because he was always so sure he'd get what he wanted.

Kat took a deep breath and began building walls inside, because that was how you kept from falling. She fought hard to appear unfazed. From a purely practical perspective, it wasn't an awful idea. She knew deep down it wasn't the worst thing in the world, to have the man you love ask you to fly across the country and move in with him. The old Kat might have even jumped at the chance. But things were so different now. She hadn't only found love on Pine Cove Island, she'd found friends and family. She had a life here now, and she'd wanted him to be in it. But she wouldn't get to have that.

A coldness settled over her. She wished she could be the woman he wanted her to be, but she couldn't. She wouldn't. "How soon are you going?" she asked calmly.

"Sooner than I'd initially anticipated, but I've got everything in order. The house is ready to sell, and I've already had some discussions with my grandmother."

Opal! In her initial shock at his proposal, Kat hadn't even thought of logistics. She took a step back. Took a deep breath. "What about Opal?"

"I'm going to move her into the assisted living facility."

"A home?" Kat's jaw dropped in disbelief. The walls inside grew stronger, because this wasn't just about her. It was about people she loved. "You can't do that to her. *This* is her home."

"She's old, and she has trouble walking." His voice had a defensive edge to it. "This farm is no place for someone in her condition."

"And you've just decided that for her?" Kat threw back. All the giddy happiness she'd felt earlier that day was gone, and in its place was a cold, hard knot of resentment.

"No." Jordan looked frustrated. "I asked her what she wanted to do, and she chose it. She said that's where all her friends lived, and she'd prefer to be closer to them."

"That's just what she told *you*. It's because she doesn't

want to be a burden." It sickened Kat to know that his grandmother was being forced to put on a brave face. Opal deserved better than that.

"She said she'd be happier there," Jordan insisted. "Why shouldn't I take her at her word?"

"Because she's telling you what you want to hear. And it's easier for you to just accept it because now you don't have to feel guilty about abandoning her!" Angry heat roiled inside her, escalating until she could feel her face grow hot. All her life, she'd moved from home to home, and she knew what it felt like when someone told you it was time to go. It felt awful. It felt like failure. She hated that this was happening to Opal.

"What about the animals?" Kat demanded. The idea of all of her precious animals having to find new homes made her heart crack. "Or were you planning to bring them all to New York City, too? I'm sure Waffles and Lulabelle would love to share your bedroom with the cats and dogs. And chickens." Her voice was sharp with bitterness, but she didn't care.

A muscle clenched in his jaw, and he shook his head. "I can't bring them all, and you know that. But you could bring Hank. We can find good homes for the rest of them. I'll help you." He looked so sincere, it just made her angrier.

"That's very noble of you," Kat scoffed. "But I'll pass on your offer to *help*." The fact that he was so easily willing to turn everyone out made her wounded heart feel like it was bleeding out. She wrapped her arms around herself and held on.

His expression grew stormy. He was angry now, too. Good. "Look, I'm doing the best I can."

"*Are you*? Stay here, then." She lifted her chin in challenge. "That's what would be easiest for everyone. I thought you said you wanted us to stay together. That you didn't want to lose me."

Jordan stared at her for a long moment. His expression was granite hard. Unreadable.

Kat could count the seconds with every beat of her pounding heart.

"My life is back there, Kat," he finally said in a low, steely voice. "Everything I've worked for. I'm asking you to be a part of it."

A heavy ache settled inside her because she knew that wasn't possible. "If I go with you, then I'm no better off than when I first came here. All my life, I've moved around and tried to fit into other people's lives. But now I know that this is *my* place. This is where I belong. I thought you could see that. I thought you understood me."

"Kat, I've always been honest with you, and I care about you. That's why I'm asking you to come."

"But what about them?" She pointed in the direction of the farmhouse. "What about Opal and the animals? How could you so easily abandon them like they're not important?"

"Dammit, Kat." He let out a harsh breath. "I can't always save everyone!" He turned and stalked across the barn, running both hands through his hair. He whirled around, gesturing to the scattered remnants of junk. "My whole existence, my whole *life* on this damned island has been about cleaning up after my parents. Taking care of everyone and everything as best I could. But I've got a new life out there now. One I made. I've worked hard for it, and I want to share it with you. Can't that be enough?"

She moved toward the door.

"Say it's enough," he insisted.

Kat fought for a calm she didn't feel. "How long before you go?"

He started toward her. "Kat—"

She held up her hands. "How long?"

He stopped a few feet away. "A week. Maybe a little

more. I'm having professional packers come to help my grandmother move."

"And the farm?" she asked quietly, grateful that her voice sounded even and neutral. The complete opposite of the cyclone that was tearing her apart inside.

"Layla's sending someone out to survey the property. It goes on the market next week."

"So. I have a week to find a new place?"

"No. I don't want you to find a new place. I want you to come with me." There was a bleak edge to his voice she hadn't expected.

Kat shook her head. "That's not going to happen."

He flinched as if she'd slapped him. "Why not?"

"Because unlike you, I believe family and community are the most important things in the world. I just found out Emma and Juliette are my cousins. I have people here who need me. Them. Smitty at the animal shelter. Opal. All the animals. I'm not going to pack up and leave just because you've offered me an easy life somewhere else. I know what's real, and what's important."

"And you don't think that what I feel for you is real or important?" His gold eyes glittered with emotion.

"Jordan, I love you," Kat said simply. It surprised her to say it so easily, especially under these circumstances. But since the entire house of cards had already come tumbling down around her, why not throw her final hand on the table? "I've loved you for a while, and I've been meaning to tell you that."

Now he looked stunned. It hurt a little, knowing it came as that much of a surprise to him. Maybe he just never felt as strongly as she did.

"I want nothing more than for you to be happy," she continued. "Since you've been here, I believed you were happy. I hoped that you would change your mind about leaving, and I hoped this place could be enough. That *I* could be enough to make you want to stay."

"Kat—"

"No." She held her hand up. "Let me finish. You know what my life has been like in the past. If you truly cared for me, then you wouldn't ask me to abandon my family. You told me we could make the family we wanted, remember? Well, I did. And my life is here now."

They both stood there with only a few feet of distance separating them, but it may as well have been a thousand miles. An eternity seemed to pass, with neither of them moving or speaking. Kat couldn't think of a single way to make it work. She loved him, but he was leaving. He wanted her to go with him, but she couldn't leave her family behind. She wouldn't. Not when she'd finally found them.

A crow's shrill cry broke the silence. Edgar swooped into the barn with a caw of alarm that seemed to echo through Kat's bones. Something was wrong. "What is it?"

Edgar flew in another circle, crying out again.

"Something's happened," Kat said, running for the door. "It's Opal."

Edgar flew out into the yard as Kat ran toward the farmhouse. Jordan was right behind her.

At the bottom of the porch steps, Opal lay in an awkward sprawl. Her purple velour track suit had gravel and dust down one side.

"Opal!" Kat cried, running toward her.

It was Jordan who reached her first. "Call nine-one-one," he said urgently, leaning over his grandmother.

Kat fumbled for her phone and managed to dial the number. She gave the address to the operator, heart thumping in her chest like a war drum. If anything happened to Opal . . .

The old woman's skin looked paper thin, and all the color had drained from her face. Her eyes fluttered, and

Jordan reached out and gently laid his hand on hers. "Grandma, can you hear me?"

Opal's eyes snapped open. "Of course I can hear you. I've got bad joints; I'm not deaf."

Jordan dipped his head, shoulders shaking. At first Kat thought he was crying. It wasn't until he spoke again that she realized he was laughing with relief. "Grandma, I thought you were dead."

Opal gave him a crooked grin. "Not dead yet, my boy. I was just coming out to tell you both I made a casserole, but I slipped on the wet steps. Now help me up off the ground. This is so undignified."

Edgar was perched on the porch railing. He cawed loudly.

"I have to agree with Edgar," Kat said. "You should stay still until the paramedics arrive."

"That bird said all that to you with one caw?" Opal asked grumpily.

"Edgar is the one who alerted us," Jordan said. "He came and told Kat you were hurt."

"Did he, now?" Opal's stern expression softened. "Remind me to give him some treats when I get back to the kitchen." She tried to rise, but Jordan placed his hand gently on her shoulder.

"No, Grandma, you need to lie still."

"On the ground?" she cried. "What kind of a grandson makes his poor grandmother lay out in the mud and rain?"

"A very terrible, no-good grandson," Jordan said, brushing her wispy hair off her forehead.

Kat watched the way he spoke to her, and how he leaned over her head to block the light rainfall. It made her heart ache to see how much he cared for his grandmother. Deep down, Kat knew he'd always been honest with her about his plans to go back to the East Coast. He'd never kept that from her, so she couldn't blame him, but it still hurt. If only he cared enough to stay.

She pressed her lips together and refused to think about it. Opal needed her, and she wasn't going to break down now. Kat ran into the house and brought out an umbrella, propping it up over their heads.

An ambulance wailed down the street, and Opal lifted her finger. "Those paramedic fellas better be good-looking, or else I did this little stunt for nothing."

"They're here now," Kat said as the ambulance pulled into the driveway. She fought to keep her voice light. "And I don't think you'll be disappointed, Opal. Everyone knows paramedic guys are good-looking. I think it's a prerequisite."

For the next fifteen minutes, three paramedics surrounded Opal, asking her questions and assessing the damage. Eventually they concluded it was a concussion, and a possible fracture of her upper ankle. After wrapping it in an inflatable air splint, they set her on a stretcher and carried her to the back of the ambulance. Kat followed, wringing her hands, wishing there was more she could do.

Once Opal was secured in the ambulance, the young paramedic turned to them and said, "Who's family?"

Jordan stepped forward. "Me."

"You coming?" the paramedic asked him, holding the door.

Jordan climbed into the ambulance, then turned to Kat, his face solemn. "Thank you."

The paramedic shut the door with a slam that seemed to echo through Kat's bones.

She slowly lowered the umbrella and watched them drive away. It was a while before she realized she was soaked to the skin and freezing. She made her way up to her apartment, heart heavier than it had ever been. *Who's family?* the paramedic had asked. *Who's family?* Not her. Not when it mattered.

Slowly, methodically, Kat dragged her old suitcase out from under her bed and began gathering her things. She folded her T-shirts and jeans into flat, neat stacks and placed them in the suitcase. Tops on one side, bottoms on the other. She was good at this—the moving on. She'd had lots of practice. There was a sharp, painful ache in the back of her throat like she'd swallowed a pine cone, and it wouldn't go away so she would just have to breathe around it. And she would not cry, because that didn't get you anywhere.

It wasn't long before Kat's belongings were packed neatly into her suitcase. She was ready. At least she wasn't on the hook for moving furniture. Silver linings.

She sagged onto the old recliner and dialed Juliette's number.

"You're moving out?" her cousin asked in surprise.

Kat knew she should tell Juliette everything—and she would—but for now, all she could manage was, "Yeah." She took a shaky breath and focused on logistics. "You okay if I sleep over at your place for a couple of days?" She just needed some time to think, away from Jordan. Of course, she would go to the farmhouse every day to take care of the animals, but the idea of being so close to him right now was too painful to contemplate.

"I'd love to have you." Juliette's voice was filled with sympathy. "My cottage is mostly empty these days, because I've been spending my time over at Logan's house. You can take the spare room. Stay as long as you like. My cat Luna hates everyone, but she'll love you."

"What about Lucky and Hank? Lucky's happiest at the farm, but I'll want to bring him home with me in the evenings to sleep with us."

Juliette laughed. "Do it. It'll be good for Luna to have some excitement in her life."

Kat thanked her and said good-bye, looking around at

the apartment. The butterfly cage was sitting empty by the window. She turned away, with Hank trotting at her heels.

In the farmhouse, Kat went to do a quick check on Clementine and the kittens, but they weren't in the downstairs bathroom. Walking through the house, Kat was beginning to panic, until Clementine greeted her from the top of the stairs. Kat followed her to Jordan's room, stunned to see the box of kittens on the floor near his desk. The bowls of food and water were lined against the wall.

"Oh." Kat swallowed past the lump in her throat, bending down to pet the happy cat. Bittersweet images flashed through her mind. Jordan working at his desk with Clementine in his lap. Jordan pulling a string across the floor for her. Jordan holding the kittens. "You did it, Clementine. You won him over," Kat whispered. Her eyes pricked with hot tears, but she blinked them back. *No crying.* She had things to figure out. She had to plan. There was no time for useless tears. It was a small comfort, at least, to know he'd take good care of the cats until he left.

She left the house and placed her keys under the mat. Then she assured the animals she'd see them very soon. "I'll be back tomorrow before work to check on all of you. I promise. And soon we'll find ourselves a new place." A new place that allowed cats, dogs, mini donkeys, and goats. Piece of cake. Kat started toward her car with a sinking feeling. What were the odds she could find a place like that? Maybe she could appeal to Smitty's good nature— which she knew was in there, somewhere—and find a way to house them at the shelter until she could come up with a more permanent solution.

As she pulled out of the driveway, she realized just how much the farm had changed since she arrived. The farmhouse looked shiny and clean with its fresh coat of paint and flowers in the mended flower boxes. The hedges were trimmed, the grass was neatly mowed, and Jordan had even painted the paddock fence. He'd done so much to fix the place up, she'd allowed herself to hope. She'd allowed herself to believe they could have a future together. A stab of grief tore through her, and she gripped the steering wheel, gritting her teeth, refusing to cry. She didn't have time to think about her own stupid heartache. Not when there were animals depending on her.

Hank sensed her sadness and climbed into her lap. "We're going to figure this out," she whispered brokenly. "I promise."

Chapter Thirty-Three

A couple of days later, Jordan walked into the hospital room to find Opal surrounded by a doctor and two laughing nurses. Opal spotted him at the door and beamed.

"And here's my grandson now," she said. "I've just been telling them about the time you decided you wanted to be a banker when you were a little boy. Do you remember that?"

"Did you really set up a stand on the side of the road with the words 'Bank of Jordan'?" one of the nurses asked.

"Yes," he said. "And would you believe not a single person wanted to invest their money? I think the safe I made out of a shoebox and duct tape didn't impress them."

"He was a very enterprising child," Opal said proudly. "Always looking for ways to make money and get ahead."

"Your grandmother can go home in the morning," the doctor said. "Though we'll miss her stories."

The doctor filled Jordan in on Opal's aftercare. She'd suffered a fracture in her upper ankle, a bruised hip, and a concussion, but she was going to be just fine.

When the staff left the room, Jordan sat beside Opal and took her hand. "Looks like I get to bust you out of here tomorrow."

"And thank the Lord for that. I've been bored to death lying around with nothing interesting to do."

"I happen to know Sam Norton's been here to visit," Jordan said. "And you seem plenty interested in him." He'd passed Sam in the hall a couple of times, grateful that his grandmother had such a good friend. There were several flower bouquets in her hospital room, and most were from Sam.

Opal blushed. "Sam is wonderful, isn't he? I'll be glad to move into the same complex so we can be closer to each other."

"Grandma, are you sure you want to leave the farmhouse?" He watched her intently, trying to gauge her true feelings. "I would hate to think you're telling me that just to make things easier for me." Kat's accusation had cut him to the bone, and for the past couple of days he couldn't stop thinking about the things she'd said. They tore him up at night. When he'd returned home from the hospital on Sunday and discovered her gone, a bleak emptiness had opened up inside him. Every day it grew bigger.

"Honest to God," Opal said. "I've been in that farmhouse far too long, and it's not set up for someone like me. That place needs a family with rowdy kids and parents who enjoy that outdoorsy, farm lifestyle. At my age, I'd be much happier over in the assisted living community. That's where all the action is."

Jordan glanced sideways at her. "What kind of action are we talking about, here? Bingo, surely."

"Yes, of course," Opal said with a mischievous grin. "Bingo, and knitting."

He laughed and squeezed her hand. He loved his grandmother. For the first time since he'd made the decision to sell, he realized just how much he was going to miss her.

"And now, we need to have a serious talk," Opal said sternly, arranging the blanket on her lap. "About you."

"What about me?" The look on her face made him nervous. "Everything's going fine. Today I've got a real estate agent showing up, and someone's coming over to assess the property. And I'll be heading out soon." *Without Kat.* The thought slammed into him like a wrecking ball every time he thought about it. He hadn't seen Kat since his grandmother's accident. Each time he went to check on the animals, they'd already been fed and cared for. He suspected Kat was coming very early in the morning so she wouldn't have to see him. Every time he'd tried to call her, the phone went straight to voice mail. It hurt to know she was avoiding him. A part of him tried to reason that maybe it was better this way. Except it all felt so wrong. All of it. He had no idea what to do.

"Kat came to see me yesterday," Opal said.

Jordan's head snapped up. He fought for composure. "And how did that go?"

Opal's expression grew pensive. "She's very worried about her animals. She's going to try to keep them over at the shelter until she finds a place that will take them all." Opal was watching him carefully, as if she was waiting for him to say something.

Jordan didn't know what to say. He felt like an ass, selling the farm and making Kat move out, but that was the plan all along. She knew that from the beginning. He'd even asked her not to bring animals home, but did she listen? No. What else could he do?

"You're stubborn as a mule, my boy," Opal finally said. "That girl is in love with you, and you're too busy with your plans to realize you're about to lose the most precious thing of all. If you let her go, then you're dumb as a box of rocks, too."

Jordan remained silent.

Opal scowled. "I mean it. You'd be a fool to lose her. Even more foolish than your parents ever were."

"I asked her to come with me," Jordan said defensively. "Did you know that? I don't want to lose her. I asked her to move back to New York with me, but she won't go."

Opal pursed her lips. "Box of rocks, I tell you."

"Grandma!"

"Listen up, Jordan. I may be old, but I'm not blind. I know you two are crazy about each other. I've seen how happy she makes you. Is all that stuff in fancy-pants New York City worth losing what you have with her? I know how hard you've worked to make a life for yourself away from here. Since you were that scrappy little boy with your Bank of Jordan stand on the side of the road, you've been trying for something better. And I don't blame you. My harebrained son and your mother didn't make things easy for you. I understand why you wanted to leave, and I understand why your business is so important. But if there's one thing I've learned in my life, one truth above all others, it's the undeniable fact that love is what matters most. Love is everything."

Jordan shifted uncomfortably on his chair. He wasn't used to having heart-to-heart talks with anyone. The only person he ever talked to about his feelings was Kat, and that realization only made him more uncomfortable.

"So," Opal said fiercely. "If you love that girl, Jordan—and I think you do—you run and grab her. You hold on to her, and never let her go." She lifted her hands, then dropped them. "Look at me. I'm almost ninety years old. I've seen fortunes rise and fall. Watched people come into this world and leave it. And I'm here to promise you that the only thing worth having is love. If you are lucky enough to find it, then you're lucky enough."

Jordan searched for an answer to give her, but he couldn't think of a single thing that could beat that. Instead he leaned forward and wrapped her hand in both of his. "I'm lucky to have you, Grandma."

* * *

An hour later, Jordan pulled into the driveway at Willow-brook Lavender Farm. He'd made arrangements the day before to show the improved property to Layla so she could put it on the market.

When he stepped out of his truck, Lucky came ambling over to greet him. The three-legged dog did not seem at all like the scared thing he'd been when Kat first brought him home. Now Lucky was full of playful energy and ecstatic to see visitors. He ran a few circles around Jordan in greeting, then nosed under a bush until he came out with his favorite toy—a tennis ball inside a filthy sock. He dropped it at Jordan's feet with a huge dog grin.

Jordan picked it up and flung it in the direction of the paddock. Inside the paddock, Waffles and Lulabelle caught sight of him. They zipped over the grass to the fence, dancing along the edge to follow him as he made his way toward the house. Waffles tossed his old bicycle tire into the air, showing off his prize as if Jordan had never seen it before.

When Jordan reached the porch steps, he sat down with a hard thud. Soon Layla would arrive, and plans would be underway. He should be glad, but instead he was overcome with how wrong it felt.

Waffles brayed from the paddock gate, as if to agree with him.

Jordan dropped his head into his hands. What was he going to do without Kat? She made everything . . . right. She'd made the farmhouse feel more like a home than it ever had before. It was the kind of home he'd always wished for as a kid. The kind where you were welcomed, and people cared, and they were happy to see you.

Lucky nudged his hand with a cold, wet nose. The dog had been so scared when Kat first brought him home, but now he laid his head in Jordan's lap like they'd known each other for years. Jordan's chest tightened.

Edgar the crow swooped down and landed on the porch railing.

Waffles brayed again and tossed the ridiculous tire into the air.

Lulabelle jumped onto a wooden platform Kat had placed in the paddock, just for her. The little goat jumped on, then off. Then on. Then off. It was exhausting just watching her, but she was happy.

They were all happy. And they *trusted* him.

Jordan rubbed a hand over the sudden ache in his chest.

A sleek white Mercedes-Benz pulled to a stop in the driveway. Layla emerged in a designer suit, mile-high stilettos, and dark sunglasses that made her look like a badass. Good for her. The little girl with the hand-me-down backpack had gone and done it. She'd made her life better, and he was glad for her.

"Hey," Layla said. "This place looks great. It's amazing what a new coat of paint and some yard work will do to make a place look like a real home."

It *was* a real home now. It had never been before, but Kat had turned it into one. She was the reason for all of this. Kat was the reason for everything. Jordan suddenly felt as though the earth's axis had tilted sideways, and he was in danger of sliding off. He gripped the edge of the step. It had always been Kat, from the moment he first saw her in that silly chicken costume at the farmer's market. He'd arrived back on Pine Cove Island believing he knew everything. But then he met Kat, and all those things that seemed so important before slipped away until the only thing left was . . . *her*.

"Layla," Jordan said, standing. "I've been an idiot."

Chapter Thirty-Four

It was unusually slow for a Wednesday at the Daisy Meadows Pet Rescue. Kat had been watching the clock for the past hour. She felt like it was ticking backward.

She dragged the elastic band from her hair and began massaging her aching scalp. For the past couple of days, she'd been like a whirlwind, spinning up one activity after another to keep herself busy. Sweeping and mopping. Cleaning the kennels. Scrubbing the windows. Calling volunteers. Sweeping and mopping again. She'd even stooped to organizing the office supplies and paperwork. Anything so she wouldn't have time to think about Jordan. How could she ever have thought things would work between them? Once again, her delusions about life had led her to hope for something that just wasn't there.

She gritted her teeth, refusing to give in to her feelings. She still hadn't cried, and it was just as well. Crying never helped anyone. What was it her grouchy gym teacher once said when she got hit in the head with a soccer ball? "Laugh and the whole world laughs with you, kid. Cry and you cry alone." She'd taken those words to heart and found that they were mostly true. Nothing good ever came from crying, and mostly it just made people uncomfortable.

She looked at the corner of her desk, remembering how

Jordan had breezed in that day, dropping off the butterfly cage with barely a backward glance. He'd been trying to escape as quickly as possible. It hurt to realize he hadn't changed; only she had. She'd fallen for him so completely, she'd been too blind to realize the home she was building back at the farm was just an illusion. She should've known it couldn't last. He'd even told her it was temporary. But as usual, she'd allowed herself to dream of something better. Something real. She'd thought maybe this time . . .

With a heavy sigh, she stood and went to the coffee maker. Hank followed closely at her heels, as if he sensed her sadness.

"Hey, gloomy," Smitty called from her back office. "Can you bring me a cup? I need to talk to you."

Uh-oh. Smitty was onto her. Kat thought she'd been pretty good at hiding her despair. She'd always been good at pretending. Apparently, Smitty wasn't fooled. Kat poured two cups of coffee and added some clumpy powdered creamer. Then she stepped into her boss's cluttered office. "Here you go."

"What's eating you?" Smitty demanded, taking the cup and setting it on her desk. "You've been moping around here all week like the ship's sinking and someone stole your lifeboat."

"I'm fine," Kat said. "I've just been keeping busy, that's all."

"Mm-hmm." Smitty eyed her shrewdly. She wasn't buying it.

Kat made a pretense of stirring her coffee with a red plastic stir stick.

"He break your heart, then?" Smitty barked.

Kat looked up, startled.

"That broody fella with the scar and the come-hither eyes." Smitty crossed her arms with an expression that said she was willing to bring out the big guns. "You want me to have a word with him?"

"What? No," Kat said quickly.

"My cousin Rocco's a bouncer over at the Siren." Smitty leaned forward in her chair. "I can get him to give that guy a"—she made air quotes with her hands—"visit."

"No!" Kat said in alarm. "I'm fine, Smitty. Really. I broke up with him, that's all. It was a mutual decision, and everything's fine now. I'll be completely fine." It wasn't a total lie. In about fifty or sixty years, she might be.

Smitty mashed her frosted red lips into a hard line. "I can't have people upsetting my favorite receptionist."

Kat felt a surge of gratitude for the older woman. Smitty was a prickly pear on the outside, but soft as sponge cake on the inside. "I'm your *only* receptionist," Kat reminded her.

"Even still. If that long, tall drink of water can't see what a catch you are, then you're better off without him."

A familiar braying sound came from the parking lot outside. Kat cocked her head and listened. It must've been her imagination. Waffles was back at the farm, of course.

A quieter sound followed. It sounded strangely like a bleating goat. *Lulabelle?*

Kat hurried to the front door. When she pushed it open, she jerked to a stop.

Jordan Prescott stood in the parking lot, leaning against the old farm truck hooked to a trailer. He looked fiercely determined. Beautiful as always, with rugged work clothes and windblown hair. He looked exactly the way Kat loved him best—a little bit wild. But it wasn't just Jordan's arrival that shocked her. It was his entourage.

Her heart began thumping madly at the sight of him. Of *them*.

Lucky stood beside Jordan with his favorite sock toy in

his mouth. When he recognized Kat, he dropped the toy and gave a happy bark.

Waffles and Lulabelle pranced around Jordan, calling out a greeting to Kat. Just when she thought the image of him and the animals couldn't get any stranger, something orange and furry jumped out of the truck's open door. It was Clementine. The cat padded over to Jordan, rubbed against his shins, then sat at his feet.

"What's going on?" Kat asked in astonishment. "Why are they here?"

"I needed backup," Jordan said.

Kat gaped in disbelief. "But . . . how did you get them to come?"

"I asked them."

She jammed her hands onto her hips. "You *asked* them. Just like that."

"Well, I did have to bring along the box of kittens to convince Clementine. And it took some coaxing to get Waffles in the trailer. But once Lulabelle hopped in, he was game."

Hank trotted over to join his friends.

Kat shook her head, incredulous. The sight of all of them together was almost painful, because it was everything she loved most.

"What are you doing here, Jordan?" she asked in a low voice. She could feel her heart cracking again, and it hurt. There wasn't much left to say.

He glanced at the ground for a moment, as if gathering his thoughts. Or was it courage? He seemed nervous.

Lulabelle butted his leg in encouragement. Clementine looked up at him and meowed.

Jordan cleared his throat, then fixed his gaze on hers. "I've been a fool, Kat. About a lot of things."

The pine cone in her throat was suddenly back, more

painful than ever. She had to work to stay in control. Why was he saying all this now?

"Yesterday, I met with Layla so we could discuss putting the farm up for sale."

Kat crossed her arms, hugging herself. "That's your business, not mine."

Jordan shook his head. "No, that's not what I'm trying to say." He swore softly and began again. "I went to the farm yesterday with the intention of selling it. But when I got there, I saw all the animals, and I realized it wasn't just a farm. It was . . . It was home."

Kat's limbs began to tingle.

Jordan stepped closer, and the animals followed right beside him like a row of soldiers on the front line. They all watched Kat expectantly, with so much hope. It made her want to cry.

"Kat, I was wrong. I should never have asked you to move back with me. I thought it was the only way to hold on to what we have together, but I was wrong. I just couldn't imagine losing you knowing how much I . . ." His voice trailed off for a moment, but he forged on. "How much I love you."

Kat blinked rapidly, ignoring the prick of tears that threatened her hard-fought composure. How in the hell was she supposed to pretend after a declaration like that?

There was a loud *caw* overhead, and Edgar swooped past her, then settled lightly on Jordan's shoulder.

Kat closed her eyes briefly. *Et tu, Edgar?*

"I love you," Jordan repeated. "I've never said it before, but I'm saying it now. You are everything that's important to me, Kat, and I didn't realize that the one thing I've always wanted the most wasn't money or that lifestyle back in Manhattan. It's been you, all along. I don't want to leave. I want to be here, with you. If you'll still have me."

Kat felt as if a dam had burst inside her, and all the

emotions she'd been suppressing for days came rushing out. The tears were really falling now. Spilling over like the stupid crier who cries alone. Except she wasn't alone. She was with her motley crew of a family.

For several moments, she was so overcome with emotion, she couldn't find any words at all.

Hank let out a little bark of encouragement.

Kat wiped her eyes, a smile hovering on her lips as she stared at the man she loved.

"Say yes, honey," Smitty's gruff voice called from the doorway. "Then you can kiss and make up and get those mangy farm animals the hell outta my parking lot."

Kat laughed through her tears. "Okay."

Jordan closed the distance between them and reached for her, burying his face in her neck. The animals surrounded them until they were anchored on all sides by a muddle of fur and feathers and joyful noises. It was the oddest, messiest group hug Kat had ever experienced, but it couldn't have been more perfect. Because these were her people. She loved them, and they loved her. And that was everything.

Epilogue

A few months later . . .

"Do you think they'll notice if we show up to the grand opening naked?" Kat dragged a towel around herself as she made a beeline for their master bedroom closet. "We're so late, we're barely going to have time to throw on clothes." She lifted a dress from a hanger, still marveling at the walk-in closet Jordan had built. One of the first things he'd done was tear down a bedroom wall in the farmhouse to make a new master bedroom for both of them. It had every luxury, and there was even a raised cushion in the corner of the room for Clementine, his "second favorite 'Kat.'"

"If you show up naked," Jordan said, coming up behind her, "customers will be fighting to get through the door."

He murmured more details about her glorious nakedness, and Kat gave him a playful shove. Then she changed her mind and pulled him closer for a quick kiss. Only it wasn't quick, because the Queen of Impulsive Decisions had other ideas. But Kat didn't mind so much anymore. She loved being impulsive, especially with him.

Jordan wrapped his arms around her, sliding his hand under her towel. Soon they were in very real danger of missing the grand opening of the new Daisy Meadows Pet Rescue.

Her phone chimed and Kat pulled away to check text messages. "It's Smitty. She's asking where we are."

"Tell her it's my fault we're running late." Jordan began buttoning his shirt. "She likes me."

"Only because you bought the building and made all the improvements she wanted for the animals. Now she thinks you walk on water." Kat quickly threw her dress over her head and began brushing her hair.

"It was the least I could do."

"It was the most anyone's ever done. Those improvements you made to the building are incredible. It's like a fancy pet hotel now." She set the brush down and held out her hand, admiring the sparkling rock of an engagement ring Jordan had surprised her with the week before. They'd been sitting under the willow trees when he proposed, and the memory would forever be at the top of her Favorite Moments of All Time list.

Together they headed down the stairs into the foyer, and the front door swung open for them.

Jordan laughed. "I wonder how long it's going to take before I get used to that."

Kat gave his hand a little squeeze, her heart overflowing with love. A couple of weeks ago, she and Emma and Juliette had finally used the "Hearth and Home" spell on the farmhouse. They'd waited for a full moon, then stood outside together, holding hands as the breeze whispered and swirled around them. It had been a simple spell, but Kat had shivered at the strength of the bond that had grown between them. Every day she thanked the universe that she'd found her cousins. Every day she felt blessed to be a Holloway.

As they left the house, Kat went to check on the animals out of habit. Waffles and Lulabelle had a new barn inside the large paddock so they could frolic. There were now ten chickens, and Jordan had built an even bigger coop for them to nest. One of the empty fields had been fenced in for potential newcomers, and the red barn had been cleared out. "Room for the family to grow," Jordan had told her. He'd also moved the bohemian caravan to a spot under the willow trees, which turned out to be one of Kat's favorite places.

When they reached the truck, Kat started to get in, but Jordan laid a hand on her shoulder. "Hold on, I have a surprise for you."

She started to grin. "What is it?"

"If I told you, it wouldn't be a surprise." He motioned for her to follow him toward the road.

At the end of the long gravel driveway, a large rectangular sign swung from a pole where the old farm sign used to be.

"I had it commissioned a few weeks ago, and they just installed it this morning." He walked with her until they were both standing in front of it.

Kat gasped in delight. It was a brilliant mosaic sign made of intricate bits of colored glass and ceramic tiles. In large, emerald green letters the sign read WILLOWBROOK LAVENDER FARM & ANIMAL SANCTUARY.

"It's by the same artist who did Emma's and Juliette's signs for their shops," Jordan said. He sounded a little nervous. "Do you like it?"

She shook her head in awe, tears pricking the corners of her eyes. It wasn't just the exquisite beauty of the sign; it was everything it represented.

"I'll have it redone," he said quickly. "Whatever you want it to say. I just thought—"

"No," she laughed, wiping her eyes. "I love it. It's the best gift I've ever received."

He gave her that slow, enchanted prince smile that made

her heart swell with so much love. The new sign sparkled in the sunlight behind him, and the farm with the animals beyond that, and the fields of lavender beyond that. And suddenly everything Kat loved most in the world was right in front of her—all her dreams in one place.

When Jordan gathered her in his arms, a thrill shot through her. Only this time it wasn't butterflies. It was the thrill of knowing that she was exactly where she was supposed to be. *Home.*

They linked hands and walked back down the path together.

*The Holloway charms are powerful. But there are other
kinds of magic in the world—like red-hot first kisses,
secret glances, and the feeling that comes
with falling truly, madly, inconveniently in love . . .*

Don't miss Emma's story in

DON'T CALL ME CUPCAKE

by Tara Sheets.

Available now from Zebra Books.

Read on for a special preview . . .

The storm on Pine Cove Island was about to make history. Thunder rumbled in the distance and the sky darkened to a charcoal gray. Clouds loomed over the sleepy island town, casting shadows against the rocky shore. For Emma Holloway, this just wasn't acceptable.

She stood in her kitchen, eyeing a mixing bowl with the single-minded focus of an ER surgeon as she whipped lemon frosting into soft peaks.

A loud clap of thunder made her jump, and she quickly scooped out a dollop of frosting and tasted it. The sharp, clean zest of lemon burst on her tongue, but it needed more vanilla to balance it out. She checked the ancient cookbook. "Close. But not quite there yet."

Lightning flashed, making the old two-story Victorian house creak. A door slammed upstairs.

"I know, I know," she called out. "I'm working as fast as I can."

Another door slammed and Emma sighed. The house was chastising her. In the seven generations her family had lived on Pine Cove Island, the house had been a part of their lives, and just like the quirky, unusual Holloways, the house had a mind of its own. It wasn't always feisty. Most of the time, it was as warm and inviting as a cozy sweater.

Doors would open for her when her arms were laden with grocery bags, and if there was a cold snap, the heater would go up a notch to chase away the winter chill.

No one in the family knew exactly how the house had become enchanted; they just accepted it as part of the Holloway family gifts. Emma shook her head and added a splash of vanilla to the frosting. *Gifts.* That's how her grandmother had lovingly explained it, but Emma could think of a few other names for the Holloway family abilities. If her mother hadn't had the "gift" of wanderlust, maybe she'd have stuck around to watch Emma grow up. Maybe Emma wouldn't be so alone, now that her grandmother was gone. She swallowed the lump in her throat and mixed faster.

Thunder struck again, and this time a hard, steady rain began pelting the windows. She spun the whisk one last time and quickly spread the frosting over the vanilla cupcakes on the counter. They smelled divine, like a warm summer day. *Perfect.*

She placed the tray of frosted cakes on the counter near the window. Heavy sheets of rain cast a dreamy quality to the gardens that lined the path to the old house. It was a typical Pacific Northwest spring morning, and any other time Emma would have already been working in her bakery down by the waterfront, but today, she couldn't leave the house defenseless.

"Okay, house. I think this will do it." She raised a cupcake to her lips and took a bite. Delicious. It was like sugared sunshine, and she smiled as the rain began to ease. Her body thrummed with warmth and she licked frosting from her fingertips, waiting.

The stairs creaked and the old house seemed to sigh. Emma sighed, too. With three holes in the attic roof, the last thing she needed was a torrential downpour. She had climbed up to the attic last week to try patching the leaks herself, but her magic skills in the bakery did not translate over to carpentry. What she really needed was decent weather until she could afford to hire a roofing contractor. With property taxes coming due soon, it was all she could do to come up with the money for either.

Emma watched out the kitchen window as the rain slowed to a steady drizzle, eventually settling into a soft mist. A few moments later, sunlight burst through the fog, and the clouds were swept away on a sudden breeze. The sky returned to a bright, clear blue and the trees swayed softly, their leaves sparkling with raindrops. Somewhere outside, a bird began to sing and Emma slapped powdered sugar off her hands. *Done and done.*

"There you have it," she told the old house. "We live another day."

The house settled in what sounded to Emma like a *hmph*. She knew her kitchen charm wouldn't last forever. A few days, at most. Mother Nature always had her way in the end, and it was never a good idea to use magic to mess with the weather. The next time the storm came around, it would be even worse. But she'd have to worry about that consequence later. At least now, she had bought some time to figure out how to get her roof patched.

Emma crossed her arms, hugging herself. By many standards the old house was falling apart, but she refused to think of it that way. Aside from her quirky cousin, the Holloway house was the only family she had left. Somehow, some way, she was going to protect and keep it.

Fairy Cakes was located near the wharf on Pine Cove Island's waterfront. Emma skirted a puddle on the sidewalk, balancing the box of lemon cupcakes as she nudged open the turquoise door to her shop. It was quiet inside, but that was to be expected for early spring. By summer it would be bustling with tourists from Seattle and British Columbia.

As always, the shop smelled heavenly. Today it smelled like toasted marshmallow buttercream frosting, and—*yes!*—freshly brewed coffee. "I brought a new batch," Emma called.

"Good, because you're going to need the extras." Her cousin Juliette stood up from behind the pastry case, licking frosting off her finger. "I've already eaten like, three of them. Seriously, if I worked here every day, I wouldn't be able to fit through that door."

Emma rolled her eyes. Juliette was one year older than her, and at twenty-six, her cousin was utterly, stupendously gorgeous. She was curvy in all the right places, and had that milky, porcelain complexion Emma had always envied growing up. "Jules, you look like you just floated off the pages of a Victoria's Secret ad. The only thing missing is a pair of wings. You have nothing to worry about."

Her cousin grinned. "See, that's why I love you so much. You're so very smart." She gave Emma's shoulder an affectionate nudge and took the box of cupcakes, inhaling. "Mmm, lemony. What are they called?"

Emma took out a scalloped tray, placing it on the counter. "They're called 'Summer Sunshine.'"

"Ha! I knew it. I *so* knew this weather was your doing. I mean, this morning there was a storm rolling in, and the forecast for the week was rain, rain, and more rain. And now we've got blue skies and even a rainbow. What gives?"

Emma leaned against the sink and balled a dishrag in her hands. "There's another hole in the roof."

Juliette nodded solemnly. "A fine reason to do a little sweet charming, then. How's the house?"

"Grumpy." Emma grabbed a flouncy black-and-white apron, cinching it around her waist.

A gift from Juliette, the apron had rows of frothy lace and looked a bit too much like a French maid costume for Emma's taste. But with business so slow, she didn't have to worry about appearances. The only customers coming through the door were the town regulars, anyway. Everyone on Pine Cove Island knew one another. It was both a blessing and a curse. "I have to get someone to fix the roof, but I can't seem to find anyone who wants to work for cupcakes."

Juliette swung a colorful bag over her shoulder. "*I* work for cupcakes."

It was true. Her cousin practically did. Emma could barely afford to pay her for the few hours she took over the shop each week. Juliette was busy enough working at Romeo's florist shop, and selling her handmade bath products to local vendors. She didn't really need the extra work. It made Emma all the more grateful. "Seriously, Jules, I don't know what I'd do without you."

"Well, since we're the last two Holloways left, you'll never have to find out. You're stuck with me." She planted a kiss on Emma's cheek. "Hey, I'm going out dancing tonight with the girls from Dazzle. You should come."

Emma thought of their two friends who worked at the local hair salon. They were always ready to paint the town red. Or a glittery shade of hot pink. "No, I don't have the energy for that right now."

"Come on, Em, it's Friday. You've been stuck here too much and you need a break. You should come out." Juliette shimmied her hips and smiled mischievously. "Shake things up for a change."

"I don't want to shake things up. I don't need change." What she needed was a truckload of money, dumped directly into her dwindling bank account.

Juliette groaned, grabbing Emma by the shoulders and shaking her dramatically. "Everyone needs change! It's good for the soul."

"My soul is fine. It just needs to finish baking. Now get out of here." Emma laughed in spite of herself.

"All right, I'm off. Everyone in my garden will be in fine form today with all this sunshine. I can't miss it."

Emma waved good-bye and began stacking the cupcakes. By "everyone," she knew Juliette meant her garden plants. That was her cousin's gift. She could make roses grow in the middle of winter, and her garden was always brilliant, with a profusion of flowers that had even the best green thumbs shaking their heads in awe.

The dragonfly wind chimes tinkled over the front door as Emma placed the last cupcake on the tray. She glanced up, then froze.

A man stood just over the threshold, surveying her tiny shop. He didn't see her at first, so she had several heartbeats to recover. He was striking: tall and broad shouldered, with sun-bronzed skin and dark hair. He wore a navy sweater over dark denim jeans, but despite the simplicity of his clothing, Emma could tell they were expensive. Cashmere maybe, and designer denim. Not the kind of relaxed, slightly outdated attire that most of the locals wore. A tourist, then. Figured. Someone like him didn't belong in her world.

He turned, his leaf green eyes sweeping over her. A dark brow rose for just a moment.

Emma suddenly remembered her French maid apron. *Crap*. Her cheeks grew hot and she cleared her throat, giving him a perfunctory nod. "Good morning." Totally professional. All business. She set the tray of cupcakes on a display stand.

He approached the pastry case slowly. "Those look amazing."

His voice was deep and smooth, reminding her of dark chocolate mixed with honey. Sweet, but with a subtle bite that made a person want to savor it on the tongue, so it would last longer. She shivered. *What the heck? Get your head in the game, Holloway.* Pretty boys like him were not a good idea. She had about a million past experiences to prove it.

He gestured to the cupcakes in the case. "What do you recommend?"

Ahh. Emma studied him for a moment. This was her favorite part of her talent—learning a little about what people needed. "Well, what do you usually like?"

He shrugged and gave her a crooked grin that sent a tiny ripple of warmth over her skin. "I like anything sweet, so I'm a pretty easy target in a place like this."

Emma felt her knees go weak. This guy was some serious kryptonite. *Focus, Holloway.* "Well, what brings you to the island?"

"How do you know I don't live here?"

It was laughable, really. As if he thought for one second that he blended in. She had lived on Pine Cove Island almost her entire life, and a man like this could never be a native. He looked like some business tycoon on holiday, or a marauding pirate from one of her romance novels. Someone who'd breeze in on a whim and then move on to his summer home in Spain or his high-rise penthouse in New York.

"Trust me, I'm good at reading people," she said. "Are you here on business or pleasure?"

"Business, as a matter of fact."

Emma noted the slight shadows under his eyes, and the way he stretched his neck as though to work out some stiffness there. For a moment he stared down at the pastry case as if he were a million miles away.

He seemed to catch himself, then glanced up. "Big day today. Lots of negotiations to handle." His smile was suddenly so warm and genuine that Emma felt as if sunlight bloomed inside her chest. On impulse, she made a decision. "*Success* is what you need, then."

"Sure," he laughed. "That would be great."

She lifted a pair of silver tongs and pulled out a chocolate cupcake with salted caramel frosting. "This one is called 'Sweet Success.' It will grant you luck in what you want most." She smiled brilliantly, wishing him all the luck in the world on his next marauding adventure.

Wide green eyes studied her for a moment. There was laughter in his gaze, but his expression remained all seriousness. "In that case, I'll take three."

Romantic Suspense from
Lisa Jackson

Absolute Fear	0-8217-7936-2	$7.99US/$9.99CAN
Afraid to Die	1-4201-1850-1	$7.99US/$9.99CAN
Almost Dead	0-8217-7579-0	$7.99US/$10.99CAN
Born to Die	1-4201-0278-8	$7.99US/$9.99CAN
Chosen to Die	1-4201-0277-X	$7.99US/$10.99CAN
Cold Blooded	1-4201-2581-8	$7.99US/$8.99CAN
Deep Freeze	0-8217-7296-1	$7.99US/$10.99CAN
Devious	1-4201-0275-3	$7.99US/$9.99CAN
Fatal Burn	0-8217-7577-4	$7.99US/$10.99CAN
Final Scream	0-8217-7712-2	$7.99US/$10.99CAN
Hot Blooded	1-4201-0678-3	$7.99US/$9.49CAN
If She Only Knew	1-4201-3241-5	$7.99US/$9.99CAN
Left to Die	1-4201-0276-1	$7.99US/$10.99CAN
Lost Souls	0-8217-7938-9	$7.99US/$10.99CAN
Malice	0-8217-7940-0	$7.99US/$10.99CAN
The Morning After	1-4201-3370-5	$7.99US/$9.99CAN
The Night Before	1-4201-3371-3	$7.99US/$9.99CAN
Ready to Die	1-4201-1851-X	$7.99US/$9.99CAN
Running Scared	1-4201-0182-X	$7.99US/$10.99CAN
See How She Dies	1-4201-2584-2	$7.99US/$8.99CAN
Shiver	0-8217-7578-2	$7.99US/$10.99CAN
Tell Me	1-4201-1854-4	$7.99US/$9.99CAN
Twice Kissed	0-8217-7944-3	$7.99US/$9.99CAN
Unspoken	1-4201-0093-9	$7.99US/$9.99CAN
Whispers	1-4201-5158-4	$7.99US/$9.99CAN
Wicked Game	1-4201-0338-5	$7.99US/$9.99CAN
Wicked Lies	1-4201-0339-3	$7.99US/$9.99CAN
Without Mercy	1-4201-0274-5	$7.99US/$10.99CAN
You Don't Want to Know	1-4201-1853-6	$7.99US/$9.99CAN

Available Wherever Books Are Sold!
Visit our website at **www.kensingtonbooks.com**